Sarah M. Anderson may live east of the Mississippi River, but her heart lies out west. *A Man of Privilege* won an *RT Book Reviews* 2012 Reviewers' Choice Best Book Award. *The Nanny Plan* was a 2016 RITA® Award winner for Contemporary Romance: Short.

Sarah spends her days talking with imaginary cowboys and billionaires. Find out more about Sarah's heroes at www.sarahmanderson.com and sign up for the new-release newsletter at www.eepurl.com/nv39b.

To Tahra Seplowin,
who once pulled my luggage
through Times Square at a dead run
so we could make the curtain call.
That's true friendship right there.

"I still don't know why you're doing this."

"Maybe you don't have to know why," Daniel said.

"That's a load of malarkey," Christine replied.

"Malarkey? That's not a word you hear every day."

"I have this daughter, you see. She has a tendency to pick up on words and repeat them loudly when it's most inconvenient."

She was looking at him again with both eyes now. "Why, Daniel?"

"I didn't want to be another person who let you down."

"I don't want you to be another person who lets me down," she said softly.

For too much of his life, he had been concerned with his own interests. It was in his best interests to keep his siblings protected and the family business solvent. But what did he have to gain from Christine? What was in it for him to shield Marie?

Nothing. He had nothing to gain by doing any of this.

Funny how that hadn't stopped him yet.

* * *

Billionaire's Baby Promise
is part of Mills & Boon Desire's No. 1 bestselling series, Billionaires and Babies: Powerful men… wrapped around their babies' little fingers.

BILLIONAIRE'S BABY PROMISE

BY
SARAH M. ANDERSON

First Published in Great Britain 2017
By Mills & Boon, an imprint of HarperCollins*Publishers*
1 London Bridge Street, London, SE1 9GF

© 2017 Sarah M. Anderson

ISBN: 978-0-263-92811-2

51-0317

One

As always, he answered the phone on the first ring. "This is Daniel."

The number was not one he recognized. The voice, on the other hand, was. "Lee! I knew I'd track your sorry butt down somehow."

"Brian," Daniel said, trying to keep the cringe out of his voice.

Brian White had plucked Daniel straight out of a political rally on the campus of Northwestern and taught him everything he knew. They had worked together for almost fourteen years on various political campaigns. Brian was a man without morals, scruples or ethics. As a result, he had an amazing track record in getting questionable candidates elected to public office.

"How have you been?" Daniel asked, stalling for time.

If Brian was calling him now, that only meant one thing. The man had been hired to run yet another political campaign and he wanted his right-hand man by his side. Never mind that Daniel Lee had walked away from politics and made it clear that he was never going back.

"I've got a job for you," Brian said, sounding sure of himself.

It was hard to surprise Daniel Lee. He made secrets his business. So he wasn't all that surprised that Brian was reaching out to him. What did surprise him was his own physical response. Daniel—a man who was rumored by his political enemies to not even have a soul—felt an anxious coiling in his stomach that was only dimly recognizable as guilt. "I have a job, Brian."

"Doing what? Running a marketing department for a beer company? Come on, Lee. We both know you're wasting your talents."

Daniel rolled his eyes. Brian didn't know the first thing about business—or loyalty. Daniel wasn't just running a marketing firm for a beer company—he was running a family business. His last name might not be Beaumont, but he was one all the same.

Every time he thought of his position here at the Beaumont Brewery—second-in-command to his half brother, Zeb Richards—he almost wished his grandfather, Lee Dae-Won, could have lived long enough to see Daniel take his rightful place in a family business—even if it wasn't Dae-Won's business. "I told you I was out."

As he spoke, he started searching. Who was Brian working for now?

"Yeah, yeah—that's what you said. But you and I both know you didn't mean it. This one's going to be fun—carte blanche." There was a pause. "You find it yet?"

Damn. Of course Brian knew him well enough to know Daniel was already looking. "You could tell me," he said as he found it.

Missouri Senator Resigns In Disgrace; Male Escort Tells All.

Missouri? The hairs on the back of Daniel's neck stood up. Brian couldn't seriously mean...

"Clarence Murray wants to hire you to work on his campaign for a special election for the Missouri Senate seat recently vacated by the disgraced Senator Struthers." Somehow, Brian managed to sound enthusiastic.

It took a lot to surprise Daniel but for a moment, he was truly stunned.

"You've got to be kidding me." It hadn't even been two years since Daniel had destroyed Clarence Murray in a bid for the Missouri governor's office. "Murray is insane."

"However true that may or may not be, he has a lot of well-funded campaign donors." Brian's voice had leveled out, which was not a good sign.

"After what we did to him two years ago, you still think he's electable?" But even as he asked, Daniel knew how Brian would respond.

"It's not my job to decide if he's electable or not. He and his donors think he's electable, so it's my job to assemble a team and get him elected. That's where you come in."

Daniel kept searching. Murray, it seemed, had spent the better part of the last two years lying low and rebuilding his supporter base. Clarence Murray was a fire-and-brimstone preacher. He played well across the Bible Belt and had a solid evangelical base. But his beliefs were extreme and would never have a crossover appeal.

"No," he told Brian.

"Come on, Lee—it'll be fun. I'm already hearing whispers that Democrats think they can win this seat."

And then, there *she* was—halfway down the list of search results. Daniel recognized that headline—he had written it himself. He had chosen the picture of her because the angle was horrible and she looked like she had three extra chins. Seeing it again hit him like a punch to the gut.

Murray's Daughter Pregnant—Who Is The Baby Daddy?

Clarence Murray might have delusions of grandeur about being God's chosen politician. But in the end, it had been his pregnant daughter who had cost him the election. His pregnant, unmarried daughter.

Christine Murray.

Because Daniel was the one who had made her a campaign issue.

All was fair in love and war—and politics. For years, Daniel had played the game as well as anyone. Sometimes his candidates lost. More often than not, they won. Each time Daniel had worked a campaign, he'd gotten better at ferreting out secrets. And if candidates had few secrets, then Daniel had...well, not invented them. But he had always found some kernel of truth that could be stretched into something resembling a scandal. Nobody was completely clean.

Not even Daniel.

He read about Christine Murray, that anxious pit in his stomach coiling more tightly, a snake getting ready to strike. It didn't seem possible that he felt bad about what he had done. He never had before. But as he looked at the images of her online—and the headlines that he had *not* written about her—he had to face the fact that he had done a terrible thing to an innocent bystander.

"You know they're going to come after his daughter again."

As odd as it seemed now, it appeared that, at the advanced age of thirty-four, Daniel Lee had developed a conscience.

Christine Murray had been twenty-four years old when

her father had run for governor. From what Daniel had been able to dig up, she hadn't lived at home since she'd gone to college at the age of eighteen. She'd had a wild youth after the death of her mother—the stereotypical preacher's daughter—but by all appearances she had quickly settled down. She'd gotten a degree in finance. By all accounts, she had very little to do with Clarence Murray. Instead, she had gotten engaged and then gotten pregnant. By itself, there really wasn't anything scandalous about that.

Except that her father was running on a faith-and-family-values platform and having an unwed, pregnant daughter was exactly the sort of ammunition Daniel had needed to knock Clarence Murray out of the race.

Daniel had dragged that woman through the mud. When her fiancé had dumped her, Daniel had made hay while the sun still shone.

"I wouldn't worry about her," Brian said, sounding smug. "I have a plan. But I need you by my side. What do you say to one more—for old time's sake?"

Consciences were messy things. Daniel's stomach turned. No wonder he hadn't had one for so long.

Christine Murray stared at him from dozens of photos on his computer screen. Blonde, petite, curvy, with huge blue eyes—absolutely beautiful, except that, in all of the pictures, she looked like a wild deer that had been cornered by a pack of hungry wolves.

"Can't help you," Daniel told Brian. Because he couldn't. He hadn't felt bad about working to defeat Clarence Murray. The man was not fit to govern.

But Christine Murray?

"Lee, quit joking around. It's going to be a bloodbath and I need you by my side. No one can uncover secrets like you."

"Good luck with your candidate," he said. "But I'm out."

Brian hesitated. "Is it just because of Murray?"

"No. I'm out for good. Don't call me again."

"Is that an order?" Brian's voice got level again—which continued to be a bad sign. "Because I thought we were friends, Lee. I thought we had been friends for a long, long time."

Daniel was no idiot. He knew a threat when he heard one. And running a political campaign involved negotiating the ever-moving line between legal and illegal, ethical and unethical. Nobody cared about morals.

Brian's threat was empty, though. He couldn't very well throw Daniel under the bus without getting his own legs run over.

"I'll cheer you on from the sidelines." As Daniel said it, Christine Murray's trapped eyes continued to stare at him from the computer screen.

Two years ago he'd realized she was stunning. A man would have to be blind not to see it. But he had ignored the attraction then. He should be able to do the same now. Something as base and inconvenient as desire screwed things up. It always did.

"You're making a mistake, Lee."

"I have a business to run. But it's been good talking to you, Brian." And with that parting line, he hung up. Daniel tried to turn his attention back to the latest reports on the marketing campaign for the Beaumont Brewery's launch of a new craft beer. But for once, Daniel couldn't focus.

He found himself staring at pictures of Christine Murray as his mind spun out all of the possibilities. Naïvely, Daniel found himself hoping that her father's opponent would leave Christine Murray out of it. He went back to his search results. There wasn't much. There was an announcement that her child had been born, a daughter. There was a teaser article that suggested she was going to sign for the next season of *Ballroom Dancing With Superstars*—but that was from the previous season. Clearly, she hadn't.

After digging deeper, he found what he was looking for—a small bio with the standard headshot attached to the First City Bank of Denver's website. It had to be her—those blue eyes were unmistakable. She was a loan officer at the First City Bank. And she was in Denver? He'd been out of the game too long—he hadn't realized she was so close.

Christine had nothing to do with her father—especially not if she had been in Denver for the last year and a half. She might not get dragged into this special election.

But Daniel knew that wasn't how things worked. The opposition's campaign manager would size up the competition. It would take all of twelve seconds to dig up every piece of useful information he could on Clarence Murray and when he did, Christine would be at the top of that list.

They would come for her again.

Daniel didn't like guilt. And he shouldn't care.

But he stared at the small picture on the bank's website. She didn't look trapped in that photo. She looked cautious, though. She looked like a woman who believed putting any picture of herself on the internet was inviting abuse.

If Daniel had any faith in Clarence Murray actually being a spiritual man, he might try to convince himself that Murray would close ranks around his daughter, try to protect her.

But Brian White wouldn't allow that to happen. Christine Murray was a liability. Daniel was willing to bet large sums of money—and he had large sums of money to bet—that Brian would attack her first. He would make an example out of her to show that Clarence Murray did not engage in nepotism and stuck by his beliefs.

Daniel picked up the phone and dialed the executive office. "Yes?" his half brother, Zeb, said into the phone. "Do you have those numbers?"

Daniel absolutely should not get involved. But two well-funded, cutthroat political campaigns were about to descend upon Christine Murray. "Not yet. I need to be out of the office for a little bit—hopefully just a couple of hours, but it has the potential to become more involved."

Zeb was quiet for a moment. "Everything okay?"

They had a tenuous relationship that was part stranger, part boss, part brother. The familial bonds felt awkward for both of them. "It should be. But if it becomes more involved, I'll let you know."

Zeb chuckled. "Yeah, that was reassuring. Good luck."

"Luck has nothing to do with it."

Which didn't change the fact that he was going to need all the luck he could get.

Christine Murray looked longingly at the coffeepot in the break room. She needed something stronger than green tea, but she had learned the hard way that if she had coffee this late in the day and then nursed Marie at bedtime, the girl would be bouncing off the walls all night long.

Not that Marie would sleep, anyway. She was teething—again—and all Christine could do was cling to her sanity in a blind stumble toward the weekend, where she would at least get to nap when Marie went down in the afternoon.

It was days like today that she gave thanks that she was a loan officer instead of a teller. She'd always liked being a teller—the job had paid her way through college. But she did not have it in her today to be perky.

Tea in hand, she settled in at her desk and stared at her computer without really seeing anything. She allowed herself a moment of indulgence to think *what if*. What if Doyle, her fiancé, had stuck by her during her father's last campaign? What if they had gotten married like they planned? What if she had some help with Marie?

But if she was going to dream about the impossible, she might as well go all out. What if her mom hadn't died? What if her father hadn't been on a quixotic journey toward political office for the last fifteen years? What if she had grown up in a normal household with normal parents?

Her phone rang, snapping her out of her reverie where life was perfect and everybody got at least seven hours of sleep every night. "Thank you for calling First City Bank of Denver, this is Christine. How can I help you?"

"Good afternoon, Ms. Murray." Something in the man's voice set her teeth on edge. "We haven't been properly introduced but my name is Brian White and I'm calling on behalf of your father, Clarence Murray," he added, as if Christine could possibly forget who her father was.

She slammed the phone down before she even realized what she was doing. She would never forget the name of the man who had ruined her life.

Brian White had been a campaign manager for the opponent in her father's last attempt at higher office.

The phone rang again and she knew it was him. She didn't want to answer it but she was at work. There was a chance that someone was calling about a loan. So, squeezing her eyes shut, she answered.

"Ms. Murray—I believe we were disconnected."

The bottom fell out of her stomach and she sat bolt upright at her desk. "What do you want?"

"Ms. Murray. There is no need to sound alarmed," he

went on in that slick voice, which of course only scared her more. "Your father has asked me to reach out to you."

"Oh?" Her voice wavered, darn it all. "He couldn't bother to call me himself, I guess? I'm only his daughter, right?"

Mentally, she high-fived herself. She was still getting used to standing up for herself. She was not going to cower before political consultants or campaign managers or even her father.

That victory was incredibly short-lived because she realized a call from a campaign manager could only mean one thing. One terrible, awful thing.

"Your father is going to be running for the US Senate seat in the state of Missouri—were you aware that it recently became open?"

Christine did not throw up all over her desk. Score one for adulting. "I was not."

"Sex scandals are such a tricky thing to negotiate. And the people of Missouri are going to be looking for someone with an unimpeachable character and record—someone like your father."

Maybe she was so tired that she had fallen asleep at her desk and was having a nightmare. *Wake up*, she told herself.

Brian White kept talking. "What we'd like to do is make you a part of this campaign. A redemption story, if you will."

Oh, God. "No, I don't think I will."

Because she had a very good idea of what a redemption story would look like to her father. There would be a public confession of her many, many sins. Probably something resembling a walk of shame. And that was just for starters. Her father would expect her to go on talk shows and accompany him on the campaign trail. Knowing him, he would expect her to find a nice man and then make Marie legitimate by getting married.

Her heart was going to beat itself right out of her chest. She had to physically hold on to the desk to keep from falling out of her chair when Mr. White said, "Oh, I think you will. You're a very important part of your father's campaign and he insists on bringing you back into the fold."

She hadn't heard from the man since his last concession speech—a garbled screed against sin and the devil where he had apologized to his faithful believers for his daughter, who had stained his quest for truth, justice and the American way. "He's had almost two years to bring me back in the fold and he can't even bring himself to do it. He has to get his lapdog to call me."

White chuckled. "I can see this is a bad time. I'll call again in a couple of days, when you've had time to think the proposition over. You are going to want my help, Ms. Murray. Because without it…"

It wasn't so much a threat as a statement of fact. She was about to lose control of her life all over again and for what? For her father's misguided attempts at winning a political office?

Last time had been bad enough. Her every misdeed, her every bad picture—all that had suddenly become fodder for the gossip mill. The television commercials had been the worst—her photos had been distorted so she looked like a stupid cow chewing cud instead of a woman who was six months pregnant. It had been the darkest time of her life.

This time would be so much worse because they wouldn't just come for her. She had survived that kind of attack once before. It was awful and painful, but she had survived.

No, this time they would come for Marie. Her precious little girl.

Christine hung up the phone and somehow made it to the ladies' room. She locked herself in a stall and sobbed. Why was her father doing this? Why was he doing it to *her*? She knew Clarence Murray didn't love her. But surely he had a little human decency—just enough that he would want to shield his only granddaughter from the media?

Oh, who was she kidding? Her father had never considered anyone else's needs. The only thing that mattered was what he decided God had meant for him to do.

"Christine? Are you okay?"

It was Sue, a teller who was Christine's best work friend. How long had she been in there? She dried her eyes on industrial-grade toilet paper and opened the door. "I'm fine."

But even as she said it, Sue gasped and recoiled in horror before throwing her arms around Christine's shoulders and hugging her. "Oh, honey—who died?"

Christine almost laughed because if she didn't, she would start crying again. "It's nothing."

The ramifications of her father's latest campaign began to spin out for her. The bank's owner, Mr. Whalen, would not appreciate this sort of attention. She might have to uproot her life. Go somewhere new and start over.

The prospect was daunting. With what money? She had a couple hundred socked away in the bank, which was not a heck of a lot. She didn't want to have to give up her life, her identity—to say nothing of her privacy and sanity—just so her father could lose a campaign again.

What was she going to do?

One of the reasons she had moved to Denver was that fewer people knew who she was. Murray was just another last name here.

So Christine did what she had to do—she lied again. "I'm hormonal and Marie is teething and I'm *so* tired." Not that it was much of a lie. She merely left out the bits about political intrigue.

"Here, let me fix you up." Sue produced her purse, which was sixty-three percent makeup. Christine felt a moment of longing for those days. Currently, her purse consisted of diapers, wet wipes, bibs, crayon stubs, random Cheerios and things she didn't want to think about. Glamour and beauty were low on her list right now.

Still, there was something comforting about letting Sue apply under-eye concealer and powder her face, especially since Sue was relatively close in coloring to Christine and was only a few inches shorter—they'd been able to swap clothes a few times.

"Am I in trouble, do you think?" She had no idea how long she had been hiding in the ladies' room. All she knew was that Brian White and Clarence Murray and the media couldn't reach her in there. If she did not have to pick up Marie tonight from day care, she would never leave the ladies' room. This place was her sanctuary.

Except for the small detail that she was still at work. "There's some guy out there waiting to talk to you." Christine must have looked stricken because Sue quickly added, "He's not mad or anything. He's *hot*. Tall, dark—extremely handsome. I didn't see a ring."

It was all she could do to get her mouth closed. "You checked him out?" But even as she said that, she felt the weight on her shoulders lighten ever so slightly. After Brian White had ruined her life, she'd looked him up on the internet. He was not tall. He was not dark. No one would ever accuse him of being handsome. The man was short, pudgy and balding.

Which meant that whoever was waiting for her at her desk was not a campaign manager representing her father.

"Of course," Sue said. "Wait until you see him. I bet he's a male model. Maybe even a movie star—he's that *hot*."

Christine snorted. She didn't need hot—she needed help. Real, tangible help. She needed someone who would get Brian White and her father to leave her alone. She needed someone who could help her protect Marie. She needed brains and brawn. And she needed enough money to pay for all of that.

She might as well ask for a unicorn for her birthday. "We don't give out loans based on hotness."

"We should. There," Sue added. "You look human again."

Christine hugged her friend and strengthened her mental resolve. "Thank you. I better get out there and meet Mr. Hot."

If she couldn't get through one day at a time, she'd take it one hour at a time. One minute at a time.

Sixty seconds. She could do this.

God, she hoped.

Two

Her courage fortified and her under-eye bags hidden, Christine headed to her desk. She rounded the corner and pulled up short—Sue had not been lying. The gentleman waiting for her was *beyond* hot. His dark hair was perfectly slicked back, giving him a smooth look. And was that suit custom-made?

Even though he was casually sitting in the chair in front of her desk, one leg crossed over the other, she got the impression of a knife—sharp and potentially dangerous. When he noticed her, he came to his feet like a cat uncoiling from a nap. She revised her earlier opinion. He was not potentially dangerous—he *was* dangerous.

"Ms. Murray." There was a tone of the familiar in his voice and she felt herself gritting her teeth. Did he know who she was?

"Welcome to the First City Bank of Denver." Because she was at work, she extended her hand in a polite businessperson's handshake. "And you are?"

He stared down at her for a moment and she almost got lost in his light brown eyes. Up close, she realized that his hair wasn't black—there was a hint of red that lightened the color to a deep mahogany. It was a striking look on the man.

Against her will, her pulse began to flutter in her neck. Men generally did not look at her with interest. She was short and chunky and she couldn't be one hundred percent sure she didn't have oatmeal stains from Marie's breakfast on her shirt.

"Lee." He slid his hand into hers but instead of the acceptable three-pump handshake, he just held her hand, palm to palm. "Daniel Lee." As he said his name—slowly and carefully—he studied her.

What was this? Was he checking to see what her reaction would be?

She swallowed nervously. Was she supposed to know who he was? Something about him seemed familiar. Maybe he was a movie star? Or at least a cable TV star? But his name didn't ring a bell. He was so incredibly gorgeous that it was making it hard for her to think.

She should have stayed in the ladies' room. "How can I help you today, Mr. Lee?" she said, taking sanctuary behind her desk. She felt better with four feet of wood between them.

He stood for a moment too long, staring down at her. Nervously, she lifted her gaze back to him. The suit was most definitely custom-made—the shirt was, also. Those trappings did little to disguise the raw power of his body. Again, she thought of a dagger in a perfectly made sheath. He was the sort of man who always got his way.

The sort she avoided like the plague. Because men like him never cared for women like her and they certainly never cared for babies like Marie. Christine was tired of being collateral damage.

She motioned toward the chair. She couldn't handle him looming over her.

He sat, somehow making her standard-issue office chair look as regal as a throne. "I don't think the question is what you can do for me, Ms. Murray. The question is what I can do for you."

She needed to start carrying pepper spray. "I'm not interested."

One corner of his mouth—not that she was staring—curved into a deadly smile. Christine was both simultaneously thankful that Sue had fixed her face and upset that she had. If only Christine looked like she was having the worst day of her life, this man might not be staring at her quite so intently. "Are you sure? You don't even know why I'm here."

This was something that was different from two years ago. Then, when the reporters had first started showing up at her home and following her to work in Kansas City, she hadn't been ready for it. Footage of her stammering and looking petrified was all over the internet. Even she had to admit that she looked guilty as sin in those videos.

But she learned how to brace herself for the attacks and how to keep her face relatively calm. She wasn't the same clueless girl she'd been back then. And besides, she already had advance warning.

"Who sent you? My father?"

That dangerous smile fell away from his face. *Ha*, Christine thought. She'd caught him off guard and that counted for something.

"No. But I'm going to make an educated guess that you received a phone call today—probably from Brian White." Although she didn't want to react, she could feel the blood draining out of her face. This guy knew who Brian White was? "Yes," he said in a voice that might have been gentle coming from anyone else. "I can see that you did. I was hoping to get to you before he did."

"Who do you work for?" And as much as she wanted to sound strong and brave, her voice came out shaky. Because how much did one woman have to endure?

Something flashed over his eyes and if she didn't know better, she would've said it was guilt. "I am the executive vice-president and chief marketing officer of the Beaumont Brewery. I do not work for your father, nor do I work for any potential opponents of his. I have no interest in forcing you to publicly..." He waved a hand, as if he could pull the right words out of thin air. "Repudiate your life choices, nor do I have any interest in using them against you."

Well. At least he hadn't called Marie a sin. Although "life choice" wasn't a huge step up.

Wait. Was that why he looked familiar? He was one of those bastards—Beaumont's bastards. His brother or half brother—she had no hope of ever keeping the Beaumonts straight—had taken over the brewery. She'd only been in Denver for a few months when that happened. And besides, she didn't drink anymore.

Why was the executive vice-president of the Beaumont Brewery offering her help? It felt like a trap. A really obvious trap. "Who are you, really?"

He didn't answer the question. "I know what's coming—and so do you. Because here's what happened. Mr. White offered to redeem your reputation and, when you refused his so-called help, he threatened to make an example of you."

Her vision swam. She wanted to go someplace quiet and dark and lie down and close her eyes and open them again and find out this entire thing had been one never-ending nightmare.

But this Daniel Lee was right. "How do you know?"

He looked pained—truly pained. He stood and pulled out a business card. He extended it to her, but she didn't take it from him and, after an awkward moment, he set it on the corner of her desk. "Because I was the one who found out you were pregnant. I'm the one who made it a news story. Everything that happened to you was a direct result of my actions, which means that—" he went on, ignoring Christine's gasp of horror "—everything that happens to you from this point on is also my responsibility. You're going to get dragged, Christine. I know what White is capable of and we both know what your father is capable of. You need my help. You can't handle this by yourself."

"Get out." She wanted to stand to make her point, but she didn't trust her legs. It was *him*. This slick, smooth, unfortunately hot man had helped Brian White ruin her life. She really was going to throw up, adulting be damned. "If I see you anywhere near me or my daughter, I'm calling the police."

He inclined his head in her direction, something that was almost a bow. "As you wish. But the offer stands. I no longer work as a political consultant, but I know how to play the game. I can protect you. You and your daughter." He touched the tip of his index finger to the top of the silver frame that held a small picture of Marie on her first birthday.

Christine's mouth was dry and her throat wasn't working. She desperately wanted to tell this man to go to hell but before she could form the words, he gave her another one of those half bows, turned on his heel, and walked away.

* * *

Christine began to search during her breaks. Although he had not officially declared his candidacy, "sources close to Clarence Murray" were leaking teasers about his upcoming campaign—the kind of leaks that were designed to inspire his political base and raise funds from the faithful.

She couldn't find *anything* about Daniel Lee. She didn't even bother looking for Brian White. White was the scum of the earth and she didn't want him to pollute her brain any more than necessary.

But Lee confused her. He had taken full credit for dragging her into the last campaign. If—and it was a huge *if*— his offer of help had been sincere, it had almost been… an apology.

But she couldn't even find a mention of him that existed before he suddenly appeared by Zeb Richards's side at the Beaumont Brewery. His official brewery biography stated that he had a long history of working for political campaigns but the man was like a ghost. And with a last name like Lee, there was no way to track him down.

She found herself staring at his official company photo. It wasn't fair how good-looking he was. If she had to guess, she would say he was at least part Asian—but that didn't exactly narrow things down. Lee was a popular name in several Asian countries. Searching "Daniel Lee" led to an overwhelming number of results.

She didn't want his help. Frankly, she didn't want anyone's help. If there was one thing she had learned, it was that relying on other people was asking to be disappointed. She had thought she could rely on Doyle. After all, they'd been engaged. They'd taken the first step in publicly declaring their love. They'd created a child together.

But when she'd really needed him, Doyle had run. Not that she could blame him—if she could have gotten away from the media attention, she would've. Still, it hurt. It hurt that he sent a monthly child support check and had nothing to do with his daughter.

It was foolish to keep hoping that no one would pay attention to Christine and her daughter. But short of calling Daniel Lee and asking what, exactly, he had in mind when he said he could protect her and Marie, she didn't know what else to do.

So she did nothing. She did her job and she took care of her daughter and foolishly hoped for the best.

"Who's the target?"

Daniel leveled a look at Porter Cole, the private investigator who'd done work for him in Denver on numerous occasions. Referring to Christine as a "target" grated on Daniel's nerves. "Christine Murray."

Porter made it his job to know things. "What are we looking for?"

Porter had done more than enough work for Daniel to trust him with sensitive directives. But Daniel wasn't about to let the man know he had suddenly developed a conscience. "You're not looking for anything about her."

Porter stared at him in confusion. "Then what are we doing?"

"I have reason to believe she's about to get a tail. I want to know who's watching her and her daughter, when and for how long. And I want the means to get them off her tail. Outstanding warrants, whatever it takes."

Seeing Christine Murray in person had made everything a thousand times worse. Had he thought she was beautiful before? In person, she was so much more than that. Delicate and vulnerable—scared and mad—but underneath was a core of strength that took everything lovely about her and made her that much more attractive.

Porter notched an eyebrow as he scanned the file on Christine. "Any particular reason?"

"None that you need to know." Which was a bit of posturing and Daniel knew it. Porter was a smart man, more than capable of connecting the dots. "As usual, do not engage unless there's a threat."

"Contact for defense only. Got it. Anything else?" He handed the file back to Daniel.

"No." Daniel took the file and put it in his desk drawer, which he then locked. "Absolute secrecy, as always."

"As always." Porter gave him a long look before standing and straightening his blazer, which concealed his gun. "If you don't mind me saying, I thought you got out of politics."

"I did. This isn't politics."

Porter smirked as he walked out of Daniel's office and said, "You'll be hearing from me," as if he didn't believe Daniel.

For once, it was the unvarnished truth.

What he was doing for Christine Murray—it wasn't politics.

It was personal.

Daniel waited impatiently. Normally, waiting was something he did well. He played a long game—always had. It was one of the things he'd learned at his grandfather's knee back in Seoul, South Korea. Most people looked at the trees. A few people could stand in front of the trees and know they were looking at the forest. But they wouldn't have any idea of how big that forest was. Daniel prided himself on knowing every tree in every acre in the never-ending forest.

He had Christine Murray figured for one of two things. One, she would either call him in a state of blind panic the moment her face appeared on the internet again. Or two, she would disappear.

Okay, maybe that was overstating. Because even though she had clearly been upset when he had approached her at work, she hadn't panicked. She'd maintained her composure and even gotten in a couple of good digs at him.

He couldn't help it. He admired her. It felt risky, this admiration. Combined with the attraction he couldn't quite rein in, it made Christine Murray feel dangerous. She made him want to do things that weren't logical.

Things like pay for private investigators to shadow her. He'd already gotten a report from Porter Cole. Porter had caught a guy trying to break into Christine's apartment while she was at work. According to his report, Porter had acted like he was a resident of the apartment complex and scared the guy off. But both Daniel and Porter knew that wouldn't be the end of it. Someone wanted inside Christine's apartment, no doubt to gather evidence that could be used against her in the court of public opinion.

Porter said there was also a woman who lingered near the child's day care. At pick up and drop off, and when the children went out to the playground, the woman was within line of sight. Probably taking pictures of the little girl Daniel had seen in the small frame on Christine's desk.

The little girl had wispy light brown hair, but her eyes were almost exactly like her mother's brilliant blue ones. Except innocent and hopeful, instead of trapped and scared.

Christine didn't want his help but she desperately needed it. It would be so much easier if she were willing to talk to him. They could coordinate and come up with a plan that would minimize this disruption to her and her daughter's lives.

But that wasn't going to happen. At least not immediately. Daniel revised his original opinion. She would not call him in a panic the moment she became an internet story. She'd already told Brian off and then told him off. She wouldn't be spooked by a little media coverage. She'd try to brazen it out just like she had at the bank. It was a brave choice. Stupid, but brave.

No, Daniel wouldn't hear from Christine when she became news. But when her daughter became news?

That was when she would either call him or disappear.

He figured he had a week before Clarence Murray announced his candidacy for the open US Senate seat in Missouri.

If only his grandfather could see him now. Lee Dae-Won wouldn't contain his disappointment at Daniel's choices—yet again. Daniel had never been smart enough or ambitious enough or legitimate enough—and certainly never Korean enough—for his grandfather. All might have been forgiven if Daniel had married any of the dozens of acceptable Korean women his grandfather had paraded in front of him over the years and started a family to carry on the family business.

Daniel had steadfastly refused to marry anyone, much less father any children. And he had refused to move to South Korea permanently and live under his grandfather's thumb. It had driven the old man insane that his only heir had rejected the family business, Lee Enterprises.

Daniel liked to think that, at least as a political consultant, he had made the old man proud. Lee Dae-Won hadn't become one of the richest men in South Korea by investing wisely in real estate and electronic manufacturing. Daniel's grandfather had gained power through manipulation, lies and outright bribery. He had trafficked in secrets and that, more than family honor or loyalty, was what Daniel had learned at his knee during summer vacations spent at the family compound in Seoul.

He who controlled the information controlled the world.

Daniel hated not being in control.

He shouldn't care about what happened to Christine or her daughter. At the very least, the basic security measures he was enacting on her behalf should relieve him of his guilt.

It didn't.

Because he had to admit that he did care. He'd catch himself staring at her photo again. And that? That had nothing to do with guilt.

He hoped she'd call him. That was all he could do. The next contact had to be hers.

That didn't mean there wasn't anything else he could be doing right now, though. He scrolled through his contacts list until he found the number he was looking for.

"Hello, Daniel," Natalie Wesley said, answering on the second ring. "Is this a business call or not?"

"What's to say it's not both?" he asked, trying to sound like he was teasing her and knowing he was failing miserably. "How are you and CJ?"

CJ Wesley was another one of Daniel's half brothers—another one of Hardwick Beaumont's bastards. CJ was the one who hadn't wanted anything to do with the Beaumont Brewery. He was a rancher up on the northeast side of Denver and he preferred his privacy. Which made it all the funnier that he had married the former television personality Natalie Baker—the same woman who had tried to expose his parentage to the world.

Natalie was one of the very few people who had been able to locate CJ and ascertain his identity. Plus, she'd had her own morning news show, *A Good Morning With Natalie Baker*, for almost a decade. She was an investigative journalist who knew how to talk to the cameras. "We're fine. You should come up and see us. CJ is determined to get you on a horse, you know."

"I'll do that sometime," Daniel said. While of course he cared for CJ—he was fond of nearly all of his half siblings—CJ was the hardest to be around. His mother had married a good man and he'd had a good life. CJ was at ease with himself in a way that Daniel could never pull off. "I have a situation that I'm going to need your help with."

Natalie sighed. "The offer stands, Daniel. But what is it?"

"What do you know about Christine Murray?"

"Who?"

So, over the next twenty minutes, Daniel filled her in. "Thus far, she hasn't accepted my help. But when she does, we'll need to do damage control."

"Manipulate the search rankings, plant positive news articles, maybe an interview?"

"Yes."

"Got it." There was a pause and Daniel braced for the sisterly concern. "We worry about you, you know."

"Why?" His health was great. He was helping to run the third-largest brewery in America and he owned a substantial share of Lee Enterprises. He owned homes in Seoul, Denver and Chicago. What was there to worry about?

Okay, so he was a little troubled about Christine Murray and her daughter. But that wasn't cause for alarm.

"Daniel…" Her voice trailed off. "Never mind. I'll look into this and get back to you if I find out anything."

It was strange that he felt disappointed she hadn't said something else. Even though he had no idea what he wanted her to say. "Thanks." He ended the call and refreshed the tab he kept open with his searches on Christine Murray. There was nothing new. Not yet, anyway.

But there would be. Soon.

Three

Everything, it seemed, happened at once. One moment, Christine was just doing her job at the bank and trying not to think about the worst-case scenarios *or* Daniel Lee and his seemingly sincere offer of help. Or the way he filled out a suit.

Suddenly, the alerts she had set up on web searches started piling up in her inbox. Clarence Murray had declared his candidacy for the open US Senate seat. Her phone started to ring, as if people had just been waiting for the official announcement. She was trying to read the article about her father and trying to answer the phone in her business-professional voice and saying no comment over and over again when *it* happened.

Will Murray's Granddaughter Cost Him This Election, Too?

And there it was—the photo of her with Marie on her hip, alongside her Honda Civic. It wasn't a good photo—

clearly, it had been taken from some distance. The image was so grainy it could have been almost anyone.

But it was her daughter. They knew where she was and they knew how to take pictures of her daughter and suddenly, Christine couldn't bear it.

With hands shaking, she pulled the nondescript business card out from underneath her office phone. She had wanted to throw Daniel Lee's card away—but she'd been unable to do it. Because what he'd said had felt true, somehow.

Would he actually help her? Or was he working an angle that she hadn't found yet?

Her phone rang again and this time, she recognized the voice on the other end. Brian White—the devil she didn't want to know. "Ms. Murray," he said, as if they were the oldest of friends. "I'm checking back in with you. As you may have heard, your father has officially declared his candidacy and I—"

She hung up the phone. She didn't want to hear his fake offers of help and she especially did not want to hear his thinly veiled threats.

She did the only thing she could—she grabbed her cell phone and hurried to the ladies' room. Daniel Lee's card was a plain white rectangle of paper with two lines of text set directly in the middle—his name and a telephone number. She was shaking so violently that she misdialed the number twice before she finally got it right and even then, she sat for a moment on the stool in the farthest stall and wondered if she wasn't about to make the biggest mistake of her life.

But then she thought about the headline, the one implying that a fourteen-month-old baby had the power to decide elections. The photos would only get better and the headlines would only get worse.

She hit the button and held the phone to her ear. "This is Daniel."

"Um, hello. You gave me your card—"

"Christine? Are you all right?"

She forced herself to take a deep breath and tried to swallow around the lump in her throat. No, she was not all right. Not even close. "Hi. Um, I need to know if what you said when you talked to me last week still applies. The offer about, um, helping me and my daughter?"

"You saw the articles?"

Her vision began to swim and she couldn't tell if she was about to pass out or if she was just crying again. "There's more than one?"

There was a long pause. "That's not important right now. What is important is that you make sure you and your daughter are safe and that we can get together and formulate a plan."

It sounded good. Someone was concerned with their safety. Someone had a plan and the means of enacting it. If life were perfect, this would be the answer to her prayers.

Life had never been perfect. "How do I know I can trust you? How do I know you didn't write those articles or take those pictures? How do I know you're not setting me up?"

"You don't."

Well, if that didn't just beat all. She let out a frustrated laugh. "You're not inspiring confidence right now."

"I'm being honest. You and I both know that if I told you I had nothing to do with those articles and promised you that you could trust me, it would only make you doubt me even more."

Darn it, he was right. But the heck of it was, she didn't have much of a choice right now. Her options were few and far between and there was no guarantee that when she went to pick up Marie after work today there wouldn't be a pack of people with cameras waiting for them. "Fine. But I don't have to like it."

"If you liked it, we wouldn't be having this conversation. Instead, you'd be holding an impromptu press conference in the bank's parking lot. We need to meet, Christine."

Her stomach turned. She leaned forward, putting her head between her knees. "I don't want you in my home. Don't take it personally."

"I don't. Besides, I'm not going to your apartment. One of the worst things that could happen would be for a strange man to be photographed entering and leaving your apartment. Similarly, you can't come to my place. If you're followed—and I think it's safe to assume you will be—that's another set of headlines that neither of us wants."

Okay, so he was being honest. "You want to meet in public?" Because that also seemed like a bad idea.

"And risk more media coverage? Out of the question."

She honestly didn't know if this conversation was making her feel better or worse. "So if we can't meet in private and we can't meet in public, how the heck are we supposed to meet?"

"You attend the Red Rock church, correct?"

She squeezed her eyes shut. "I suppose I shouldn't be surprised you know that."

Red Rock was her attempt to bridge the evangelical teachings of her childhood with the faith that was in her heart. She needed a spiritual home and a nondenominational megachurch was a good place to disappear.

Plus, they had a nice child care center. Going to Sunday services was as close as she got to a weekly break.

"Which service do you normally attend—the nine a.m. or the ten forty-five?"

"The later one." This seemed like a bad idea. Meeting

with a—well, she didn't really know what to call Daniel
Lee. He certainly wasn't a friend. Maybe a spy? Finally,
she decided on *associate*. Meeting an associate like Daniel Lee in church seemed colossally wrong.

But sometimes, there simply was no right option.

"Which side of the chapel do you sit on?"

"I'm surprised you don't know," she snapped. Immediately, she added, "Sorry. I'm under a lot of stress right
now."

"There's no need to apologize. If I know which side
you sit on, it'll make it easier to find you. I don't want it to
look like you're looking for me. I would like you to think
if there is a classroom or a small alcove—an out-of-the-
way place where we could chat without being conspicu-
ous about it. Can you do that?"

"There will be people around. Over two thousand people go to this church."

"We're not hiding. We're merely being inconspicuous."

Was she supposed to understand that distinction? "I
sit on the far left side. It's close to the aisle and closer to
the child care center if there's a problem. And there are a
few places where we could talk with minimal interruptions." She hoped.

Actually, the idea of meeting in a semipublic place like
the church wasn't half-bad. She didn't want to be alone
with him. But if they were in the church, there would be
people around. It was probably as safe as it was going to
get.

"Excellent. I'll find you after the service. But don't
hesitate to call me before then if there's something you
need help with."

"All right." It was Friday. Surely, she could make it
through a day and a half, right?

"Christine, I'm serious. If you see someone around who

makes you uncomfortable, try to get a picture of them, then call me immediately."

"What are you going to do that the police couldn't?"

There was another pause, one that felt heavy and ominous. "I'll see you on Sunday," he said, completely avoiding the question. "Keep a low profile until then."

That made her laugh even as her eyes began to water again. "I've been doing that for the last year and a half. I go to work, I go grocery shopping and I go home. I do my laundry and then take care of my daughter. I don't have wild nights on the town. I don't take lovers. I'm the most boring person I know and see what good it's done me?" She only realized she was shouting because her voice echoed off the tiled walls of the bathroom. "It doesn't matter how low my profile is. I'm nothing but bait in a sea of sharks. And it's all your fault."

She didn't know what she expected him to do. Defend himself? Yell? Point out that, if she had managed to get married before she'd gotten pregnant, none of this would have happened? That was her father's favorite. This was nobody's fault but her own.

Daniel Lee said none of those things. "I know. Just remember that help is a phone call away. You're not alone." And just like that, he ended the call, leaving her in a state of shock.

Had he just admitted that she was right? That didn't seem possible. Someone as gorgeous and refined as Daniel Lee—he wasn't the kind of person who owned up to his mistakes—was he?

As tempting as it was, she knew she could not hide out in the ladies' room for the rest of her workday. Sooner or later, her bosses would send Sue to find her and then there would be another makeover session and she would have to go back to her desk and stare at the voicemail, which by now was probably approaching hundreds of messages.

But she couldn't move just yet. She didn't trust that man. She wasn't entirely sure she trusted anyone.

You're not alone.

Oh, if only that were true.

One of the many things Daniel had learned at a young age was how to blend in. Going to school in Chicago had been easy. He had been surrounded by children of Korean descent and other Asians, Eastern Europeans and Africans, in addition to Americans of all colors. Americans could look like anyone and *be* like anyone.

It hadn't been that way in Seoul. Even as a child, he had stuck out. By the age of ten, he'd been taller than his mother and by the age of twelve, taller than his grandfather. His hair and eyes weren't black. His eyes would never be as green as his half brother Zeb's, but they were a light brown and his hair had an almost reddish look to it.

Most Americans guessed he was Asian, but Koreans knew he was American on sight.

So he had learned how to blend in. His grandfather had paid for a private tutor to instruct him on Korean social manners and Daniel had been an eager student—first, in the hope that he would fit into his grandfather's world and then, when it became apparent he never would, just to show up the old man. Similarly, every fall when he came back to Chicago after three long months in Seoul, he had to relearn how to shake hands, how to tell American jokes— hell, even how to walk. He took longer strides in Chicago.

He was good at blending, though. Sometimes, due to his coloring, people thought he might be Hispanic. Daniel had learned not to mind. People saw what they wanted to see, which made it easier to blend in.

Take this Sunday morning, for instance. People wanted to see a potential new church member and Daniel gave them what they wanted. He was wearing a pair of brown corduroys and a thick cable knit sweater over a denim shirt. On top of all of that, he had on a ski jacket and snow boots and a knit cap pulled over his ears. He'd added a pair of glasses. In other words, he looked nothing like Daniel Lee but everything like a hipster attendee of a megachurch.

Daniel wanted to see Christine with his own eyes. He was responsible for dragging her name through the mud—that wasn't even a question. But what if...

What if she was just as crazy as her father was? What if she was a manipulative, coldhearted woman?

He didn't think so. When he had dug up all that dirt on her two years ago, he hadn't found anyone who'd described her that way. She'd gone through a wild phase in high school, but lots of teenagers rebelled. Besides, Christine had settled down in college. She'd met the man who'd fathered her daughter and gotten her life together.

Until Daniel had blown it up.

It was easy to get lost in a crowd of this size. The day was cold and everyone was bundled up. Aside from his clothing, all he needed was a friendly smile and a certain eagerness in his gaze.

He let the crowd carry him into the lobby. He snagged a program and pretended to read it as he studied the crowd. He didn't see anyone out of the ordinary, but then again, whoever was shadowing Christine was probably trying to blend in just as much as he was.

And then she walked right past him, that little girl in her arms. Marie, he mentally corrected himself. She wasn't just a little girl. She was the child Christine would do anything to protect.

Christine didn't notice him. She was busy chatting with

her daughter, getting her puffy pink coat unzipped and the stocking cap off her head. It was the first time he'd seen Christine smile. God, she was stunning when she was happy.

Marie had a red nose and redder cheeks, but a big smile that she spread around the room. She even looked at Daniel and grinned, her blue eyes lighting up as if she had been waiting for him all this time.

It felt like someone had punched him in the chest. Marie really did have Christine's eyes, hopeful and happy. And it seemed like Marie's little face answered at least some of Daniel's questions.

Then they were gone, disappearing down a long hallway with a steady stream of parents jostling other small children. The crowd began to move into the auditorium and Daniel moved with them, trying to stick to the back. He didn't see either of the people Porter had identified as watching Christine, which was good.

Daniel had grown up going to a church where the service was performed in Korean in Chicago, but he was not deeply religious. He knew too much about people in power, which included religious leaders.

Nonetheless, it felt awkward to be spying on the woman in the house of God and even more wrong to be looking for other spies. He wanted at least one place to be a sanctuary for Christine.

She was one of the last people to come back into the auditorium as the band started up. This was the kind of church that had a rock 'n' roll band in addition to gospel singing and hymns. It had a little bit of everything, with high definition video presentations and surround-sound audio.

He watched Christine without staring at her. As she settled into her seat, she nodded and smiled and said a few things to the people around her. People treated her as they would any good acquaintance they saw once a week—they were friendly, but not overly warm. Which was good. He wasn't sure how far that first story had gotten. Christine as a news item hadn't been picked up by network television yet. Wonky political sites didn't have much reach outside of the political set. Plus, they were in Colorado, not Missouri.

The service was a solid hour and a half of preaching and singing and clapping. It was an engaging service, but Daniel wasn't really paying attention. He was mentally running through all the potential outcomes.

Natalie had already started flooding the internet with positive mentions of Christine. Even if Christine wasn't actually discussed in the article, Natalie was referencing her in the title to drive down search engine results on the other news articles. More official press releases would be released on Monday and Tuesday.

As tempting as it would be to think that would be that, Daniel knew better. Christine and her daughter were too tempting a target, the political writ large on something that should've been personal. The primary voting for the special election was a mere two months away and, God forbid Murray actually get his party's nomination, the election was only two months after that. A lot could happen in four months.

The service ended with a thundering song that brought everyone to their feet and they stayed there, chatting with friends as the crowd thinned. Other parents made a beeline for the direction of the day care—but not Christine. She leaned on a pew, smiling at the person who'd been sitting in front of her—but Daniel noticed the way she was surreptitiously glancing around the room. Looking for him.

Suddenly, he was gripped with a strange urge to make

her *see* him. He wanted her to look at him and recognize
him and—he knew it was completely unreasonable—he
wanted her to be happy to see him.

He had no business wanting such a thing. Obviously,
what he really wanted was to be absolved of any guilt he
had about the situation she now found herself in.

And then it almost happened. She *did* notice him. Her
eyes grew wide with recognition. But it wasn't with hap-
piness. At best, he would call her expression one of grim
acceptance.

He deserved nothing more.

He gently inclined his head to the left, gesturing toward the hallway. Her chin moved down ever so slightly.

Daniel headed into the hall, which was bustling with
parents trying to get their children back into winter gear
and children refusing to be coddled. The hallway was almost as loud as the band had been—and that was saying
something. Another few minutes passed before Christine
appeared. Daniel did not follow her. He focused on looking lost and overwhelmed. In all this noise, it wasn't hard.

By the time Christine and Marie reappeared, many
families had left and it was starting to quiet down. Christine was tickling the little girl's tummy and Marie was
shrieking with joy. Unexpectedly, Daniel felt an overwhelming urge to protect her. Marie was completely innocent and for the time being, anyway, he was glad Christine
had called him.

She was looking for him this time. Her gaze met his
and the lines around her mouth tightened. It was not a reaction he enjoyed inspiring in people.

That wasn't entirely true. When he was looking at an
opponent, the little sign of displeasure would be a good
thing. But it bothered him coming from her.

She said loudly, "Sweetie, I think we left your hat in the day care," before turning around.

Daniel followed at a safe distance. No one else did. The day care was downstairs and, outside of the room, there was a grouping of chairs and a sofa, along with some toys and books on a beat-up coffee table. It looked like someone had donated a living room and the church had stuck the whole set in a glorified hallway, but it was quiet and no one else came in or out of the day care.

Christine settled onto the couch and clutched Marie as if she were afraid to let her go. "I wasn't sure if you would actually come."

"I gave you my word."

Her brow wrinkled. An irrational need to wipe away the doubt hit him. He wanted to make her smile, like he'd seen before the service. He wanted that smile all for himself.

He wasn't going to get it. "You'll forgive me if that doesn't mean a lot to me at this point."

She still had a lot of fight in her. A grin tugged at his lips, which made her eyes widen. "Understood, but when I make a promise to you, I'm going to keep that promise."

He hadn't always operated like that. But he had turned over a new leaf when he had accepted his role in the Beaumont Brewery and the Beaumont family. He did not lie to his relatives. And he wouldn't lie to Christine.

She gave him a long look, as if she were debating whether or not to believe this particular statement. "So, what do we do now?" But the words had barely left her mouth when Marie squirmed off her lap. Christine set her down and the little girl began to sidestep her way around the coffee table.

"I have a few questions and a couple of suggestions. And then we'll come up with a plan that minimizes the disruption to your life and keeps Marie as safe as possible."

She took a deep breath and let it out slowly before nodding her head. "All right. Although I can't imagine there's something about me you don't know. Not if you're the one who found out about her first."

He felt a pang of regret—but at the same time, he was encouraged. That backbone of steel gave a flinty edge to Christine's vulnerability and damned if he didn't like it.

No, no—not like. *Appreciate*. He appreciated her resolve. "Again, let me apologize for that."

She tried to shrug, as if his destroying her life had been just another day. "All's fair in love and politics."

"No, it's not." She looked up at him sharply, but he went on, "How much contact do you have with Marie's father?"

She winced. "I don't. Every now and then, I'll send him a picture, but he doesn't even reply to those anymore. He pays child support on time, though—my father made sure of that. It's the only thing he's ever done for me."

"That's my next question," Daniel said, forcing himself to ignore the pain in her voice. He was trying to make it better. "How much contact do you have with your father?"

She shook her head. "He doesn't want to breathe the same air as me. He blames me for his last loss—even though he's lost so many elections. He's convinced himself that if it hadn't been for me, he would've won that one."

"You don't think he would have?"

She slumped in the chair. "Of course not. His world is black and white. He's right and everyone who doesn't agree with him is wrong. Most people can't live like that. I know I couldn't." She grimaced, something that was supposed to look like a smile and failed. "Needless to say, I was always wrong."

Her words made sense on a level Daniel didn't want to inspect too closely. "I don't think you're wrong, Christine."

Whatever attempt at a smile she had made faded. "It's

nice of you to say that but I still don't know why you're here or what you think you're going to get out of helping me."

"What I want isn't important. It's my responsibility to shield you and your daughter from the coming storm. That's all there is to it."

As he said it, he looked down at the little girl who was still cruising around the coffee table. As if she knew she was being talked about, she looked up at him and smiled a drooly smile. She made her way over to him and then, in a moment of bravery, let go of the coffee table and all but fell into his legs.

Acting on instinct, Daniel caught her. He had not dealt with children a great deal. He was an uncle several times over, thanks to all of his various half siblings. He had even held Zeb's daughter, Amanda. But that had been when the baby was asleep.

Marie was much larger, squirming and laughing as she looked up at him with those trusting blue eyes. "Hello, Marie."

Marie giggled in response to this and leaned in to him. She was warm and heavy and impossibly cute.

It felt like something shifted in his chest as he stared down at her, the past and future all mixed up in one innocent child.

Then she squirmed and pointed at the coffee table, leaning so far that he had to hold on to her to keep her from toppling over. "She wants to read you a book," Christine said, a note of caution in her voice.

"All right." He scooped one of the dog-eared books off the table. He flipped it open and the little girl began to make babbling sounds. She pointed at a picture and then looked up at him, her eyes so big and so blue. Then she paused.

"She's waiting for you to respond," Christine said. Daniel glanced up at her to see that she was watching this entire scene unfold with interest.

Respond? "Really?" he said, hoping that was what Marie wanted to hear.

It was, apparently. She turned the page and chattered before waiting for Daniel. So he said, "Really?" again, this time with more emphasis. Marie nodded, her downy hair floating around her head.

There was something awkward about this entire arrangement. He was sitting in the basement of a church that he did not attend, holding a child who was not his. But at the same time, there was something that felt…right about it, too. Marie was proof there could still be sweetness and innocence in the world.

That realization he'd had earlier hit him again, harder this time.

He had to protect her. He had to protect them both.

Four

Christine sat in utter confusion. She'd thought she was meeting with the slick, smooth-talking, dangerous man who had made vague promises about helping her weather the oncoming storm. But that's not what was happening.

When she'd seen him earlier, she'd almost jumped out of her skin. Gone was the executive vice-president of the Beaumont Brewery. And in his place was a man who was taking her breath away again and again. Seriously, if Sue had thought he was hot before, she would die of gorgeousness now.

Christine had no idea a cable-knit sweater could be so danged sexy. And the way he was cuddling her daughter? She'd say this was a dream come true but her dreams were never this good.

She shook her head. They had a limited amount of time before either Marie had a meltdown or someone noticed them and began to ask questions. She still had no idea if she could trust Daniel Lee, much less accept his help. She couldn't let her attraction to him muddy the waters, either. She was done being dependent on other people to protect her name or family.

So why couldn't she do anything but sit here and stare as Marie curled into his lap and read him a story as if her daughter had known him all of her young life?

And Daniel—the smooth, dangerous man who had showed up at Christine's work—he was playing along. He was turning the pages for Marie and saying "Really?" a lot—which was what Marie wanted. He wasn't checking his phone or his watch. He wasn't complaining about Marie's very existence.

He was the executive vice-president of the Beaumont Brewery. He was a political consultant who had screwed up her life.

He was a man holding her daughter as if he truly cared about her. A man who looked at her as if she were worth something.

Not even Doyle had held Marie like this. He had never come to see his own daughter. He hadn't replied to the last pictures Christine had sent from her first birthday. Marie was a persona non grata with both her father and her grandfather. They had never seen her as a person. She'd always been a chess piece, a pawn that they moved at will around the board for a game Christine didn't want to play.

And Daniel—he had been the one to start it all. Okay, that wasn't fair. She bore some of the responsibility. But she couldn't look at Marie and think of her perfect angel as a mistake.

"Really?" Daniel said again, cracking a huge smile when Marie drooled on him.

Christine was having trouble breathing. Daniel wasn't looking at Marie like she was a mistake or an accident. He was treating her as a perfectly normal fourteen-month-old baby. Was it wrong to want that?

No. It wasn't. It was the whole reason Christine was here with this man that she still did not trust.

Then Daniel leaned down and rested his cheek on the top of Marie's head. Christine saw him breathe deeply and she knew what he was smelling—Marie's sweet baby scent. Daniel sighed and in that moment, he looked so different from the man who had walked into the bank a week ago that she wouldn't have recognized him. He didn't look hard and sharp. He looked...

He looked perfect.

No. It was probably an act. She didn't believe he felt a responsibility for her and Marie. She absolutely could not let herself buy into whatever fiction he presented. She could not be seduced by tenderness *or* a chiseled jaw—or any combination of the two.

Marie finished the book and squirmed off his lap to go back to cruising around the table. Daniel watched her for a moment and then turned his eyes to Christine's. Heat flashed through her body, an awareness that she didn't want but couldn't seem to ignore. What was wrong with her?

"Where were we?"

Right. Yes. The point—that had nothing to do with the way her skin warmed under his gaze. "Neither my ex-fiancé nor my father has any contact with us."

A change came over his face. It didn't matter how cuddly he'd looked—he was still a weapon that could be used against her.

"And just so we're clear, do you have any interest in publicly reconciling with your father?"

"Why? He'll want me to repent, tell everyone I've seen the light and that his way is the one true way. He'll want me to go to campaign events and dress Marie as a little princess. He might even want me to get married—to someone he approves of, of course—so that Marie is no longer illegitimate." Christine shuddered at the thought of the man her father would approve of. "No. I'm not interested in being a bullet point in a fund-raising email or his mouthpiece and they *cannot* have my daughter."

He considered this statement for so long that she began to fidget. "It might shield you from some of the worst of it."

Was he seriously trying to talk her into this? "Let's say I go along with this insanity. I get an image makeover and follow my father's path. I marry someone who 'redeems' me. Then what? God forbid my father actually wins the election. Instead, he'll probably lose. Will he blame me for it again? Or—more likely—I'll break one of his rules. I *always* do, just by existing. Then what? Another public shaming? No."

Daniel was staring at her and she knew she needed a thicker skin. She knew that this was probably the most sympathetic audience she would get. But he was unnerving her anyway.

God, she was so tired of being judged. "You don't know what it's like," she went on bitterly, "never being good enough. Maybe if I'd been born a boy, it would've been different. But I can't change the fact that, in his eyes, I am marked by sin. You wouldn't understand."

And then she realized what she had just said—and who she had said it to. Maybe Daniel Lee, the political consultant, couldn't understand. But Daniel Lee, the illegitimate son of Hardwick Beaumont, might. "I'm sorry," she stammered. "I didn't mean…"

One corner of his mouth curved up. "It's perfectly fine. I do understand—I had a complicated relationship with my grandfather. I never knew my father." He said it so casually, as if being cut off from half of his heritage was no big deal.

Marie was going to grow up like that, too. She would never know Doyle or Doyle's family. They wanted nothing to do with either of them. Marie picked up on her distress and looked up, her lower lip quivering.

"I'm sorry," Christine repeated, smiling big to show her daughter that all was well. "That was rude of me. I... Well, I don't know anything about you and I think you know a lot about me and this is the most awkward thing ever, isn't it?"

He shrugged, somehow managing to look nonchalant and glamorous at the same time. He really was unfortunately hot. Hot and patient with small children and inexplicably offering to protect her. If circumstances weren't what they were, she could easily develop a huge crush on the man.

She'd always liked boys. *Always*. And the more her father had scolded her about her clothes, her attitude and especially her boyfriends, the more attractive boys had become.

Once, a lifetime ago, she'd started sneaking out of the house when she was fourteen. She'd been smoking by fifteen, drinking by then, too. And the boys...

But as she squirmed under Daniel's direct gaze, she realized that he was nothing like the boys she'd run wild with. He wasn't a boy in any sense of the word. Tall and lean, his hair that unusual mahogany color—so beautiful it was almost painful to look at him straight on—yeah, he was way hotter than any of the boys from her teen years.

But Daniel's appeal went way beyond his physical attributes. Because all of those guys she'd dated in high school and college—none of them would have stood by her side when the crap hit the fan. Doyle certainly hadn't—and

Doyle had been a pretty good guy. He'd paid his part of the bills and asked her to marry him and joked about her crazy dad with her. Sure, he hadn't made her wild with lust—but she'd always chalked that up to maturity. She'd gotten tired of fighting her father's dictates and she'd settled down.

What if it hadn't been maturity? What if it'd just been exhaustion?

Oh, it would be too easy to lust after this man. So she decided she wouldn't. "Look, Mr. Lee—"

He interrupted her. "Call me Daniel, Christine."

She didn't want to. It felt too intimate, to say his name like that. It was definitely too intimate to hear her name on his lips and intimacy was the last thing she needed if she was going to *not* lust after him.

She knew she was blushing and she was completely powerless to stop it. What she wouldn't give to face this man with cool indifference.

Then Marie piped up. "Daniel Tiger!" she said, looking up at Daniel with wild enthusiasm.

At least, that was what Marie meant. Christine had no trouble understanding her even if her pronunciation left something to be desired.

But that's not what Daniel heard. His eyes got wide as Marie banged on the top of the coffee table, warming to her theme and repeated *"anal grr!"* in a volume that was just short of a tornado siren.

"What did she say?" Daniel said, staring at Christine in shock. His cheeks had darkened as she got the distinct feeling he was trying not to laugh.

"Daniel Tiger. It's one of her favorite shows." When he blinked, she added, "He was a minor character on *Mr. Roger's Neighborhood*? They animated him and gave him his own show. She loves it."

"Daniel Tiger!" Marie screeched even louder. It still came out sounding like *"anal grr!"* though.

Daniel blinked a few more times, his eyes getting wider and wider. Then he hid his mouth behind his hand. "Kids say the darndest things?"

He was completely flustered, Christine realized. All it took was a fourteen-month-old with a lisp to knock him completely out of his groove. She allowed herself to smile as she wondered how many people got to see him like this. She was tempted to let Marie keep going—and she knew her daughter could—but time was of the essence.

"Honey," she said to Marie, "why don't you read me a story while Mr. Lee and I keep talking?"

For a moment, she thought her daughter would balk but then she spotted a *Pat the Bunny* book. She slid along the coffee table and cuddled into Christine's arms, ready to tell some long-winded story about a bunny that even Christine wouldn't be able to understand.

"Sorry for the interruptions. This is life with a toddler."

Daniel still had his mouth hidden behind his hand, but she could tell he was grinning wildly. "Not a problem. Although it would probably be best if we didn't let her say that near any microphones."

She wanted to laugh but the mention of microphones reminded her why she was here. "You don't think I'm a bad person for letting her watch television, do you? Or is that the sort of thing people will say makes me an unfit mother?"

The smile fell away from his eyes as his hand fell away from his mouth. "I'm sure there are a few sanctimonious idiots who'd make that case. But in reality, letting a young child watch an age-appropriate television show while you cook dinner or breakfast, I assume, is what everyone does."

Marie looked up at her and Christine said, "Oh, really?" which was what Marie wanted to hear. She turned the page and kept on telling her story.

"It won't matter if that's what almost everyone else does. It'll still get twisted around." Christine exhaled heavily. "What should I do? I'd really rather not quit my job and go on the lam."

"Are you seeing anyone now?"

The question caught her off guard. "Oh, yes—in all of my free time, I have an exciting social life where I juggle countless men effortlessly." The corner of his mouth quirked up again but she was absolutely not looking at that smile. "This is it. I go to church. That's my social life. Even if I had time to date, finding a man who doesn't consider my daughter a roadblock to romance is challenging." His piercing stare made her nervous. "Why? You're not going to suggest that I get a boyfriend, are you? Or…"

He wasn't about to suggest that *he* become her boyfriend, was he? Because a man she didn't trust offering to protect her from a media frenzy by pretending to be a romantic interest—that seemed like a setup.

"Absolutely not," he said quickly. "That would only add fuel to the fire. No, I don't want you to find a boyfriend or a fiancé. Instead, I want you to keep doing what you always do."

"You want me to be boring?"

Something deepened in his eyes and, fool that she was, she wanted to think it was approval. "I want you to be the most boring person in the world, Christine." More flutters set off along her stomach at the way he said her name, but she ignored them. "The news cycle moves fast—even faster than it did two years ago. Doing anything interesting—including suddenly developing a love life—would only prolong your time in the spotlight."

They were back to awkward again. Because there was no way to convince her it wasn't awkward to have a man casually dismissing the possibility of her social life. Even though she knew he was right. "Got it. No fun."

He looked almost sympathetic at that. "You're not going to like this next part."

"I haven't liked any part so far."

He dropped his gaze and looked guilty again. It was unsettling. "I've already taken a number of steps to insulate you from the worst of the damage."

He was right. She didn't like the sound of that. "What kind of steps?"

Marie demanded her attention. When Christine looked back at Daniel, he was staring at her again. He needed to stop doing that. She was already struggling to not lust after him and having him look like he actually cared what happened to her wasn't helping. "I've arranged with a freelance journalist to flood the internet with articles that will drive down less positive articles about you in the search results. I've set up a phone number and email address so your phone at work isn't ringing off the hook and I've assigned a twenty-four-hour security detail to you."

She gaped at him, stunned. "You did *what*?"

For a moment, he looked uncomfortable. "I also know the names of the people currently tailing you and I'm working to make sure they leave you alone. I've already had one of them arrested on an outstanding warrant, but someone else will replace him, I'm sure."

She began to shake again with impotent anger. Which part of this was worse—the fact that he'd "taken the liberty" to set up phone numbers in her name or that the people who had been following her and Marie were the kind of people who had outstanding warrants?

None of it was good. "You did all of that without my permission?"

"Yes."

"After I told you to leave me alone?"

He didn't look away. "Yes."

She stood abruptly, gathering Marie to her chest. "Explain to me again why I'm supposed to trust you?"

He stood as well, his hands in his pockets. He looked contrite, but it was probably an act. "You need me, Christine."

"That's no explanation at all." Marie started to fuss. Christine grabbed her puffy coat and shoved the little girl's arms into it. "Why did you even ask me to meet with you, if you weren't going to listen to me anyway? God, I am *so* tired of other people deciding for me."

She spun on her heels to walk away, but Daniel's hand closed around her arm, bringing her to a halt. She could feel the warmth of his body heat through her sweater but it didn't matter. None of it mattered. "Let me go."

"Christine."

Then she made the mistake of looking at him. His eyes—they were huge and pleading and she didn't see dishonesty there. Why was the one man who gave a damn about her the one who'd ruined her life? It wasn't fair.

"And stop saying my name like that, darn it."

He was genuinely confused. "Like what?"

"Like I mean something to you. Because I don't. *We* don't. Stay away from me, Mr. Lee. Stop trying to rescue me from your own guilt."

She jerked away from him and this time, he didn't stop her. Marie looked back over her shoulder as Christine all but ran for the stairs and called out, *"anal grr!"* as she waved goodbye.

Christine was so mad that she struggled to keep the

tears from spilling over as she rushed out to her car. Because she couldn't cry. Someone might be watching. Doing something as unforgivably human as having a bad day would doom Christine to yet more hell on earth.

So, despite her anger and frustration and the sheer hopelessness, she kept a big smile pasted on her face, just in case someone was watching. Even if that someone was Daniel Lee. She wouldn't give him the satisfaction of knowing he'd upset her.

He was perfect and he was one hundred percent wrong and somehow, he was both of those things at the exact same time. He'd gotten her into this mess and she wanted nothing more than for him to make it go away, too.

But only fools clung to hopes and prayers and Christine was done being made the fool by any man. No more.

God, she hoped she never saw that man again.

Five

Over the course of the next week, Daniel tried to stop thinking about Christine.

He couldn't, actually. Because even though his actions had infuriated her, he still couldn't bring himself to abandon her to the winds of fate. She didn't have to like it and she didn't have to like him. But he was not going to let her be dragged through the muck and he especially was not going let Marie be dragged. The little girl was too innocent—and too helpless.

So he tried to think about her as a client—a non-paying one, but still, one who required a high level of personalized service without any active involvement in…anything.

It didn't work. Because although he was usually perfectly able to separate his personal life from his business endeavors, he was struggling this time.

He couldn't stop thinking about the way Christine had looked at him during their meeting—cautious and wary, then warm and happy when her little girl had mangled an animated tiger's name. Repeatedly. That smile—God. And she had no idea what she did to him, either.

It'd been a long time since he'd felt this kind of attraction to a woman. And even then, it wasn't the same. This wasn't merely an awareness of Christine on a sexual level. He was concerned about her. He wanted to make up for what he'd done, yes—but he didn't just want to shield her from the fallout. He wanted...

Hell, he didn't know what he wanted. Something more from her.

And he couldn't stop thinking about Marie, either. He hadn't expected how deeply it would affect him to hold the little girl on his lap and smell her baby smell and listen to her babble at him.

So, yeah—he was going to keep right on protecting the Murray women, whether Christine liked it or not. If anything happened to Marie because of something he'd started two years ago, he wasn't sure he could live with himself.

The hell of it was, he'd always been able to live with himself. So what was it about Christine and her daughter that was different? Had he gone soft?

If he was being honest, the situation struck a chord with him. Because the truth was, he knew what it was to grow up with a shadow permanently following him. Every time his mother had put him on the airplane to fly to Korea for the summer, he'd had to lock a part of himself away in a small box where his grandfather wouldn't be able to get to him.

He'd had to. His grandfather would never let Daniel forget that he was a bastard. As if Daniel had any choice in the matter. He hadn't, but that hadn't saved him from the old man's ire. No matter what he had done, no matter how hard he had worked, he had always been a stain on the Lee family honor.

He didn't want that for Marie. And if White or someone else made that child into a campaign issue, the stain of her birth—the stain Daniel had made—would follow her for the rest of her life. Those internet stories would never die. Marie would never have the chance to be her own person instead of the person everyone had already decided she was.

Just like he had made an executive decision two years ago about who Christine Murray was—a wild child, an embarrassment to her father's name. She'd been a liability. He'd turned up the witnesses with stories of parties and drinking. He'd dug up the truth about her pregnancy and he had constructed a fiction around those things—an out-of-control girl who was a risk to everyone around her.

She'd spent the last year and a half trying to live down that reputation. All because of him.

So he kept Porter Cole on the case and he kept his sister-in-law Natalie busy manipulating web rankings. He crafted several statements that he could put out on Christine's behalf. And he monitored the media requests. Occasionally, he had to contact a customer over a legitimate banking request who'd looked up Christine's number online, but that was an inconvenience he was willing to bear.

If Christine knew Daniel had hacked into her bank's website and changed two numbers on the direct line listed for her, she would kill him. At the very least, she might have him arrested. But given that he had racked up an impressive four hundred and thirty seven messages in a week, he was willing to risk that. Besides, her bosses would fail to appreciate it if their employee's phone rang so much that she couldn't do her job.

Maybe he was working overtime to justify his intrusion

into her life. But every time he felt bad about that, he'd remember the way Marie had waved goodbye to him and then another news article with a click-bait headline would pop up and Daniel would renew his resolve.

But most of all, he stayed alert. The campaign hadn't even really begun yet. These first few articles had merely been warning shots across the bow. The next attack would be coming soon and he needed to be ready.

"Daniel?"

Daniel started, then realized his brother Zeb stood in the doorway looking concerned. "Yes?"

"I said, is everything all right?"

Daniel let that question hang in the air for a moment. He and Zeb had been working together for almost a year, first to get control of the brewery and then to actually run it. But as for having a close brotherly relationship, that was still a work in progress. "Fine. Why do you ask?"

He could tell Zeb was trying not to laugh. "Oh, no reason. I've only been standing here for three minutes, trying to get your attention. Casey wants to get your opinion on the new pale ale brews. Do you have time?"

Zeb had married the brewmaster of the Beaumont Brewery. Together, she and Zeb had remade the Beaumont Brewery into a family business all over again. Daniel would like to take credit for that, but he wouldn't. He never did.

"Of course." He had been—well, not exactly neglecting his duties as the executive vice-president of the Beaumont Brewery—but he had certainly been distracted recently. If Zeb was noticing, it had become a problem.

Daniel stood, putting on his suit jacket. But before he could get the button buttoned, an alert chimed on his computer. "One second."

"She Tricked Me." The Father Of Clarence Murray's Granddaughter Speaks Out.

A sharp stabbing pain began to beat behind his eyeballs. Wasn't it a little early for this? It'd been less than two weeks since Murray had announced his candidacy.

"What's the matter?"

Daniel looked up at his brother. "Nothing."

"Are you sure?" Zeb leaned forward. "Because you look like someone just killed your dog and if it's something that affects you, it's something that affects me."

It was a noble sentiment. In fact, Daniel was pretty sure he had said something along those lines to Zeb when they had first joined forces to get control of the brewery. He had positioned himself as the all-knowing, all-seeing Beaumont bastard. He couldn't be surprised and he always had a plan.

He needed a better plan because no amount of misdirected phone numbers or web ranking manipulations were going to bury this particular lede.

"It's nothing," he repeated. He wasn't surprised that someone had gone after Marie's father—but he was disappointed that he hadn't gotten to the man first. "It's something going back to my previous career. It doesn't affect you or the brewery at all."

Zeb looked like he was debating whether or not to accept that statement at face value. "You'd tell me if you're in trouble?"

"I'm not." Zeb gave him a long look and, against his better judgment, Daniel buckled. "I'm just helping a friend." Although Christine would probably string him up by his toenails if she heard him describe her as a friend. The alerts chimed again—damn it. This was about to snowball. "Look, I need to deal with this. My apologies to Casey about the beer."

He grabbed his coat and started texting before he even got to the door. Bradley needed to bring the car around *now*.

As he brushed past Zeb, the man put a hand on Daniel's arm and stopped him. "She must mean a great deal to you, this friend."

That was a fishing expedition if Daniel had ever heard one. Zeb was a brilliant businessman, but he didn't seriously think that a leading question like that would get him anywhere, did he? "I'll keep you apprised of my whereabouts."

Zeb's eyebrows jumped. "Are you going to be gone for a while?"

"I don't know." Daniel thought he'd had a little more time than this. But watching and waiting was over. He needed to secure Christine and Marie. He didn't want to leave it to Porter or his associates.

He and Christine might not be friends, but he was beginning to think she might mean something to him, anyway.

Christine had thrown herself into work for the last week. She had loan applications to process, credit checks to run, a teething toddler who drooled more than the Mississippi River—more than enough to keep her busy. There was no time in her life to think about Daniel Lee, much less her father's political campaign. She didn't even go on the internet on her work computer unless she was specifically looking for something online. Ignorance was bliss and she simply did not want to know what her father or anyone connected with Missouri politics was doing at any given moment. To heck with whatever they said about her. She wouldn't give them any power over her and that was final.

It was a nice idea.

She still couldn't believe Daniel Lee was having her watched. Or that he was manipulating the internet, somehow. But she was forced to admit that, whatever he was doing, it appeared to be working. She hadn't seen anyone unusual loitering around her apartment or the day care. Her work phone had stopped ringing off the hook. In fact, she had gotten almost no phone calls for the last week, which was odd. Not that she was complaining. In fact, she was kind of relieved.

Maybe she wouldn't hate him. She found herself going over the way he'd let Marie read him a story, the way he'd laughed at her mispronunciations.

The way the heat of his hand had warmed Christine through her clothes and the way his eyes had watched her.

The way he'd looked at her like she mattered.

He was so far out of her league—that much was obvious. And lusting after the man—no matter how deeply she buried that lust—would only complicate every single problem in her life.

Besides, she didn't trust him. Or like him. Only a fool would crush on the man.

"Christine?"

Shaking herself out of her reverie, she looked up to see Sue standing before her, looking seriously worried. At the exact same moment, she realized that there was a dull roar coming from downstairs. "What's wrong?"

"There are reporters in the lobby," Sue said in confusion. "They're demanding to see you?"

"What?"

Just then, her phone buzzed. She looked at it in confusion. Where are you? It was from Daniel.

That realization, coupled with the fact that there were reporters in the building, made the bottom of her stomach fall out. "What's happening?" she asked Sue in a shaky whisper.

"I don't know," Sue replied, twisting her fingers together. "Mr. Whalen is trying to get them out of the building. But there's a *lot* of them. Some of them have really big cameras. Are you going to talk to them?"

Christine knew how this worked because this was what had happened last time. She'd been trying to come to grips with Doyle's sudden reluctance to set a date for their wedding even though she was four months pregnant when she had left work to find a reporter lying in wait for her, shouting rude questions about her pregnancy and her father's campaign. She hadn't known then that she had just become a centerpiece of the opponent's campaign. All she had known was that it felt like she was being attacked— because she was. By Daniel Lee.

This was no different. Those people expected her to come down there and maybe offer some weak statement of innocence or something. And then they would descend upon her like a pack of dogs and she was nothing but fresh meat for the next round of web hits.

"Absolutely not." She wished she had told Sue or even her bosses that this was a possibility. But denial wasn't just a river in Egypt.

Her phone buzzed again. Christine. Please let me help you.

She wanted to hate Daniel so much right now. But she needed help more. There are reporters downstairs. I don't want to talk to them.

"What are you going to do?" Sue asked, staring nervously over her shoulder as the volume downstairs increased.

Is there another way out of the building?

Yes. There was a staff exit by the drive-up windows.

A picture popped up in the text window of a gruff-looking man with a flattop and square jaw. It was followed by the text, This is Porter. He's a private investigator who works for me. Do you feel comfortable getting into a car with him?

The ludicrousness of the situation began to catch up with her. Maybe she should just go back and hide in the ladies' room. It didn't make any less sense than getting into a strange car with a strange investigator who was being paid by a strange man to protect her from her father's insanity.

Maybe this was how Alice felt when she sat down for tea with the Mad Hatter and the March Hare. Because Christine felt like there should be rules, a code of conduct for governing behavior—and nobody but her was trying to make those rules apply.

No, she texted back.

I'm fifteen minutes away. Will you feel safe getting into a car with me?

He was already on his way? He was coming here—for her? Where are we going if I get into a car with you? She was being snippy, but she couldn't help it. Once again, control over her life had been ripped away from her and this time she wasn't even sure why.

Well, to heck with that. She opened a web browser and searched. Immediately, she saw what the problem was.

"She Tricked Me." The Father of Clarence Murray's Granddaughter Speaks Out.

Dear God, Doyle had talked. Worse, she scrolled through the article and saw that he had included one of the pictures Christine had sent him from Marie's first birthday party. The very same picture that sat on her desk, crisp and clear for all the world to see.

White-hot rage blurred out everything but Marie's happy little face. She was going to *kill* Doyle. That was all there was to it. The man did not deserve to live after throwing his own daughter to the wolves.

Waves of fury and fear crashed into each other inside of her head, leaving her with a dull roaring in her ears. That also could be the reporters clamoring downstairs.

"Christine? Sue asked, looking like she was on the verge of crying.

"I'm going to leave," she told her best friend. "A friend of mine is going to pick me up and we're going to go. Somewhere." She didn't know where but, given the racket coming from downstairs, she almost didn't care.

Christine? Daniel texted her.

I'm not sure safe is the right word, but I can't stay here and face these reporters.

Thirteen minutes away. I'll have Porter create a disturbance.

Thirteen minutes. She could make it thirteen minutes, right? Come to the drive-up window.

Then she looked up at Sue. Sue, who was only a few inches taller than Christine and heavyset. Sue, who had overhighlighted her hair, making it blondish. Sure, Sue had a square jaw and brown eyes and freckles and was bottom-heavy instead of top-heavy like Christine was. The women didn't really look that much alike. But to someone who didn't know either of them...

Sue was close enough.

"Christine?"

"Sue, I need a favor," she said, digging out her sunglasses and handing over her knit cap. "I need your winter coat and you're going to take mine."

"What? Why?"

I have a distraction, she texted to Daniel. Then, to Sue, she added, "You're going to pretend to be me."

Six

Daniel wasn't sure if Christine's bait and switch was going to work. She claimed her coworker bore a passing resemblance to her. In a flurry of texts, Daniel had arranged for Porter to muscle his way into the bank, escort the other woman to his car, and drive off. After five or ten minutes, Porter would switch vehicles, come back to the drive-through, and hopefully, the coworker would slip back into the building with no one else the wiser.

But then what? For the first time in a very long time, Daniel didn't have a plan A, plan B or even a plan C.

He was getting soft. That was the only possible explanation for why he hadn't planned for this contingency.

There were two different ways to get to the drive-through—the parking lot and the alley. As Bradley swung around to the second entrance, Daniel could see the crowd churning in the parking lot, like sharks at a feeding frenzy. He just caught a glimpse of Porter muscling people aside, a smallish woman tucked under his arm, when the car turned into the alley, bringing it to the drive-through. He rolled down his window as the teller behind the glass said, "May I help you?"

"I'm picking up a delivery." As the words crackled across the microphone, he saw Christine peek around the corner, an unfamiliar hat scrunched low over her head.

The teller shut off the microphone and turned. She and Christine said a few words, then Christine pulled the hat down even lower, completely obscuring her blond hair.

A minute later, a small side door opened and she slipped out. Daniel did a quick look around, but he didn't see any reporters lying in wait. Christine came around the side of the vehicle, opened the door and climbed in. The moment she shut the door behind her, Bradley began to drive.

"Are you all right?" Daniel asked after a moment of silence.

"Oh, sure. It's just the end of the world. I'll be fine." Christine said the whole thing in a monotone voice.

Was she quoting song lyrics? "You're in shock."

That caught her attention. She rolled her head to look at him and then kept right on rolling her eyes. "Do you think? I'm at least glad to see you're not texting and driving." She looked around at the car. "I was sort of expecting you to be in a little sports car."

For some reason, this response made him grin. She hadn't given up. She still had a lot of fight in her and, oddly, he was glad to see her. "We could change, if you'd like. Would you rather avoid the press in a Corvette or a Maserati?"

"I was joking."

Daniel felt his grin grow. "I wasn't. But to do that, we would have to go back to my place and I'm not sure you'd be comfortable doing that." Oddly, though, he wanted her to be comfortable with it. If he had her back at his condo, there would be additional levels of security between her and the rest of the world.

"I'm not comfortable doing any of this. But I can't just sit there and wait for them to find me again."

"I agree."

She exhaled heavily, staring out the window. "I suppose this is the moment you tell me that it's not safe for me to go home?"

Guilt hit him again, a feeling he didn't want and didn't have time to deal with. "If you'd really like to go home, I am more than happy to take you there. However, I don't feel that's the safest option for you."

"Because they already know where I live?"

She was not going to like this. Daniel braced for the worst. "Because someone has already tried to break into your place."

She jolted as if he had jabbed her with a pin. "What? When?"

"Before we met at the church. My associate scared the guy off. They did not gain access to your apartment or your personal things, but I realize that must be little comfort to you now."

She squeezed her eyes shut tight as the blood drained from her face and Daniel wished he could stop being the bearer of bad news. He wished he had never heard the name Christine Murray. Or Clarence Murray, for that matter.

In that moment, he wished, for the first time in a very long time, that he had been someone else. Someone better. Someone who could have done and said the right things at the right time.

He wished that he were the kind of person who would've

protected someone like Christine the first time, instead of using her.

Sadly, he had very little idea of what a man like that would look like.

"Is this the part where I get to run away and hide?" she asked in a shaky voice. To his horror, a tear escaped her closed eyes and trickled down her cheek.

It hit him harder than any name she could've called him, any insult she could've shouted. And he would give anything to make it better.

He reached over and cupped her cheek, his thumb brushing that tear away. "Is that what you want?"

When she opened her eyes, the world stopped spinning. She looked at him with such longing and hopelessness all mixed together and he knew he needed to drop his hand away. But he couldn't. He couldn't leave her alone. "You know that you're the only man who asks me that? But I don't know what the point of answering it is. Because I still don't know if you listen to me and I still don't know why I should trust you."

"I want to make this better for you," he told her honestly, his thumb still moving over her cheek. It felt so unusual to be honest.

"Just because you feel guilty about what you did to me?"

Somehow, he was getting closer to her and he desperately wanted to believe she was getting closer to him, too. "No."

That's where it started—but that wasn't the position from which he was operating now.

"I want the world to go back to normal. I want to raise my daughter in peace and quiet. I want to do my job without fear that the next time the phone rings, it'll start all over again. That's what I want."

"It will," he promised her. "It just won't happen today. Or tomorrow."

Another tear slipped free and rolled down her cheek. "I should hate you," she said in a voice so soft he had to lean even closer to hear it. Only a few inches separated them now. "You ruined everything. Why don't I hate you?"

In some distant part of his mind, he was calculating the extensive list of reasons why she should hate him. But that list wasn't the reason he wiped this second tear away with his thumb, nor was it the reason he lifted her chin, pulling her closer. Because she didn't hate him. "Because I'm trying to take care of you."

This close, her eyes were an impossible shade of blue, like sapphires catching the light. And the fact that he was even thinking such trite thoughts about any woman— much less *this* woman—was so far out of character for him that he almost didn't recognize himself.

"Why?" Her breath was warm against his cheek. He was close enough to feel that breath, close enough to taste her.

He was going to. He forgot about campaigns and illegitimate children and breweries and terrible fathers. His hand slid down her cheek to her neck and he could feel her pulse throbbing just underneath her delicate skin— skin he wanted to press his lips against. For the few moments they had near privacy in the back of his car, he didn't want to think about the past or the future. Just her. Just him and her.

He brushed his lips over hers, a request more than a kiss. At first, he thought she was going to kiss him back— she sighed against his lips and leaned into him. When she did so, all he could think was *mine*.

Mine.

Then she pulled away, her cheeks blushing a brilliant

crimson. She snapped her gaze out the window and then startled again. "Wait—why are we here?"

Daniel forcibly shook back to himself. Had he lost his mind? Had he almost kissed Christine Murray in the backseat of his car as they were making a getaway of sorts?

She completely turned him around. Did she have any idea how hard it was to do that? He never lost control—or failed to see the big picture.

Except when it came to her, apparently.

"Ah. You didn't think I was going to help you disappear without getting your daughter, did you?"

Christine looked stunned as the driver pulled around the back of the day care. "What did you do?" she asked in that voice that he didn't like—distant and scared.

He didn't want her to feel like she had lost control of her life, even if she had. "I told them you would be picking Marie up early and if they could somehow find a car seat for her, that would be great."

Christine turned back to look at him. "They're going to think you're kidnapping us."

"I'm not. You know that, right? If you wanted, I could leave you here. I'll have Bradley and Porter bring you your car. I will leave you alone if you want me to, Christine." As the words hung in the air, he found himself fervently hoping that she wouldn't want him to.

An older woman with a helmet of curls peeked out the back door. That was probably Mrs. McDonald, the day care operator he'd spoken to on the phone. Christine shot a concerned look at Daniel, but then got out. Daniel let the women speak in private.

As he waited, he got a text from Porter that the investigator had safely returned Christine's coworker to the bank through the staff door. Most of the reporters had dispersed—but Porter warned they could be heading for the day care next.

They didn't have much time. Christine needed to decide what she wanted to happen next. Would she be able to trust him? And if she did, where would he take her? Denver wasn't safe. If someone connected him with her, it would only make the situation worse.

No, they had to go somewhere else. Somewhere where he was not the executive vice-president of the Beaumont Brewery and she was not Clarence Murray's daughter.

If it were just the two of them, he would fly her to Seoul. He maintained a condo in the city and usually spent at least a few weeks a year there, monitoring his business interests and honoring his grandparents' graves.

Christine went inside with Mrs. McDonald. No, he absolutely did not want to bustle a toddler onto a plane for an eighteen-hour flight. Which left only one option.

He called up the number of his pilot. "Lennon, get the jet ready. I'm leaving for Chicago and I'll have two guests, a woman and a baby. Please plan accordingly."

"Are you *sure* everything is okay?" Mrs. McDonald asked for the fifteenth time. "Because if it's not..."

Christine sighed. At this point, all she could do was hide but where would she go? She had limited funds for things like hotels and airline tickets.

"Everything is fine. Mr. Lee is a family friend. My father is in the news again and there were a bunch of reporters at work and I'm afraid that they're going to be on their way here next and I need to keep Marie safe. That's all this is."

When she said it like that, it all sounded perfectly reasonable.

Unlike that near kiss in the backseat of Daniel's very

expensive car. There hadn't been a single reasonable thing about that—not the way he'd touched her and not the way her body had responded to him and not the way that, even now, she wished she'd let him kiss her.

But Daniel had a driver, for God's sake, sitting right there in the front seat. She couldn't kiss Daniel with witnesses.

She was in Mrs. McDonald's office, a closet-sized room with a huge glass window so she could see who came and went from the Gingerbread Day Care. It was nap time and, for once, the building was quiet. "I just find it odd that a strange man calls up and asks me to find a child seat and get Marie ready and he's not on your preferred list. And then you show up with him in a car like that? You have to admit, Ms. Murray, that the whole thing is odd."

"Daniel is a friend," Christine repeated. "I promise there's nothing hinky about this."

God, how she wished that was true.

Mrs. McDonald fretted. "Well, if you say so." She led the way out of the tiny office to where all of the children were sprawled out on miniature cots.

Christine moved as if she were in a daze. Daniel had almost kissed her. In the movies, a kiss was a moment of clarity, a declaration. It made everything make sense.

This wasn't the movies and Christine had never been more confused in her entire life. Everything had spiraled out of control—including her good sense. Because Daniel Lee's lips should be nowhere near hers.

But there was one thing that hadn't changed—that was her daughter. Christine bent over Marie's sleeping form. "Honey, we're going for a ride, okay?" Marie didn't stir.

Mrs. McDonald appeared with Marie's backpack and a car seat that had seen better days. Christine lifted her daughter and the two women moved silently to the back door. Marie stirred in Christine's arms, so warm and heavy with sleep.

The driver, whose name Christine did not know, was waiting for them. He took the car seat from Mrs. McDonald and started to install it where Christine had been sitting.

At the same time, Daniel came over to speak to Mrs. McDonald. As Christine watched, he thanked her warmly and handed her a check for the car seat. He even made sure she had his cell phone number, inviting her to call at any time. He talked about this Porter Cole guy again, the private investigator who had apparently been watching Christine for some time. He promised Mrs. McDonald that, if anyone from the media showed up and started making a nuisance of themselves, Porter would help her handle it.

That was when Mrs. McDonald surprised Christine. "*The* Porter Cole? The hotshot detective that does all that work for the Beaumont family?" Honest to God, Mrs. McDonald's eyes lit up.

Christine had never heard of Porter—but then again, she wasn't exactly plugged into the heartbeat of the Denver social scene.

As Daniel and Mrs. McDonald discussed the private investigator, the driver got the car seat installed and Christine got Marie belted in. Daniel walked Christine around to the other side of the car and held the door for her, and then circled back around to sit in the passenger seat in front.

And just like that, they were off. Destination unknown.

She felt she should be panicking more but she was drained. "We're going by my apartment?"

"No. Not unless there's something that you absolutely cannot live without. Medicines, for example."

She got the feeling he was asking about birth control. She'd had an IUD installed after Marie's birth for obvious reasons. "No, no medicines." She rifled through Marie's backpack. Oh, thank goodness—there was Pooh Bear, her stuffed animal. "If we don't go back to the apartment, where are we going, Daniel?"

He turned around in the seat, his gaze meeting hers. "You want to disappear until this blows over, right?"

"Yes." But even as she said it, another wave of exhaustion hit her. Would this ever really blow over?

"Chicago, then. We're going to Chicago."

Her mouth fell open and she couldn't do anything but stare at him for a long moment. Then the moment got longer she tried to make sense of what he'd just said. "Chicago? As in, Illinois?"

An almost smile ghosted over his lips. "There's only one. I maintain a residence there. The other alternative was Seoul, South Korea—but I didn't think your daughter would do well on a flight that long."

She blinked. "You maintain a residence in South Korea?"

"Of course," he said, as if it was no big deal to own homes in multiple countries. "Now, if you're comfortable..." She began to laugh, but he ignored the outburst. "Could you give me your size and preferences for clothing and toiletries?"

God, just when she thought it couldn't get any worse—now this gorgeous, apparently filthy-rich man who had almost kissed her wanted to know what size she wore. "Why?"

"You can sleep in those clothes if you want, but I think you and your daughter will be more comfortable if you have a change of clothes. And Marie needs diapers?" It came out as a question.

Despite the insanity of it all, she smiled at him. "That would probably be a good idea. Can I make a list?" That way, at least, she wouldn't have to say *size twelve* out loud.

He nodded and produced a small notepad. She wrote down a basic list of things they would need and handed it over to him.

This wasn't a stretch limo so there was no partition dividing the front and the back. But after she handed over the list, it was almost as if a wall was raised between them. Marie had fallen back asleep once the car started to move and Daniel turned his attention to his phone. He was texting and then he made some calls. He spoke in a language she assumed was Korean.

He owned a home in Korea. In her internet searches, she hadn't turned up anything that even hinted at that.

It just reminded her once again that he knew practically everything about her—including her jeans size—and she knew practically nothing about him.

She looked out the window and realized that instead of heading north toward the Denver International Airport, they were heading south. "I thought you said we were flying to Chicago?"

"We are. I keep my private jet at Centennial Airport. It's easier."

She hadn't even realized there were other airports in Denver. Once again, she felt woefully out of her league. "You have a private jet?"

Daniel looked back at her over his shoulder and shot her a quick but intense smile. "Is this going to be a problem? If you changed your mind, we can make other plans."

"I don't think we can go to Seoul. Marie doesn't have a passport and mine might be expired and even if it wasn't, I'd have to look for it."

Besides, there were advantages to going to Chicago. There, no one probably cared about Beaumonts or Clarence Murray and his delusional quest for public office. No one could tail them in a private jet. And Chicago was a very big city. Maybe they would disappear into the teeming mass of humanity.

So she made her decision. "Chicago is fine."

He gave that little nod with his head that was almost more of a bow and then turned his attention back to his phone.

Christine reached over and covered Marie's hand with hers. This was a level of insane she had never anticipated—but if it managed to keep her daughter safe from the onslaught of reporters there'd been at the bank, it was worth it.

An hour later, they pulled onto a runway, right alongside of Daniel's private jet. It was sleek and powerful-looking, and in that way, it reminded her of Daniel. There wasn't anything wasted about it.

Marie woke up as they were unbuckling her and was now full of postnap energy and grumpiness. Luckily, a woman was waiting for them with a few bags of supplies, including a box of diapers. Daniel said a few words to her.

Christine watched as the woman got into a car and sped off. "Who was that?"

"Someone who works for me. Don't worry about it."

Christine snorted. "You realize that I'm about to get on a private jet with a man I barely know and a toddler who's never flown before because it's better than the alternative of waiting for the reporters to break into my house. What part of *that* am I not supposed to worry about?"

Daniel paused, his hand on the railing that led up the steps into his jet. "Christine, I know this is a difficult time, but I would never hurt you or your daughter."

She so desperately wanted to believe his words. "Again, you mean?"

The look of pain flashed over his face. "Again. Shall we?"

She was surprised to see a car seat already installed in

one of the leather chairs—chairs that were nicer than any furniture she owned. They swiveled and had extendable footrests and she was willing to bet the leather was Italian, just like his shoes. "You really do own your own jet."

"I do. Here." He held out his hands for Marie. "I'd recommend using the facilities before we take off."

"Good idea." But she didn't move immediately because she was busy looking at Daniel.

"Anal grr," Marie said in a sleepy voice as she lurched toward him.

The smile on Daniel's face hit Christine like a hammer because he looked so happy to see Marie, happier to be holding her. God help Christine, but Daniel looked like he really cared about her daughter. That feeling only got stronger when he said, "Hi, sweetie," in a tender voice as he tickled Marie's tummy. Marie giggled and Christine's heart clenched.

In another life, this would be everything she'd never allowed herself to dream of. A hot, rich man who cared about her and her daughter? Her fantasies definitely weren't this good.

But in this life, she hurried to the back of the plane to one of the nicest bathrooms she had ever been in. There was even a shower.

She took a moment after she was done to wash her face. There was still a chance this was a dream. Possibly a nightmare. She was going to wake up in her own bed in her own apartment with her own boring life stretching out before her. Marie would keep teething, they would keep working on potty training and hot, insanely rich guys wouldn't make what sounded like sincere promises to her. Because this wasn't her life any more than her father's strict rules and regulations for governing female behavior had been her life.

It was only when Christine realized that she was, once again, hiding out in the ladies' room that she forced herself back to the front of the plane. The door had been sealed, but the plane wasn't moving yet. Marie was cruising from chair to table to chair. And Daniel? Daniel was sitting on the floor, smiling wildly as Marie got grubby fingerprints all over his pristine plane.

If this was a dream, perhaps she didn't want to wake up. Perhaps she wanted to stay in this not-reality where an eligible, insanely rich man saved the day.

"Are you married?" she asked before she could stop the words from coming out of her mouth.

Daniel's eyebrows jumped up, but he didn't look like she had trapped him in a corner. "No. Despite my grandfather's best attempts to find me a proper wife to carry the family name, I remain unattached and uninvolved." Before she could make sense of *that* statement, Daniel rose to his feet. "If you'll excuse me, you might want to get Marie into her seat. We'll be taking off shortly."

"Oh. Sorry." Dying of self-inflicted embarrassment, she scooped Marie out of Daniel's way. Once the door had closed behind him, she looked around. The sofa would have to do as a changing table.

There was a blanket in the bags—Christine would've preferred to wash it first, but beggars couldn't be choosers. She laid it out on the sofa and quickly changed Marie's diaper.

"Baby," she tried to explain, "we're going to take a trip with Mr. Daniel. It's going to be a lot of fun." She hoped.

"Anal grr!"

Christine grinned. *"Daniel*, baby. Can you say Daniel?"

"ANAL!"

Christine couldn't help it. She began to laugh. There was no other response possible.

Really, getting into the car and then the plane with him—that was the sort of impulsive, half-baked thing she would've done back when she was a teenager. It had only been since Marie had arrived and Christine had been raked over the coals publicly that she had stopped acting out. If she weren't so worried, she would be enjoying the hell out of this.

Maybe that's what she needed to do—worry less, enjoy more. While it was still a possibility that Daniel could turn out to be an ax murderer, she doubted it. In fact, aside from the fact that he had openly admitted to destroying her life two years ago, he didn't seem particularly evil at all.

If that was as good as it got—not particularly evil— then that's what she was going with. Because the alternatives were not pretty. Brian White, who worked for her father? He was evil. And her father? Evil was a strong word but...

She got Marie strapped into her new car seat and found a bag of Goldfish crackers from the supplies that Daniel's associate had provided. There was a sippy cup as well. Christine noticed there was a wet bar tucked back in the corner near the bathroom, so she quickly rinsed out the cup. Next to the wet bar, there were several mini fridges tucked under a cabinet. In one there was a variety of alcohol—including stuff that looked really expensive. He flew with champagne? Was that even a good idea? But in the other one there were more normal beverages—soda, sparkling water and apple juice. Bingo.

She filled the sippy cup. She turned back to Marie just as the door to the bathroom opened and Daniel emerged. They almost collided, but he caught her in time. "Ah," he said, taking in the sippy cup. "I see you're finding your way around."

"It's not that big of a plane." His hand was still on her arm and she was blushing terribly.

His eyes crinkled with what she hoped was amusement. "Size isn't everything, or so I've heard."

He was teasing her, she realized. Teasing her and rubbing small circles on her inner arm with his thumb. The flush of embarrassment caught and flamed into something hotter. Something needier.

How long had it been? Too danged long.

"Thank you," she said softly.

Something in his eyes shifted. How could he look at her like that? Like she was somehow glamorous and desirable instead of a disaster with a daughter?

His head tilted toward hers, but he didn't kiss her. He didn't even come close to it—not this time. "Thank you for trusting me." Before she could respond to that, he took the sippy cup and went to sit down by Marie.

No, if this was a dream, she definitely didn't want to wake up.

Seven

"Oh, thank goodness," Christine said, exhaustion in her voice as she slumped back into the plush seating of Daniel's Chicago car.

This Mercedes was longer than his Denver car, the better to accommodate the divider between the driver and the passengers.

"I have to ask—is it always that much fun?" He didn't know a lot about babies but it'd been obvious that Marie had not enjoyed her first flight.

Christine shot him a weak smile. "Sometimes, it's even more entertaining. She's teething. She hasn't figured out yet how to tell me she doesn't feel good without crying. The doctor says she's normal." She notched an eyebrow at him, her eyes tired. "Didn't you grow up with any brothers and sisters?"

"No." That was all he would've said to anyone else, but Christine gave him a measured look and he remembered her saying that he knew everything about her and she knew nothing about him. "My mother never married and she was an only child. And, as you know, I didn't grow up with any of my half siblings on my father's side."

She gave him a tired smile. What was it about that look that made him want to pull her into his arms and let her rest? Maybe she could relax at the condo. There, at least, no reporters would be lying in wait. Plus, Chicago did have one advantage over Seoul, Korea—his mother, Minnie.

But even as he thought it, he worried. His mother had been almost as bad as his grandfather about wanting grandchildren. Daniel had refused to get married in Korea, no matter what his grandfather said. He wouldn't give the old man the satisfaction.

His mother, however, was a different matter entirely. She didn't want grandchildren to carry on the Lee family name and restore the Lee family honor.

She wanted grandchildren because she wanted *grand-children*. And here he was, bringing an adorable baby girl and a single mother back to his condo. Would his mother restrain herself?

Christine slumped back in her seat. "I grew up in Missouri—we had our own local brewery with its own family drama. I don't know very much about the Beaumonts."

It was a relief. Being an acknowledged Beaumont brought a measure of personal scrutiny that he didn't enjoy. "There's not much to know."

She lifted her head up and squinted at him through one eye.

"My family legacy—my American family, that is—was something we didn't talk about growing up," he said.

He hadn't even known who his father was until he'd turned six. Apparently, being in kindergarten had made him mature enough in Lee Dae-Won's eyes to inform him that his real father was a heartless businessman from Colorado who, along with Daniel's mother, had stained the Lee family honor.

But he pushed that frustration away because Christine had rested her head back against the seat. He thought she might fall asleep—which was fine. Given current traffic conditions, they had about an hour from the airport to his condo on the lakefront. She needed the rest.

What he really wanted to do was slide into the seat next to her, wrap his arm around her shoulders and tuck her in close. He wanted to physically take the burden from her shoulders and let her know she was safe with him.

He also wanted to finish the kiss they'd started in Colorado. Which was not the same as making sure she felt safe. In fact, he was pretty sure those two desires didn't mesh at all.

So he did the only thing he could do—he stayed on his side of the car. He couldn't allow this attraction to distract him from the matter at hand—deflecting media attention and protecting the Murray women. He'd just taken out his phone to check his messages when she spoke again. "Was it rough, growing up without any contact with your father or his family?"

The question took him by surprise. No one had ever asked that question before. Not even Zeb.

He didn't answer fast enough, because she went on, "I'm sorry if I'm prying. Marie's father doesn't want anything to do with her, either. Or," she added with a bitter laugh, "he didn't, until he realized he could use her for his own aims."

He set his phone down. "It wasn't bad. It wasn't as good as CJ had it—you know CJ, my other half brother?"

"I used to watch *A Good Morning With Natalie Baker* when I first moved here. She married him, right?"

"Yes, that brother. His mother married and he had a

happy childhood. But I think that's rare for anyone, to have two parents who are completely committed to making sure you have a stable upbringing. The fact that I had one parent committed to that was a gift. I think you're going to be that person for Marie, too."

Her head popped up. "You think?"

He couldn't fight the grin if he'd wanted to—and he didn't want to. "I *know*. You're an amazing mom doing the best you can with what you've got—even if what you've got is a toxic relative with deep pockets."

With a groan, she let her head fall back again. "Don't remind me." There was another moment of silence before she added, "How much worse is this going to get?"

"Actually, now that we're on ground level, I think it's only going to get better from here."

She snorted, an indelicate noise that made him smile. "I wasn't talking about Marie screaming. I was talking about the scandal. About what's happening between us."

Daniel froze, but she still wasn't looking at him. There wasn't anything happening between them.

All right, in a misguided attempt to comfort her earlier, he had touched her. And almost kissed her. And yes, he had flown her across the country and was actively taking her to his condominium—where he had never brought a woman before. And, sure—his mother was going to be waiting there to meet them and would undoubtedly take one look at Marie and fall head over heels in love.

None of that meant anything was happening between *them*.

Really.

He exhaled heavily. Perhaps if he kept telling himself that lie, he might even start believing it.

Because the truth was, it did feel like something was happening, something strange and unexpected. He had started this endeavor from a position of weakness—he had allowed himself to feel guilt over his actions. Christine didn't seem to realize how unusual that was—maybe it was better that she didn't. Maybe he didn't want her to know how much of a coldhearted bastard he could be. She knew enough, anyway.

He didn't have an answer for her so he kept quiet, hoping she would doze off. And it seemed like that was what happened because she was silent for several minutes. Then, out of nowhere, her voice came again. "I still don't know why you're doing this."

She sounded sleepy and he had an overwhelming urge to be the soft place where she could land. He had never had that particular urge before. "Maybe you don't have to know why."

"That's a load of malarkey."

Even though she couldn't see it, he cracked a wide grin. "Malarkey? That's not a word you hear every day."

"I have this daughter, you see. She has a tendency to pick up on words and repeat them loudly when it's most inconvenient." She lifted her head and cracked one eye open. "Do I need to remind you about the Daniel Tiger incident?"

He chuckled. "Trust me, I won't ever forget the Daniel Tiger incident."

She was looking at him again with both eyes now. "Why, Daniel?"

"I didn't want to be another person who let you down." This was the problem with honesty. Once a person started being honest, it became almost addictive. There was a certain measure of freedom in the truth. He felt like he could breathe.

Something in the air changed between them, charging the space in the limo with electricity. "I don't want you to be another person who lets me down," she said softly.

For too much of his life, he had been concerned with his own interests. And his mother's, of course. He was even concerned with his grandfather's business interests—up to a point. He wasn't going to marry anyone for family honor—but Lee Enterprises had made Daniel an insanely wealthy man.

He cared for his siblings—in a fashion. It was in his best interest to keep his siblings protected and the family business solvent.

But what did he have to gain from Christine? What was in it for him to shield Marie?

Nothing. He knew it and Christine knew it, too. He had nothing to gain by doing any of this.

Funny how that hadn't stopped him yet.

"I won't be." It wasn't an empty promise but, given the worry that crept into the corner of Christine's eyes, he wasn't sure that she believed him.

Which was smart. She should absolutely not put her full faith and trust in him. She should keep her guard up.

But he wanted that trust. Suddenly, he needed it.

The car turned and Daniel became aware of his surroundings. They were on Lower Wacker Drive, turning toward Navy Pier.

Quickly, Daniel checked his messages. There were no emergencies from Zeb, so that was good. Natalie had forwarded him several new links to articles that were full of content scraped from Marie's father's original interview. Some days, it was like playing whack-a-mole on the internet.

"Where are we?" Christine asked.

"Home." Huang, his driver, pulled into the garage and parked at the entrance. The doorman had the door open before Christine could blink.

"Welcome home, Mr. Lee."

"It's good to be home, Rowell. These are my guests. They have complete access to my condo." Behind him, he heard Christine give a little squeak. The staff here was highly trained to keep their mouths shut. He turned and held out a hand.

After a moment's hesitation, she took it and let him help her to her feet. "Hello," she said nervously to the doorman.

"We have a few things in the trunk." With a small salute, Rowell went to the trunk. Daniel leaned in to unbuckle Marie. The little girl startled as he lifted her out and handed her to her mother. Christine tucked her daughter to her chest, rubbing her back. It was such a sweet image that Daniel wished he could take a picture of it.

What would it be like, if this were real? If he were returning with his wife and daughter after a business trip, everyone tired and happy to be home? They'd go upstairs and unpack, give Marie a bath and, once the little girl was asleep, he and Christine would...

Would *what*? Fall into bed, taking comfort in each other? No. He didn't take comfort from anyone, much less a woman who was still well within her rights to view his every single action as suspect. Even if he wanted to strip her out of her rumpled business suit and make love to her until she was sated, he couldn't get any closer.

He shook his head at his own foolishness. He was about to introduce Christine to his mother. It didn't get much closer than that.

In short order, he was leading them down the hall to his corner condo. Before he could get his keys out, the door swung open and there stood his mother, hope all over her face.

This was a mistake, but it was too late now.

"Dae-Hyun," she said, using his real name. *"Naega geogjeonghaessda."* I was worried.

That was just like her, to worry about him despite the fact that he'd been in Denver for a few months. Even though she had lived in Chicago for almost thirty-five years, she spoke Korean with him when they were alone.

Daniel stepped inside and kissed his mother on the cheek. *"Annyeong eomma,"* he said, telling her hi. Then he stepped to the side and switched to English. "Mom, I'd like to introduce you to Christine Murray and her daughter, Marie."

Her eyes lit up as she turned to Christine and Marie. "Welcome," she said, her English softly accented. Mom bowed in their direction. Daniel had been embarrassed by that bow when he was growing up. It had always marked his mother as a foreigner. But now, it was comforting. "I'm so glad Daniel brought you for a visit."

Which was a nice way of phrasing "mad dash to get away from the press." He snorted. "Christine, this is my mother, Minnie Lee."

"Hello," Christine said nervously, clutching Marie to her chest. Her gaze cut back to Daniel.

He set down the bags his assistant, Beth, had gotten them for the airplane ride. "Mom, have the other things been delivered yet?"

Minnie didn't hear him. She had eyes for one person and one person only. "Oh," she cooed, stepping in to place a hand on Marie's back. "Was the plane ride very hard?"

Christine glanced over his mother's head—which was saying something, because Christine was not that tall to begin with—and made eye contact with Daniel. He could see the second she made up her mind, the tension in her eyes fading as she smiled a warm smile at his mother. "It was a little bit of a rough flight. She's never been on an airplane before."

Mom clucked sympathetically. "You must be so tired. Both of you. I have some snacks in the kitchen. Some fresh fruit and milk? You could take a few moments to freshen up. I had a guest room set up for you."

Christine blinked in surprise at this, but Minnie turned back to Daniel. "The crib proved to be a problem, but they sent over a portable one." She turned back to Christine. "I hope that will be all right?"

"Um...yes?"

Mom's eyes crinkled with warmth. "Come with me. I'm so glad Daniel brought you here," she repeated.

As if Daniel hadn't already known this was a mistake, that sentence sealed the deal. His mother was already painting rosy pictures of happy babies and little granddaughters.

With another look, Christine followed Minnie into the apartment. He heard her gasp when she rounded the corner and saw the view. When he caught up with her in the living room, she was standing openmouthed and staring out at the never-ending sky. "This is amazing."

"I like it."

Which was something of an understatement. He liked being above everyone on the top floor. He liked looking down on Navy Pier, at the scurrying little dots that were the rest of humanity. He liked being unreachable and untouchable—and of course the privacy that went with both of those things.

Christine turned to his mother. "How long have you lived here?"

His mother's laugh tinkled lightly. "Oh, I don't live here. This is Dae-Hyun's home. I live in Wheeling."

When Christine looked confused by this statement, Daniel added, "That's close to where we landed. Mom volunteers at the Korean Cultural Center located there."

"Oh. Okay." He could tell that it still didn't make much sense to her.

At that moment, Marie seemed to come fully awake. She squirmed in Christine's arms. Christine tried to set her down and hold on to her hand, but the little girl was a lot faster than she looked. She fell to her hands and knees and crawled over to the windows, where she got back to her feet and began cruising and banging on the glass. "Pretty!" she crowed.

Christine gasped, but Daniel put a hand on her arm. "That glass is inches thick. She is not going to knock it out. I promise."

Mom hurried over and crouched down beside the little girl. "Pretty, isn't it?"

Marie turned a wide smile to the older woman and Daniel felt something tighten in his chest. It only got worse when his mother clapped her hands and giggled like a schoolgirl.

He leaned down and spoke softly in Christine's ear. "I think the two of them will be fine for a few minutes. Would you like to see your room?"

She nodded and, without taking his hand away from her arm, he led her through his apartment. He pointed out things like the kitchen and the dining room—which was really an extension of the living room. Then he led her down the hall to the extra bedrooms. "I keep a room here for Mom when she wants to stay in town but she won't be here tonight, so you can take her room," he explained. "I have two other guestrooms, but I use one as an office. So you'll have to let me know if you want Marie to stay in the room with you or if you would like her to be next door." He showed her the bathrooms and then opened the door to the guestroom.

"You really do live here," Christine said, a note of

amazement in her voice as she stepped away from him to look around.

"Yes, I do. Did you think I would bring you to some dungeon and keep you locked away?"

She shot him a look. "I hadn't ruled it out. And besides, you don't need a dungeon to keep someone trapped."

"You're free to leave whenever you want," he said, stepping closer. Too close. He was close enough to touch her now and that was exactly what he did. He took her bag from her shoulder and set it on the bed, next to the boxes he'd ordered from Saks Fifth Avenue.

For the second time today, he brushed his fingertips over her cheek. She didn't pull away—although she didn't exactly throw herself into his arms, either. Instead, she stood looking at him as if he were a space alien. "But I'd like you to stay for a little while."

That was the wrong thing to say. But he wasn't sure what the right thing would have been. She took in a shuddering breath and stepped back. "You shouldn't look at me like that."

"Like what?"

"Like...*that*." She waved her hand in the air, as if that magically explained anything. The color rose in her cheeks. "You know."

"No, I don't."

Now she waved both hands in the air, looking like a panicked bird. "You're being intentionally obtuse. You shouldn't look at me like you *like* me because we both know you don't."

Now it was his turn to blink at her in wonder. "Whatever gave you that idea?"

"Seriously?"

"Putting aside the events of several years ago—"

She snorted. "That's one way to put it."

Daniel pressed on, undeterred. "When have I given you the impression at any point in the last several weeks that I don't like you?"

He really was trying to understand. And failing.

"You can stop making fun of me now." She turned to walk out of the bedroom.

"Christine."

Eight

He put a hand on her shoulder to stop her. "I am *not* making fun of you."

"Aren't you? What other possible explanation could there be?"

He stepped close enough to brush her hair away from her cheek. "Has it ever occurred to you that I'm attracted to you?"

He didn't know how he'd expected her to react to that statement—but barking out a bitter laugh wasn't it. "Oh, that's rich. How could a man like you be attracted to a woman like me?"

Daniel stared at her in confusion. "What are you talking about?"

She spun away from him again, but she didn't head for the door. She began to pace in small circles next to the bed. "Really? Do you have to make me say it out loud?"

"*Christine*. Do you mind explaining what you think I'm

thinking? Because I think I'm thinking something completely different from what you think I'm thinking." He shook his own head at that linguistic nightmare, no matter how true it was.

She rolled her eyes at him. "I'm no supermodel—I never have been. I haven't lost the baby weight, either. And look at you. You're so handsome it hurts to watch you play with Marie. And you own a private jet and this condo with this view—clearly, you are richer than sin while I struggle to make rent and day care every month."

"I don't care about any of that," he put in quietly, but she ignored him.

"I'm impulsive and unnatural. I can't follow the rules and I never do the right thing. I don't even know if coming here with you was the right thing or the most spectacularly stupid thing in a long line of stupid things." She glared at him. "And you shouldn't try to make me think that you like me, that you could even like Marie. It's not fair to her." She dropped her gaze, looking defeated. "To either of us."

"He was wrong."

She jerked her head up, her eyes wide. "What?"

"Your father. He was wrong about you. If it's any consolation, he's wrong about everything, but most especially you." This time, he didn't just stroke his fingertips over her cheek. He cupped her face in his hands so she had no choice but to look at him. "You listen to me, Christine Murray. You were a teenager. All teenagers are impulsive. But that's not who you are now. I don't care what he says about you. Because the woman you are now would do anything to protect her daughter. The woman you are now is kind and thoughtful and cautious. You're the only person trying to play by the rules and if you don't let me help you, those rules will crush you. And I can't stand by and watch that happen."

He slid his hands down her shoulders and over her back, letting them settle around her waist. "I don't give a damn about the baby weight or how much you do or do not earn. I don't define your worth by your size. I define it by your actions and your actions tell me you're a woman that I could…"

That he could *what*? Trust with his own secrets? She didn't trust him and it wasn't any smarter for him to trust her.

Her eyes shone and she swallowed nervously. "Why are you saying these things to me?"

He bent his head down to meet hers. "Because I do like you."

This time, she didn't pull away. This time, he kissed her—slow and gentle at first and then, when her lips parted and welcomed him, with more heat.

Daniel had always been something of a monk. While women had always been plentiful and available, he hadn't trusted them.

In America, he was tall, dark and mysterious. In Korea, he had a hint of exoticism to him. Despite many offers, he'd taken very few lovers. When he was younger, he'd been convinced his grandfather was behind every come-on. He'd avoided dating and sex simply because he hadn't wanted to be trapped by the old man's notions of honor and duty. And then, when he began his career as a political operative, he'd gotten even more cautious, unwilling to let a one-night stand turn out to be a political liability.

So, it'd been a while. A *long* while. And when Christine sighed into his mouth and her arms came around his neck, he was almost overwhelmed by the sweetness of it all. She still tasted faintly of the ginger ale she'd drunk on the plane, but underneath that was a taste of warmth and even familiarity. He curled his fingers into her hips, pulling her closer. Her curves felt right against his chest, under his hands. He hardened as she softened against him.

Kissing Christine Murray was like finally coming home.

Then she pushed him away. Chest heaving, she closed her eyes. "Did you bring me here to seduce me?"

There was a part of him that wanted to tell her not to be so suspicious. There really weren't any ulterior motives behind the kiss, behind any of it.

But she was still Christine Murray and Daniel had to face the fact that if she was suspicious, it was because he'd made her that way.

And, just like that, they were right back to where they started. He stepped away, knowing there was nothing he could say to convince her. So he didn't. Instead, he motioned to the bed. "If you'd like to change, I had some things brought up for you. Don't worry about Marie. I'm sure my mom's having the time of her life with her. When you have the chance to…recover, we can reconvene and discuss the situation."

Her lips twisted and he couldn't tell if she was grimacing in frustration or trying not to laugh. "And which situation would *that* be?"

"Whichever situation you'd like it to be." With that, he turned and walked out.

He stopped in the kitchen to get his thoughts in order. This wasn't like him. He did not get personally involved. He did not bring people back to his apartment. And he never introduced women to his mother.

And yet, here they all were. He could hear his mom cooing with Marie and he knew that, when he went in to check on them in a few moments, his mother would ask about Christine.

Running a political campaign meant ignoring rules in favor of bigger and better stories, higher polling numbers, and victories. Especially victories. Christine hadn't been a part of her father's campaign until Daniel had made her a part of it. But he never could've predicted that it would have led to this.

Because he hadn't lied. He *did* like her. She was handling this horrible situation with a surprising amount of grace. Unlike her own father, she was fiercely loyal to her daughter. And she *was* beautiful. She was soft and curved in all the right places and she made him ache. Like right now, he thought darkly as he adjusted his trousers. He *ached* for her.

In his time, he'd lusted. But that was sex. This? This was something else.

Dimly, he was aware that she was exactly the kind of woman who would have given his grandfather an apoplectic stroke. Christine was too blonde, too blue-eyed, too outspoken and far too American to have ever satisfied Lee Dae-Won. Was that part of her appeal? Was he still trying to irritate the old man?

This should have been a simple job of salvaging a woman's reputation and shielding an infant from the media. Daniel should've manipulated the web rankings and guarded her apartment without caring for her. Hell, he could've done what he'd always done—operate behind the scenes, in secrecy, pulling the strings as he saw fit.

But he hadn't. Instead, he'd walked right into that bank of hers and made his intentions known. He'd gone to her church and flown her to Chicago and installed her in his own personal guestroom instead of a nice hotel under an assumed name. And now he had to go into the living room and watch his mother fall in love with Marie.

He had never in his life made such a mess of things and the hell of it was, even knowing it would only get messier, he wasn't sure he'd change any of it.

Because he had kissed her and because she had kissed him back and it had felt like *home*.

He grabbed a sparkling water from the fridge and went to check on his mother. She was kneeling next to the coffee table and Marie, as usual, was cruising around the edges. A plate with sliced fruit and a sippy cup half full of milk were within reach. Marie looked bright-eyed and bushy-tailed and his mother had a matching smile upon her face. She didn't even look up when he entered the room. As he removed his coat and loosened his tie, she said to him in Korean, "Is she all right?"

Daniel collapsed into a chair. Truthfully, he didn't know. "She's had a long day," he replied in Korean.

His mother slanted him a knowing look. "Did you tell her you were going to introduce her to me?"

Busted. "No…"

His mother leaned over and patted him on the knee. Marie saw this and decided to do the same, lurching toward Daniel's knees.

Minnie clucked at him. "She's been through quite a lot."

Daniel sighed heavily and caught Marie up in his arms. Marie giggled, which made him feel like he was doing something right. "She's been through a lot because of me."

Minnie came to her feet. "Did she know you were bringing her here?"

Shame heated his cheeks. His mother was the only person who could inspire this reaction in him. He had long ago learned that pissing off his grandfather was a victory and he certainly didn't give a damn what anyone else thought. But a single look from Minnie Lee and he was a misbehaving kid all over again. "I'm just trying to keep her safe. I didn't think she'd come if she knew I was bringing her here."

His mother stroked Marie's hair with such tenderness that Daniel wished he could be someone else. A more dutiful son, at least. The kind of man who would've settled down and given his mother the grandchildren she desperately wanted.

Marie obviously knew who was the soft touch in the room. She looked up at Minnie and then, grinning wildly, reached up her hands in a gesture that even Daniel knew meant she wanted to be picked up. Minnie was only too happy to oblige. She began to sing an old song in Korean, one that Daniel hadn't heard in years, *Santoki*—a song about a bunny.

Daniel thought he was off the hook, but when his mother reached the end of the first verse, she paused and looked back at him. "You have to trust her if you want her to trust you." She said it in English, which somehow made it worse.

"I do trust her," he replied, also in English. "I trusted her enough to bring her here, didn't I?"

His mother shook her head, a small gesture that still spoke loudly of her disappointment with his answer. She had never been one to bluster, like her own father had been. She was a quiet woman who lived a quiet life surrounded by fellow Korean Americans in her adopted city. Sometimes, Daniel forgot that she had been a young girl who left home and carved out a place for herself in a strange country. She had raised her son on her own, more or less. She had found her place in this world, straddling two cultures with apparent ease.

So why did he feel like he didn't belong anywhere?

"You must trust her with the truth, Dae-Hyun."

His phone chimed again—he had ignored reality for long enough. "I have some things I need to do," he said, glancing at the screen. Crap. It was Brian White. Again. Had someone connected him and Christine?

If his mother was disappointed by Daniel's announcement, she didn't show it. Instead, she said, "Don't you worry about us. Come along, Miss Marie." She began singing the bunny song again as she carried Marie over to the windows.

When they were out of earshot, Daniel answered the call. "I'm still not interested."

Brian let loose with a string of curse words. "Where the hell is she?" he finished, sputtering.

All right, so Daniel had not had the foresight to get to Marie's father first. But he had the distinct satisfaction of having pulled a fast one on Brian White.

"Who?" he asked in as innocent a voice as he could manage.

"You know goddamned well who—Christine Murray. Where is she?"

"I don't know. I would assume that she's at work?" It was a challenge to keep the humor out of his voice.

"Don't try that bullshit with me, Lee. She's disappeared off the face of the earth and I can only think of one person would have a vested interest in hiding her and that's you. So where is she?"

Daniel couldn't remember ever having this much fun. "You all right?" he asked, trying not to overdo the innocent tone. "You don't sound good."

"Answer the goddamn question. *Someone* has been burying the lede on internet stories. *Someone* has had private investigators roughing up my associates. And now *someone* has helped that girl fall off the face of the earth."

"Oh, are you talking about the Murray girl?"

Brian let loose with another string of obscenities.

"I told you I was out," Daniel said, letting anger seep into his voice.

"You better be. If I find out you're working for Rosen…"

That was it. "Is that a threat?" Because he was not going to let this man act like he still pulled the strings.

Brian must've finally recognized the warning in Daniel's tone. "Don't mess with me on this, Lee. I'm running a campaign for Clarence Murray and my employer has requested that I bring his daughter in for a chat."

"I'm skimming the search results now—it seems like someone beat you to the punch with her ex." It probably wasn't wise to pour salt into the wound, but Daniel felt a powerful need to remind Brian he was not all-knowing. "You're slipping, Brian. It's not like you."

"You're nothing but a bastard, Lee. A bastard through and through."

"Name-calling isn't very original, Brian." Even if it was true. "I'm out. I'm not working for you and I'm not working for Rosen and even if I knew where the Murray girl was, I wouldn't tell you."

"I *will* find her and I *will* bring her back into the fold. That's a promise. I just hope, for your sake, I don't find her with you."

That was most definitely a threat. In a perverse way, Daniel took pride in it. It meant that, despite the fact that he and Brian had worked together for a dozen years on political campaigns across the country, Brian had never figured out the extent of Daniel's wealth and power.

"I'll say this one more time—I'm out. But if you bother me again, I'll be back in and you won't like what happens next."

"You forget that I know your secrets," Brian sneered.

And the truth was, he probably believed that. He would be only too happy to smear Daniel's name in the press, linking him to dozens of dirty campaign tricks over the years. It might be bad press for the Beaumont Brewery— but then again, there was no such thing as bad press.

Trust her with the truth. That's what his mother had said. But she couldn't honestly mean everything. Maybe— *maybe*—Christine would understand his family history. But things like owning the majority of Lee Enterprises? He'd watched her struggle to get her mind wrapped around his plane and his condo. He'd listened to her explain in excruciating detail why she wasn't good enough for him.

He didn't know how much more truth Christine Murray could handle, frankly.

Brian, on the other hand, needed a reality check in the worst sort of way. "And I know yours. Don't make me bury you." He hung up.

He sat there, trying to look at the forest and all of the trees. He tried to envision the strings he'd need to pull to get the outcome he preferred.

But instead of mentally mapping out the playing field, his thoughts kept turning back to Christine. To the warm way her flesh had molded against his, to the sweet taste of her against his mouth. To the way he'd wanted *more*.

No. He couldn't afford to let himself get distracted now, not if Brian was already suspicious.

It was time to take this to the next level. Daniel made the call. "Natalie? When can you get to Chicago?"

Nine

This was ridiculous. Christine stared down at what was most likely several thousand dollars–worth of clothing from a department store she had never visited.

Ridiculous.

At least this time, she wasn't hiding in the ladies' room. She was hiding in the guest room. It made all the difference in the world.

She knew these were designer labels—Tahari, Calvin Klein—for pity's sake, there was even a silk Gucci top in the mix. These brands cost more than her rent for a month. Heck, even more than day care for Marie. And the bag of makeup from MAC and Chanel? In colors that would look good on her?

And it all just magically appeared because Daniel made some calls. Because Daniel liked her.

She couldn't believe that. Obviously, he had more money than she could comprehend. He owned homes in at least two countries, had his own private jet, and this condo was the kind of place that didn't come cheap. Just like the clothing.

She touched the Gucci top, letting the cool silk slip over her fingers. The tags had all been removed, but she was willing to bet this top alone was worth at least five hundred dollars, maybe more.

In other words, it was not the kind of top a dumpy single mom wore. Marie would destroy this thing within seconds, if not sooner.

Christine should've been more specific when she had given Daniel her clothing size. She should have said some yoga pants and T-shirts would've been fine. That's what she would've packed, if she had gone home.

But even as she thought that, she cringed. Would she really have sat around in this glamorous condominium with this glamorous view next to this glamorous man in her decidedly nonglamorous yoga pants?

What the heck. If he'd paid for these clothes, she'd wear them. And Marie would destroy them, of that she had no doubt. But for at least five minutes she would pretend that she fit into Daniel's world.

She fixed her face—and danged if her skin didn't look amazingly dewy with those high-end cosmetics. Then she slid the silk shirt on and was pleased to see her boobs looked great. The pair of embellished dark-wash jeans slid on like second skin. There was even a thick chocolate brown cardigan because, after all, March in Chicago was not any warmer than March in Denver.

She eyed the long flannel nightgown with matching robe. Oscar de la Renta. Even the nightie was designer.

She didn't know how she would go out there and look at him—or his mother. He had kissed her and she had kissed him back. For a little while, anyway.

What if she were wrong? What if she were looking for a

deeper meaning here and there just wasn't one? Could she seriously take Daniel at his word? She wanted to. Desperately, she wanted to. But every time she felt herself being swayed by his thoughtfulness, by the way he played with Marie—by the way he touched Christine, like she was a delicate thing to be treasured—she would remember the truth of the situation.

She'd gotten pregnant out of wedlock. But he'd made it national news.

So she was wearing designer clothes. That didn't mean she trusted him. It didn't mean she wanted him to kiss her again. She didn't want it and she didn't need it.

Yeah, right.

From somewhere inside this cavernous apartment, she heard Marie giggling and a soft feminine voice responding. Everything seemed fine, just as he'd promised it would be.

And that was another thing. He hadn't told her where they were going—other than the generic *Chicago*. He hadn't told her that his mother would be here. Not that Christine was complaining about that. Luxury was not only wearing designer clothes, but it was having half an hour to wash her face and get dressed.

It was all so different from her normal life. She pressed the palms of her hands into her temples, trying to get her head to stop spinning.

"Are you all right?"

Christine let out a little gasp. Daniel had appeared out of nowhere to stand in front of her, worry etched on his face. She was instantly aware of him on a different level. A physical level.

"Oh, fine," she said, trying to sound nonchalant and failing miserably. "Everything about this is fine."

His suit jacket and tie were gone and he had unbuttoned

the top two buttons on his pristine white dress shirt. He had even cuffed the sleeves, revealing forearms that were far more muscular than she expected.

Her gaze slid over the V of his waist. Without the jacket—or the bulky cable-knit sweater he'd worn to church—she could see the shape of his legs. And he had taken off his shoes! Instead of basic socks that matched his gray trousers, he wore socks with wildly colorful paisleys. She felt like she should have noticed those socks earlier.

"Yes, I can tell." Daniel's gaze swept over her, warming her from the inside out. "I see the clothes worked. That top suits you perfectly."

Christine could feel her cheeks burning up at his leisurely perusal of her person. "It really wasn't necessary to spend that much money on clothes Marie is going to destroy, you know."

"It was worth it."

All of her warm feelings took a hard right into embarrassment. Why did he keep doing this? Was it because of the kiss? "Stop."

His gaze hardened as he took another step closer. "Why can't you take a compliment?"

Instinctively, she took a step back, which brought her up hard against the countertop. "What?"

"You are a lovely woman and the clothing looks nice on you. I'm trying to compliment you. Not because I'm trying to seduce you and not because I want something out of you." His eyes glittered with emotion that she was afraid to identify. Lust? Anger? "I like you and I am expressing that in a commonly accepted form. Stop tearing yourself down. You look *nice*," he said, leaning in. Less than a foot separated them now. When Christine couldn't come up with a response, he added with an amused grin, "This is the part where you say *thank you*."

She blinked hard, tears stinging her eyes and she wasn't sure why. "Thank you. The clothes are lovely."

"Closer," he murmured, putting a hand on the counter on either side of her. She was trapped and that was maybe a bad thing but she desperately wanted it to be good.

Her body pulsed with need and this time, that need wouldn't be ignored. Especially not when Daniel said, "The clothes are lovely because *you* make them lovely, Christine."

She wasn't strong enough, darn it all. "You're trying to make me like you." He moved closer and she put a hand on his chest. It was the first time she'd touched him and, through the fine cotton of his shirt, she could feel the warmth of his body.

In another life, she'd do more than just rest her palm against his chest. The old Christine would still be in the back bedroom with him. The old Christine would've thrown herself into that kiss because he truly was her knight in shining armor—well, her knight in a suit, anyway.

But the new woman she was didn't do that. She didn't even slide her hand around his waist or pull him in until her breasts were flush against his chest. She just…touched him. It shouldn't have been a big deal, that touch.

But it was.

His eyes darkened. "I'd like to think I don't have to try that hard." Smoothly, he pushed off the counter and put more space between them. He did so in a way that kept her hand from dropping away from his chest. She wasn't pushing him, but she wasn't breaking the contact, either. "There's something about you…" he said, his voice trailing off as he leaned into her touch.

Please say the right thing—something she could believe in.

"But," he said, going on in a more formal voice, "I understand if you don't feel the same way after what I did to you two years ago."

She let her hand fall away as she opened her mouth to try and make sense of the confusion. But at that moment, Marie let out a familiar shriek of, "Mama!"

"Oh," Christine said dully. "I need to check on her."

She went to step around him, but he put a hand on her waist, stopping her when she was parallel with him. God, he was so hot—heat radiated from his side, where it was pressed against hers. "Maybe we can talk tonight?"

She should say no. She shouldn't believe anything he said at this point or at any other point. She shouldn't agree to being alone with him, especially not under cover of darkness. It was too risky and there was too much at stake. This was all happening far too fast.

But he was looking down at her with those beautiful eyes. He liked her. He had already kissed her. He wasn't working for her father and she didn't think he was working for the opposition.

She had tried to be good for two years and what had it gotten her? Hounded by the press and dragged through the mud. Again. Maybe she didn't want to be good anymore. That had to be the reason she lifted her hand and stroked it over his smooth cheek.

"Okay," she said in a soft voice. "Tonight, we'll talk."

Then she slipped out of his grasp and went to check on her daughter.

Daniel had a feast of Korean food delivered and opened a good bottle of wine. Christine didn't even have to clean up—she offered, but he waved her away. He stacked the dishes and threw away the take-out boxes, but he said he had a maid who cleaned up for him. Then Minnie swept Marie up and declared that the child needed a bath.

All in all, it was one of the nicer evenings Christine had had in a long time. She sent a text to Sue at the bank, assuring her that Christine was all right. She called Mrs. McDonald, too. She sent a message to her boss, explaining that she'd be back to work in a few days and apologizing for the whole mess.

Between the low-pressure meal and the wine, Christine was able to relax—something she didn't really allow herself to do anymore. She rarely drank because she was always the responsible parent on duty.

Far removed from the reporters and the daily struggle of caring for her daughter, Christine began to think of this interlude as a vacation. After all, she was staying with a gorgeous man who provided child care and all accommodations—while looking at her with desire in his eyes.

Sooner or later, she would to go back to her decent job at the bank and her daily struggle to get Marie to bed early so Christine could have fifteen minutes to herself before she collapsed from exhaustion.

She wanted to enjoy this. More than that, she wanted to enjoy it without having to pay for it later. That was the sticking point. Would all this come back to haunt her tomorrow? That was the question she had to ask as Daniel came to sit beside her on his massive couch. It stretched out for almost fifteen feet—far larger than any regular couch. And it faced the floor-to-ceiling windows that looked out over Lake Michigan. Even as dusk faded into night, the view was amazing.

"She's in love with that baby," Daniel said as Minnie carried a squirming Marie, wrapped in a fluffy towel that looked like a duck, into the living room so Christine could see how good her daughter had been. Then they were off again, Minnie singing Korean lullabies and armed with a small stack of brand-new children's books.

"I picked up on that, it's true." There were cookie crumbs on the coffee table and random toys scattered all over the place, but he didn't seem to mind. Minnie and Daniel cared about Marie.

God, how Christine needed more of that in her life.

To her horror, she heard herself ask, "How come you're not married? You know your mom would adore grandchildren."

After a long pause, Daniel said, "We need to talk a little business," in a voice that was regretful. "If you're up to it."

"All right." *Business* seemed like a nice way of saying the complete and total collapse of her life. *Business*, she repeated to herself several more times.

She'd like some more wine before they got down to *business*, but she hadn't nursed Marie yet. She needed the closeness with her daughter, the one single thing that was a familiar part of their routine.

"Natalie Wesley will be here tomorrow evening," Daniel announced into the silence.

"She will?" Christine wasn't normally the kind to get starstruck but… "Why?"

"I'd like her to conduct a sit-down interview with you where we're in complete control of the conversation."

Okay, her heart was definitely pounding. "Is that a good idea?"

The apartment was dark, with only a few lamps lit at the far ends of the couch. Christine could see, but she felt less exposed.

Then Daniel reached over and curled his fingers around hers. It wasn't the same kind of touch that had led to the kiss earlier—but it still sent sparks of electricity over her skin. "You can't hide forever, Christine, as nice as it might be for all of us." She swung her head around at that statement but Daniel went on in a gentle voice, "It's better to control your narrative than to let someone else control it. You have to tell your own story."

Hadn't that been the problem the last time? He'd defined her first. "Do I have to?"

"Absolutely not." He squeezed her fingers and then slid his hand around so they were palm to palm. "But Natalie and I agree that it's a good idea. I promise she won't ask any gotcha-style questions. She's working up the questions and answers now."

"The answers? Good Lord, you don't leave anything to chance, do you?"

He chuckled, a rich sound that surrounded her. "I try not to. I don't mean that she'll have a script for you to read from—that wouldn't be believable. It'll be more like talking points."

She mulled that over—while also trying to figure out if she wanted to pull her hand away or not.

She didn't want to. His hand was warm and heavy, almost a promise of good things to come. She felt safe with him. She had all along, she had to admit. Because if she hadn't, she wouldn't have met him in the church, wouldn't have let Marie grow attached to him and she certainly wouldn't have let him whisk them away.

She trusted him. If that made her a fool, then, she was a fool. She gave his hand a little squeeze. "Like... I wish my father all the luck in his campaign but I'm far too busy raising my daughter to join him on the campaign trail?"

He turned to look at her, warmth in his eyes. "Yes," he murmured, the space between them closing, "exactly like that."

He was going to kiss her again and she was going to let him. This time, she was going to enjoy it, by God.

"Here we are," Minnie's chipper voice announced seconds before she came back into the living room with Marie curled against her shoulder. "It's bedtime for a sleepy little girl, isn't it, sweetheart?" She sighed and kissed the top of Marie's head. "And I need to head home."

Christine and Daniel both jerked back like they were teenagers caught kissing by, well, his mother. "I'll call the car for you, Mom," Daniel said, looking completely unflustered while Christine knew her face was burning.

She stood. "I usually nurse her at night," she said, holding out her arms. Marie leaned toward her and Christine let her daughter's heavy body ground her in reality. "If you'll excuse us. Minnie, thank you so, so much. This has been a wonderful evening. Will we get to see you again before we go back to Denver?"

"Oh, I hope so." The older woman's eyes lit up. "I have something to do tomorrow morning but I'd love to come back over in the afternoon?" She looked longingly at Marie and Christine knew she hadn't been wrong. Minnie Lee had grandbabies on the brain. "You two could go out, do something fun. Miss Marie and I will be just fine."

Daniel cleared his throat and, finally, he looked embarrassed. "Mom, that's not a smart idea right now. We're trying to keep Christine out of the public eye. But," he went on before his mother could respond, "Natalie will be here tomorrow evening to interview Christine and it'd be a huge help if you could entertain Marie for us during that." He turned to Christine. "Wouldn't it?"

She would have sworn there was a hint of pleading in his tone, a need to keep his mother happy. "It would be wonderful," she agreed, patting Marie's back.

Minnie clapped her hands. "Is three okay? I could cut one meeting short…"

"No," Christine said quickly, "three is fine. She'll probably be waking up from her nap by then."

"Wonderful." Minnie moved as if she wanted to hug Marie—and, by extension, Christine—before pulling to a stop. "Tomorrow, then."

Christine nodded and carried Marie back to where the portable crib had been set up. That man had even had a glider delivered. Everything she needed had appeared out of thin air. Clothes, food—compliments. Sincere, dangerous compliments.

He was, in a word, perfect.

God, she hoped she wasn't about to make a fool of herself.

Ten

"I'm exhausted. I might just turn in," Christine said, already moving down the hall.

Of course she was. It'd been a day. But that didn't make him any less disappointed that she wouldn't be back out—where they would finally be alone. "That's fine. Get some sleep."

The moment Christine was out of earshot, his mother rounded on him. "Dae-Hyun," she said, using his Korean name and that particular tone of voice that made him feel like he was six. "Why haven't you told her?"

"About what?"

They both knew what. His mother shook her head and Daniel had to force back the uncomfortable feeling that he had disappointed her. "About you. Does she know who you really are?"

If he had less self-discipline, he'd throw his hands up in frustration. But he had a lot of self-discipline. "That's not some deep mystery, Mom. I'm the former political campaign operative who ruined her life."

If there were one person in the whole world he couldn't fool, though, it was his mother. Only Minnie could cut through the crap with one well-placed look. With a sigh of resignation, she stepped closer and patted him on the cheek. "There is more to you than that. And more to her than just a woman whose life you ruined." Her eyes twinkled. "She's the first woman you've ever shown your home to—as far as I know," she said before Daniel could say the exact same thing. "You can't tell me that's just because you're trying to make up for what happened before."

He wasn't going to win an argument with his mother. Especially not when there was a distinctive chance she was right. So Daniel leaned down and kissed his mom on the cheek. "Thanks for your help today. We'll see you tomorrow?"

She notched an eyebrow at him. "You can't avoid the truth forever, you know," she said softly in Korean. Then she went to get her things.

He saw her out. He wasn't avoiding anything. He *wasn't*. He was a full-grown man who was helping to manage one business and keeping tabs on another. He ran his business interests and protected his family members. He...

He'd never brought a woman back to his place. The few times he had taken a lover—he was no saint—he had arranged for five-star hotels.

Damn it, he hated it when his mother could see right through him.

Because there hadn't been a single good reason to bring Christine back here. He could have gotten her a penthouse suite and had all the clothes and things for her daughter delivered there. He could have stayed there as well, if that was what she'd been comfortable with.

But that's not what he'd done. He'd brought her straight here, straight to his mother.

What had he done?

What made it worse was the fact that he wanted to talk to Christine tonight. He wanted reassurances that she was okay with what was happening. He wanted to know that…

Well, that she didn't hate him. He was willing to accept that she didn't like him, that she might not ever like him. But in some perverse way, he wanted to make sure he was making things better instead of worse.

He wanted to know he wasn't failing her. That's really what it came down to.

He wasn't going to find out tonight—whether she liked him, whether she wanted him to kiss her again. He wanted to kiss her again, he had to admit to himself as he sat down on the couch and refilled his wineglass. She'd barely had a glass and he hated to see a good bottle go to waste.

She was a little right, he thought halfway through the glass. She wasn't his type. Did he *have* a type? The few women he'd had affairs with had some things in common. They hadn't been looking for a relationship any more than Daniel had. They had wanted certain needs fulfilled to their satisfaction—discreetly. There hadn't been a common look, despite what Christine seemed to think. He'd simply wanted his affairs to be casual and easy.

There was nothing casual or easy about Christine Murray. Not only did she have more baggage than the average woman, she had more skin in the game. She had Marie.

It should have sent him running. The man he'd been when his grandfather had been alive would have put as much distance between himself and Christine as physically possible.

So why hadn't he? She kept asking him that same question—why was he doing this?

He knew he hadn't answered Christine's questions. And the truth was, he didn't have answers. He didn't know why he was inserting himself into her life. He didn't know why, for the first time in his life, he cared.

Except that he felt the pull to protect her. That was how it had started. He had wanted to make things right. And then he had seen her daughter and he'd wanted to protect the little girl. And through it all, no matter what curveball he threw at her, Christine kept herself together with grace and dignity. She might be the strongest woman he'd ever met.

His mother had suggested she could watch Marie while he and Christine went out and did something fun and he'd shot her down. But why couldn't they? The odds of Christine being recognized in Chicago were slim and the odds of Marie being recognized were so small as to be laughable. There were two pictures of her on the internet, neither of them great.

With a few precautions, they should be able to go out. He found himself looking down to where Navy Pier was lit up. The whole front of the Pier was a gigantic children's museum—the kind where kids could play and parents could watch or join in.

In the reflection of the glass, he saw the light in the hall flick on behind him, saw Christine silhouetted in the doorway. He turned, feeling ridiculously hopeful. She'd come back out and damned if she didn't look like an angel, backlit by the hall light. The gold in her hair and the white robe, with the silhouette of her body just hinted at...

She simply took his breath away. That ache came back and it took everything he had not to stride over to her and pull her into his arms and pick up where that earlier kiss had left off. And this time, he didn't want to stop.

He didn't move.

"Oh," she said, twisting her hands in the belt of the bathrobe. "I didn't know you were still up."

"I was just thinking." Not strategizing, not working—just thinking. About her. "Is everything all right?"

She dropped her hands to her sides. "I wanted a cup of tea. I didn't mean to disturb you."

He moved toward the kitchen and was gratified when she followed him. He filled the electric kettle. "Chamomile?"

He set the tea caddy before her and tried not to stare. He hadn't specified what kind of clothing he'd wanted for her. He had merely called in her size, her coloring and what he thought she might need for an extended visit. The personal shoppers had done everything else—and they had done their job well. The nightgown was long, brushing the tops of her toes. It was awfully modest, a heavyweight cotton flannel, maybe. And a matching robe had come with it. She was, in essence, covered from head to toe. She shouldn't have looked sensual. She should have looked like she was wrapped in a sheet.

But even that thought spiraled another set of images through his mind, ones of her wearing his sheet and nothing else. Nothing except a smile—that he'd put there.

He couldn't read the look on her face—was it confusion or amusement? "Every time I think I have you figured out, you throw me for another loop."

He frowned, leaning on the counter. "How so?"

She looked down at the gown and robe. "When a man buys a woman a nightgown, it rarely involves this much fabric."

And he remembered her asking if he had planned on seducing her. "I wanted you to be warm."

He thought she blushed. "I am."

He might have had too much wine because suddenly

he couldn't fight it any longer. He had to hold her, feel the weight of her body against his. He pulled her into his arms. A miracle occurred—she let him. Her arms came around his waist and she nuzzled against him. She was soft and warm and he closed his eyes and inhaled deeply.

"Christine…" he said softly, against her hair. He wanted to say so much but for once in his life, he didn't know how.

She did this to him, turned him inside out and upside down. She made him ache for her, for a glimpse of a man that he'd be in another life. A man she trusted. A man she *wanted*. Because he wanted her. He couldn't ignore it any longer.

"Don't talk," she said in a voice that he felt more than heard. "Just…don't."

So he didn't. Instead, he held her as tightly as he could, letting his body take some of the weight off her shoulders. Her breasts were barely contained by the fabric and they pressed against his chest with each breath she took. And him? His blood was pounding in his veins and that physical ache had focused where she was touching him, making him hard.

But he was oddly happy anyway. There was an intimacy to this that he didn't want to take for granted. He couldn't remember the last time he had held a woman like this.

The kettle clicked, jarring them out of the moment. Reluctantly—at least, Daniel hoped it was reluctantly—Christine pulled away from him. But she stayed within the space between his legs and his hands settled on her hips. He'd slid down against the counter so far that he could almost look her in the eye. Her face was nearly lost in the shadows, but she was staring at him. He could feel it.

"My bedroom's on the far side of the condo," he said in a quiet voice. "If you need anything at all, don't hesitate to come get me."

He meant it sincerely. But it was only after her eyes widened slightly that he realized there was an additional meaning to his words. Damn it.

But then she said, "I won't."

He wanted to kiss her—he wanted so much from her. But he didn't want to put her in a position where she felt trapped.

Yet he couldn't *not* touch her. So instead, he cupped her face and kissed her forehead. Heat flooded his body, a raw physical reaction that wasn't something he'd planned for.

He made himself break the contact. He'd had wine and she'd had a terrible day and the fastest way to make sure she didn't trust him would be to seduce her.

So he was shocked when, after he pulled away, she leaned up on her toes and pressed her lips against his.

If he'd ached before, the lust that roared through his body now was just shy of sheer pain. Desire hit him low and hard. There was a hunger to her mouth that set his blood humming and made him dizzy. The kiss was far sweeter than the one he had taken earlier because Christine gave it to him. She'd come to his arms. She'd kissed him.

He didn't want to be noble. He wanted to take and give—especially give. He wanted to peel Christine out of this nightgown and lay her out on his bed and kiss every single inch of her luscious body. He slid his hands down her waist, cupping her bottom and pulling her against his erection.

Which was a mistake. Too much, too fast. She rocked back on her heels, her chest heaving. He caught her around the waist. "We...we can't."

He didn't let go of her. He wasn't sure he could even if he wanted to. Instead, he dug his fingertips into her skin. "We can't?"

"I..." she took a deep breath—but she hadn't stepped

clear of him yet. "I can't make another mistake," she told him in a whisper, her voice shaking. "I can't be hurt again."

It damn near broke his heart to hear that, to know he was the reason for that pain. "I won't hurt you. Not ever again."

"How can I believe you?" Her voice was stronger, suddenly—an edge to it.

"Let me show you, babe." He pulled her into another kiss, rougher this time. She melted into him, a small sound of need coming from high in her throat. "Let me take care of you."

He could do that for her. Put her first. Let her call the shots while he took care of everything else.

"Daniel," she whispered against his mouth as her arms went around his neck.

Yes. Her body was flush against his, the delicious weight of her breasts pressing against his chest. He ran his hands up and down her back, squeezing her bottom again, harder this time. "Tell me what you want, babe," he asked as he brushed kisses over her cheeks, her forehead, her lips.

Because what he wanted was to pick her up and carry her back to his bed. Or the couch. Hell, he'd settle for laying her out on the damned dining room table—anywhere was fine, as long as he could make her cry out with pleasure. But he wouldn't do anything without her permission. He wanted her to trust that, deep down, he wanted her. This wasn't because she was convenient and available.

Nothing about her was convenient, was it?

She gripped his head between her hands. In the dim light, she looked like an avenging angel, come down to earth to mete out the punishment for his sins. "I don't want to regret this." Oh, yeah—she was definitely angry now.

He deserved that anger. He honestly didn't even know how she could want him. But she did because even as she said it, she hitched one of her legs up as high as the nightgown would allow and wrapped it around his leg. He could feel the tantalizing heat of her, so close to his throbbing erection. "I don't want to regret you, Daniel." It was an order.

One he'd follow if it killed him. "God help me, you won't." He lifted her against him, his hips already moving against her. She gasped as he thrust against her, so close but yet so far away. "I promise, Christine—you won't." He pushed himself away from the counter, lifting her as he stood. "Yes?"

She hesitated, but only for a second. "Yes."

He wanted to shout with an excitement he hadn't felt in a long time. Holding her up, her legs around his hips and her mouth against his, he kissed her with a passion so intense he barely recognized it.

She pulled away. "I shouldn't like you, damn it. Start walking."

Had he ever heard her curse before? "But you do, anyway."

"You ruined everything," she whispered, and then her lips fastened on to his neck, moving down until she was below the collar of his shirt. "Everything," she repeated. Then she bit him.

A spike of pain and pleasure jerked his dick to attention. He groaned as she sucked at his neck, punishing him and rewarding him all at the same time.

"Are you going to make me pay for it?" He couldn't walk with this hard-on, couldn't carry her while she was taking all of her frustrations out on him. He collapsed onto the couch.

She straddled him and he hiked her nightgown up to her

hips. "Yes," she hissed before crushing her mouth down onto his. He tried to pull the nightgown up even farther—off would be great—but she grabbed his hands and pinned them against the back of the couch.

She was fierce, his Christine, holding him down and taking what she wanted. He could have pulled free, rolled her onto her back and taken her—but this wasn't about him. This was about her—her life, her taking control.

So he let her exact her revenge one bruising kiss at a time. He'd never had angry sex before. His affairs had always been detached, almost, focused on the physical with as little emotion as possible.

But this? Christine grinding down on his erection, holding him by the wrists and nipping at his lower lip while her breasts rubbed against his chest?

This was all about the emotion.

"I don't like you," she whispered fiercely as she pushed herself up and let go of his wrists. "I don't."

He heard the lie in her voice and felt it in her hands as she jerked the fly of his pants open. He wouldn't have thought he could get any harder—but this thing between them—it wasn't like anything he'd ever felt before.

The fact that she made him feel at all—it was something. Did she even realize that? "I want you so bad," he groaned again as her fingertips stroked over him through his boxer briefs.

"Stop talking." She yanked his pants down a little and shoved his briefs aside. "Just stop talking, Daniel. I had to change who I was because of you—" she stroked him once, "and move to a new place." She rose over him again and positioned him at her entrance. "I had to leave behind my friends and my job and—" She bore down on him and he slid up into her in one hard thrust. "Oh, God," she moaned.

"Christine," he got out through gritted teeth. She was hot and wet and tight around him, gripping him with such urgency that he almost came right then and there.

He cupped her breasts in his hands, trying to figure out how to get to her skin. Her body and the way she was surrounding him was all he could see and feel and think. But it wasn't enough. He needed more. God, he'd never needed more in his life.

"No." For a split second, he thought she'd changed her mind and a part of him nearly died. But instead of throwing herself off him, she grabbed his hands and held them against the back of the couch. "I'm doing this, Daniel." With that, she began to rise and fall.

"You're in charge," he managed to say before his mind quit trying to think. "That's it. Ride me. Ride me hard."

"Shut up." Her mouth crushed down onto his again with such savage fury that he knew he was going to be bruised and he didn't care.

He took it all—all of her rage, her lust, her burdens. He took everything she had to give him. He thrust up into her and, when her head fell back with a low moan, he leaned forward and dragged his teeth over the layers of flannel, biting and sucking until he had one of her nipples hard and pointed. He nipped at her again until she released one wrist and, threading her fingers through his hair, shoved his head back. "You do that again and I'll stop."

That noise—needy, almost a whimper—that wasn't him, was it? It was. She'd reduced him to this—and God help him, he liked it.

He did what he could—thrusting up into her with a steady rhythm, rolling with her when she shifted from side to side. He let her chase her orgasm at her own speed. It was hers to take.

Still, his control started to fray as she rode him. She

felt so good that, although he needed to come, he didn't want to. He didn't want this to end.

"Daniel," she moaned, falling and rising faster and faster. "Oh—*Daniel*."

"Yeah," he said, encouraging her. "You feel so good."

"Shh," she hissed before grinding down on him.

Daniel felt her body tighten, heard the noises of desire from high in the back of her throat. "Take it, Christine," he said as her grip on his hands tightened.

And then he couldn't hold back. As her body held his in the throes of her climax, his control slipped and he came with her.

She collapsed onto his shoulder, panting heavily. Her arms went around his neck and his went around her waist and they were right back to where they'd started in the kitchen—except it was more intimate now because he was still inside of her.

His head began to clear from the fog of lust—and that wasn't necessarily a good thing.

He'd just had sex with Christine.

On the couch. Without a condom.

In his condo.

Where he'd never even brought a woman home before.

And then it only got worse because Christine pushed off him and then completely off the couch. She stood while the hem of her nightgown floated back down to her feet and then, before Daniel could do anything, *say* anything, she whispered, "Good night," and moved away from him.

He hadn't even been able to come up with a reasonable compliment, for God's sake.

She had taken everything he had.

Turnabout was fair play, it seemed.

Eleven

After tossing and turning most of the night—plus getting up with Marie at two—Christine wasn't feeling as fresh as a daisy when she dragged herself out of bed.

Last night, she had kissed Daniel. And slept with him.

Well, there hadn't been a lot of actual sleeping. That was a dodge on the truth and the truth was…

She'd had sex with Daniel. Raw, hard, desperate, *angry* sex. Because she'd been furious with him for putting her in the spotlight two years ago, angry that she was back in the spotlight. But under that anger, the sparks of attraction were too hot to ignore.

Lord, it'd been amazing. It'd been two years since she'd had sex—but she didn't remember it being that electric—or intense. She shivered thinking about the climax that had ripped through her.

However, once again, that physical act hadn't brought clarity. If anything, she was more confused now than ever.

Because she'd had sex with Daniel. It was exactly the

same kind of impulsive, careless act that had gotten her here. Except now, the potential for blowback was even more dangerous because of Marie.

Christine's baby girl was still asleep in her crib and Christine needed a shower. There was no way she was going to face Daniel with yesterday's deodorant under her armpits.

The bathroom was outfitted with all the luxuries she never got to enjoy. The shampoo was the finest. The soap was the finest. The conditioner was the finest. The lotion was the finest. The towels—good Lord, she could write poetry about the towels. They were heated.

She showered and shaved and dried off, telling herself she wasn't getting all pretty for Daniel and knowing that was a lie. She cracked open the bathroom door but didn't hear any sounds from Marie, so she closed it again and found a blow dryer.

When she had her hair looking decent, she pulled the robe back on and went to the guest room. She found a tank top, along with a pale peach tunic shirt and another cardigan, this one longer and a soft gray. There was even a pair of riding boots—real leather. And the crazy thing was, it all fit. She tucked the jeans into the boots and zipped them up, the calf just making it closed.

Layers were good. Layers would hide her lumps and stretch marks. Layers would protect her from Daniel's intense gazes.

Another lie. Because the layers of nightgown and robe last night hadn't done a darned thing to slow them down.

Doyle had been gone by the time she was six months pregnant. But the two months between finding out she was pregnant and Doyle bailing on her had not been a time of great intimacy and togetherness. The moment she'd become a news story, Doyle had started putting space between them. In public, he had stood by her side and held her hand—but in private...

They'd barely spoken. She'd been with him and yet *not* with him at the same time and she had known long before she had come home to the empty apartment that she had lost him.

She'd been alone since then—but she was too drained at the end of the day to feel sorry for herself. Self-pity was a luxury she simply didn't have the time or energy for. And in all honesty, she hadn't missed the sex. Well, she'd missed the crazy sex she and Doyle had had when they'd first hooked up. But not the lifeless going-through-the-motions sex that had marked their last months as a couple.

But last night, Daniel holding her like she meant something to him—she hadn't felt completely alone in the world.

That was all it took to make her revert back to her wild ways, apparently. Five minutes in the kitchen and she'd all but dragged him to his couch and had her way with him. For Pete's sake, they hadn't even made it to a bed. They hadn't even gotten undressed.

And now she had to go out there and face him, wearing clothes he had purchased for her. He would probably try and tell her how nice she looked again and she would struggle to accept a compliment.

She listened hard, but couldn't hear any fussing from Marie. If Christine was going to face this man, it was going to involve under-eye concealer.

Finally, dressed and ready for whatever the day held— she didn't even want to think about the possibilities—she tiptoed into Marie's room.

Only to find that the crib was empty.

Oh, crap. She flew out of the bedroom, torn between

stark panic and the logical explanation that Marie couldn't have gotten out of the apartment and probably hadn't done anything as deadly as stick a fork in an electrical outlet.

Christine skidded into the living room and came to a dead halt when she saw Daniel, sprawled out on the couch, Marie resting on his chest. A thick throw was tucked around them and in one hand, Daniel held a book. The other rested on Marie's stomach, keeping her from rolling off.

Marie was telling him the story and he was listening.

Oh, it simply wasn't *fair* how perfect he was. Never mind the fact that Christine hadn't had a date in twenty months. Never mind the fact that she might not have another date for another twenty months, if ever.

Daniel Lee was in the process of ruining her for any other man. He was too handsome, too rich, too good at sex—but that wasn't the issue. No, the thing that was going to be the death of her was the way he held her as if she was precious to him, the way he was saying, "Oh, really?" every time Marie looked up at him.

He was taking care of her and her daughter and Christine wasn't an idiot. She knew exactly how rare both of those things were.

No one else would ever meet this impossibly high bar that Daniel Lee was setting. If she weren't careful, he would make her fall in love with him and then where would she be?

He looked up, his gaze meeting hers and she could feel his mouth against hers, feel the hard planes of his body pressing into hers. She could feel the physical pain of loneliness all over again and it scared her because she knew what would happen if she let that rule her. She'd spent a good six years chasing away that loneliness and she had been paying the price for it since.

So it was settled. She was absolutely not going to fall in love with Daniel Lee.

"Good morning," he said in his silky voice. He looked rumpled, his hair mussed from where she'd driven her fingers through it.

She swallowed hard, trying to remember who she'd been before she'd straddled him. On this very couch.

Hell. At least he and Marie were sitting on the far side, a good ten feet from what had happened last night. "Good morning. How is everyone today?"

Marie looked up at her, grinning wildly. Christine could tell that her daughter was still a little fuzzy from sleep, her hair sticking out wildly on all sides. But the baby made no move for Christine to pick her up from Daniel's chest. If anything, Marie seemed to burrow deeper.

A sound came from the kitchen behind her and she jumped in surprise. "Don't worry," Daniel said quickly. "It's only the maid."

She blinked at him. "Oh, of course. Only the maid."

He slanted a smile in her direction and then, without breaking eye contact, leaned down and kissed the top of Marie's head. "Sunny has some coffee going and she's making breakfast, if you're interested."

"Coffee would be good." It would be *great*. She needed something to help her make sense of this world she found herself in. She felt a little like Alice having stumbled through the looking glass, where nothing made sense.

Sunny, it turned out, was a young Korean woman and she was pulling a pan of fresh-baked muffins out of the oven. She nodded shyly at Christine.

"Thank you," Christine said as the smell of the muffins—blueberry?—hit her nose. "Is there coffee?"

The young woman crinkled her eyes as if she didn't understand completely, but she pointed at the coffeepot and Christine nodded, hoping she was being encouraging and not patronizing. "Yes, thank you."

Strangely, the maid's presence reassured Christine. With another person in the apartment, she didn't think there'd be awkwardness about what had happened last night.

Sex. Angry sex. *Great* angry sex.

"I need to talk to you," Daniel said right in her ear.

She spun around, nearly clocking Marie upside her head. "What?"

Daniel said something in Korean to Sunny, who smiled and bobbed her head as she rushed forward to lift Marie from Daniel's arms and carry her over to the high chair.

Daniel slid his hand under Christine's arm and pulled her close to the windows. "About last night…"

"Do you have to make this awkward?" Although, given the way his thumb was rubbing little circles on the inside of her elbow and given the way she wanted to do nothing more than throw herself at him again, it appeared there wasn't any way to make this *not* awkward. "Or are you going to throw this back in my face as concrete proof that you were right about me two years ago?"

His face hardened and he said in a low voice, "Yes, I have to make this awkward. We didn't use a condom."

Flames licked up the side of her face—that's how hot her cheeks burned. "Oh." She dropped her gaze to where he was still holding on to her and his hand fell away. "Don't worry about it."

"I think I'm entitled to worry about it. What if, Christine?" he asked, which was both touching, that he cared whether or not he got her pregnant, and infuriating all the same and she didn't know why.

Of course he didn't want to get her pregnant. Because if he did, he'd be tied to her forever, his name dragged through the mud with hers. Another baby would simply be another problem to manage.

"I have an IUD. I can't get pregnant," she blurted out. Daniel's eyebrows shot up at this, so Christine lowered her voice. "I had one put in after Marie was born. I couldn't risk another surprise pregnancy. Which is funny, since last night was the first time I've had sex in…"

Her voice trailed off because she made the mistake of looking up at him. Instead of shocked or angry, his mouth had curved up on one side. Was he smiling? At her?

Darn his hide. "So don't worry about it," she whispered angrily, stepping around him and heading back to where Marie was banging on the high chair tray.

In short order, Christine had eggs, bacon and fresh blueberry muffins to go with some of the best coffee she had ever had in her life. Daniel followed her to the table and they sat down to eat as if this were an everyday occurrence.

Was this just how it was going to be? Everything was the best when it came to Daniel. The best food, the best clothes, the best apartment—and who could forget the best sex?

She exhaled heavily, trying not to be angry at Daniel or at the situation or at life, in general. She wasn't sure she was making it, though. Last night, she'd done something selfish. And wonderful. Was it wrong if she didn't want to face any fallout from that?

As Marie made headway into destroying her muffin, Christine decided to cut straight to the chitchat. "So, what are we doing today? Just hanging out here?" It would be peaceful and quiet and there was a lot to be said for that right now.

"We can," Daniel replied. "But we have another option.

If you want to, there's the Chicago Children's Museum down at the Pier. We could take Marie."

Christine gaped at him, wondering if she really had fallen through the looking glass. "Didn't you tell your mother that we were trying to lie low last night? I didn't hallucinate that, did I?"

He shrugged, looking completely innocent. It didn't look right on him. "It's one of those big areas with lots of fun things. It'll be crowded and noisy on a cold day like today. Everyone's going to be paying attention to their kids—not to each other. But we can stay in if you'd like. Natalie won't get here until about six tonight."

She looked out the expansive floor-to-ceiling windows where the maid was now wiping Marie's fingerprints off everything. If they stayed in all day, her daughter would continue to destroy this pristine apartment. But if they went to a children's museum...

"You don't think we'll get caught?" She winced at how juvenile she sounded.

But he didn't react as if she had said something dumb. "We didn't get caught at your church—and those were people who knew who you were. I think you're relatively safe here." She must've frowned or something because he added, "If I didn't think it was safe, I wouldn't suggest it. It'll be fun."

She eyed him. "You don't strike me as the kind of guy who has a lot of fun."

Something in his gaze shifted, sending tingles of electricity racing down her back. "I know how to have a good time." His voice came out husky and deep and her body responded.

Oh, how it responded. Her nipples tightened and her pulse raced and she was right back to where she'd been last night, wanting to climb him like a tree in the kitchen and hold him down on the couch.

They needed to get out of this apartment. "We can try the museum." Because someplace loud and crowded and focused on a small child—she wouldn't be thinking about the way his eyes darkened when he looked at her or wondering if he looked as good without clothing as he did fully dressed.

No, no—she wasn't thinking about what his body looked like or how it'd felt under her hands or on top of her. Or in her. Or what might happen tonight after Marie went to bed.

She shifted in her chair. Nope. Not thinking about any of it.

"It's a date," Daniel said with a smile that bordered on wicked and Christine had to wonder how true that was.

Even when Daniel dressed down, he was sinfully gorgeous. Really, no one man should be able to make sweaters look that good—but Daniel did. Effortlessly.

What was ridiculous was that Daniel was crawling through a tunnel, chasing a squealing Marie and looking like he was having the time of his life. He wasn't normal, Christine realized. Normal men did not take an interest in other men's children. Normal men did not happily play with little girls. Normal men didn't...

Christine was off to the side, keeping an eye on the action in the tunnels from the ground. In that moment, she looked around and she saw something that surprised her.

There were a lot of men playing with a lot of children in this museum. Daniel by no means stuck out. What if Daniel *was* normal? Okay, overlooking the condo and the jet and the cars—what if he was a regular guy on the inside? What if...

Her father had never really played with her. She couldn't remember a single time she and her dad had done something fun together. Children were to be seen and not heard. Spare the rod and spoil the child.

She mentally flipped back through the few photo albums she'd studied before she'd left home for college. She'd known then that she'd never return because she couldn't live with her father's dictates for her behavior, her dress—the way she fixed her coffee, even. He had some ideal of what a daughter was and it'd been obvious that Christine wasn't it. She never would be.

She didn't remember a single photo of him holding her like Daniel had been holding Marie this morning. Not even when she was a baby. All the pictures were of her mother and Christine.

She wondered if Donna Murray would've liked Daniel. Her mother had been dead for almost ten years and in that time, Christine had learned to live with the loss. But now Christine couldn't help but wonder what her mom would've thought about all of this.

What if Daniel *was* normal and all the other men Christine had known weren't? What if Doyle was the aberration because he didn't want his own child? And her father— well, he was a megalomaniac.

Lost in thought, she watched Daniel carry Marie back to her as if they were walking out of a dream. What if this was a new normal?

Christine realized just from looking at her daughter that Marie was about ten minutes away from a total fun-based meltdown. Christine checked her phone—it was already eleven forty-five.

"Lunchtime—and then nap time." When Marie fussed at this announcement, Christine knew it was time to go.

Predictably, lunchtime was a disaster. Marie did not

want to leave the museum. She did not want to sit in a high chair. She did *not* want to be quiet. She didn't want Christine to hold her. She wanted Daniel, who had been upgraded from *"anal grr"* to *"my anal."*

Daniel did his best to help, but his mere presence only wound Marie up more and finally, Christine had to ask him to step back. She closed the door to Marie's room and sat in the glider with Marie in her arms, riding out the storm.

It took almost half an hour, but Marie finally cried herself out. Even better, Christine was able to get her into the portable crib without waking her up. She laid her daughter down and Marie rolled over, sound asleep.

Thank God. For a moment, Christine debated just curling up in the bed next to the crib and zoning out.

But then she thought of Daniel. At this very moment, he was somewhere in this condo, effortlessly making a sweater look hot. Would he be waiting on her, or would he merely be thankful that the screaming had stopped?

If she walked back into his living room, would he look at her like a woman or a problem?

She found him on the couch, toggling between a laptop and a cell phone. Crap, he was working. She started to back out, but he looked up.

"I didn't mean to bother you," she said quickly. "I'll let you get some work done."

He'd taken so much time off to fly her across the country and entertain her daughter. She didn't know how much longer this little time-out was going to last, but she couldn't expect him to put his entire life on hold because of her.

"Christine?" His voice stopped her and she turned back. He'd closed the computer and set it on the coffee table.

"I'll go. I should nap." It had been such a crazy couple of days and she was supposed to do an interview this evening. "I'll go," she said again, as if saying it would make it true.

It didn't. Because Daniel was already moving, his long legs effortlessly closing the distance between them. He looked at her with naked want.

"Stay," he said and then his hands were on her, sliding around her waist and pulling her into his chest. *"Stay."*

And fool that she was, she did. Last night, she'd taken what she'd wanted from him like a brazen hussy. Because that's who she was—who she'd always been. Desperate and needy and shamelessly chasing the high of a climax, no matter the cost. And Daniel had just…taken it. He'd taken everything she'd dished out—the anger, the lust, the need.

But today? Today, Daniel was in charge. She could feel it in the way his mouth moved over hers, the way his hands roved over her backside, pushing her closer to him. If she had half a brain, she'd stop this and go take that damned nap. Because she didn't need this and she didn't need him. All she needed was to know that her daughter was safe. Nothing else mattered.

"I want you," he growled against her neck—and then his teeth bit into her skin.

"Daniel," she moaned, digging her hands into his sweater and holding him close.

No. A moment of panic spiked through her. She couldn't do this. This wasn't who she was, not anymore. She was Christine Murray, loan processor and mom. Nothing more—and certainly not the kind of woman a man like Daniel went for.

She shoved him back, her chest heaving as if she'd run up all sixty-seven flights of stairs. "We can't do this." When he notched an eyebrow at her, heat rushed to her face and she added, "Again."

Daniel's hands slipped up her back and over her shoulders, stroking her lightly. "Why not?" he asked, his voice deceptively innocent. "We're two consenting adults. I enjoyed last night. I thought…" His hands stilled. "I thought you did, too."

"I did." He was easily the best lover she'd ever had. "But that doesn't change things."

"What things?" He cupped her cheeks in his hands again and stroked his thumbs over her skin.

She shouldn't lean into his touch, shouldn't want him. But she couldn't help it. "I don't know anything about you and I shouldn't trust you. And when this is all over, I'm going back to being a dumpy single mom and you'll go back to doing…whatever it is you do."

Everything about him sharpened. *Dangerous* was all she had time to think before he spoke. "You know more about me than anyone else does."

She stared at him—no way would she buy that line. But before she could tell him that, he went on, "And you do trust me. You trust me enough to get into a car and a plane with me. You trust me to play with your daughter. And," he said, which was when she realized he was backing her up, one slow step at a time, "you trust me with your body."

"I'm not worried about my body," she got out as they crossed the threshold into his bedroom.

He tilted his head to one side and leaned back, his hot gaze raking over her. "You're not? Then what's the problem?"

My heart, she wanted to tell him. She couldn't risk falling for him any more than she already had. Which was a battle she'd already lost because he was too perfect and she couldn't fight this attraction anymore.

His lips curved into a sinful smile. "Let me take care

of you, Christine," he said in a voice that made her want to do bad, bad things—like peel him out of that sweater.

Hell, she already wanted to do that. Last night on the couch had taken the edge off but she had a backlog of physical need that went well past a one-time thing.

"Why?" The younger Christine would've fallen right out of her pants by now—especially after what had happened last night.

But last night, she had been mad at him, at herself—at the world. The anger had tripped some sort of mental wire, sure. But today?

Today she was tired and worried. And Daniel was still…perfect.

"Why do you want me?"

Part of her hoped he would whisper sweet nothings, easy-to-believe lies about how pretty and special she was. But part of her knew that if he said things like that, she wouldn't believe him, no matter how sincere his earlier compliments had seemed. Having him think she was pretty wasn't enough for her to give her heart away again.

"Because you are the strongest woman I have ever met," he said in a serious voice that was a balm for her soul. "But even strong women need a soft place to land every now and then."

Oh, sweet heavens. She needed him and if that made her an unnatural thing, a sinner of the first order, then so be it.

And then he was kissing her, pulling her cardigan off and Christine gave in to the strength of his body and the sweetness of his lips. She gave in to this place out of time, this life that wasn't hers.

Daniel sat her down on the edge of the bed and pulled the tunic off over her head in one smooth movement. "Last night, you showed me what you wanted, Christine. So let me give it to you." When she shivered as the cold air rushed to her bare skin, he paused and said, "Okay?"

"Yeah. Kiss me." Because she didn't want to stop and think about this, or what would come after. She just wanted Daniel to take care of her.

With a wicked grin, he pushed her back on the bed. She yanked at the sweater, trying to get it over his head. Back in her wild youth, she would've let the guy take the lead. Whatever worked for him worked for her. She wasn't that girl anymore, thank God.

"I want you naked."

"The feeling is mutual." He pushed off her and peeled his sweater, shirt and undershirt off. So many layers. The joys of sex in the winter. But eventually, he was down to his bare chest. "Oh, my," Christine said, running her hands over his sculpted muscles. She jerked her gaze up to his face. "You really are perfect, aren't you?"

He chuckled, a throaty noise that was definitely strained with need. "Far from it." When she went for the button fly of his jeans, he grabbed her hands. "Patience," he hissed.

"I don't want to be patient." She didn't want time to think of all the reasons that doing this—again—was a bad idea. And she didn't want Marie to wake up before…

Well. Before Daniel unleashed another mind-blowing orgasm upon her body.

That's all this was, she tried to tell herself as she grabbed for his jeans again—something physical. A way to take the edge off.

This time, he was faster than she was. He dodged and grabbed her tank top, stripping it over her head.

And then she was in nothing but her bra and jeans. Daniel froze, staring down at her with what she desperately wanted to believe was reverence. "God, Christine—look at you." His hands drifted over her collarbones and to the tops of her breasts above her bra. "You are amazing."

She didn't want to think. "Less talk." This time, she got her hands on his jeans and began jerking the buttons open. Talking meant thinking and thinking wasn't what she wanted right now. She just wanted to feel *good*.

Daniel kicked out of his jeans but before he could get out of his boxer briefs, he had her on the bed, his mouth covering hers, his body covering hers. He was hot to the touch, so hot it made her sweat with need.

They rolled under the covers together. His hands were everywhere and his mouth followed in hot pursuit.

Christine's mind tried to drift off into the quicksand of worries and regrets—because she knew those things were real and unavoidable and would be waiting for her the moment the fun stopped.

But Daniel simply would not let her mind wander because he took full possession of her body. His erection rubbed against her in languid strokes, his mouth and hands demanding her full attention.

"All day," he murmured against the sensitive skin on the underside of her breasts, "I thought of doing this to you."

"You did?" Then she gasped when his fingers slid over her sex.

"I didn't get to touch you last night," he said, sounding cool when she was about to lose her mind. "At your request. But I want to touch you. All of you, Christine."

With that, he slid a finger inside of her. "Oh," she moaned, her hips writhing at his touch. Because he wasn't just stroking in and out of her body. Oh, no. He was kissing his way down to the juncture of her legs, rubbing his thumb over the very center of her sex—he was going to drive her insane.

"Daniel," she gasped as he worked over her body, his

mouth settling where his thumb had been. She laced her fingers into his short hair and held him against her.

Everything fell away as he drove her higher and higher. Good Lord, had anyone ever done this for her?

Daniel made a humming sound that rocketed through her and she couldn't help herself. Her back came off the bed and she made some kind of noise but her mind blanked out in white-hot pleasure and all she could think was how much she'd missed this.

How much she would miss this.

But before that thought could take hold and drag her to the future where she was alone, except for her daughter, Daniel moved over her. "That's better," he murmured, settling his weight on top of her. "God, you're so beautiful, Christine."

And she was so relaxed from the orgasm that she believed him. Because right now, she felt beautiful and desirable and special. He'd given that to her—all that and an orgasm, too. "You're very good at that."

He chuckled, a confident sound deep in his throat. Who knew chuckling could be so sensual? "I told you I'd take care of you," he said, pressing his erection against her opening. "And I always keep my promises." But instead of thrusting in, he paused. "Okay?"

She lifted her hips to meet him. "Please," she whimpered as he teased her.

"Hmm," he said, but this time, she heard the crack in his cool demeanor. "Which is better?" As he spoke, he flexed, driving his erection into her a teasing inch at a time. "When you're mad at me? Or when you're begging?"

She dug her nails into his back. "I'll show you mad…"

But that was all it took. He sank into her, filling her so completely that she almost came again. She must have really scratched him because, with a grunt, he grabbed her hands from around his waist and held her wrists against the bed. "Last night I was at your mercy," he said, driving into her with such ruthlessness that it was all she could do to meet him. "Now you're at mine and so help me, Christine, you will come again."

"Oh, God," she whispered as she gave herself up to him.

For all his perfection, they fit together. He was relentless, driving into her over and over. She came and then came again as he groaned and collapsed onto her and she knew—

She was forever ruined for anyone but this man. Which was a damn shame because time was not their friend.

Exhaustion clawing at her, she hugged him tight, not caring that he was crushing her with his weight. She didn't want to let him go.

"Christine," Daniel said, his voice shaky as he leaned up on his forearms and brushed a lock of hair from her face.

She'd never heard him so uneven before. She got her eyes open to find him staring down at her, a look so intense that she was almost afraid—because this was the man who stopped at nothing.

Just when she couldn't take another second of being in his sights, he kissed her. "We've got some time," he said, rolling to the side and tucking her in his arms. "Sleep."

She might have protested but honestly? She was completely wrung out and even the simple touch of his arm around her waist and his heartbeat against her ear from where she was resting on his chest—everything pulled her into the nap.

So she went. Willingly.

Twelve

Daniel was a mess. His mother was on the way—which was fine. That was a part of the plan.

Natalie had also landed—again, all part of the plan. But she was bringing her husband, CJ, with her.

Daniel's brother.

And the hell of it was, he wasn't sure why the idea of Natalie and CJ waltzing into his apartment had him on edge. After the explosive afternoon sex with Christine, Daniel would have thought he'd be achieving peak mellow right about now.

After all, he'd essentially taken the morning off. He'd played with Marie and made love to Christine and…

And for one too-brief morning, he'd gotten a glimpse of what a different life looked like, one where he was a normal man instead of the heir to the Lee Enterprises fortune and Hardwick Beaumont's bastard son.

He did not enjoy this level of personal confusion. This

was exactly why he didn't let people just walk into his house—or his life. The results were too messy.

Still, when he went to wake up Christine, he found himself staring at her. All of this upset—it was because of her. She made him feel things, want things, that he'd long ago decided he'd never have and, therefore, never want.

But here she was, anyway—in his house and in his bed. She was in his life now and he had no idea what to do next. Except wake her up. After all, he still had most of a fully functional plan to protect her and Marie, thwart Brian White and Clarence Murray and...

And then what? After the dust had settled—and he'd been doing this long enough to know that the dust would settle eventually—what came next? Where were plans A, B and C?

For the first time in his life, he wasn't sure what came next. "Christine," he said gently, leaning down to touch her hair. Her eyelids fluttered. "You need to get up and get dressed."

Her eyes scrunched shut. "Why?" she murmured groggily. "Wanna stay here."

God, he'd love that—her in his bed?

But the moment the thought crossed his mind, he heard his grandfather's voice in his head, telling him had to marry the "right" girl. "People will be here soon. Do you really want Natalie to interview you nude in my bed?"

That did the trick. She sat up, clutching the sheet to her chest. "Oh, Lord, no. How long?"

Daniel knew he needed to put some distance between them. But she looked so gorgeous, her hair mussed and her shoulders bare. He knelt, one knee on the bed, and kissed her.

"Twenty minutes," he murmured against her lips. A man could get a lot done in twenty minutes.

She shoved him back. "I've got to—oh, Lord!" She hopped out of bed, pulling the sheet with her. "I've got to…" she repeated, gathering up her clothes and dashing into his bathroom.

Just before she closed the door, she turned around, the sheet falling to reveal the creamy sweep of her breast. His blood quickened as he jerked his gaze up to her face.

She shot him a knowing little smile—and then shut the door.

"Wow," he exhaled, forcing his body to stand down. He had to get through some unexpected family socializing and media management before he could follow up on that smile.

"Where is my little Marie?" Minnie said, all but running into the apartment, bags of toys hanging from her arms as she ignored Daniel completely.

Marie looked up from her bowl of Cheerios and squealed. Christine came running—Daniel noticed that she came from the direction of the guest room, not from his bathroom. "Is everything—oh, Minnie," she said with a warm smile, "you're here."

"Christine," Minnie said, a warm smile on her face as she dropped her presents for Marie and scooped the little girl up. "You're looking better. Did you sleep well?"

Christine flushed and, for a second, Daniel wondered if she was about to give them away. Not that there was anything wrong with consenting adults enjoying some time together.

But that's not how his mom would look at it. A physical relationship between him and Christine would only be further proof that Daniel had found a ready-made family.

"Yes—the bed was wonderful," Christine said, slanting him a sideways look.

That answer was good enough for his mother. She and Marie were off, talking in a mixture of English, Korean and Baby that not even Daniel had a hope of understanding.

Daniel moved to Christine's side, but he was surprised to see a look of sadness on her face as she watched his mom and Marie. "Okay?"

"It's fine," she said too quickly. She caught him staring at her and gave him a weak smile. "It's just going to be hard when we leave all of this behind. I mean, for Marie. She's not used to being spoiled like this—that's all," she said, color washing over her pale cheeks.

"Christine—" he started, but stopped because she was right. It would be hard when this ended. But end it would.

The amount of work he was ignoring to take care of this was snowballing and if he didn't get a handle on things soon, he'd be buried in an avalanche.

Besides, it wasn't like he could keep Christine and Marie here. They had their own lives. He couldn't imagine Christine giving up her job because doing so would put her at the mercy of someone else and she wouldn't do that.

"It'll be fine," she said, watching Minnie and Marie. But her eyes revealed the lie of her words.

Once again, Daniel was seized with some sort of urge to do something—anything—to make it better. But what? It was no stretch to say that he was out to sea here. His entire involvement with Christine Murray should have been limited to protecting Marie from the press. That was what he knew how to do—a concrete plan with actionable steps that led to a desired—and predictable—outcome.

At no point did any of those steps include him and Christine naked. Or even partially naked, as they had been last night.

Or as they would be again tonight.

Jesus, what was wrong with him? The fact that he was thinking about tonight instead of the interview or the imminent arrival of his brother—this was a problem.

He could work around problems. Through them, if he had to. And his attraction to Christine… Well, he didn't want to call it a problem. Even if it was on the verge of becoming one.

His phone buzzed—the text from the doorman. Natalie and CJ were here. Which was good. It would keep Daniel from thinking about Christine and her sleepy smiles and the way she had felt beneath him, over him. "They're on their way up."

Christine patted her hair. "Do I look all right?"

"Gorgeous. As usual." Even as the words were leaving his mouth he wondered where they had come from. He did not flirt. He didn't even sweet talk. He was all business.

Except with her. And he didn't know why.

Luckily, he was saved from any further fruitless introspection by a knock on the door. He opened it to see CJ wearing a giant cowboy hat. "You really do live here," his half brother said, an easy smile on his face. But that's how CJ was. He was open and happy, honest almost to a fault.

"I really do live here." It struck Daniel that, if not for Christine, he had no idea when he might've invited his brother to Chicago. "Come on in. Thanks for making the trip, you two."

"And miss the chance to get a glimpse into the life of Daniel Lee?" Natalie said, launching a professional smile in his direction. "We wouldn't miss *this* for the world."

Daniel knew that she was teasing him—they both were. But it bothered him, anyway. He didn't really have close friends. He suddenly had a huge family—but they were mostly strangers. It had always been easier that way. Safer, too. "It's not that big of a deal, guys."

It was supposed to be a joke. But he didn't miss the look that Natalie and CJ shared, the way they seemed to understand each other without saying a word.

He shook his head. He shouldn't have stayed in bed with Christine until she'd fallen asleep. It had messed with his normal routine and that was throwing him for a loop. "My mother is here. She's going to watch Marie during the interview," he told them as he led them into the front room.

CJ whistled at the view, which got Christine's attention. She hopped to her feet and said, "Hello. I'm Christine Murray," in a surprisingly even voice, given the circumstances.

"CJ Wesley," CJ said, giving her a big handshake and another easy smile. "It's a pleasure to make your acquaintance. This is my wife, Natalie."

Daniel watched Christine closely as she and Natalie made their introductions. He could tell Christine was nervous but she was doing an admirable job of hiding it. That was encouraging.

Minnie came over with Marie. Daniel introduced his mother and Christine introduced her daughter and Marie introduced Daniel to everyone as *"my anal!"* which sent CJ into snorting peals of laughter. It should have been awful. All of these people were in Daniel's condo where, prior to this, only his mother and the maid had ever set foot.

He didn't know what to do. For all of his training on manners, Grandfather had never prepared Daniel for this—his brother was talking to his mother and Natalie talking to Christine and Marie being passed around and smiling big for everyone. It wasn't bad. He watched all the pieces of his life collide head-on and it was...

Okay. This was okay. He could have his half brother and his mother and his—well, he wasn't sure what Christine was. But he could have all of them here together and somehow, it worked.

Christine looked up at him, her eyes wide. She quirked an eyebrow and he could almost hear her saying, *are you all right?* And he realized he was standing off to the side, watching them, without being a part of the conversation.

Natalie noticed Christine's distraction and turned to face him. "We should get started. Where do you want us?"

Yes, it would probably be best to cut the chitchat short and focus on the reason they were all here today. This wasn't a party, after all.

"This way." He led them back to his office.

While Christine had slept, he had arranged some lights and chairs. "Do you need me for anything?"

Natalie smiled at the setup. "We'll go over the talking points and then take a run at it. But," she added, looking up, "I want a tour when we're done. We came all this way—don't think you're going to get us out of here without at least showing us around."

He scowled at her. "You know you're more than welcome to—"

She made shooing gestures, which made Christine giggle. "I've got this. Go have a beer with CJ."

Right. That was probably what normal people did—grabbed a beer with their brother. Except Daniel had never done that. Not outside of the Beaumont Brewery and tastings with Zeb, that was.

Feeling awkward in his own home, Daniel found his brother standing by the window, looking down on Navy Pier.

"Damn, if I had any idea that you had a place like this, I would've invited myself a long time ago," he said in a quiet voice when Daniel approached with two Beaumont beers in hand. CJ took one and said, "You don't mind that I came, do you?"

"Of course not. You're family."

They stood for a moment, the silence uncomfortable. Or maybe it wasn't. Daniel didn't like the way he was suddenly unsure. Uncertainty was a liability and liabilities were dangerous.

CJ leaned to one side and looked over Daniel's shoulder to where Minnie and Marie were singing. "Your mom seems like a nice person."

"She is."

For some reason, that statement made CJ smile. "I wonder about you sometimes, man."

Daniel took a long pull of his beer, trying to figure out which way this conversation was going. "How so?"

CJ still had that easygoing smile, but there was a hardness to his eyes that Daniel recognized. As much as he didn't want to admit it, CJ was a Beaumont, just like Daniel. "You do realize that I've never even been to your place in Denver? If it hadn't been for Christine, how long would it have been before I saw this fabulous view?"

Daniel tried to shrug nonchalantly. "You're welcome anytime. You know that."

"Do I?" CJ chuckled, but it wasn't a happy sound. "I guess I'm not surprised," he said, turning his attention back to the view.

"About what?"

"This," CJ said, gesturing to the world below. "This is just how you are, isn't it? You keep yourself removed from the rest of us—even those who care for you. You're always distant and remote and watching."

He'd argue that—but he couldn't because it was true. Hadn't he just stood on the perimeter of his own living room and watched everyone else talk—without him? Instead, Daniel heard himself ask, "Does it bother you?"

"What?" CJ asked, taking another pull of his beer.

"Well, your mom's Mexican American but your dad—both of your dads," he hurried to add, "are American. Does it ever bother you, trying to be both?"

CJ gave him a look of utter confusion. "No," he said slowly. "It's never been an either/or thing."

Of course it wasn't for CJ and Daniel felt stupid for having asked. But who else besides Zeb and CJ would ever understand?

Except even they couldn't, of course. It was one thing to be one of Beaumont's biracial bastards—but there was no way to compare Zeb being half black or CJ being half Mexican with Daniel being half Korean. Minnie was a citizen now—but she hadn't been when Daniel had been born.

CJ took another drink. "I will say this, though—I'm still working on how to be a Wesley and a Beaumont. There's been a hard line between those two things my entire life and it's only since I've known Natalie that I've been able to think about crossing the streams. It's a difficult thing, trying to carve out a place to exist where people said you couldn't." He was silent for a moment longer and then slid a sideways glance to Daniel. "Why?"

"No reason." Unexpectedly, Daniel was glad CJ had come. His brother might not ever understand what it was like to be Lee Dae-Won's grandson, but he knew what it was like to be Hardwick Beaumont's bastard.

Because hadn't that been at the center of Daniel's entire relationship with his grandfather? He'd stained the honor of the Lee family name by being born. It was his duty to restore that honor—or else.

Marie squealed behind them and both men turned to

look. "She seems nice—Christine, not the baby. Although the baby seems nice, too. As far as babies go, anyway."

"Don't read anything into it." It was bad enough that Daniel's mother was already seeing grandbabies. He didn't need CJ joining in. "This was simply the best way to make sure she was protected until the dust settled."

CJ gave him another long look and Daniel knew he wasn't buying that line. "Whatever, man. You don't have to justify your actions to me." For a moment, Daniel thought CJ wouldn't let it go. Then he sighed deeply. "Again, I'm sorry for crashing. Natalie's settling into ranch life but... I think she needed a break and I sure as hell wasn't going to pass up the chance to see Chicago." He smacked Daniel on the shoulder. "Thanks for getting us that room at the Drake."

"No problem," Daniel said, more relieved than he expected to be at the subject change. "My driver will take you wherever you guys want to go after Natalie and Christine are done."

"But until then," CJ said, with a gleam in his eyes that Daniel didn't necessarily like, "I'm going to hang out with your mom and see what I can learn about the mysterious Daniel Lee."

Daniel groaned. But even as he cringed at the thought of his mother sharing baby stories with CJ, he felt a little excited about it, too. He wasn't any good at having brothers—but even though the situation made him uncomfortable, there was something reassuring about the way things had played out.

Natalie and Christine were talking. CJ started rolling a ball to Marie, all while talking and joking with Minnie. And Daniel?

He was glad they were here. But more than that, he didn't want to stand on the edge, watching from a distance.

What if CJ were right? What if it were possible to carve out a new space—a place where he could be both Daniel and Dae-Hyun? A place where he could honor his father and his grandfather and still be his own man?

Daniel looked toward his office, where Natalie and Christine were conducting their interview. He had dragged Christine through the mud two years ago. And yet she'd put her trust in him—that he could shield her and Marie, that he could take care of her. She made him want things he hadn't thought he could want.

In her eyes, Daniel was almost...forgiven.

Christine waited awkwardly while Natalie set up tripods with phones and tablets attached to them. She would record from several different angles so they had options when Natalie spliced the video. Christine thought. She hadn't understood all the technical terms.

"So tell me," Natalie said, adjusting one of the devices. "How did you wind up here with Daniel?" When Christine didn't answer immediately, Natalie went on, "I'm not recording. I'm just curious. I've been working with him for months now and he's like Fort Knox. We can't get him out to the ranch. CJ wasn't even invited today but he couldn't pass up the opportunity to find out a little bit more about his half brother."

"Honestly? I have no idea. One moment, there were reporters barking at the bank and I was afraid. The next thing I know, Daniel's whisked me away on his private jet and I'm meeting his mother in this condo." Natalie notched an eyebrow at her and Christine realized that might have sounded whiny. "It's great—don't get me wrong. But it all happened so fast."

Too fast, it seemed. If she stopped and thought about it—like she was doing right now—everything was a blur.

Except for the part where Daniel took her to bed. And made her climax three times before letting her nap. *That* she remembered perfectly.

She desperately hoped that whatever was happening between her and Daniel wasn't just really good sex. The kind of sex she wasn't sure she'd ever had before.

The kind of sex she was not going to regret. Sleeping with Daniel was the same as wearing these expensive clothes or jetting around the country in his private plane. This wasn't real life and it wouldn't last.

She started to tell herself that she still didn't trust him—but she knew that wasn't true. He was right—she trusted him with her life, with her daughter's life. She trusted him with her body.

But she didn't know him. Even if what he had said was true, that she knew more about him than almost anyone else in the world—she still didn't know who Daniel Lee was.

And she had to accept the fact that she wasn't going to find out. She didn't need to find out, either. She just needed to...get back to normal.

Back to her job at the bank while Marie was in day care. Back to the long nights and the housework that piled up. Back to the crushing loneliness.

Boy, she was really selling it.

"I hope you don't mind me saying so, but that's just... Well, that's not like Daniel. I assume. He's family, but we know so little about him." Natalie adjusted one of the monitors and asked, "Can you sit back just a few inches— perfect." She sat in the chair opposite of Christine. "I tried to look him up, you know. Before I went digging for CJ."

"You did?" Because Christine had also tried looking Daniel up and hadn't been able to find anything. She'd assumed that was because she hadn't been looking in the right places. "What did you find?"

Natalie leaned back in her chair, looking defeated. "Nothing. Not a damn thing. And it's not because he never did anything newsworthy. It was like there was a Daniel Lee–shaped black hole where nothing existed. He's still like that. I mean, I had no idea what his mother's name was. And he stood up with CJ at our wedding!" she said, her frustration bleeding through.

Christine could sympathize. "I didn't know I was going to meet her until she opened the door. I think she was almost as surprised as I was, frankly." She debated whether or not she should tell Natalie what she had learned—but then again, what *had* she learned? Not much. "He told you what happened two years ago, didn't he?"

Natalie nodded. "But that's the other thing," she said, reaching over and adjusting a light. "I honestly think he feels bad about what he did to you—and trust me, he is not the kind of guy to experience guilt. Before you came along, if someone had told me that underneath that handsome face, he was actually a robot, I wouldn't have been surprised."

Christine felt her cheeks heat as she dropped her gaze to her lap. "He's apologized for dragging my name through the mud. I guess all of *this*," she said, waving her hands over her clothes and around the room and toward Natalie, "is his way of making up for it."

Natalie didn't say anything and Christine glanced up to find the other woman staring at her. "Well," she said slowly, "I'm glad to hear it. Are you ready to get started?"

Not really. She understood why she needed to do this interview, but that didn't make it any better. She was so loath to have her name out there in any capacity that it was almost physically painful to say, "We might as well get this over with."

"Okay," Natalie said as she reached over and tapped the

screens. Then, in what Christine recognized as Natalie's television voice, she said, "Ms. Murray, how would you describe your relationship with your father?"

Thirteen

Christine woke with a start, her heart pounding. Fragments of a dream where she was being interviewed not by Natalie but by her father—"Tell me about your relationship with me," he asked—floated through her mind. It took a moment to remember where she was.

She was in Daniel's bed. After his family had left and Marie had gone to sleep, he had carried her back to his bed and made love to her again. She'd felt safe and happy and beautiful.

She flung out her arm at the same time a noise hit her ears. The bed was empty.

Now fully awake, she got up and fumbled with her nightgown. As she dressed, she strained to hear the familiar sounds of Marie's cries and checked the clock.

2:00 a.m. Right on schedule.

Except the sound she heard wasn't Marie. She tiptoed out into the hall and saw a dim glow in the living room. She saw Daniel sitting on the couch, bathed in the blue light of computer screens. He was speaking Korean and sounding angry.

Quietly, Christine went to check on Marie. But for once, the little girl was sound asleep in the middle of the night. Christine felt awful for being awake when her daughter was out like a light, but...

She slipped back into the living room. Daniel turned and, without missing a beat in whatever he was saying, held out his hand for her.

She took it and sank against his side of the couch. He had a headset on, so she couldn't hear the other half of the conversation—not that she would've understood it, anyway. Daniel's laptop was open and he was toggling between several screens—all of which were filled with numbers and Korean writing she had no hope of understanding.

But he tucked his arm around her shoulders and she nestled in, letting the flow of his words lull her into a daze. It was silly to think that this felt right. The last time she'd thought things felt right between her and a man, it had been with Doyle and see where that had gone? And besides, this wasn't her life. In a few short days, things would go back to normal and she would be okay. Really.

"Sorry about that," Daniel said some time later as he pulled his headset off and closed the laptop. "I didn't mean to wake you, but it was a meeting I couldn't miss."

"It's all right." They sat for a moment longer before she asked, "Would you tell me something about yourself?"

She expected him to tense up and pull away. But he didn't. "Like what?"

She snuggled in deeper. He was *so* warm. "Anything. No one knows anything about you. Natalie said she didn't even know your mother's name before today."

He sighed and she wondered if he would avoid this

topic—again. Then he opened the laptop. After several clicks, she found herself looking at a website. It was in Korean, but there were pictures. An older man scowled out at them, looking harsh and unforgiving—and vaguely like Daniel. With a few keystrokes, the page was translated into English.

"This is my grandfather," he said in a soft voice. "Lee Dae-Won. He was the founder of Lee Enterprises, and he helped industrialize Korea after the Korean War."

Christine stared at the man. "He doesn't look very happy."

"In Korea, it's not common to smile for pictures." He chuckled. "But you're right. He wasn't the jolliest of men. I spent every summer with him, whether I wanted to or not. I was his only grandchild."

They sat in silence while Christine skimmed the text. Lee Enterprises had been founded in 1973 by Lee Dae-Won. It started with one factory making parts for transistor radios and from there had spawned an empire—factories, real estate—a little bit of everything. "Wow," she said when she read that the company was valued at $200 billion. The number was almost too big to be real. "So your grandfather was one of the richest men in Korea?"

"Pretty much. And as much as he hated it, I was his only heir."

There was something in his voice that made her pause. "Why did he hate it?"

"Because I was his great shame," Daniel said, leaning his head back. "Not only was I born out of wedlock, but my father was American. For three months every year, my grandfather did his best to make me into the perfect heir. He wanted me to marry a good Korean girl—from a family of his choosing—so the line would continue. That was the only way he thought I could redeem my bad birth." He sat up and smirked at her, as if what he'd just said wasn't that important, when Christine had the feeling that it was everything. "In the end, I won. I refused to marry and when he died, I took control of the company."

This, Christine realized, was the Daniel Lee–shaped black hole Natalie had been referring to. "No one knows this about you?"

"No." He turned his attention back to the laptop. With a few more keystrokes, he pulled up a different page. "Because, in Korea, my name is Lee Dae-Hyun. He didn't allow me to be Daniel when I was with him." Christine stared at the website. There was his name, listed on the board of directors. But there was no picture and no biography.

"I thought…" she said slowly, trying to wrap her head around it. "I thought you were a political consultant."

"I am. I mean, I was. My grandfather taught me a lot about manipulating the press and controlling appearances. By the time I went to college, I'd learned how to cover my tracks. I didn't want him watching me and I didn't want people to find out how much I was worth. If men like Brian White—" Christine physically shuddered at the mention of the name. "Yeah, that. If he knew that I was a billionaire…"

"Wait." Christine sat up. "You're a *billionaire*?"

His smile tightened. "It changes things, I know."

She didn't know why she was surprised. After all, it made sense. He owned three homes in two different countries. He had a private jet on standby at all times. Everything in this apartment—he really *was* rich. She just hadn't put a dollar amount to that. "Does it, though?"

It was physically painful, the way his self-deprecating smile faded into something that looked much sadder. "It does." He cupped her cheek in his hand. "You're the first woman I've ever brought home with me. I don't know what it is about you, Christine. Two years ago, I knew that I was crossing a line. But it was too late—I couldn't stop what I'd started." He stroked his thumb over her cheek. "I don't regret making sure your father lost. But after what I did to you, I realized—that was what my grandfather would have done. He would've looked for weaknesses and exploited them mercilessly. It didn't matter how innocent anyone was, not to him. And I..." his voice trailed off.

"And you're not him," she said, her voice gentle.

She could tell by the way he grimaced that he didn't quite believe that. "After the election, I got out of the game. Zeb had decided to get control of the brewery and I knew I could help him accomplish his goals." He touched his forehead to hers. "I spent so long trying not to be the man my grandfather demanded but when it came down to the important things—to someone like you—I realized I was exactly the man he'd created. And I couldn't be that person anymore."

She tucked her head back against his chest and tried to make sense of it all. Even if it were the middle of the afternoon and she was fully awake, she wasn't sure she could.

As she thought back through everything he had just said—all those secrets he carried—one thing stuck out. She pushed herself off his chest and looked him in the eyes. "He was wrong about you," she told him, hearing echoes of something he had said to her just a few days ago.

His gaze shuttered. "What?"

"All those things he said—because he said them to you, right? That you weren't Korean enough, that you weren't *good* enough? He was wrong. Just as my father is wrong about me."

He looked away. "I know that. I've known that for years."

"But it's one thing to *know* it and another thing to *believe* it," she pressed. "I don't know what it's like to have an unforgiving grandfather or what it's like to be a part of two cultures or two families who don't know what to do with you. But I do know what it's like to grow up with a man who believes your very existence was a mistake and I know what it's like to have that voice in your head reminding you how wrong you are no matter what you do or how hard you try."

That had been her whole life, hadn't it? Trying to meet some impossible standard that would always be out of reach because, according to her father, she was a daughter of Eve and therefore a sinner. And she'd long ago decided that if she would always be a sinner, she might as well earn that title.

"You don't have to be the person he says you are or should be. And…" Unexpectedly, her eyes started to water. "And you don't have to prove anything to him. My father will never know me and he'll never know his granddaughter because that's his choice. Who am I to argue with him?"

She'd thought she had made peace with this years ago. But she had proven herself wrong. The first time she'd had sex with Daniel—hadn't she decided that if wanting him made her an unnatural sinner of the first order, so be it? Those weren't her words—they were her father's. Even when she'd thought she had built a wall between them, he *still* found his way into her head.

Daniel looked at her with such tenderness that she didn't know what to make of it. "How can you stand it?" he asked. "How can you sit there and treat me like I'm a decent human being, after what I did to you?"

She'd spent the better part of the last few weeks asking herself the same question. And she wasn't any closer to an answer. "I don't know. But we were both different people then, weren't we? I changed because of what happened two years ago. And I think..." she touched his face. "I think you did, too."

"I don't know. I don't think I changed enough." He tried to look away, back to the computer screen and the other half of his life that no one else knew about.

But she wouldn't let him. "Why did you tell me about this?" she asked, waving at the screen.

He shrugged as if he were trying to look nonchalant and failing miserably. "You're here. I owe you an explanation for why I was calling into a board meeting at two in the morning."

"I don't believe that for one second, Daniel Lee. It's because you trust me." She took a deep breath, knowing it was the truth. "Just like I trust you. I forgive you for what happened two years ago, Daniel. I forgive you," she repeated and the words seemed to lift a weight off her shoulders.

Something flitted across his face that she couldn't interpret. "I can't promise you anything, Christine. We've got another day or two but beyond that..."

Beyond that, there couldn't be anything between them. Their worlds were too different. "I don't want any promises, Daniel." Because if he didn't make any promises, then, when they went their separate ways, she wouldn't be disappointed if he didn't keep them. "Let's just enjoy what we've got for the time being."

He stared at her for the longest moment. "Come on," he said, pulling her to her feet. "It's time to go to bed."

Like all good things, Daniel's time with Christine came to an end. And when it did, he wished that it hadn't.

For two more days, they essentially played house.

Christine slept in his bed. They ate their meals around the table and visited the Chicago Children's Museum at the Pier a second time. Minnie came over to play with Marie.

Daniel got the chance to do something he rarely did—he relaxed and had fun. True, he couldn't ignore reality for long. He had to get up for another middle of the night call to the board of Lee Enterprises. And he constantly monitored the impact of Christine's interview. But when all that was done, she was waiting for him in bed.

Something had changed between them. He didn't want to be so naïve as to think those three little words—"I forgive you"—were the reason why. They were just words and, besides, he didn't exactly deserve her forgiveness.

He didn't deserve her at all—not her affection, not her trust. He didn't deserve Marie's sweet smiles or her silly nickname for him. Christine was convinced she wasn't good enough for him because of her past and his wealth—but she had it all wrong.

He wasn't good enough for her. Because if he were, he'd be able to keep his hands off her. He'd be able to give her space.

And he couldn't, selfish bastard that he was.

As a piece of marketing, the interview was a success. It got some good press and one cable news show spent an hour debating whether or not Christine really had an impact on any election, present or past. Natalie fielded the media requests, but—aside from one or two news outlets that were clearly looking to sell a particular angle—the interview diffused the gossip.

It also helped that Clarence Murray got a challenger in the Republican field—a state senator who just happened to be a moderate while at the same time being a Methodist minister. He was conservative but not on the fringe.

Daniel could see Brian White's hand at work as the Murray campaign pivoted, leaving Christine behind.

Which meant their time was almost up. Daniel needed to get her back to her life. But more than that, he needed to get back to his own—board meetings and beer tastings and expensive condominiums around the world, always watching. Back to being alone and somehow thinking that kept his grandfather from dictating his choices in life.

No, that wasn't true. He had things to do—companies to run, situations to monitor. He had plenty to keep him busy. Except…

If Daniel chose to be alone in order to spite the old man—who'd been dead for almost thirteen years—then wasn't he still letting his grandfather dictate his choices?

It didn't matter. What mattered was that he made his peace with Christine and fulfilled his promise to protect her and Marie. He was a man of honor. Maybe his grandfather would've been proud of him for that, if nothing else.

Christine refused to take any of the clothes and toiletries, so Daniel left instructions to have everything boxed up and mailed to her. It wasn't like he had any use for ladies' tops or toddler jammies.

His mother came over to say goodbye and Daniel was stunned when Minnie got teary. "You take care," she told Christine, sniffing, patting Christine's cheek and rubbing Marie's back. "And if there's anything I can ever do for you, please let me know."

"I will," Christine said, wrapping an arm around his mother and hugging her tight.

This tearful farewell made him feel things he didn't think he was capable of feeling.

Emotion was a weakness, a vulnerability. If he cared about something, that something—or someone—could be used against him. At one point, he had loved his grandfather. He had wanted his grandfather's approval and the old man had used that against him, always dangling a kind word or an affectionate pat on the shoulder just out of Daniel's reach, like a carrot tied to the end of the long stick.

That hadn't changed. If Brian White ever figured out that Daniel cared for Christine and Marie, Daniel knew what would happen. The man would come after them with guns drawn and murder in his eyes. White would convince himself his actions were justified because Daniel had dared care about someone.

Because he did. It was pointless to deny it. He cared for Christine. He cared for Marie.

So the best way to keep them safe was to stay away from them. He would go back to doing what he should have done from the very beginning—monitoring the situation from a distance, running interference with an invisible hand. He would keep Natalie involved for as long as needed. He would be vigilant. There was no room for error.

So why did this feel like such a mistake?

The flight back to Denver was nearly silent. What was there to say? He had already screwed up her life enough. Doing anything foolish like asking to see her again or even asking her to come home with him—even for one more night—would only prolong the inevitable.

Daniel had, of course, planned for every contingency upon their arrival back in Denver. When the jet doors opened, suddenly he found himself talking. "Porter Cole is here with your car. I've arranged for him or one of his associates to shadow you for the next week or two, just to be safe." Her eyebrows jumped up. "But I don't think you'll have any problems. The news cycle has moved on. You should be fine from here on out."

She was silent as they gathered up Marie and walked

down the jet's stairs. "So," Christine said as they headed to her car. "This is it?"

What he should've said was *yes*. A clean break. No one would ever draw a connection between Christine Murray and Daniel Lee. It was better this way.

But that's not what came out of his mouth. "For now. You still have my number?" She nodded. "Call me anytime, if there's anything you need. Anytime," he repeated, pointedly *not* cupping her cheek in his hand and *not* pulling her into an embrace.

Marie blinked up at him sleepily. *"My anal,"* she murmured around the thumb in her mouth.

"My Marie," he said, patting her back. "You be good for Mommy, okay?"

Christine buckled her daughter into the car seat and then turned back to Daniel, her face so blank it hurt to see it. "You won't call me, will you?"

Daniel had never let himself fall in love and, therefore, had never let his heart get broken. He wondered if this was what it felt like. "No."

She tried to smile, but the corner of her mouth pulled down into a frown. "I see." Then, unexpectedly, she threw her arms around his neck and kissed him and, fool that he was, he let her. He did more than that. He held her tight and kissed her back, thinking that this was it. *The End.*

"Phones work both ways," she whispered. With that, she climbed into her car. With a dawning sense of horror, all Daniel could do was watch her drive away.

"That must have been some trip to Chicago," Porter said as he walked over to Daniel. "You're really going to let her go?"

"Aren't you supposed to be following her?" he demanded, trying his best to ignore the stab of... something Porter's observation sparked in his chest.

"Yes, sir," Porter said with a mocking salute. He climbed into his own vehicle and took off, leaving Daniel alone.

Just like always.

He could call her. Just to check in, see how she was doing. He could ask about Marie, make sure she got the clothes and things. He could...

No. To keep in contact with Christine—or, worse, see her—would be a risk. To both of them.

So what if he'd been able to relax around her? So what if he'd brought her to his home, his bed? So what if he'd told her who he really was and so the hell *what* that she had understood, damn it—understood the impossible burdens his grandfather had put upon Daniel's shoulders at an age when most kids were worried about learning to ride bikes and play video games?

None of it mattered, as long as she was safe from the damage he'd unleashed upon her life. From him.

She might have forgiven him.

But he couldn't forgive himself.

Fourteen

A week passed. Christine tried to go back to normal. She returned to her job at the bank and made up a story about staying with an old college friend. Not that Sue or anyone else at the bank bought that, but they didn't press her.

Things with Marie were rough. The little girl wanted to do all of the fun things with Daniel and Minnie. And when neither of those two people appeared, she threw a fit that seemed to last for days.

Which just reminded Christine how much she had enjoyed the vacation, as well. It'd been such a relief to have Minnie there to watch Marie for a little bit while she…

It felt wrong to admit that it had been a relief not to have to think about Marie—but it was the truth. For a few days, she had taken some time for herself.

And what had she done with that time?

Nothing much. She'd only fallen in love with Daniel. She wanted to think that, with time and space, she would get over it. The daily grind would wear her down until that time in Chicago was little more than a dream.

It had very nearly been a dream come true.

More than once, Christine called up Daniel's contact information. She hadn't heard from him. She hadn't expected to—but there'd been a kernel of hope that he'd miss her, that maybe she'd meant something to him.

After all, he'd told her about his life in Korea and his grandfather and the fact that Daniel was a billionaire but worked as an executive vice-president in a midsized brewery in Denver, of all things. He trusted her. He liked her. He'd introduced her to his mother, for crying out loud.

These thoughts were the quickest way to madness because he had also told her he would always keep his word and he had, for better or for worse, promised that he would not call her again. And he hadn't.

She knew he wouldn't. The simple fact was that, until he accepted that she'd forgiven him for what had happened two years ago, he wouldn't.

No, that wasn't right. She wouldn't hear from him until he'd forgiven himself. And she didn't know if he was capable of doing that.

Which was reassuring, in an odd sort of way. He wasn't treating her like a convenient bed buddy. Which was why she wasn't going to call him, either. She simply didn't want him to think she was only interested in him because of what he could do for her—the clothes, the jet, the luxury condo.

All of those things were nice but they weren't what made Daniel who he was.

He was gorgeous and rich, true. And maybe for a lot of people, that would've been enough. But he was also the only man who had ever stood up for her, with her. Every other man had cut her loose the moment the shit hit the fan. Her father had turned on her and Doyle had abandoned her. But Daniel?

He ran toward the danger. He told her she was worth defending.

More than that, he made her feel beautiful and whole and valuable—things she had been taught she didn't deserve.

Then the boxes arrived—four boxes of designer clothes and makeup, toys and outfits for Marie. There was no note—of course there wasn't. But they were from him.

She sat in her bedroom, staring at it all and trying not to cry. The cardigan she'd worn the afternoon he'd taken her to bed was in there—she lifted it out and it smelled like him.

This was fine. Everything was okay. All these things were just…souvenirs from the most unusual, wonderful vacation she'd ever had. Yes, that was it. And she was only sad because the vacation was over. Not because she didn't know if Daniel had sent her these boxes to purge any trace of her from his apartment—and his life—or if he'd wanted to make sure she had something to remember him by.

Because she certainly wasn't ever going to forget him.

It was Sunday—two and a half weeks since Christine had returned to Denver a changed woman. Marie was having a fussy morning after a night of broken sleep but Christine was going to church, darn it. Because if she sat home with Marie, she would start to wallow in unproductive self-pity and who had time for that? Not her. Besides, Marie was already wallowing enough for both of them.

Marie cried all the way to the church and Christine felt like crying, too. She just needed to get her bearings again, she decided. Work had been blissfully quiet and political consultants had left her alone. But it was perfectly reasonable to say that the events of the previous month had left her shaken. She and Marie just had to get back to normal, that was all.

Which was all well and good—but try telling a fourteen-month-old that.

By the time they made it to the Red Rock church, Marie had almost cried herself out. Christine carried her inside, already mentally apologizing to the day care ladies and hoping that Marie would keep it together long enough that Christine could find some comfort in the service.

"I want my Daniel," Marie whimpered pitifully, although it came out sounding like *"Wan anal."*

"I know, sweetie. But you'll have fun today," Christine promised in a voice that was obnoxiously perky even to her own ears.

Normally, Christine could lose herself in the service. She enjoyed the chance to reconnect with her faith and the music wasn't bad either. But today, all she could think about was how she would cushion her little girl's disappointment that "her Daniel" wasn't here and then, when Marie finally went to bed, how Christine would deal with her own disappointment that Daniel wasn't going to call.

No. Better not think of it.

After the service, she went down to get Marie from the day care. Marie fussed some more as they followed the crowd out of the building. Then, suddenly, she squirmed in Christine's arms and squealed in what sounded like… excitement?

"Hey!" Christine said, struggling to hold on to her daughter. But Marie somehow wiggled out of her coat and slid to the floor with an unceremonious *plop*. Then she was off, walking on wobbly legs through the crowded lobby.

"Marie!" Christine cried, struggling to get through the crowd before her daughter got trampled. She lost sight of

Marie for just a second and then, when the crowd parted, Marie wasn't there.

Panic dumped into Christine's bloodstream as she frantically looked around—who had her daughter? Marie wasn't fast enough to just *disappear*.

Then she came to a screeching halt because someone did have Marie. Someone tall and dark, someone who made cable-knit sweaters look surprisingly glamorous.

Oh, God—*Daniel*.

She'd never been so glad to see anyone in her entire life. "You're here," she said in shock.

"I am," he agreed, giving Marie a hug. The little girl threw her arms round his neck, screaming with delight.

Christine's heart melted at the sight of them together. "What are you doing here?"

He smiled hesitantly. "Is there someplace we can go to talk?" he asked, his eyes intent as the rest of the church slowly emptied out around them. "Someplace inconspicuous?"

He had come for her. Not under the cover of darkness, not just for sex. At least, she hoped. That kernel of hope took root in her chest and began to blossom into something far greater. "Come with me."

They went back down to the place where it all started—the old living room set outside the day care. Back to the place where it had first occurred to her that maybe he'd come to help after all.

As they walked down the stairs, though, a horrible thought occurred to her. What if he wasn't here for her? What if something else had happened and she was back in the news again? What if he were only here because of his misguided sense of protecting her?

What if he didn't feel about her the way she felt about him?

Paralyzed by this thought, she sat awkwardly in the

exact spot she had sat so many weeks ago. "Has something gone wrong?"

He cuddled Marie, then put her down. She went off to get a book, chattering happily about "her Daniel." "No," he said, standing in front of her. "Nothing's happened."

"Okay…" How she was supposed to take that?

"I mean—something did happen." He looked anxious again, which didn't help her nerves. "But it doesn't concern your father's political campaign or your reputation on the internet."

"That's…good?"

She hadn't seen him this unsettled since he'd told her about his grandfather and his business in Korea.

"I miss you," he blurted out. "I didn't expect to. I've never missed anyone before. But I miss you."

He said it like it'd come as a complete and total surprise to him. And frankly, she was a little surprised herself. "I miss you, too," she said, pushing herself out of the chair. She didn't want him looking down on her. She wanted to meet him as an equal. "But you made it clear that there wasn't anything else to our relationship. You've atoned for your mistakes in the past and I've forgiven you. Everything else was just an…unexpected bonus."

Somehow, he managed to look ashamed by this statement. "That's how it was supposed to be. But that's not how it worked out. I…" He took a deep breath and took her hands in his. "I thought I could go back to the way I was before. I thought I would be fine without you—without anyone. Watching and waiting—always *above* everyone else. Never *with* them. Does that even make sense?"

She thought back to his apartment, looking down on the world but never touching it—or anyone in it. "I think so. You never had anyone come over to your place before and then suddenly Marie and I were there and your brother and Natalie…"

He stepped in closer, close enough that she could feel the warmth of his chest through her layers. "I thought I could go back to watching you from a distance—monitoring you online, having Porter shadow you. But I missed you, Christine." He sounded continually surprised by this realization.

She smiled in spite of herself. "You said that already."

He took a deep breath and for some reason, she thought of a man standing on a bridge, ready to jump. "I thought about what you said to me that one night on the couch. I don't have to prove anything to my grandfather. I never did. But I thought that, by keeping my distance from my family and never getting involved with anyone, hiding behind my political work—somehow I was showing him how wrong he was about me. But I was still letting him make my choices for me. I never wanted to be alone. I just didn't want to marry the person he said I had to and I didn't want to marry someone who saw me as a family name first and my wealth second. I didn't want to be used like he wanted to use me."

At that moment, Marie bumped into his leg, a book in her hand. He leaned down and picked her up, but his gaze never left Christine.

"That's all I wanted, too," she told him. "I didn't want to be a cog in my father's political machine and I didn't want Marie to be one, either. I just wanted to be accepted as I am. I just wanted to be good enough. And then I wanted to be good enough for you." She hung her head. Even now—with him right here—she couldn't believe he thought she was on the same level as he was.

"But you are," he said. Then, turning his attention to Marie, he said, "I need to talk to Mommy. Can you sit on the couch and read quietly?"

And, miracle of miracles, Marie nodded. He sat her down and she curled up on the couch, intent on her story.

Daniel turned his attention back to her. "You changed me, Christine. You're the one thing I never saw coming. I couldn't plan for you and the thought of not having a plan scares me—but not as much as the thought of not having you in my life. I always believed that I didn't fit anywhere but when I'm with you, I feel like I belong. I want to belong to you, Christine. Not to my grandfather and not to someone like Brian White. I don't want to live my life on the fringe of humanity anymore. I want to play with Marie in the park and have breakfast with you in the morning and I want to know that, at the end of the day—no matter what state or country I'm in—that I'm coming home to you."

One thing was clear. Daniel Lee had ruined her for anyone else. Even now—he was saying all the things she needed to hear. But there was one thing that still worried her. "I don't want this to be all because of some misguided notion that you're protecting me or that you owe it to me. And I don't want you to think that I only care for you because you're this elusive billionaire."

His eyes got wide. "Do you? Care for me, that is?"

"Oh, Daniel," she whispered, stretching up on her tiptoes and brushing her lips over his. "You ruined me for any other man. You stood by me when I needed you and you make things better. You're kind to my daughter and you make me feel like the woman I was always meant to be. How could I *not* love you?"

His arms went around her waist, holding her tight. "Do you really love me? Because I love you, too. I know it's quick, but I kept waiting for things to go back to normal again after you left and they didn't."

"Me, too," she said, her eyes stinging. "And they didn't."

"We can't go back," he said with a grin that got more confident by the second. "You changed me, Christine— for the better. You forgave me and I...this sounds crazy, but I think I've forgiven myself. This isn't about rescuing you. This is about having you by my side because I can't stand back and watch you walk away."

Her heart was pounding. Was this really happening? "So what are you saying? Do you want to try dating? Or..."

"I want more than that. I don't want you one night a week or lunch every other Thursday. I want you all the time. I want you *always*. Would you marry me, Christine?" From behind them, Marie trilled. Daniel smiled and, turning to the little girl, said, "Would you be my family, too, Marie?"

Christine gaped at him. *"What?"*

His grin sharpened and there it was, that intense feeling of being in Daniel Lee's sights. "Marry me, Christine. You're the strongest woman I know, but let me be the soft place you can land. Let me show you every day that you're the only woman for me. I want to adopt Marie. I want to be the man I think I was always meant to be. That's who I am when I'm with you."

Christine didn't even bother to blink back the tears. As far as proposals went, it was perfect—just like Daniel. Oh, she was under no illusions that he *was* perfect. But he was perfect for her and that was the most important thing of all. "Yes," she said, laughing and crying at the same time. "But promise me that you won't listen to *his* voice inside your head more."

With a huge grin on his face, he picked her up and spun her in a small circle. "The only voice I want inside my head is yours," he told her, lowering her back down to the ground and touching his forehead to hers. "Your voice is the only one that matters to me."

And then he kissed her and no one said anything at all for quite some time.

* * * * *

If you liked this story of a billionaire tamed by the love of the right woman—and her baby— pick up these other novels from Sarah M. Anderson.

*A MAN OF DISTINCTION
EXPECTING A BOLTON BABY
THE NANNY PLAN
HIS SON, HER SECRET
HIS FOREVER FAMILY*

Available now from Mills & Boon!

***

And don't miss the next
BILLIONAIRES AND BABIES *story,*

*TEN-DAY BABY TAKEOVER
by Karen Booth.*

Available April 2017!

***

If you're on Twitter, tell us what you think of Mills & Boon! #mills&boon

"You can't play these kinds of games. You don't know the rules."

"I don't know what your problem is. You don't want me, so what do you care if they do?"

"Hayley, honey, I don't *want* to want you, but that is not the same thing as not wanting you. It is not even close. What I want is something you can't handle."

She tilted her head to the side, her hair falling over her shoulder like a glossy curtain. "Maybe I want to be shocked. Maybe I want something I'm not quite ready for."

"No," he said, his tone emphatic now. "You're on a big kick to have experiences. But there are much nicer men you can have experiences with."

She bared her teeth. "I was trying! You just scared them off."

"You're not having experiences with those clowns. They wouldn't know how to handle a woman if she came with an instruction manual. And let me tell you, women do not come with an instruction manual. You just have to know what to do."

"And you know what to do?"

"Damn straight," he returned.

"So," she said, tilting her chin up, looking stubborn. "Show me."

* * *

Seduce Me, Cowboy
is part of *New York Times* bestselling
author Maisey Yates's Copper Ridge series.

SEDUCE ME, COWBOY

BY
MAISEY YATES

First Published in Great Britain 2017
By Mills & Boon, an imprint of HarperCollins*Publishers*
1 London Bridge Street, London, SE1 9GF

© 2017 Maisey Yates

ISBN: 978-0-263-92811-2

51-0317

Printed and bound in Spain
by CPI, Barcelona

Maisey Yates is a *New York Times* bestselling author of more than thirty romance novels. She has a coffee habit she has no interest in kicking and a slight Pinterest addiction. She lives with her husband and children in the Pacific Northwest. When Maisey isn't writing, she can be found singing in the grocery store, shopping for shoes online and probably not doing dishes. Check out her website, www.maiseyyates.com.

To the whole Harlequin team.
This is the best job ever.
Thank you for letting me do it.

One

Hayley Thompson was a good girl. In all the ways that phrase applied. The kind of girl every mother wished her son would bring home for Sunday dinner.

Of course, the mothers of Copper Ridge were much more enthusiastic about Hayley than their sons were, but that had never been a problem. She had never really tried dating, anyway. Dates were the least of her problems.

She was more worried about the constant feeling that she was under a microscope. That she was a trained seal, sitting behind the desk in the church office exactly as one might expect from a small-town pastor's daughter—who also happened to be the church secretary.

And what did she have to show for being so good? Absolutely nothing.

Meanwhile, her older brother had gone out into the

world and done whatever he wanted. He'd broken every rule. Run away from home. Gotten married, gotten divorced. Come back home and opened a bar in the same town where his father preached sermons. All while Hayley had stayed and behaved herself. Done everything that was expected of her.

Ace was the prodigal son. He hadn't just received forgiveness for his transgressions. He'd been rewarded. He had so many things well-behaved Hayley wanted and didn't have.

He'd found love again in his wife, Sierra. They had children. The doting attention of Hayley's parents—a side effect of being the first to supply grandchildren, she felt—while Hayley had...

Well, nothing.

Nothing but a future as a very well-behaved spinster.

That was why she was here now. Clutching a newspaper in her hand until it was wrinkled tight. She hadn't even known people still put ads in the paper for job listings, but while she'd been sitting in The Grind yesterday on Copper Ridge's main street, watching people go by and feeling a strange sense of being untethered, she'd grabbed the local paper.

That had led her to the job listings. And seeing as she was unemployed for the first time since she was sixteen years old, she'd read them.

Every single one of them had been submitted by people she knew. Businesses she'd grown up patronizing, or businesses owned by people she knew from her dad's congregation. And if she got a job somewhere like that, she might as well have stayed on at the church.

Except for one listing. Assistant to Jonathan Bear, owner of Gray Bear Construction. The job was for him personally, but would also entail clerical work for his company and some work around his home.

She didn't know anything about the company. She'd never had a house built, after all. Neither had her mother and father. And she'd never heard his name before, and was reasonably sure she'd never seen him at church.

She wanted that distance.

Familiar, nagging guilt gnawed at the edges of her heart. Her parents were good people. They loved her very much. And she loved them. But she felt like a beloved goldfish. With people watching her every move and tapping on the glass. Plus, the bowl was restricting, when she was well aware there was an entire ocean out there.

Step one in her plan for independence had been to acquire her own apartment. Cassie Caldwell, owner of The Grind, and her husband, Jake, had moved out of the space above the coffee shop a while ago. Happily, it had been vacant and ready to rent, and Hayley had taken advantage of that. So, with the money she'd saved up, she'd moved into that place. And then, after hoarding a few months' worth of rent, she had finally worked up the courage to quit.

Her father had been… She wouldn't go so far as to say he'd been disappointed. John Thompson never had a harsh word for anyone. He was all kind eyes and deep conviction. The type of goodness Hayley could only marvel at, that made her feel as though she could never quite measure up.

But she could tell her father had been confused. And she hadn't been able to explain herself, not fully. Because she didn't want either of her parents to know that ultimately, this little journey of independence would lead straight out of Copper Ridge.

She had to get out of the fishbowl. She needed people to stop tapping on her glass.

Virtue wasn't its own reward. For years she'd believed it would be. But then…suddenly, watching Ace at the dinner table at her parents' house, with his family, she'd realized the strange knot in her stomach wasn't anger over his abandonment, over the way he'd embarrassed their parents with his behavior.

It was envy.

Envy of all he had, of his freedom. Well, this was her chance to have some of that for herself, and she couldn't do it with everyone watching.

She took a deep breath and regarded the house in front of her. If she didn't know it was the home and office of the owner of Gray Bear Construction, she would be tempted to assume it was some kind of resort.

The expansive front porch was made entirely out of logs, stained with a glossy, honey-colored sheen that caught the light and made the place look like it was glowing. The green metal roof was designed to withstand harsh weather—which down in town by the beach wasn't much of an issue. But a few miles inland, here in the mountains, she could imagine there was snow in winter.

She wondered if she would need chains for her car. But she supposed she'd cross that bridge when she came to it. It was early spring, and she didn't even have the job yet.

Getting the job, and keeping it through winter, was only a pipe dream at this point.

She took a deep breath and started up the path, the bark-laden ground soft beneath her feet. She inhaled deeply, the sharp scent of pine filling her lungs. It was cool beneath the trees, and she wrapped her arms around herself as she walked up the steps and made her way to the front door.

She knocked before she had a chance to rethink her actions, and then she waited.

She was just about to knock again when she heard footsteps. She quickly put her hand down at her side. Then lifted it again, brushing her hair out of her face. Then she clasped her hands in front of her, then put them back at her sides again. Then she decided to hold them in front of her again.

She had just settled on that position when the door jerked open.

She had rehearsed her opening remarks. Had practiced making a natural smile in the mirror—which was easy after so many years manning the front desk of a church—but all that disappeared completely when she looked at the man standing in front of her.

He was… Well, he was nothing like she'd expected, which left her grappling for what exactly she had been expecting. Somebody older. Certainly not somebody who towered over her like a redwood.

Jonathan Bear wasn't someone you could anticipate.

His dark, glittering eyes assessed her; his mouth pressed into a thin line. His black hair was tied back, but it was impossible for her to tell just how long it was from where she stood.

"Who are you?" he asked, his tone uncompromising.

"I'm here to interview for the assistant position. Were you expecting someone else?" Her stomach twisted with anxiety. He wasn't what she had expected, and now she was wondering if she was what *he* had expected. Maybe he wanted somebody older, with more qualifications.

Or somebody more… Well, sexy secretary than former church secretary.

Though, she looked very nice in this twin set and pencil skirt, if she said so herself.

"No," he said, moving away from the door. "Come in."

"Oh," she said, scampering to follow his direction.

"The office is upstairs," he said, taking great strides through the entryway and heading toward a massive curved staircase.

She found herself taking very quick steps to try and keep up with him. And it was difficult to do that when she was distracted by the beauty of the house. She was trying to take in all the details as she trailed behind him up the stairs, her low heels clicking on the hardwood.

"I'm Hayley Thompson," she said, "which I know the résumé said, but you didn't know who I was… So…"

"We're the only two people here," he said, looking back at her, lifting one dark brow. "So knowing your name isn't really that important, is it?"

She couldn't tell if he was joking. She laughed nervously, and it got her no response at all. So then she was concerned she had miscalculated.

They reached the top of the stairs, and she followed him down a long hallway, the sound of her steps dampened now by a long carpet runner the colors of the nature that surrounded them. Brown, forest green and a red that reminded her of cranberries.

The house smelled new. Which was maybe a strange observation to make, but the scent of wood lingered in the air, and something that reminded her of paint.

"How long have you lived here?" she asked, more comfortable with polite conversation than contending with silence.

"Just moved in last month," he said. "One of our designs. You might have guessed, this is what Gray Bear does. Custom homes. That's our specialty. And since my construction company merged with Grayson Design, we're doing design as well as construction."

"How many people can buy places like this?" she asked, turning in a circle while she walked, daunted by the amount of house they had left behind them, and the amount that was still before them.

"You would be surprised. For a lot of our clients these are only vacation homes. Escapes to the coast and to the mountains. Mostly, we work on the Oregon coast, but we make exceptions for some of the higher-paying clientele."

"That's...kind of amazing. I mean, something of this scale right here in Copper Ridge. Or I guess, technically, we're outside the city limits."

"Still the same zip code," he said, lifting a shoulder.

He took hold of two sliding double doors fashioned to look like barn doors and slid them open, revealing a huge office space with floor-to-ceiling windows and a view that made her jaw drop.

The sheer immensity of the mountains spread before them was incredible on its own. But beyond that, she could make out the faint gray of the ocean, white-capped waves and jagged rocks rising out of the surf.

"The best of everything," he said. "Sky, mountains, ocean. That kind of sums up the company. Now that you know about us, you can tell me why I should hire you."

"I want the job," she said, her tone hesitant. As soon as she said the words, she realized how ridiculous they were. Everybody who interviewed for this position would want the job. "I was working as a secretary for my father's…business," she said, feeling guilty about fudging a little bit on her résumé. But she hadn't really wanted to say she was working at her father's church, because… Well, she just wanted to come in at a slightly more neutral position.

"You were working for your family?"

"Yes," she said.

He crossed his arms, and she felt slightly intimidated. He was the largest man she'd ever seen. At least, he felt large. Something about all the height and muscles and presence combined.

"We're going to have to get one thing straight right now, Hayley. I'm not your daddy. So if you're used to a kind and gentle working environment where you get a lot of chances because firing you would make it awkward around the holidays, this might take some adjustment for you. I'm damned hard to please. And I'm not a very nice boss. There's a lot of work to do around here. I hate paperwork, and I don't want to have to do any form twice. If you make mistakes and I have to sit at that desk longer as a result, you're fired. If I've hired you to make things easier between myself and my clients, and something you do makes it harder, you're fired. If you pass on a call to me that I shouldn't have to take, you're fired."

She nodded, wishing she had a notepad, not because she was ever going to forget what he'd said, but so she could underscore the fact that she was paying attention. "Anything else?"

"Yeah," he said, a slight smile curving his lips. "You're also fired if you fuck up my coffee."

This was a mistake. Jonathan Bear was absolutely certain of it. But he had earned millions making mistakes, so what was one more? Nobody else had responded to his ad.

Except for this pale, strange little creature who looked barely twenty and wore the outfit of an eighty-year-old woman.

She was... Well, she wasn't the kind of formidable woman who could stand up to the rigors of working with him.

His sister, Rebecca, would say—with absolutely no tact at all—that he sucked as a boss. And maybe she was right, but he didn't really care. He was busy, and right now he hated most of what he was busy with.

There was irony in that, he knew. He had worked hard all his life. While a lot of his friends had sought solace and oblivion in drugs and alcohol, Jonathan had figured it was best to sweat the poison right out.

He'd gotten a job on a construction site when he was fifteen, and learned his trade. He'd gotten to where he was faster, better than most of the men around him. By the time he was twenty, he had been doing serious custom work on the more upscale custom homes he'd built with West Construction.

But he wanted more. There was a cap on what he could make with that company, and he didn't like a ceiling. He wanted open skies and the freedom to go as high, as fast as he wanted. So he could amass so much it could never be taken from him.

So he'd risked striking out on his own. No one had believed a kid from the wrong side of the tracks could compete with West. But Jonathan had courted business across city and county lines. And created a reputation beyond Copper Ridge so that when people came look-

ing to build retirement homes or vacation properties,
his was the name they knew.

He had built everything he had, brick by brick. In a
strictly literal sense in some cases.

And every brick built a stronger wall against all the
things he had left behind. Poverty, uncertainty, the lack
of respect paid to a man in his circumstances.

Then six months ago, Joshua Grayson had approached
him. Originally from Copper Ridge, the man had been
looking for a foothold back in town after years in Seattle.
Faith Grayson, Joshua's sister was quickly becoming the
most sought after architect in the Pacific Northwest. But
the siblings had decided it was time to bring the business back home in order to be closer to their parents.

And so Joshua asked Jonathan if he would consider
bringing design in-house, making Bear Construction
into Gray Bear.

This gave Jonathan reach into urban areas, into Seattle. Had him managing remote crews and dealing
with many projects at one time. And it had pushed him
straight out of the building game in many ways. He had
turned into a desk drone. And while his bank account
had grown astronomically, he was quite a ways from
the life he thought he'd live after reaching this point.

Except the house. The house was finally finished.
Finally, he was living in one of the places he'd built.

Finally, Jonathan Bear, that poor Indian kid who
wasn't worth anything to anyone, bastard son of the
biggest bastard in town, had his house on the side of
the mountain and more money than he would ever be
able to spend.

And he was bored out of his mind.

Boredom, it turned out, worked him into a hell of

a temper. He had a feeling Hayley Thompson wasn't strong enough to stand up to that. But he expected to go through a few assistants before he found one who could handle it. She might as well be number one.

"You've got the job," he said. "You can start tomorrow."

Her eyes widened, and he noticed they were a strange shade of blue. Gray in some lights, shot through with a dark, velvet navy that reminded him of the ocean before a storm. It made him wonder if there was some hidden strength there.

They would both find out.

"I got the job? Just like that?"

"Getting the job was always going to be the easy part. It's keeping the job that might be tricky. My list of reasons to hire you are short—you showed up. The list of reasons I have for why I might fire you is much longer."

"You're not very reassuring," she said, her lips tilting down in a slight frown.

He laughed. "If you want to go back and work for your daddy, do that. I'm not going to call you. But maybe you'll appreciate my ways later. Other jobs will seem easy after this one."

She just looked at him, her jaw firmly set, her petite body rigid with determination. "What time do you want me here?"

"Seven o'clock. Don't be late. Or else…"

"You'll fire me. I've got the theme."

"Excellent. Hayley Thompson, you've got yourself a job."

Two

Hayley scrubbed her face as she walked into The Grind through the private entrance from her upstairs apartment. It was early. But she wanted to make sure she wasn't late to work.

On account of all the firing talk.

"Good morning," Cassie said from behind the counter, smiling cheerfully. Hayley wondered if Cassie was really thrilled to be at work this early in the morning. Hayley knew all about presenting a cheerful face to anyone who might walk in the door.

You couldn't have a bad day when you worked at the church.

"I need coffee," Hayley said, not bothering to force a grin. She wasn't at work yet. She paused. "Do you know Jonathan Bear?"

Cassie gave her a questioning look. "Yes, I'm friends

with his sister, Rebecca. She owns the store across the street."

"Right," Hayley said, frowning. "I don't think I've ever met her. But I've seen her around town."

Hayley was a few years younger than Cassie, and probably a bit younger than Rebecca, as well, which meant they had never been in classes together at school, and had never shared groups of friends. Not that Hayley had much in the way of friends. People tended to fear the pastor's daughter would put a damper on things.

No one had tested the theory.

"So yes, I know Jonathan in passing. He's... Well, he's not very friendly." Cassie laughed. "Why?"

"He just hired me."

Cassie's expression contorted into one of horror and Hayley saw her start to backpedal. "He's probably fine. It's just that he's very protective of Rebecca because he raised her, you know, and all that. And she had her accident, and had to have a lot of medical procedures done... So my perception of him is based entirely on that. I'm sure he's a great boss."

"No," Hayley said, "you were right the first time. He's a grumpy cuss. Do you have any idea what kind of coffee he drinks?"

Cassie frowned, a small notch appearing between her brows. "He doesn't come in that often. But when he does I think he gets a dark roast, large, black, no sugar, with a double shot of espresso."

"How do you remember that?"

"It's my job. And there are a lot of people I know by drink and not by name."

"Well, I will take one of those for him. And hope that it's still hot by the time I get up the mountain."

"Okay. And a coffee for you with room for cream?"

"Yes," Hayley said. "I don't consider my morning caffeination ritual a punishment like some people seem to."

"Hey," Cassie said, "some people just like their coffee unadulterated. But I am not one of them. I feel you."

Hayley paid for her order and made her way to the back of the store, looking around at the warm, quaint surroundings. Locals had filed in and were filling up the tables, reading their papers, opening laptops and dropping off bags and coats to secure the coveted positions in the tiny coffee shop.

Then a line began to form, and Hayley was grateful she had come as early as she had.

A moment later, her order was ready. Popping the lid off her cup at the cream and sugar station, she gave herself a generous helping of both. She walked back out the way she had come in, going to her car, which was parked behind the building in her reserved space.

She got inside, wishing she'd warmed up the vehicle before placing her order. It wasn't too cold this morning, but she could see her breath in the damp air. She positioned both cups of coffee in the cup holders of her old Civic, and then headed to the main road, which was void of traffic—and would remain that way for the entire day.

She liked the pace of Copper Ridge, she really did. Liked the fact that she knew so many people, that people waved and smiled when she walked by. Liked that there were no traffic lights, and that you rarely had to wait for more than one car at a four-way stop.

She loved the mountains, and she loved the ocean.

But she knew there were things beyond this place, too. And she wanted to see them.

Needed to see them.

She thought about all those places as she drove along the winding road to Jonathan Bear's house. She had the vague thought that if she went to London or Paris, if she looked at the Eiffel Tower or Big Ben, structures so old and lasting—structures that had been there for centuries—maybe she would learn something about herself.

Maybe she would find what she couldn't identify here. Maybe she would find the cure for the elusive ache in her chest when she saw Ace with Sierra and their kids.

Would find the freedom to be herself—whoever that might be. To flirt and date, and maybe drink a beer. To escape the confines that so rigidly held her.

Even driving out of town this morning, instead of to the church, was strange. Usually, she felt as though she were moving through the grooves of a well-worn track. There were certain places she went in town—her parents' home, the church, the grocery store, The Grind, her brother's brewery and restaurant, but never his bar—and she rarely deviated from that routine.

She supposed this drive would become routine soon enough.

She pulled up to the front of the house, experiencing a sharp sense of déjà vu as she walked up to the front porch to knock again. Except this time her stomach twisted with an even greater sense of trepidation. Not because Jonathan Bear was an unknown, but because she knew a little bit about him now. And what she knew terrified her.

The door jerked open before she could pound against it. "Just come in next time," he said.

"Oh."

"During business hours. I was expecting you."

"Expecting me to be late?" she asked, holding out his cup of coffee.

He arched a dark brow. "Maybe." He tilted his head to the side. "What's that?"

"Probably coffee." She didn't know why she was being anything other than straightforward and sweet. He'd made it very clear that he had exacting standards. Likely, he wanted his assistant to fulfill his every whim before it even occurred to him, and to do so with a smile. Likely, he didn't want his assistant to sass him, even lightly.

Except, something niggled at her, telling her he wouldn't respect her at all if she acted like a doormat. She was good at reading people. It was a happy side effect of being quiet. Of having few friends, of being an observer. Of spending years behind the church desk, not sure who might walk through the door seeking help. That experience had taught Hayley not only kindness, but also discernment.

And that was why she chose to follow her instincts with Jonathan.

"It's probably coffee?" he asked, taking the cup from her, anyway.

"Yes," she returned. "Probably."

He turned away from her, heading toward the stairs, but she noticed that he took the lid off the cup and examined the contents. She smiled as she followed him up the stairs to the office.

The doors were already open, the computer that faced the windows fired up. There were papers everywhere. And pens sat across nearly every surface.

"Why so many pens?" she asked.

"If I have to stop and look for one I waste an awful lot of time cussing."

"Fair enough."

"I have to go outside and take care of the horses, but I want you to go through that stack of invoices and enter all the information into the spreadsheet on the computer. Can you do that?"

"Spreadsheets are my specialty. You have horses?"

He nodded. "This is kind of a ranch."

"Oh," she said. "I didn't realize."

"No reason you should." Then he turned, grabbing a black cowboy hat off a hook and putting it firmly on his head. "I'll be back in a couple of hours. And I'm going to want more coffee. The machine is downstairs in the kitchen. Should be pretty easy. Probably."

Then he brushed his fingertips against the brim of his hat, nodding slightly before walking out, leaving her alone.

When he left, something in her chest loosened, eased. She hadn't realized just how tense she'd felt in his presence.

She took a deep breath, sitting down at the desk in front of the computer, eyeing the healthy stack of papers to her left. Then she looked over the monitor to the view below. This wouldn't be so bad. He wasn't here looking over her shoulder, barking orders. And really, in terms of work space, this office could hardly be beat.

Maybe this job wouldn't be so bad, after all.

By the time Jonathan made a run to town after finishing up with the horses, it was past lunchtime. So he brought food from the Crab Shanty and hoped his new assistant didn't have a horrible allergy to seafood.

He probably should have checked. He wasn't really used to considering other people. And he couldn't say he was looking forward to getting used to it. But he would rather she didn't die. At least, not while at work.

He held tightly to the white bag of food as he made his way to the office. Her back was to the door, her head bent low over a stack of papers, one hand poised on the mouse.

He set the bag down loudly on the table by the doorway, then deposited his keys there, too. He hung his hat on the hook. "Hungry?"

Her head popped up, her eyes wide. "Oh, I didn't hear you come in. You scared me. You should have announced yourself or something."

"I just did. I said, 'hungry?' I mean, I could have said I'm here, but how is that any different?"

She shook her head. "I don't have an answer to that."

"Great. I have fish."

"What kind?"

"Fried kind."

"I approve."

He sighed in mock relief. "Good. Because if you didn't, I don't know how I would live with myself. I would have had to eat both of these." He opened the bag, taking out two cartons and two cans of Coke.

He sat in the chair in front of the table he used for drawing plans, then held her portion toward her.

She made a funny face, then accepted the offered lunch. "Is one of the Cokes for me, too?"

"Sure," he said, sliding a can at her.

She blinked, then took the can.

"What?"

She shook her head. "Nothing."

"You expected me to hand everything to you, didn't you?"

She shook her head. "No. Well, maybe. But, I'm sorry. I don't work with my father anymore, as you have mentioned more than once."

"No," he said, "you don't. And this isn't a church. Though—" he took a french fry out of the box and bit it "—this is pretty close to a religious experience." He picked up one of the thoughtfully included napkins and wiped his fingers before popping the top on the Coke can.

"How did you know I worked at the church?" she asked.

"I pay attention. And I definitely looked at the address you included on your form. Also, I know your brother. Or rather, I know of him. My sister is engaged to his brother-in-law. I might not be chummy with him, but I know his dad is the pastor. And that he has a younger sister."

She looked crestfallen. "I didn't realize you knew my brother."

"Is that a problem?"

"I was trying to get a job based on my own merit. Not on family connections. And frankly, I can't find anyone who is not connected to my family in some way in this town. My father knows the saints, my brother knows the sinners."

"Are you calling me a sinner?"

She picked gingerly at a piece of fish. "All have sinned and so forth."

"That isn't what you meant."

She suddenly became very interested in her coleslaw, prodding it with her plastic fork.

"How is it you know I'm a sinner?" he asked, not intending to let her off the hook, because this was just so fun. Hell, he'd gone and hired himself a church secretary, so might as well play with her a little bit.

"I didn't mean that," she insisted, her cheeks turning pink. He couldn't remember the last time he'd seen a woman blush.

"Well, if it helps at all, I don't know your brother well. I just buy alcohol from him on the weekends. But you're right. I am a sinner, Hayley."

She looked up at him then. The shock reflected in those stormy eyes touched him down deep. Made his stomach feel tight, made his blood feel hot. All right, he needed to get a handle on himself. Because that was not the kind of fun he was going to have with the church secretary he had hired. No way.

Jonathan Bear was a ruthless bastard; that fact could not be disputed. He had learned to look out for himself at an early age, because no one else would. Not his father. Certainly not his mother, who had taken off when he was a teenager, leaving him with a younger sister to raise. And most definitely not anyone in town.

But, even he had a conscience.

In theory, anyway.

"Good to know. I mean, since we're getting to know each other, I guess."

They ate in relative silence after that. Jonathan took that opportunity to check messages on his phone. A damn smartphone. This was what he had come to. Used to be that if he wanted to spend time alone he could unplug and go out on his horse easily enough. Now, he could still do that, but his business partners—dammit all, he had business partners—knew that he should be accessible and was opting not to be.

"Why did you leave the church?" he asked after a long stretch of silence.

"I didn't. I mean, not as a member. But, I couldn't work there anymore. You know, I woke up one morning and looked in the mirror and imagined doing that exact same thing in forty years. Sitting behind that desk, in the same chair, talking to the same people, having the same conversations… I just didn't think I could do it. I thought…well, for a long time I thought if I sat in that chair life would come to me." She took a deep breath. "But it won't. I have to go get it."

What she was talking about… That kind of stability. It was completely foreign to him. Jonathan could scarcely remember a time in his life when things had stayed the same from year to year. He would say one thing for poverty, it was dynamic. It could be a grind, sure, but it kept you on your toes. He'd constantly looked for new ways to support himself and Rebecca. To prove to child services that he was a fit guardian. To keep their dwelling up to par, to make sure they could always afford it. To keep them both fed and clothed— or at least her, if not him.

He had always craved what Hayley was talking about. A place secure enough to rest for a while. But not having it was why he was here now. In this house, with all this money. Which was the only real damned security in the world. Making sure you were in control of everything around you.

Even if it did mean owning a fucking smartphone.

"So, your big move was to be my assistant?"

She frowned. "No. This is my small move. You have to make small moves before you can make a big one."

That he agreed with, more or less. His whole life had been a series of small moves with no pausing in between. One step at a time as he climbed up to the top. "I'm not sure it's the best thing to let your employer know you think he's a small step," he said, just because he wanted to see her cheeks turn pink again. He was gratified when they did.

"Sorry. This is a giant step for me. I intend to stay here forever in my elevated position as your assistant."

He set his lunch down, leaning back and holding up his hands. "Slow down, baby. I'm not looking for a commitment."

At that, her cheeks turned bright red. She took another bite of coleslaw, leaving a smear of mayonnaise on the corner of her mouth. Without thinking, he leaned in and brushed his thumb across the smudge, and along the edge of her lower lip.

He didn't realize it was a mistake until the slug of heat hit him low and fast in the gut.

He hadn't realized it would be a mistake because she was such a mousy little thing, a church secretary. Because his taste didn't run to that kind of thing. At least, that's what he would have said.

But while his brain might have a conscience, he discovered in that moment that his body certainly did not.

Three

It was like striking a match, his thumb sweeping across her skin. It left a trail of fire where he touched, and made her feel hot in places he hadn't. She was... Well, she was immobilized.

Like a deer caught in the headlights, seeing exactly what was barreling down on her, and unable to move.

Except, of course, Jonathan wasn't barreling down on her. He wasn't moving at all.

He was just looking at her, his dark eyes glittering, his expression like granite. She followed his lead, unsure of what to do. Of how she should react.

And then, suddenly, everything clicked into place. Exactly what she was feeling, exactly what she was doing...and exactly how much of an idiot she was.

She took a deep breath, gasping as though she'd been submerged beneath water. She turned her chair sideways, facing the computer again. "Well," she said, "thank you for lunch."

Fiddlesticks. And darn it. And fudging graham crackers.

She had just openly stared at her boss, probably looking like a guppy gasping on dry land because he had wiped mayonnaise off her lip. Which was—as things went—probably one of the more platonic touches a man and a woman could share.

The problem was, she couldn't remember ever being touched—even platonically—by a man who wasn't family. So she had been completely unprepared for the reaction it created inside her. Which she had no doubt he'd noticed.

Attraction. She had felt *attracted* to him.

Backtracking, she realized the tight feeling in her stomach that had appeared the first moment she'd seen him was probably attraction.

That was bad. Very bad.

But what she was really curious about, was why this attraction felt different from what she'd felt around other men she had liked. She'd felt fluttery feelings before. Most notably for Grant Daniels, the junior high youth pastor, a couple years ago. She had really liked him, and she was pretty sure he'd liked her, too, but he hadn't seemed willing to make a move.

She had conversations with him over coffee in the Fellowship Hall, where he had brought up his feelings on dating—he didn't—and how he was waiting until he was ready to get married before getting into any kind of relationship with a woman.

For a while, she'd been convinced he'd told her that

because he was close to being ready, and he might want to marry her.

Another instance of sitting, waiting and believing what she wanted would come to her through the sheer force of her good behavior.

Looking back, she realized it was kind of stupid that she had hoped he'd marry her. She didn't know him, not really. She had only ever seen him around church, and of course her feelings for him were based on that. Everybody was on their best behavior there. Including her.

Not that she actually behaved badly, which was kind of the problem. There was what she did, what she showed the world, and then there were the dark, secret things that lived inside her. Things she wanted but was afraid to pursue.

The fluttery feelings she had for Grant were like public Hayley. Smiley, shiny and giddy. Wholesome and hopeful.

The tension she felt in her stomach when she looked at Jonathan…that was all secret Hayley.

And it scared her that there was another person who seemed to have access to those feelings she examined only late at night in the darkness of her room.

She had finally gotten up the courage to buy a romance novel when she'd been at the grocery store a month or so ago. She had always been curious about those books, but since she'd lived with her parents, she had never been brave enough to buy one.

So, at the age of twenty-four, she had gotten her very first one. And it had been educational. Very, *very* educational. She had been a little afraid of it, to be honest.

Because those illicit feelings brought about late at

night by hazy images and the slide of sheets against her bare skin had suddenly become focused and specific after reading that book.

And if that book had been the fantasy, Jonathan was the reality. It made her want to turn tail and run. But she couldn't. Because if she did, then he would know what no one else knew about her.

She couldn't risk him knowing.

They were practically strangers. They had nothing in common. These feelings were ridiculous. At least Grant had been the kind of person she was suited to.

Which begged the question—why didn't he make her feel this off-kilter?

Her face felt like it was on fire, and she was sure Jonathan could easily read her reaction. That was the problem. It had taken her longer to understand what she was feeling than it had likely taken him. Because he wasn't sheltered like she was.

Sheltered even from her own desire.

The word made her shiver. Because it was one she had avoided thinking until now.

Desire.

Did she desire him? And if she did, what did that mean?

Her mouth went dry as several possibilities floated through her mind. Each more firmly rooted in fantasy than the last, since she had no practical experience with any of this.

And it was going to stay that way. At least for now.

Small steps. This job was her first small step. And it was a job, not a chance for her to get ridiculous over a man.

"Did you have anything else you wanted me to do?"

she asked, not turning to face him, keeping her gaze resolutely pinned to the computer screen.

He was silent for a moment, and for some reason, the silence felt thick. "Did you finish entering the invoices?"

"Yes."

"Good," he said. "Here." He handed her his phone. "If anyone calls, say I'm not available, but you're happy to take a message. And I want you to call the county office and ask about the permits listed in the other spreadsheet I have open. Just get a status update on that. Do you cook?"

She blinked. "What?"

"Do you cook? I hired you to be my assistant. Which includes things around the house. And I eat around the house."

"I cook," she said, reeling from the change of topic.

"Great. Have something ready for me, and if I'm not back before you knock off at five, just keep it warm."

Then he turned and walked out, leaving her feeling both relieved and utterly confused. All those positive thoughts from this morning seemed to be coming back to haunt her, mock her.

The work she could handle. It was the man that scared her.

The first week of working with Hayley had been pretty good, in spite of that hiccup on the first day.

The one where he had touched her skin and felt just how soft it was. Something he never should have done.

But she was a good assistant. And every evening when he came in from dealing with ranch work his dinner was ready. That had been kind of a dick move, asking her to cook, but in truth, he hadn't put a very detailed job description in the ad. And she wasn't an employee of Gray Bear. She was his personal employee, and that meant he could expand her responsibilities.

At least, that was what he told himself as he approached the front porch Friday evening, his stomach already growling in anticipation. When he came in for the evening after the outside work was done, she was usually gone and the food was warming in the oven.

It was like having a wife. With none of the drawbacks *and* none of the perks.

But considering he could get those perks from a woman who wasn't in his house more than forty hours a week, he would take this happily.

He stomped up the front steps, kicking his boots off before he went inside. He'd been walking through sludge in one of the far pastures and he didn't want to track in mud. His housekeeper didn't come until later in the week.

The corner of his mouth lifted as he processed that thought. He had a housekeeper. He didn't have to get on his hands and knees and scrub floors anymore. Which he had done. More times than he would care to recount. Most of the time the house he and Rebecca had shared while growing up had been messy.

It was small, and their belongings—basic though they were—created a lot of clutter. Plus, teenage boys weren't the best at keeping things deep cleaned. Especially not when they also had full-time jobs and were trying to finish high school. But when he knew child services would be by, he did his best.

He didn't now. He paid somebody else to do it. For a long time, adding those kinds of expenses had made both pride and anxiety burn in his gut. Adjusting to living at a new income level was not seamless. And since things had grown exponentially and so quickly, the adjustments had come even harder. Often in a million ways he couldn't anticipate. But he was working on it. Hiring a housekeeper. Hiring Hayley.

Pretty soon, he would give in and buy himself a new pair of boots.

He drew nearer to the kitchen, smelling something good. And then he heard footsteps, the clattering of dishes.

He braced his arms on either side of the doorway. Clearly, she hadn't heard him approach. She was bending down to pull something out of the oven, her sweet ass outlined to perfection by that prim little skirt.

There was absolutely nothing provocative about it. It fell down past her knees, and when she stood straight it didn't display any curves whatsoever.

For a moment, he just admired his own commitment to being a dick. She could not be dressed more appropriately, and still his eyes were glued to her butt. And damn, his body liked what he saw.

"You're still here," he said, pushing away from the door and walking into the room. He had to break the tension stretching tight inside him. Step one was breaking the silence and making his presence known. Step two was going to be calling up one of the women he had associations with off and on.

Because he had to do something to take the edge off. Clearly, it had been too long since he'd gotten laid.

"Sorry," she said, wiping her hands on a dishcloth and making a few frantic movements. As though she wanted to look industrious, but didn't exactly have a specific task. "The roast took longer than I thought it would. But I did a little more paperwork while I waited. And I called the county to track down that permit."

"You don't have to justify all your time. Everything has gotten done this week. Plus, inefficient meat preparation was not on my list of reasons I might fire you."

She shrugged. "I thought you reserved the right to revise that list at any time."

"I do. But not today."

"I should be out of your hair soon." She walked around the counter and he saw she was barefoot. Earlier, he had been far too distracted by her backside to notice.

"Pretty sure that's a health code violation," he said.

She turned pink all the way up to her scalp. "Sorry. My feet hurt."

He thought of those low, sensible heels she always wore and he had to wonder what the point was to wearing shoes that ugly if they weren't even comfortable. The kind of women he usually went out with wore the kinds of shoes made for sitting. Or dancing on a pole.

But Hayley didn't look like she even knew what pole dancing was, let alone like she would jump up there and give it a try. She was… Well, she was damn near sweet.

Which was all wrong for him, in every way. He wasn't sweet.

He was successful. He was driven.

But he was temporary at best. And frankly, almost everyone in his life seemed grateful for that fact. No one stayed. Not his mother, not his father. Even his sister was off living her own life now.

So why he should spend even one moment looking at Hayley the way he'd been looking at her, he didn't know. He didn't have time for subtlety. He never had. He had always liked obvious women. Women who asked for what they wanted without any game-playing or shame.

He didn't want a wife. He didn't even want a serious girlfriend. Hell, he didn't want a casual girlfriend. When he went out it was with the express intention of hooking up. When it came to women, he didn't like a challenge.

His whole damned life was a challenge, and always had been. When he'd been raising his sister he couldn't bring anyone back to his place, which meant he needed someone with a place of their own, or someone willing to get busy in the back of a pickup truck.

Someone who understood he had only a couple free hours, and he wouldn't be sharing their bed all night.

Basically, his taste ran toward women who were all the things Hayley wasn't.

Cute ass or not.

None of those thoughts did anything to ease the tension in his stomach. No matter how succinctly they broke down just why he shouldn't find Hayley hot.

He nearly scoffed. She *wasn't* hot. She was… She would not be out of place as the wholesome face on a baking mix. Much more Little Debbie than Debbie Does Dallas.

"It's fine. I don't want you going lame on me."

She grinned. "No. Then you'd have to put me down."

"True. And if I lose more than one personal assistant that way people will start asking questions."

He could tell she wasn't sure if he was kidding or not. For a second, she looked downright concerned.

"I have not sent, nor do I intend to send, any of my employees—present or former—to the glue factory. Don't look at me like that."

She bit her lower lip, and that forced him to spend a moment examining just how lush it was. He didn't like that. She needed to stop bending over, and to do nothing that would draw attention to her mouth. Maybe, when he revised the list of things he might fire her for, he would add drawing attention to attractive body parts to the list.

"I can never tell when you're joking."

"Me, either," he said.

That time she did laugh. "You know," she said, "you could smile."

"Takes too much energy."

The timer went off and she bustled back to the stove. "Okay," she said, "it should be ready now." She pulled a little pan out of the oven and took the lid off. It was full of roast and potatoes, carrots and onions. The kind of home-cooked meal he imagined a lot of kids grew up on.

For him, traditional fare had been more along the lines of flour tortillas with cheese or ramen noodles. Something cheap, easy and full of carbs. Just enough to keep you going.

His stomach growled in appreciation, and that was the kind of hunger associated with Hayley that he could accept.

"I should go," she said, starting to walk toward the kitchen door.

"Stay."

As soon as he made the offer Jonathan wanted to bite his tongue off. He did not need to encourage spending more time in closed off spaces with her. Although dinner might be a good chance to prove that he could easily master those weird bursts of attraction.

"No," she said, and he found himself strangely re-lieved. "I should go."

"Don't be an idiot," he said, surprising himself yet again. "Dinner is ready here. And it's late. Plus there's no way I can eat all this."

"Okay," she said, clearly hesitant.

"Come on now. Stop looking at me like you think I'm going to bite you. You've been reading too much *Twilight*. Indians don't really turn into wolves."

Her face turned really red then. "That's not what I was thinking. I don't... I'm not afraid of you."

She was afraid of something. And what concerned him most was that it might be the same thing he was fighting against.

"I really was teasing you," he said. "I have a little bit of a reputation in town, but I didn't earn half of it."

"Are you saying people in town are...prejudiced?"

"I wouldn't go that far. I mean, I wouldn't say it's on purpose. But whether it's because I grew up poor or it's because I'm brown, people have always given me a wide berth."

"I didn't... I mean, I've never seen people act that way."

"Well, they wouldn't. Not to you."

She blinked slightly. "I'll serve dinner now."

"Don't worry," he said, "the story has a happy end-ing. I have a lot of money now, and that trumps anything else. People have no issue hiring me to build these days. Though, I remember the first time my old boss put me on as the leader of the building crew, and the guy whose house we were building had a problem with it. He didn't think I should be doing anything that required too much skill. Was more comfortable with me just swinging the hammer, not telling other people where to swing it."

She took plates down from the cupboard, holding them close to her chest. "That's awful."

"People are awful."

A line creased her forehead. "They definitely can be."

"Stop hugging my dinner plate to your shirt. That really isn't sanitary. We can eat in here." He gestured to the countertop island. She set the plates down hurriedly, then started dishing food onto them.

He sighed heavily, moving to where she was and taking the big fork and knife out of her hands. "Have a seat. How much do you want?"

"Oh," she said, "I don't need much."

He ignored her, filling the plate completely, then filling his own. After that, he went to the fridge and pulled out a beer. "Want one?"

She shook her head. "I don't drink."

He frowned, then looked back into the fridge. "I don't have anything else."

"Water is fine."

He got her a glass and poured some water from the spigot in the fridge. He handed it to her, regarding her like she was some kind of alien life-form. The small conversation had really highlighted the gulf between them.

It should make him feel even more ashamed about looking at her butt.

Except shame was pretty hard for him to come by.

"Tell me what you think about people, Hayley." He took a bite of the roast and nearly gave her a raise then and there.

"No matter what things look like on the surface, you never know what someone is going through. It surprised me how often someone who had been smiling on Sunday would come into the office and break down in tears on Tuesday afternoon, saying they needed to talk to the pastor. Everyone has problems, and I do my best not to add to them."

"That's a hell of a lot nicer than most people deserve."

"Okay, what do you think about people?" she asked, clasping her hands in front of her and looking so damn interested and sincere he wasn't quite sure how to react.

"I think they're a bunch of self-interested bastards. And that's fair enough, because so am I. But whenever somebody asks for something, or offers me something, I ask myself what they will get out of it. If I can't figure out how they'll benefit, that's when I get worried."

"Not everyone is after money or power," she said. He could see she really believed what she said. He wasn't sure what to make of that.

"All right," he conceded, "maybe they aren't all after money. But they are looking to gain something. Everyone is. You can't get through life any other way. Trust me."

"I don't know. I never thought of it that way. In terms of who could get me what. At least, that's not how I've lived."

"Then you're an anomaly."

She shook her head. "My father is like that, too. He really does want to help people. He cares. Pastoring a small church in a little town doesn't net you much power or money."

"Of course it does. You hold the power of people's

salvation in your hands. Pass around the plate every week. Of course you get power and money." Jonathan shook his head. "Being the leader of local spirituality is power, honey, trust me."

Her cheeks turned pink. "Okay. You might have a point. But my father doesn't claim to have the key to anyone's salvation. And the money in that basket goes right back into the community. Or into keeping the doors of the church open. My father believes in living the same way the community lives. Not higher up. So whatever baggage you might have about church, that's specific to your experience. It has nothing to do with my father or his faith."

She spoke with such raw certainty that Jonathan was tempted to believe her. But he knew too much about human nature.

Still, he liked all that conviction burning inside her. He liked that she believed what she said, even if he couldn't.

If he had been born with any ideals, he couldn't remember them now. He'd never had the luxury of having faith in humanity, as Hayley seemed to have. No, his earliest memory of his father was the old man's fist connecting with his face. Jonathan had never had the chance to believe the best of anybody.

He had been introduced to the worst far too early.

And he didn't know very many people who'd had different experiences.

The optimism she seemed to carry, the softness combined with strength, fascinated him. He wanted to draw closer to it, to her, to touch her skin, to see if she was strong enough to take the physical demands he put on a woman who shared his bed.

To see how shocked she might be when he told her what those demands were. In explicit detail.

He clenched his jaw tight, clamping his teeth down hard. He was not going to find out, for a couple reasons. The first being that she was his employee, and off-limits. The second being that all those things that fascinated him would be destroyed if he got close, if he laid even one finger on her.

Cynicism bled from his pores, and he damn well knew it. He had earned it. He wasn't one of those bored rich people overcome by ennui just because life had gone so well he wanted to create problems so he had something to battle against.

No. He had fought every step of the way, and he had been disappointed by people in every way imaginable. He had earned his feelings about people, that was for damn sure.

But he wasn't certain he wanted to pass that cynicism on to Hayley. No, she was like a pristine wilderness area. Unspoiled by humans. And his first inclination was to explore every last inch, to experience all that beauty, all that majesty. But he had to leave it alone. He had to leave it looked at, not touched.

Hayley Thompson was the same. Untouched. He had to leave her unspoiled. Exploring that beauty would only leave it ruined, and he couldn't do that. He wouldn't.

"I think it's sad," she said, her voice muted. "That you can't see the good in other people."

"I've been bitten in the ass too many times," he said, his tone harder than he'd intended it to be. "I'm glad you haven't been."

"I haven't had the chance to be. But that's kind of the point of what I'm doing. Going out, maybe getting bitten in the ass." Her cheeks turned bright red. "I can't believe I said that."

"What?"

"That word."

That made his stomach feel like it had been hollowed out. *"Ass?"*

Her cheeks turned even redder. "Yes. I don't say things like that."

"I guess not... Being the church secretary and all."

Now he just felt... Well, she made him feel rough and uncultured, dirty and hard and unbending as steel. Everything she was not. She was small, delicate and probably far too easy to break. Just like he'd imagined earlier, she was...set apart. Unspoiled. And here he had already spoiled her a little bit. She'd said ass, right there in his kitchen.

And she'd looked shocked as hell by her own behavior.

"You don't have to say things like that if you don't want to," he said. "Not every experience is a good experience. You shouldn't try things just to try them. Hell, if I'd had the choice of staying innocent of human nature, maybe I would have taken that route instead. Don't ruin that nice vision of the world you have."

She frowned. "You know, everybody talks about going out and experiencing things..."

"Sure. But when people say that, they want control over those experiences. Believe me, having the blinders ripped off is not necessarily the best thing."

She nodded slowly. "I guess I understand that. What kinds of experiences do you think are bad?"

Immediately, he thought of about a hundred bad things he wanted to do to her. Most of them in bed, all of them naked. He sucked in a sharp breath through his teeth. "I don't think we need to get into that."

"I'm curious."

"You know what they say about curiosity and the cat, right?"

"But I'm not a cat."

"No," he said, "you are Hayley, and you should be grateful for the things you've been spared. Maybe you should even go back to the church office."

"No," she said, frowning. "I don't want to. Maybe I don't want to *experience everything*—I can see how you're probably right about that. But I can't just stay in one place, sheltered for the rest of my life. I have to figure out…who I am and what I want."

That made him laugh, because it was such a naive sentiment. He had never stood back and asked himself who the hell Jonathan Bear was, and what he wanted out of life. He hadn't given a damn how he made his money as long as he made it.

As far as he was concerned, dreams were for people with a lot of time on their hands. He had to *do*. Even as a kid, he couldn't think, couldn't wonder; he had to act.

She might as well be speaking a foreign language. "You'll have to tell me what that's like."

"What?"

"That quest to find yourself. Let me know if it's any more effective than just living your life and seeing what happens."

"Okay, now you've made me feel silly."

He took another bite of dinner. Maybe he should back down, because he didn't want her to quit. He would like to continue eating her food. And, frankly, he would like to keep looking at her.

Just because he should back down didn't mean he was going to.

"There was no safety net in my life," he said, not bothering to reassure her. "There never has been. I had to work my ass off from the moment I was old enough to get paid to do something. Hell, even before then. I would get what I could from the store, expired products, whatever, so we would have something to eat. That teaches you a lot about yourself. You don't have to go looking. In those situations, you find out whether you're a survivor or not. Turns out I am. And I've never really seen what more I needed to know."

"I don't… I don't have anything to say to that."

"Yeah," he returned. "My life story is kind of a bummer."

"Not now," she said softly. "You have all this. You have the business, you have this house."

"Yeah, I expect a man could find himself here. Well, unless he got lost because it was so big." He smiled at her, but she didn't look at all disarmed by the gesture. Instead, she looked thoughtful, and that made his stomach feel tight.

He didn't really do meaningful conversation. He especially didn't do it with women.

Yet here he was, telling this woman more about himself than he could remember telling anyone. Rebecca knew everything, of course. Well, as much as she'd observed while being a kid in that situation. They didn't need to talk about it. It was just life. But other people… Well, he didn't see the point in talking about the deficit he'd started with. He preferred people assume he'd sprung out of the ground powerful and successful. They took him more seriously.

He'd had enough disadvantages, and he wouldn't set himself up for any more.

But there was something about Hayley—her openness, her honesty—that made him want to talk. That made him feel bad for being insincere. Because she was just so…so damn real.

How would he have been if he'd had a softer existence? Maybe he wouldn't be as hard. Maybe a different life would have meant not breaking a woman like this the moment he put his hands on her.

It was moot. Because he hadn't had a different life. And if he had, he probably wouldn't have made half as much of himself.

"You don't have to feel bad for wanting more," he said finally. "Just because other people don't have it easy, doesn't mean you don't have your own kind of hard."

"It's just difficult to decide what to do when other people's expectations feel so much bigger than your own dreams."

"I know a little something about that. Only in my case, the expectations other people had for me were that I would end up dead of a drug overdose or in prison. So, all things considered, I figured I would blow past those expectations and give people something to talk about."

"I just want to travel."

"Is that it?"

A smile played in the corner of her lips, and he found himself wondering what it might be like to taste that smile. "Okay. And see a famous landmark. Like the Eiffel Tower or Big Ben. And I want to dance."

"Have you never danced?"

"No!" She looked almost comically horrified. "Where would I have danced?"

"Well, your brother does own a bar. And there is line dancing."

"I can't even go into Ace's bar. My parents don't go. We can go to the brewery. Because they serve more food there. And it's not called a bar."

"That seems like some arbitrary shit."

Her cheeks colored, and he didn't know if it was because he'd pointed out a flaw in her parents' logic or because he had cursed. "Maybe. But I follow their lead. It's important for us to keep away from the appearance of evil."

"Now, that I don't know anything about. Because nobody cares much about my appearance."

She cleared her throat. "So," she said. "Dancing."

Suddenly, an impulse stole over him, one he couldn't quite understand or control. Before he knew it, he was pushing his chair back and standing up, extending his hand. "All right, Hayley Thompson, Paris has to wait awhile. But we can take care of the dancing right now."

"What?" Her pretty eyes flew wide, her soft lips rounded into a perfect O.

"Dance with me, Hayley."

Four

Hayley was pretty sure she was hallucinating.

Because there was no way her stern boss was standing there, his large, work-worn hand stretched toward her, his dark eyes glittering with an intensity she could only guess at the meaning of, having just asked her to dance. Except, no matter how many times she blinked, he was still standing there. And the words were still echoing in her head.

"There's no music."

He took his cell phone out of his pocket, opened an app and set the phone on the table, a slow country song filling the air. "There," he said. "Music accomplished. Now, dance with me."

"I thought men *asked* for a dance, I didn't think they demanded one."

"Some men, maybe. But not me. But remember, I don't give a damn about appearances."

"I think I might admire that about you."

"You should," he said, his tone grave.

She felt… Well, she felt breathless and fluttery, and she didn't know what to do. But if she said no, then he would know just how inexperienced she was. He would know she was making a giant internal deal about his hand touching hers, about the possibility of being held against his body. That she felt strange, unnerving sensations skittering over her skin when she looked at him. She was afraid he could see her too clearly.

Isn't this what you wanted? To reach out? To take a chance?

It was. So she did.

She took his hand. She was still acclimating to his heat, to being touched by him, skin to skin, when she found herself pressed flush against his chest, his hand enveloping hers. He wrapped his arm around her waist, his palm hot on her lower back.

She shivered. She didn't know why. Because she wasn't cold. No. She was hot. And so was he. Hot and hard, so much harder than she had imagined another person could be.

She had never, ever been this close to a man before. Had never felt a man's skin against hers. His hand was rough, from all that hard work. What might it feel like if he touched her skin elsewhere? If he pushed his other hand beneath her shirt and slid his fingertips against her lower back?

That thought sent a sharp pang straight to her stomach, unfurling something inside her, making her blood run faster.

She stared straight at his shoulder, at an innocuous spot on his flannel shirt. Because she couldn't bring herself to raise her eyes and look at that hard, lean face, at the raw beauty she had never fully appreciated before.

He would probably be offended to be characterized as beautiful. But he was. In the same way that a mountain was beautiful. Tall, strong and unmoving.

She gingerly curled her fingers around his shoulder, while he took the lead, his hold on her firm and sure as he established a rhythm she could follow.

The grace in his steps surprised her. Caused her to meet his gaze. She both regretted it and relished it at the same time. Because it was a shame to stare at flannel when she could be looking into those dark eyes, but they also made her feel…absolutely and completely undone.

"Where did you learn to dance?" she asked, her voice sounding as breathless as she had feared it might.

But she was curious about this man who had grown up in such harsh circumstances, who had clearly devoted most of his life to hard work with no frills, who had learned to do this.

"A woman," he said, a small smile tugging at the edges of his lips.

She was shocked by the sudden, sour turn in her stomach. It was deeply unpleasant, and she didn't know what to do to make it stop. Imagining what other woman he might have learned this from, how he might have held her…

It hurt. In the strangest way.

"Was she…somebody special to you? Did you love her?"

His smile widened. "No. I've never loved anybody. Not anybody besides my sister. But I sure as hell *wanted* something from that woman, and she wanted to dance."

It took Hayley a while to figure out the meaning behind those words. "Oh," she said, "she wanted to dance and you wanted…" That feeling in her stomach intensified, but along with it came a strange sort of heat. Because he was holding *her* now, dancing with her. *She* wanted to dance. Did that mean that he…?

"Don't look at me like that, Hayley. This," he said, tightening his hold on her and dipping her slightly, his face moving closer to hers, "is just a dance."

She was a tangle of unidentified feelings—knots in her stomach, an ache between her thighs—and she didn't want to figure out what any of it meant.

"Good," she said, wishing she could have infused some conviction into that word.

The music slowed, the bass got heavier. And he matched the song effortlessly, his hips moving firmly against hers with every deep pulse of the beat.

This time, she couldn't ignore the lyrics. About two people and the fire they created together. She wouldn't have fully understood what that meant even a few minutes ago, but in Jonathan's arms, with the heat that burned from his body, fire was what she felt.

Like her nerve endings had been set ablaze, like a spark had been stoked low inside her. If he moved in just the wrong way—or just the right way—the flames in him would catch hold of that spark in her and they would combust.

She let her eyes flutter closed, gave herself over to the moment, to the song, to the feel of him, the scent of him. She was dancing. And she liked it a lot more than she had anticipated and in a way she hadn't imagined she could.

She had pictured laughing, lightness, with people all around, like at the bar she had never been to before.

But this was something else. A deep intimacy that grew from somewhere inside her chest and intensified as the music seemed to draw them more tightly together.

She drew in a breath, letting her eyes open and look up at him. And then she froze.

He was staring at her, the glitter in his dark eyes almost predatory. She didn't know why that word came to mind. Didn't even know what it might mean in this context. When a man looked at you like he was a wildcat and you were a potential meal.

Then her eyes dipped down to his mouth. Her own lips tingled in response and she was suddenly aware of how dry they were. She slid her tongue over them, completely self-conscious about the action even as she did it, yet unable to stop.

She was satisfied when that predatory light in his eyes turned sharper. More intense.

She didn't know what she was doing. But she found herself moving closer to him. She didn't know why. She just knew she had to. With the same bone-deep impulse that came with the need to draw breath, she had to lean in closer to Jonathan Bear. She couldn't fight it; she didn't want to. And until her lips touched his, she didn't even know what she was moving toward.

But when their mouths met, it all became blindingly clear.

She had thought about these feelings in terms of fire, but this sensation was something bigger, something infinitely more destructive. This was an explosion. One she felt all the way down to her toes; one that hit every place in between.

She was shaking. Trembling like a leaf in the wind. Or maybe even like a tree in a storm.

He was the storm.

His hold changed. He let go of her hand, withdrew his arm from around her waist, pressed both palms against her cheeks as he took the kiss deeper, harder.

It was like drowning. Like dying. Only she didn't want to fight it. Didn't want to turn away. She couldn't have, even if she'd tried. Because his grip was like iron, his body like a rock wall. They weren't moving in time with the music anymore. No. This was a different rhythm entirely. He propelled her backward, until her shoulder blades met with the dining room wall, his hard body pressed against hers.

He was hard. Everywhere. Hard chest, hard stomach, hard thighs. And that insistent hardness pressing against her hip.

She gasped when she realized what that was. And he consumed her shocked sound, taking advantage of her parted lips to slide his tongue between them.

She released her hold on him, her hands floating up without a place to land, and she curled her fingers into fists. She surrendered herself to the kiss, to him. His hold was tight enough to keep her anchored to the earth, to keep her anchored to him.

She let him have control. Let him take the lead. She didn't know how to dance, and she didn't know how to do this. But he did.

So she let him show her. This was on her list, too, though she hadn't been brave enough to say it, even to herself. To know passion. To experience her first kiss.

She wanted it to go on and on. She never wanted it to end. If she could just be like this, those hot hands cupping her face, that insistent mouth devouring hers, she was pretty sure she could skip the Eiffel Tower.

She felt him everywhere, not just his kiss, not just his touch. Her breasts felt heavy. They ached. In any other circumstances, she might be horrified by that. But she didn't possess the capacity to be horrified, not right now. Not when everything else felt so good. She wasn't ashamed; she wasn't embarrassed—not of the heavy feeling in her breasts, not of the honeyed, slick feeling between her thighs.

This just made sense.

Right now, what she felt was the only thing that made sense. It was the only thing she wanted.

Kissing Jonathan Bear was a necessity.

He growled, flexing his hips toward hers, making it so she couldn't ignore his arousal. And the evidence of his desire carved out a hollow feeling inside her. Made her shake, made her feel like her knees had dissolved into nothing and that without his powerful hold she would crumple onto the floor.

She still wasn't touching him. Her hands were still away from his body, trembling. But she didn't want to do anything to break the moment. Didn't want to make a sound, didn't want to make the wrong move. She didn't want to turn him off or scare him away. Didn't want to do anything to telegraph her innocence. Because it would probably freak him out.

Right, Hayley, like he totally believes you're a sex kitten who's kissed a hundred men.

She didn't know what to do with her hands, let alone her lips, her tongue. She was receiving, not giving. But she had a feeling if she did anything else she would look like an idiot.

Suddenly, he released his hold on her, moving away

from her so quickly she might have thought she'd hurt him.

She was dazed, still leaning against the wall. If she hadn't been, she would have collapsed. Her hands were still in the air, clenched into fists, and her breath came in short, harsh bursts. So did his, if the sharp rise and fall of his chest was anything to go by.

"That was a mistake," he said, his voice hard. His words were everything she had feared they might be.

"No, it wasn't," she said, her lips feeling numb, and a little bit full, making it difficult for her to talk. Or maybe the real difficulty came from feeling like her head was filled with bees, buzzing all around and scrambling her thoughts.

"Yes," he said, his voice harder, "it was."

"No," she insisted. "It was a great kiss. A really, really good kiss. I didn't want it to end."

Immediately, she regretted saying that. Because it had been way too revealing. She supposed it was incredibly gauche to tell the guy you'd just kissed that you could have kissed him forever. She tried to imagine how Grant, the youth pastor, might have reacted to that. He would have told her she needed to go to an extra Bible study. Or that she needed to marry him first.

He certainly wouldn't have looked at her the way Jonathan was. Like he wanted to eat her whole, but was barely restraining himself from doing just that. "That's exactly the problem," he returned, the words like iron, "because I *did* want it to end. But in a much different way than it did."

"I don't understand." Her face was hot, and she was humiliated now. So she didn't see why she shouldn't go whole hog. Let him know she was fully outside her comfort zone and she wasn't keeping up with all his implications. She needed stated facts, not innuendo.

"I didn't want to keep kissing you forever. I wanted to pull your top off, shove your skirt up and bury myself inside of you. Is that descriptive enough for you?"

It was. And he had succeeded in shocking her. She wasn't stupid. She knew he was hard, and she knew what that meant. But even given that fact, she hadn't really imagined he wanted... Not with her.

And this was just her first kiss. She wasn't ready for more. Wasn't ready for another step away from the person she had been taught to be.

What about the person you want to be?

She looked at her boss, who was also the most beautiful man she had ever seen. That hadn't been her immediate thought when she'd met him, but she had settled into it as the truth. As certain as the fact the sky was blue and the pine trees that dotted the mountains were deep forest green.

So maybe... Even though it was shocking. Even though it would be a big step, and undoubtedly a big mistake... Maybe she did want it.

"You better go," he said, his voice rough.

"Maybe I don't—"

"You do," he said. "Trust me. And I want you to."

She was confused. Because he had just said he wanted her, and now he was saying he wanted her to go. She didn't understand men. She didn't understand this. She wanted to cry. But a lick of pride slid its way up her spine, keeping her straight, keeping her tears from falling.

Pride she hadn't known she possessed. But then, she hadn't realized she possessed the level of passion that had just exploded between them, either. So it was a day for new discoveries.

"That's fine. I just wanted to have some fun. I can go have it with someone else."

She turned on her heel and walked out of the dining room, out the front door and down the porch steps as quickly as possible. It was dark now, trees like inky bottle brushes rising around her, framing the midnight-blue sky dotted with stars. It was beautiful, but she didn't care. Not right now. She felt…hurt. Emotionally. Physically. The unsatisfied ache between her thighs intensified with the pain growing in her heart.

It was awful. All of it.

It made her want to run. Run back to her parents' house. Run back to the church office.

Being *good* had always been safe.

She had been so certain she wanted to escape safety. Only a few moments earlier she'd needed that escape, felt it might be her salvation. Except she could see now that it was ruin. Utter and complete ruin.

With shaking hands, she pushed the button that undid the locks on her car door and got inside, jamming the key into the ignition and starting it up, a tear sliding down her cheek as she started to back out of the driveway.

She refused to let this ruin her, or this job, or this step she was taking on her own.

She was finding independence, learning new things.

As she turned onto the two-lane highway that would take her back home, she clung to that truth. To the fact that, even though her first kiss had ended somewhat disastrously, it had still shown her something about herself.

It had shown her exactly why it was a good thing she

hadn't gotten married to that youthful crush of hers. It would have been dishonest, and not fair to him or to her.

She drove on autopilot, eventually pulling into her driveway and stumbling inside her apartment, lying down on her bed without changing out of her work clothes.

Was she a fallen woman? To want Jonathan like she had. A man she wasn't in love with, a man she wasn't planning to marry.

Had that passion always been there? Or was it created by Jonathan? This feeling. This *need*.

She bit back a sob and forced a smile. She'd had her first kiss. And she wouldn't dwell on what it might mean. Or on the fact that he had sent her away. Or on the fact that—for a moment at least—she had been consumed with the desire for more.

She'd had her first kiss. At twenty-four. And that felt like a change deep inside her body.

Hayley Thompson had a new apartment, a new job, and she had been kissed.

So maybe it wasn't safe. But she had decided she wanted something more than safety, hadn't she?

She would focus on the victories and simply ignore the rest.

No matter that this victory made her body burn in a way that kept her up for the rest of the night.

Five

He hadn't expected her to show up Monday morning. But there she was, in the entryway of the house, hands clasped in front of her, dark hair pulled back in a neat bun. Like she was compensating for what had happened between them Friday night.

"Good morning," he said, taking a sip of his coffee. "I half expected you to take the day off."

"No," she said, her voice shot through with steel, "I can't just take days off. My boss is a tyrant. He'll fire me."

He laughed, mostly to disguise the physical response those words created in him. There was something about her. About all that softness, that innocence, combined with the determination he hadn't realized existed inside her until this moment.

She wasn't just soft, or innocent. She was a force to

be reckoned with, and she was bent on showing him that now.

"If he's so bad why do you want to keep the job?"

"My job history is pathetic," she said, walking ahead of him to the stairs. "And, as he has pointed out to me many times, he is not my daddy. My previous boss was. I need something a bit more impressive on my résumé."

"Right. For when you do your traveling."

"Maybe I'll get a job in London," she shot back.

"What's the biggest city you've been to, Hayley?" he asked, following her up the stairs and down the hall toward the office.

"Portland," she said.

He laughed. "London is a little bit bigger."

"I don't care. That's what I want. I want a city where I can walk down the street and not run into anybody that I've ever seen before. All new people. All new faces. I can't imagine that. I can't imagine living a life where I do what I want and not hear a retelling of the night before coming out of my mother's mouth at breakfast the next morning."

"Have you ever done anything worthy of being re-counted by your mother?"

Color infused her cheeks. "Okay, specifically, the in-cident I'm referring to is somebody telling my mother they were proud of me because they saw me giving a homeless woman a dollar."

He laughed. He couldn't help himself, and her cheeks turned an even more intense shade of pink that he knew meant she was furious.

She stamped. Honest to God stamped, like an old-time movie heroine. "What's so funny?"

"Even the gossip about you is good, Hayley Thompson. For the life of me, I can't figure out why you hate that so much."

"Because I can't *do* anything. Jonathan, if you had kissed me in my brother's bar... Can you even imagine? My parents' phone would have been ringing off the hook."

His body hardened at the mention of the kiss. He had been convinced she would avoid the topic.

But he should've known by now that when it came to Hayley he couldn't anticipate her next move. She was more direct, more up-front than he had thought she might be. Was it because of her innocence that she faced things so squarely? Because she hadn't experienced a whole range of consequences for much of anything yet?

"I wouldn't do that to you," he said. "Because you're right. If anybody suspected something unprofessional had happened between us, it would cause trouble for you."

"I didn't mean it that way." She looked horrified. "I mean, the way people would react if they thought I was... It has nothing to do with you."

"It does. More than you realize. You've been sheltered. But just because you don't know my reputation, that doesn't mean other people in town don't know it. Most people who know you're a good girl know I am a bad man, Hayley. And if anyone suspected I had put my hands on you, I'm pretty sure there would be torches and pitchforks at my front door by sunset."

"Well," she said, "that isn't fair. Because *I* kissed *you*."

"I'm going out on a limb here—of the two of us, I have more experience."

She clasped her hands in front of her and shuffled her feet. "Maybe."

"Maybe nothing, honey. I'm not the kind of man you need to be seen with. So, you're right. You do need to get away. Maybe you should go to London. Hell, I don't know."

"Now you want to get rid of me?"

"Now you're just making it so I can't win."

"I don't mean to," she said, with that trademark sincerity that was no less alarming for being typical of her. "But I don't know what to do with...with this."

She bit her lip, and the motion drew his eye to that lush mouth of hers. Forced him back to the memory of kissing it. Of tasting her.

He wanted her. No question about it.

He couldn't pretend otherwise. But he could at least be honest with himself about why. He wanted her for all the wrong reasons. He wanted her because some sick, caveman part of him wanted to get all that *pretty* dirty. Part of him wanted to corrupt her. To show her everything she was missing. To make her fall from grace a lasting one.

And that was some fucked up shit.

Didn't mean he didn't feel it.

"Well, after I earn enough money, that's probably what I'll do," she said. "And since this isn't going anywhere... I should probably just get to work. And we shouldn't talk about it anymore."

"No," he said, "we shouldn't."

"It was just a kiss."

His stomach twisted. Not because it disappointed him to hear her say that, but because she had to say it for her own peace of mind. She was innocent enough that a kiss worked her up. It meant something to her. Hell, sex barely meant anything to him. Much less a kiss.

Except for hers. You remember hers far too well.

"Just a kiss," he confirmed.

"Good. So give me some spreadsheets."

The rest of the week went well. If well meant dodging moments alone with Jonathan, catching herself staring at him at odd times during the day and having difficulty dreaming of anything except him at night.

"Thank God it's Friday," she said into the emptiness of her living room.

She didn't feel like cooking. She had already made a meal for Jonathan at his house, and then hightailed it out of there as quickly as possible. She knew that if she'd made enough for herself and took food with her he wouldn't have minded, but she was doing her best to keep the lines between them firm.

She couldn't have any more blurred lines. They couldn't have any more…kissing and other weirdness. Just thinking about kissing Jonathan made her feel restless, edgy. She didn't like it. Or maybe she liked it too much.

She huffed out a growl and wandered into the kitchen, opening the cupboard and pulling out a box of chocolate cereal.

It was the kind of cereal her parents never would have bought. Because it wasn't good for you, and it was expensive. So she had bought it for herself, because she had her own job, she was an adult and she made her own decisions.

Do you?

She shut out that snotty little voice. Yes, she *did*

make her own decisions. Here she was, living in her own place, working at the job she had chosen. Yes, she very much made her own decisions. She had even kissed Jonathan. Yes, that had been her idea.

Which made the fallout her fault. But she wasn't going to dwell on that.

"I'm dwelling," she muttered. "I'm a liar, and I'm dwelling." She took down a bowl and poured herself a large portion of the chocolaty cereal. Then she stared at it. She didn't want to eat cereal by herself for dinner.

She was feeling restless, reckless.

She was feeling something a whole lot like desperation.

Because of that kiss.

The kiss she had just proposed she wasn't going to think about, the kiss she couldn't let go of. The kiss that made her burn, made her ache and made her wonder about all the mysteries in life she had yet to uncover.

Yeah, *that* kiss.

She had opened a floodgate. She'd uncovered all this potential for passion inside herself, and then she had to stuff it back down deep.

Jonathan Bear was not the only man in the world. Jonathan Bear wasn't even the only man in Copper Ridge.

She could find another guy if she wanted to.

Of course, if she went out, there would be all those gossip issues she and Jonathan had discussed earlier in the week.

That was why she had to get out of this town.

It struck her then, like a horse kicking her square in the chest, that she was running away. So she could be who she wanted to be without anybody knowing about it. So she could make mistakes and minimize the consequences.

So she could be brave and a coward all at the same time.

That's what it was. It was cowardice. And she was not very impressed with herself.

"Look at you," she scolded, "eating cold cereal on a Friday night by yourself when you would rather be out getting kissed."

Her heart started to beat faster. Where would she go?

And then it hit her. There was one place she could go on a Friday night where nobody from church would recognize her, and even if they did recognize her, they probably wouldn't tell on her because by doing so they would be telling on themselves.

Of course, going there would introduce the problem of her older brother. But Ace had struck out on his own when he was only seventeen years old. He was her inspiration in all this. So he should understand Hayley's need for independence.

And that was when she made her decision. It was Friday night, and she was going out.

She was going to one of the few places in town where she had never set foot before.

Ace's bar.

Six

"I'd like a hamburger," Hayley said, adjusting her dress and trying not to look like she was about to commit a crime.

"Hayley?" Her brother looked at her as if she had grown another head. "What are you doing in my bar?"

"I'm here to have a hamburger. And…a beer."

Ace shook his head. "You don't want beer."

Darn him for being right. She couldn't stand the smell of the stuff, and she'd honestly never even been tempted to taste it.

"No," she agreed. "I want a Coke."

"I will get you a Coke. Are Mom and Dad here?"

She sighed heavily. "No, they're not. I do go places without them. I moved out."

"I know. We talked about it last time Sierra and I went over for dinner."

Hayley's brother had never much cared about his

reputation, or about what anyone thought of him. She had been jealous of that for a long time. For years, Ace had been a total hellion and a womanizer, until he'd settled down and married the town rodeo princess, Sierra West. Now the two of them had one child and another on the way, and Ace's position in the community had improved vastly.

"Right. Well, I'm just saying." She traced an imaginary pattern over the bar top with the tip of her finger. "Did I tell you I quit working at the church?"

Ace look surprised by that. "No."

"Well," she said, "I did. I'm working for Jonathan Bear. Helping out with things around the house and in the office."

Ace frowned. "Well, that probably isn't very much fun. He's kind of a grumpy sumbitch."

"I didn't know you knew him all that well."

"He's my future sister-in-law's brother," Ace said, "but no, I don't know him *well*. He's not very sociable. It's not like he comes to the West family gatherings."

"He said he knows you because he buys beer from you."

"That's how everybody knows me," Ace said.

"Except for me."

"You were *trying* to buy beer from me. I'm just not going to sell one to you."

"That's not fair."

"Sure it is," he said, smiling. "Because you don't actually want to buy beer from me. You're just trying to prove a point."

She scowled. She hated that Ace seemed to understand her so well. "Okay, maybe so. I'm kind of proving a point by being here, I guess."

"Well," he said, "it's all right by me."

"Good."

"I kind of wish you would have come on another night, though," he said, "because I have to go. I promised Sierra I would be home early, so I'm about to take off. But I'll tell Jasmine to keep an eye on you."

"I don't need anybody to keep an eye on me."

"Yes," Ace said, laughing, "you do."

Hayley frowned, and plotted how to order a beer when her brother was gone. Ultimately, she decided to stick with Coke, but when the dancing started, she knew that while she might stay away from alcohol, she didn't want to stay seated. She had danced once. And she had liked it.

She was going to do it again.

Jonathan didn't know what in blazes he was doing at Ace's. Sure, he knew what he'd told himself while getting ready, his whole body restless thanks to memories of kissing Hayley.

He had continued to push those thoughts down while pacing around the house, and then, after a while, he'd decided to go out and find someone to hook up with. He didn't do that kind of thing, not anymore. He had a couple of women he called; he didn't go trawling bars. He was too old for that.

But right now, he was too much of a hazard to his innocent assistant, and he needed to take the edge off.

And it occurred to him that if he went to Ace's bar and found somebody, the news might filter back to Hayley.

Even though she might find it upsetting, it would be beneficial in the long run. She didn't want to mess with a man like him, not really. It was only that she was too innocent realize the dangers. But she would, eventually, and she would thank him.

That decision made, he'd hauled his ass down to the bar as quickly as possible.

By the time he walked in, his mood had not improved. He had thought it might. The decision to find a willing woman should have cheered him up. But he felt far from cheered. Maybe because an anonymous body was the last thing he wanted.

He wanted *Hayley*.

Whether he should or not. But he wasn't going to have Hayley. So he would have to get the hell over it.

He moved to the bar and then looked over at the dance floor. His chest tightened up. His body hardened. There was a petite brunette in a formfitting dress dancing with no one in particular. Two men hovered nearby, clearly not minding as she turned to and away from each of them, giving them both just a little bit of attention.

She reminded him of Hayley. Out there on the dance floor acting like nothing close to Hayley.

Then she turned, her dark hair shimmering behind her in a stream, a bright smile on her face, and he could barely process his thoughts. Because it was Hayley. *His* Hayley, out there in the middle of the dance floor, wearing a dress that showed off the figure her clothes had only hinted at before. Sure, in comparison to a lot of women, there was nothing flashy about it, but for Hayley Thompson, it was damned flashy.

And he was… Well, he would be damned if he was going to let those guys put their hands on her.

Yeah, he was bad news. Yeah, he was the kind of guy she should stay well away from. But those guys weren't any better. College douche bags. Probably in their twenties, closer to her age, sure, but not the kind of men who knew how to handle a woman. Especially not one as inexperienced as Hayley.

She would need a man who could guide the experience, show her what she liked. A man who could unlock the mysteries of sex, of her body.

Dickwads that age were better off with an empty dorm room and a half bottle of lotion.

And there was no way in hell they were getting their hands on her.

Without ordering, he moved away from the bar and went out on the dance floor. "You're done here," he said to one of the guys, who looked at him as though Jonathan had just threatened his life. His tone had been soft and even, but it was nice to know the younger man had heard the implied threat loud and clear.

Hayley hadn't noticed his approach, or that the other guy had scurried off to the other end of the dance floor. She was too involved with the guy she was currently dancing with to notice. She was shaking her head, her eyes closed, her body swaying to the music. A completely different kind of dancing than the two of them had done last week.

Then her current dance partner caught Jonathan's eye and paled. He slunk off into the shadows, too.

If Jonathan hadn't already found them wanting when it came to Hayley, he would have now. If they were any kind of men, they would have stood up and declared their interest. They would have proclaimed their desire for her, marked their territory.

He still would have thrown punches, but at least he would've respected them a bit.

Not now.

"Mind if I dance with you?"

Her eyes flew open and she looked around, her head whipping from side to side, her hair following suit. "Where are…"

"Tweedledee and Tweedledum had somewhere to be."

"Where?"

"Someplace where I wouldn't beat their asses."

"Why are you going to beat their…butts?"

"What are you doing here, Hayley?"

She looked around, a guilty expression on her face. "I was just dancing. I have to say, when I imagined getting in trouble in a bar, I figured it would be my dad dragging me outside, not my boss."

"I haven't dragged you outside. *Yet.*" He added that last bit because at this point he wasn't sure how this night was going to end. "What are you doing?"

She lifted a shoulder. "Dancing."

"Getting ready to have your first threesome?"

Her mouth dropped open. "I don't even know how that would work."

He huffed out a laugh. "Look it up. On second thought, don't."

She rolled her eyes like a snotty teenager. "We were just dancing. It wasn't a big deal."

"Little girl, what you don't know about men could fill a library. Men don't *just want to dance.* And men don't *just want to kiss.* You can't play these kinds of games. You don't know the rules. You're going to get yourself into trouble."

"I'm not going to get myself into trouble. Did it ever occur to you that maybe some men are nicer than you?"

He chuckled, a low, bitter sound. "Oh, I know that most men are a lot nicer than me. Even then, they want in your pants."

"I don't know what your problem is. You don't want me, so what do you care if they do?"

"Hayley, honey, I don't *want* to want you, but that is not the same thing as not wanting you. It is not even close. What I want is something you can't handle."

"I know," she said, looking to the right and then to the left, as though making sure no one was within earshot. Then she took a step toward him. "You said you wanted to…be inside of me."

That simple statement, that repetition of his words, had him hard as an iron bar. "You better back off."

"See, I thought you didn't want me. I thought you were trying to scare me away when you said that. Because why would you want me?"

"I'd list the reasons, but I would shock you."

She tilted her head to the side, her hair falling over her shoulder like a glossy curtain. "Maybe I want to be shocked. Maybe I want something I'm not quite ready for."

"No," he said, his tone emphatic now. "You're on this big kick to have experiences. And there are much nicer men you can have experiences with."

She bared her teeth. "I was trying! You just scared them off."

"You're not having experiences with those clowns. They wouldn't know how to handle a woman if she came with an instruction manual. And let me tell you, women do not come with an instruction manual. You just have to know what to do."

"And you know what to do?"

"Damn straight," he returned.

"So," she said, tilting her chin up, looking stubborn. "Show me."

"Not likely, babe."

He wanted to. He wanted to pick her up, throw her over his shoulder and drag her back to his cave. He wanted to bury himself inside her and screw them both senseless, breathless. He wanted to chase every man in the vicinity away from her. He wanted to make it known, loud and clear that—for a little while at least—she was his.

But it was wrong. On about a thousand levels. And the fact that she didn't seem to know it was just another bit of evidence that he needed to stay away.

"You're playing with fire," he said.

"I know. When you kissed me, that was the closest to being burned I've ever experienced in my life. I want more of that."

"We're not having this conversation in the middle of a bar." He grabbed her arm and hauled her off the dance floor, steering them both to the door.

"Hayley!"

He turned and saw one of the waitresses standing by the bar with her hands on her hips.

"Is everything all right?" she asked.

"Yes," Hayley responded. "Jasmine, it's fine. This is my boss."

Jasmine arched her brow. "Really?"

Hayley nodded. "Really. Just work stuff."

Then she broke free of him and marched out ahead of him. When they were both outside, she rounded on him, her words coming out on a frosty cloud in the night air.

"You're so concerned about my reputation, but then you wander in and make a spectacle."

"You were dancing with two men when I got there," he said. "And what's happening with that dress?"

"Oh please," she said, "I wear this dress to church. It's fine."

"You wear that to *church*?" He supposed, now that he evaluated it with more neutrality, it was pretty tame. The black stretch cotton fell past her knees and had a fairly high neckline. But he could see the curves of her breasts, the subtle slope of her waist to her hips, and her ass looked incredible.

He didn't know if hers was the sort of church that did confession, but he would sure as hell need to confess if he were seated in a row behind her during service.

"Yes," she said. "And it's fine. You're being crazy. Because…because you…*like* me. You *like me* like me."

There she went again, saying things that revealed how innocent she was. Things that made him want her even more, when they should send him running.

"I don't have relationships," he said. He would tell her the truth. He would be honest. It would be the fastest way to chase her off. "And I'm betting a nice girl like you wants a relationship. Wants romance, and flowers, and at least the possibility of commitment. You don't get any of those things with me, Hayley."

She looked up at him, her blue eyes glittering in the security light. He could hear the waves crashing on the shore just beyond the parking lot, feel the salt breeze blowing in off the water, sharp and cold.

"What would I get?" she asked.

"A good, hard fuck. A few orgasms." He knew he'd shocked her, and he was glad. She needed to be shocked. She needed to be scared away.

He couldn't see her face, not clearly, but he could

tell she wasn't looking at him when she said, "That's… that's a good thing, right?"

"If you don't know the answer, then the answer is no. Not for you."

The sounds of the surf swelled around them, wind whipping through the pines across the road. She didn't speak for a long time. Didn't move.

"Kiss me again," she said, finally.

The words hit him like a sucker punch. "What? What did I just tell you about men and kissing?"

"It's not for you," she said, "it's for me. Before I give you an answer, you need to kiss me again."

She raised her head, and the light caught her face. She stared at him, all defiance and soft lips, all innocence and intensity, and he didn't have it in him to deny her.

Didn't have it in him to deny himself.

Before he could stop, he wrapped his arm around her waist, crushed her against his chest and brought his lips crashing down on hers.

Seven

She was doing this. She wasn't going to turn back. Not now. And she kept telling herself that as she followed Jonathan's pickup truck down the long, empty highway that took them out of town, toward his house.

His house. Where she was going to spend the night.

Where she was going to lose her virginity.

She swallowed hard, her throat suddenly dry and prickly like a cactus.

This wasn't what she had planned when she'd started on her grand independence journey. Yes, she had wanted a kiss, but she hadn't really thought as far ahead as having a sexual partner. For most of her life she had imagined she would be married first, and then, when she'd started wavering on that decision, she had at least imagined she would be in a serious relationship.

This was… Well, it wasn't marriage. It wasn't the beginning of a relationship, either. Of that, she was certain. Jonathan hadn't been vague. Her cheeks heated at the memory of what he'd said, and she was grateful they were driving in separate cars so she had a moment alone for a private freak-out.

She was so out of her league here.

She could turn around. She could head back to town, back to Main Street, back to her little apartment where she could curl up in bed with the bowl of cereal she'd left dry and discarded on the counter earlier.

And in the morning, she wouldn't be changed. Not for the better, not for the worse.

She seriously considered that, though she kept on driving, her eyes on the road and on Jonathan's taillights.

This decision was a big deal. She wouldn't pretend it wasn't. Wouldn't pretend she didn't put some importance on her first sexual experience, on sex in general. And she wouldn't pretend it probably wasn't a mistake.

It was just that maybe she needed to make the mistake. Maybe she needed to find out for herself if Jonathan was right, if every experience wasn't necessary.

She bit her lip and allowed herself a moment of undiluted honesty. When this was over, there would be fallout. She was certain of it.

But while it was happening, it would feel really, really good.

If the kissing was anything to go by, it would be amazing.

She would feel…wild. And new. And maybe sex with Jonathan would be just the kind of thing she needed. He was hot; touching him burned.

Maybe he could be her own personal trial by fire.

She had always imagined that meant walking through hard times. And maybe, conventionally, it did. But she was walking into the heat willingly, knowing the real pain would come after.

She might be a virgin, but she wasn't an idiot. Jonathan Bear wasn't going to fall in love with her. And anyway, she didn't want him to.

She wanted freedom. She wanted something bigger than Copper Ridge.

That meant love wasn't on her agenda, either.

They pulled up to the house and he got out of his truck, closing the door solidly behind him. And she... froze. Sitting there in the driver's seat, both hands on the steering wheel, the engine still running.

The car door opened and cool air rushed in. She looked up and saw Jonathan's large frame filling the space. "Second thoughts?"

She shook her head. "No," she said, and yet she couldn't make herself move.

"I want you," he said, his voice rough, husky, the words not at all what she had expected. "I would like to tell you that if you are having second thoughts, you should turn the car around and go back home. But I'm not going to tell you that. Because if I do, then I might miss out on my chance. And I want this. Even though I shouldn't."

She tightened her hold on the steering wheel. "Why shouldn't you?" she asked, her throat constricted now.

"Do you want the full list?"

"I've got all night."

"All right. You're a nice girl. You seem to believe the best of people, or at least, you want to, until they absolutely make it so you can't. I'm not a nice man. I don't believe the best of anyone, even when they prove I should. People like me, we tend to drag people like you down to our level. Unfortunately. And that's likely what's going to happen here. I'm going to drag you right down to my level. Because let me tell you, I like dirty. And I'm going to get you filthy. I can promise you that."

"Okay," she said, feeling breathless, not quite certain how to respond. Part of her wanted to fling herself out of the car and into his arms, while another, not insignificant part wanted to throw the car in Reverse and drive away.

"I can only promise you two things. This—you and me—won't last forever. And tonight, I will make you come. If you're okay with those promises, then get out of the car and up to my room. If you're not, it's time for you to go."

For some reason, that softly issued command was what it took to get her moving. She released her hold on the steering wheel and turned sideways in her seat. Then she looked up at him, pushing herself into a standing position. He had one hand on the car door, the other on the side mirror, blocking her in.

Her breasts nearly touched his chest, and she was tempted to lean in and press against him completely.

"Come on then," he said, releasing his hold on the car and turning away.

The movement was abrupt. It made her wonder if he was struggling with indecision, too. Which didn't really make sense, since Jonathan was the most decisive man she had ever met. He seemed certain about everything, all the time, even if he was sure it was a bad decision.

That certainty was what she wanted. Yeah, she was certain this was a bad decision, too, but she was going for it, anyway.

She had walked into this house five days a week for the past couple weeks, yet this time was different. Because this time she wasn't headed to the office. This time she was going to his bedroom. And she wasn't his employee; he wasn't her boss. Not now.

Her stomach tightened, her blood heated at the idea of following orders. His orders. Lord knew she would need instruction. Direction. She had no idea what she was doing; she was just following her gut instinct.

When they reached the long hallway, they stopped at a different door than usual. His bedroom. She had never been inside Jonathan's bedroom. It was strange to be standing there now. So very deliberate.

It might have been easier if they had started kissing here in the house, and let things come to their natural conclusion… On the floor or something. She was reasonably sure people did it on the floor sometimes.

Yeah, that would have been easier. This was so *intentional*.

She was about to say something about the strangeness of it when he reached out, cupped her chin and tilted her face upward. Then he closed the distance between them, claiming her mouth.

She felt his possession, all the way down to her toes.

He didn't wait for her to part her lips this time. Instead, he invaded her, sliding his tongue forcibly against hers, his arms wrapped tight around her like steel bands. There was nothing gentle about this kiss. It was consuming, all-encompassing. And all her thoughts about the situation feeling premeditated dissolved.

This time, she didn't stand there as a passive participant. This time, she wrapped her arms around his neck—pressing her breasts flush against his chest, forking her fingers through his hair—and devoured him right back.

She couldn't believe this was her. Couldn't believe this was her life, that this man wanted her. That he was hard for her. That he thought she might be a mistake, and he was willing to make her, anyway. God knew, she was willing to make him.

Need grew inside her, prowling around like a restless thing. She rocked her hips forward, trying to tame the nameless ache between her thighs. Trying to calm the erratic, reckless feeling rioting through her.

He growled, sliding his hands down her back, over her bottom, down to her thighs. She squeaked as he gripped her tightly, pulling both her feet off the ground and picking her up, pressing that soft, tender place between her legs against his arousal.

"Wrap your legs around me," he said against her mouth, the command harsh, and sexier because of that.

She obeyed him, locking her ankles behind his back. He reversed their positions, pressing her against the wall and deepening his kiss. She gasped as he made even firmer contact with the place that was wet and aching for him.

He ground his hips against her, and her internal muscles pulsed. An arc of electricity lanced through her. She gripped his shoulders hard, vaguely aware that she might be digging her fingernails into his skin, not really sure that she cared. Maybe it would hurt him, but she wasn't exactly sure if he was hurting her or not. She was suspended between pleasure and pain, feelings so intense she could scarcely breathe.

And through all that, he continued to devour her mouth, the rhythm of his tongue against hers combining with the press of his firm length between her thighs, ensuring that her entire world narrowed down to him. Jonathan Bear was everything right now. He was her breath; he was sensation. He was heaven and he was hell.

She needed it to end. Needed to reach some kind of conclusion, where all this tension could be defused.

And yet she wanted it to go on forever.

Her face was hot, her limbs shaking. A strange, hollow feeling in the pit of her stomach made her want to cry. It was too much. And it was not enough. That sharp, insistent ache between her legs burrowed deeper with each passing second, letting her know this kiss simply wasn't enough at all.

She moved her hands up from his broad shoulders, sliding them as far as she could into his long, dark hair. Her fingers snagged on the band that kept his hair tied back and she internally cursed her clumsiness, hoping he wouldn't notice. She had enthusiasm guiding her through this, but that was about it. Enthusiasm and a healthy dose of adrenaline that bordered on terror. But she didn't want to stop. She couldn't stop.

Those big, rough hands gripped her hips and braced her as he rocked more firmly against her, and suddenly, stars exploded behind her eyes. She gasped, wrenching her lips away from his as something that felt like thunder rolled through her body, muscles she'd never been aware of before pulsing like waves against the shore.

She pressed her forehead against his shoulder, did her best to grit her teeth and keep herself from crying out, but a low, shaky sound escaped when the deepest wave washed over her.

Then it ended, and she felt even more connected to reality, to this moment, than she had a second ago. And she felt...so very aware that she was pressed against the wall and him, that something had just happened, that she hadn't been fully cognizant of her actions. She didn't know what she might have said.

That was when she realized she was digging her nails into his back, and she had probably punctured his skin. She started to move against him, trying to get away, and he gripped her chin again, steadying her. "Hey," he said, "you're not going anywhere."

"I need to... I have to..."

"You don't have to do anything, baby. Nothing at all. Just relax." She could tell he was placating her. She couldn't bring herself to care particularly, because she needed placating. Her heart was racing, her hands shaking, and that restlessness that had been so all-consuming earlier was growing again. She had thought the earthquake inside her had handled that.

That was when she realized exactly what that earthquake had been.

Her cheeks flamed, horror stealing through her. She'd had... Well, she'd had an orgasm. And he hadn't even touched her. Not with his hands. Not under her clothes.

"I'm sorry," she said, putting her hands up, patting his chest, then curling her hands into fists because she had patted him and that was really stupid. "I'm just sorry."

He frowned. "What are you sorry about?"

"I'm sorry because I—I... I did that. And we didn't..."

He raised one eyebrow. "Are you apologizing for your orgasm?"

She squeezed her eyes tightly shut. "Yes."

"Why?"

She tightened her fists even more, pressing them against her own chest, keeping her eyes closed. "Because we didn't even... You didn't... We're still dressed."

"Honey," he said, taking hold of her fists and drawing them toward him, pressing them against his chest. "You don't need to apologize to me for coming."

She opened one eye. "I... I don't?"

"No."

"But that..." She looked fully at him, too curious to be embarrassed now. "That ruins it, doesn't it? We didn't..."

"You can have as many orgasms as I can give you. That's the magical thing about women. There's no ceiling on that."

"There isn't?"

"You didn't know?"

"No."

"Hayley," he said, his tone grave, "I need to ask you a question."

Oh great. Now he was actually going to ask if she was a virgin. Granted, she thought he'd probably guessed, but apparently he needed to hear it. "Go ahead," she said, bracing herself for utter humiliation.

"Have you never had an orgasm before?"

"Yes," she said, answering the wrong question before he even got his out. "I mean... No. I mean, just a minute ago. I wasn't even sure what it was right when it was happening."

"That doesn't… Not even with yourself?"

Her face felt so hot she thought it might be on fire. She was pretty sure her heart was beating in her forehead. "No." She shook her head. "I can't talk to you about things like that."

"I just gave you your first orgasm, so you better be able to talk to me about things like that. Plus I'm aiming to give you another one before too long here."

"I bet you can't."

He chuckled, and then he bent down, sweeping her up into his arms. She squeaked, curling her fingers around his shirt. "You should know better than to issue challenges like that." He turned toward the bedroom door, kicking it open with his boot before walking inside and kicking it closed again. Then he carried her to the bed and threw her down in the center.

"Wait," she said, starting to feel panicky, her heart fluttering in her chest like a swarm of butterflies. "Just wait a second."

"I'm not going to fall on you like a ravenous beast," he said, his hands going to the top button of his shirt. "Yet." He started to undo the button slowly, revealing his tan, muscular chest.

She almost told him to stop, except he stripped the shirt off, and she got completely distracted by the play of all those muscles. The sharp hitch of his abs as he cast the flannel onto the floor, the shift and bunch of his pectoral muscles as he pushed his hand over his hair.

She had never seen a shirtless man that looked like him. Not in person, anyway. And most definitely not this close, looking at her like he had plans. Very, very dirty plans.

"I'm a virgin," she blurted out. "Just so you know."

His eyes glowed with black fire. For one heart-stopping moment she was afraid he might pick up his shirt and walk out of the room. His eyes looked pure black; his mouth pressed into a firm line. He stood frozen, hands on his belt buckle, every line in his cut torso still.

Then something in his expression shifted. Nearly imperceptible, and mostly unreadable, but she had seen it. Then his deft fingers went to work, moving his belt through the buckle. "I know," he said.

"Oh." She felt a little crestfallen. Like she must have made some novice mistake and given herself away.

"You're a church secretary who confessed to having never had an orgasm. I assumed." He lowered his voice. "If you hadn't told me outright, I could have had plausible deniability. Which I was sort of counting on."

She blinked. "Did you…need it?"

"My conscience is screwed, anyway. So not really."

She didn't know quite what to say, so she didn't say anything.

"Have you ever seen a naked man before?"

She shook her head. "No."

"Pictures?"

"Does medieval art count?"

"No, it does not."

"Then no," she said, shaking her head even more vigorously.

He rubbed his hand over his forehead, and she was sure she heard him swear beneath his breath. "Okay," he said, leaving his belt hanging open, but not going any further. He pressed his knee down on the mattress, kneeling beside her. Then he took her hand and placed it against his chest. "How's that?"

She drew shaking fingers across his chest slowly, relishing his heat, the satiny feel of his skin. "Good," she said. "You're very...hot. I mean, temperaturewise. Kind of smooth."

"You don't have to narrate," he said.

"Sorry," she said, drawing her hand back sharply.

"No," he said, pressing her palm back against his skin. "Don't apologize. Don't apologize for anything that happens between us tonight, got that?"

"Okay," she said, more than happy to agree, but not entirely sure if she could keep to the agreement. Because every time she moved her hand and his breath hissed through his teeth, she wanted to say she was sorry. Every time she took her exploration further, she wanted to apologize for the impulse to do it.

She bit her lip, letting her hands glide lower, over his stomach, which was as hard and rippled as corrugated steel. Then she found her hands at the waistband of his jeans, and she pulled back.

"Do you want me to take these off?" he asked.

"In a minute," she said, losing her nerve slightly. "Just a minute." She rose up on her knees, pressed her mouth to his and lost herself in kissing him. She really liked kissing. Loved the sounds he made, loved being enveloped in his arms, and she really loved it when he laid them both down, pressing her deep into the mattress and settling between her thighs.

Her dress rode up high, and she didn't care. She felt rough denim scraping her bare skin, felt the hard press of his zipper, and his arousal behind it through the thin fabric of her panties.

She lost herself in those sensations. In the easy, sensual contact that pushed her back to the brink again. She could see already that Jonathan was going to win the orgasm challenge. And she was okay with that.

Very, very okay with that.

Then he took her hem and pulled the cotton dress over her head, casting it onto the floor. Her skin heated all over, and she was sure she was pink from head to toe.

"Don't be embarrassed," he said, touching her collarbone, featherlight, then tracing a trail down to the curve of her breast, to the edge of her bra. "You're beautiful."

She didn't know quite how to feel about that. Didn't know what to do with that husky, earnest compliment. She wasn't embarrassed because she lacked beauty, but because she had always been taught to treasure modesty. To respect her body, to save it.

He *was* respecting it, though. And right now, she felt like she had been saving it for him.

He reached behind her, undoing her bra with one hand and flicking the fabric to the side.

"You're better at that than I am," she said, laughing nervously as he bared her breasts, her nipples tightening as the cold air hit her skin.

He smiled. "You'll appreciate that in a few minutes."

"What will I appreciate?" she asked, shivering. She crossed her arms over her chest.

"My skill level." Instead of moving her hands, he bent his head and nuzzled the tender spot right next to her hand, the full part of her breast that was still exposed. She gasped, tightening her hold on herself.

He was not deterred.

He nosed her gently and shifted her hand to the side, pressing a kiss to her skin, sending electric sensations firing through her. "Don't be shy," he said, "not with me."

She waited for a reason why. He didn't give one, but she found that the more persistent he was—the more hot, open-mouthed kisses he pressed to her skin—the less able she was to deny him anything. Anything at all. She found herself shifting her hands and then letting them fall away.

As soon as she did, he closed his lips over her nipple, sucking deep. She gasped, her hips rocking up off the bed. He wrapped his arm around her, holding her against his hardness as he teased her with his lips and tongue.

Every time she wiggled, either closer to him, or in a moment of self-consciousness, away, it only brought him more in contact with that aching place between her thighs, and then she would forget why she was moving at all. Why she wasn't just letting him take the lead.

So she relaxed into him, and let herself get lost. She was in a daze when he took her hand and pushed it down his stomach, to the front of his jeans. She gasped when his hard, denim-covered length filled her palm.

"Feel that? That's how much I want you. That's what you do to me."

A strange surge of power rocketed through her. That she could cause such a raw, sexual response... Well, it was intoxicating in a way she hadn't appreciated it could be.

Especially because he was such a man. A hot man. A sexy man, and she had never thought of anyone that way in her life. But he was. He most definitely was.

"Are you ready?" he asked.

She nodded, sliding her hand experimentally over

him. He moved, undoing his pants and shoving them quickly down, hardly giving her a chance to prepare. Her mouth dried when she saw him, all of him. She hadn't really... Well, she had been content to allow her fantasies to be somewhat hazy. Though reading that romance novel had made those fantasies a little sharper.

Still, she hadn't really imagined specifically how large a man might be. But suffice it to say, he was a bit larger than she had allowed for.

Her breath left her lungs in a rush. But along with the wave of nerves that washed over her came a sense of relief. "You are... I like the way you look," she said finally.

A crooked smile tipped his mouth upward. "Thank you."

"I told you, I've never seen a naked man before. I was a little afraid I wouldn't like it."

"Well, I'm glad you do. Because let me tell you, that's a lot of pressure. Being the first naked man you've ever seen." His eyes darkened and his voice got lower, huskier. "Being the first naked man you've ever touched." He took her hand again and placed it around his bare shaft, the skin there hotter and much softer than she had imagined. She slid her thumb up and down, marveling at the feel of him.

"You're the first man I've ever kissed," she said, the words slurred, because she had lost the full connection between her brain and her mouth. All her blood had flowed to her extremities.

He swore, and then crushed her to him, kissing her deeply and driving her back down to the mattress. His erection pressed into her stomach, his tongue slick against hers, his lips insistent. She barely noticed when he divested her of her underwear, until he placed his hand between her legs. The rough pads of his fingers sliding through her slick flesh, the white-hot pleasure his touch left behind, made her gasp.

"I'm going to make sure you're ready," he said.

She had no idea what that meant. But he started doing wicked, magical things with his fingers, so she didn't much care. Then he slid one finger deep inside her and she arched away, not sure whether she wanted more of that completely unfamiliar sensation, or if she needed to escape it.

"It's okay," he said, moving his thumb in a circle over a sensitive bundle of nerves as he continued to slide his finger in and out of her body.

After a few passes of his thumb, she agreed.

He shifted his position, adding a second finger, making her gasp. It burned slightly, made her feel like she was being stretched, but after a moment, she adjusted to that, too.

That lovely, spiraling tension built inside her again, and she knew she was close to the edge. But every time he took her to the brink, he would drop back again.

"Please," she whispered.

"Please what?" he asked, being dastardly, asking her to clarify, when he knew saying the words would embarrass her.

"You know," she said, placing her hand over his, like she might take control, increase the pressure, increase the pace, since he refused.

But, of course, he was too strong for her to guide him at all. "I need to hear it."

"I need… I need to have an orgasm," she said quickly.

For a moment, he stopped. He looked at her like she

mystified him. Like he had never seen anything like her before. Then he withdrew his hand and slid down her body, gripping her hips roughly before drawing her quickly against his mouth.

She squeaked when his lips and tongue touched her right in her most intimate place. She reached down, grabbing hold of his hair, because she was going to pull him away, but then his tongue touched her in the most amazing spot and she found herself lacing her fingers through his hair instead.

She found herself holding him against her instead of pushing him away.

She moved her hips in time with him, gasping for air as pleasure, arousal, built to impossible heights. She had been on the edge for so long now it felt like she was poised on the brink of something else entirely. But right when she was about to break, he moved away from her, drawing himself up her body. He grabbed a small, round packet from the bedspread that she hadn't noticed until now, and tore it open, quickly sheathing himself before moving to position the blunt head of his arousal at her entrance.

He flexed his hips, thrusting deep inside her, and her arousal broke like a mirror hit with a hammer. She gritted her teeth as pain—sharp and jagged—cut through all the hidden places within her. But along with the pain came the intense sensation of being full. Of being connected to another person like she never had been before.

She reached up, taking his heavily muscled arms and holding him, just holding him, as he moved slowly inside her.

He was *inside* her.

She marveled at that truth even as the pain eased, even as pleasure began to push its way into the foreground again.

"Move with me," he said, nuzzling her neck, kissing the tender skin there.

So she did, meeting his every thrust, clinging to him. She could see the effort it took for him to maintain control, and she could see when his control began to fray. When his thrusts became erratic, his golden skin slick with sweat, his breathing rough and ragged, matching her own.

When he thrust deep, she arched her hips, an electric shower of sparks shimmering through her each time.

His hands were braced on either side of her shoulders, his strong fingers gripping the sheets. His movements became hard, rough, but none of the earlier pain remained, and she welcomed him. Opened her thighs wider and then wrapped her legs around his lean hips so she could take him even deeper.

There was no pain. There was no shame. There was no doubt at all.

As far as she was concerned, there was only the two of them.

He leaned down, pressing his forehead against hers, his dark gaze intense as his rhythm increased. He went shallow, then deep, the change pushing her even closer to the edge.

Then he pulled out almost completely, his hips pulsing slightly. The denial of that deep, intimate contact made her feel frantic. Made her feel needy. Made her feel desperate.

"Jonathan," she said. "Jonathan, please."

"Tell me you want to come," he told her, the words a growl.

"I want to come," she said, not wasting a moment on self-consciousness.

He slammed back home, and she saw stars. This orgasm grabbed her deep, reached places she hadn't known were there. The pleasure seemed to go on and on, and when it was done, she felt like she was floating on a sea, gazing up at a sky full of infinite stars.

She felt adrift, but only for a moment. Because when she came back to herself, she was still clutching his strong arms, Jonathan Bear rooting her to the earth.

And then she waited.

Waited for regret. Waited for guilt.

But she didn't feel any of it. Right now, she just felt a bone-deep satisfaction she hoped never went away.

"I..." He started to say something, moving away from her. Then he frowned. "You don't have a toothbrush or anything, do you?"

It was such a strange question that it threw her for a loop. "What?"

"It doesn't matter," he said. He bent down, pressing a kiss to her forehead. "We'll work something out in the morning."

She was glad he'd said there was nothing to worry about, because her head was starting to get fuzzy and her eyelids were heavy. Which sucked, because she didn't want to sleep. She wanted to bask in her newfound warm and fuzzy feelings.

But she was far too sleepy, far too sated to do anything but allow herself to be enveloped by that warmth. By him.

He drew her into his arms, and she snuggled into his chest, pressing her palm against him. She could feel his heartbeat, hard and steady, beneath her hand.

And then, for the first time in her life, Hayley Thompson fell asleep in a man's arms.

Eight

Jonathan didn't sleep. As soon as Hayley drifted off, he went into his office, busying himself with work that didn't need to be done.

Women didn't spend the night at his house. He had never even brought a woman back to this house. But when Hayley had looked up at him like that... He hadn't been able to tell her to leave. He realized that she expected to stay. Because as far as she was concerned, sex included sleeping with somebody.

He had no idea where she had formed her ideas about relationships, but they were innocent. And he was a bastard. He had already known that, but tonight just confirmed it.

Except he had let her stay.

He couldn't decide if that was a good thing or not. Couldn't decide if letting her stay had been a kindness or a cruelty. Because the one thing it hadn't been was the reality of the situation.

The reality was this wasn't a relationship. The reality was, it had been... Well, a very bad idea.

He stood up from his desk, rubbing the back of his neck. It was getting light outside, pale edges beginning to bleed from the mountaintops, encroaching on the velvet middle of the sky.

He might as well go outside and get busy on morning chores. And if some of those chores were in the name of avoiding Hayley, then so be it.

He made his way downstairs, shoved his feet into his boots and grabbed his hat, walking outside with heavy footsteps.

He paused, inhaling deeply, taking a moment to let the scent of the pines wash through him. This was his. All of it was his. He didn't think that revelation would ever get old.

He remembered well the way it had smelled on his front porch in the trailer park. Cigarette smoke and exhaust from cars as people got ready to leave for work. The noise of talking, families shouting at each other. It didn't matter if you were inside the house or outside. You lived way too close to your neighbors to avoid them.

He had fantasized about a place like this back then. Isolated. His. Where he wouldn't have to see another person unless he went out of his way to do so. He shook his head. And he had gone and invited Hayley to stay the night. He was a dumb ass.

He needed a ride to clear his head. The fact that he got to take weekends off now was one of his favorite things about his new position in life. He was a workaholic, and he had never minded that. But ranching was the kind of work he really enjoyed, and that was what he preferred to do with his free time.

He saddled his horse and mounted up, urging the bay gelding toward the biggest pasture. They started out at a slow walk, then Jonathan increased the pace until he and his horse were flying over the grass, patches of flowers blurring on either side of them, blending with the rich green.

It didn't matter what mess he had left behind at the house. Didn't matter what mistakes he had made last night. It never did, not when he was on a horse. Not when he was in his sanctuary. The house... Well, he would be lying if he said that big custom house hadn't been a goal for him. Of course it had been. It was evidence that he had made it.

But this... The trees, the mountains, the wind in his face, being able to ride his horse until his lungs burned, and not reach the end of his property... That was the real achievement. It belonged to him and no one else. In this place he didn't have to answer to anyone.

Out here it didn't matter if he was bad. You couldn't let the sky down. You couldn't disappoint the mountains.

He leaned forward to go uphill, tightening his hold on the reins as the animal changed its gait. He pulled back, easing to a stop. He looked down the mountain, at the valley of trees spread out before him, an evergreen patchwork stitched together by rock and river. And beyond that, the ocean, brighter blue than usual on this exceptionally clear morning, the waves capped with a rosy pink handed down from the still-rising sun.

Hayley would love this.

That thought brought him up short, because he wasn't exactly sure why he thought she would. Or why he cared. Why he suddenly wanted to show her. He had never shown this view to anybody. Not even to his sister, Rebecca.

He had wanted to keep it for himself, because growing up, he'd had very little that belonged to him and him alone. In fact, up here, gazing at everything that belonged to him now, he couldn't think of a single damn thing that had truly belonged to him when he'd been younger.

It had all been for a landlord, for his sister, for the future.

This was what he had worked for his entire life.

He didn't need to show it to some woman he'd slept with last night.

He shook his head, turning the horse around and trotting down the hill, moving to a gallop back down to the barn.

When he exited the gate that would take him out of the pasture and back to the paddock, Jonathan saw Hayley standing in the path. Wearing last night's dress, her hair disheveled, she was holding two mugs of coffee.

He was tempted to imagine he had conjured her up just by thinking of her up on the ridge. But if it were a fantasy, she would have been wearing nothing, rather than being back in that black cotton contraption.

She was here, and it disturbed him just how happy that made him.

"I thought I might find you out here," she said. "And I figured you would probably want your coffee."

He dismounted, taking the reins and walking the

horse toward Hayley. "It's your day off. You don't have to make me coffee."

Her cheeks turned pink, and he marveled at the blush. And on the heels of that marveling came the sharp bite of guilt. She was a woman who blushed routinely. And he had... Well, he had started down the path of corrupting her last night.

He had taken her virginity. Before her he'd never slept with a virgin in his damn life. In high school, that hadn't been so much out of a sense of honor as it had been out of a desire not to face down an angry dad with a shotgun. Better to associate with girls who had reputations worse than his own.

All that restraint had culminated in him screwing the pastor's daughter.

At least when people came with torches and pitchforks, he would have a decent-sized fortress to hole up in.

"I just thought maybe it would be nice," she said finally, taking a step toward him and extending the coffee mug in his direction.

"It is," he said, taking the cup, knowing he didn't sound quite as grateful as he might have. "Sorry," he conceded, sipping the strong brew, which was exactly the way he liked it. "I'm not used to people being nice. I'm never quite sure what to make of it when you are."

"Just take it at face value," she said, lifting her shoulder.

"Yeah, I don't do that."

"Why not?" she asked.

"I have to take care of the horse," he said. "If you want story time, you're going to have to follow me."

He thought his gruff demeanor might scare her off,

but instead, she followed him along the fence line. He tethered his horse and set his mug on the fence post, then grabbed the pick and started on the gelding's hooves.

Hayley stepped up carefully on the bottom rung of the fence, settling herself on the top rung, clutching her mug and looking at him with an intensity he could feel even with his focus on the task at hand.

"I'm ready," she said.

He looked up at her, perched there like an inquisitive owl, her lips at the edge of her cup, her blue eyes round. She was…a study in contradictions. Innocent as hell. Soft in some ways, but determined in others.

It was her innocence that allowed her to be so open— that was his conclusion. The fact that she'd never really been hurt before made it easy for her to come at people from the front.

"It's not a happy story," he warned.

It wasn't a secret one, either. Pretty much everybody knew his tragic backstory. He didn't go around talking about it, but there was no reason not to give her what she was asking for.

Except for the fact that he never talked to the women he hooked up with. There was just no point to it.

But then, the women he usually hooked up with never stumbled out of his house early in the morning with cups of coffee. So he supposed it was an unusual situation all around.

"I'm a big girl," she said, her tone comically serious. It was followed by a small slurp as she took another sip of coffee. The sound should not have been cute, but it was.

"Right." He looked up at her, started to speak and then stopped.

Would hearing about his past, about his childhood, change something in her? Just by talking to her he might ruin some of her optimism.

It was too late for worrying about that, he supposed. Since sleeping with her when she'd never even kissed anyone before had undoubtedly changed her.

There had been a lot of points in his life when he had not been his own favorite person. The feeling was intense right now. He was a damned bastard.

"I'm waiting," she said, kicking her foot slightly to signify her impatience.

"My father left when I was five," he said.

"Oh," she said, blinking, clearly shocked. "I'm sorry."

"It was the best thing that had happened to me in all five years of my life, Hayley. The very best thing. He was a violent bastard. He hit my mother. He hit me. The day he left... I was a kid, but I knew even then that life was going to be better. I was right. When I was seven, my mom had another kid. And she was the best thing. So cute. Tiny and loud as hell, but my mother wasn't all that interested in me, and my new sister was. Plus she gave me, I don't know...a feeling of importance. I had someone to look after, and that mattered. Made me feel like maybe I mattered."

"Rebecca," Hayley said.

"Yeah," he replied. "Then, when Rebecca was a teenager, she was badly injured in a car accident. Needed a lot of surgeries, skin grafts. All of it was paid for by the family responsible for the accident, in exchange for keeping everything quiet. Of course, it's kind of an open secret now that Gage West was the one who caused the accident."

Hayley blinked. "Gage. Isn't she... Aren't they... Engaged?"

Familiar irritation surged through him. "For now. We'll see how long that lasts. I don't have a very high opinion of that family."

"Well, you know my brother is married into that family."

He shrugged. "All right, maybe I'll rephrase that. I don't have anything against Colton, or Sierra, or Maddy. But I don't trust Gage or his father one bit. I certainly don't trust him with my sister, any more now than I did then. But if things fall apart, if he ends up breaking off the engagement, or leaves her ten years into the marriage... I'll have a place for her. I've always got a place for her."

Hayley frowned. "That's a very cynical take. If Rebecca can love the man who caused her accident, there must be something pretty exceptional about him."

"More likely, my sister doesn't really know what love looks like," he said, his voice hard, the words giving voice to the thing he feared most. "I have to backtrack a little. A few months after the accident, my mom took the cash payout Nathan West gave her and took off. Left me with Rebecca. Left Rebecca without a mother, when she needed her mother the most. My mom just couldn't handle it. So I had to. And I was a piss-poor replacement for parents. An older brother with a crappy construction job and not a lot of patience." He shook his head. "Every damn person in my life who was supposed to be there for me bailed. Everyone who was supposed to be there for Rebecca."

"And now you're mad at her, too. For not doing what you thought she should."

Guilt stabbed him right in the chest. Yeah, he was angry at his sister. And he felt like he had no damn right to be angry. Shouldn't she be allowed to be happy? Hadn't that been the entire point of taking care of her for all those years? So she could get out from under the cloud of their family?

So she'd done it. In a huge, spectacular way. She'd ended up with the man she'd been bitter about for years. She had let go of the past. She had embraced it, and in a pretty damned literal way.

But Jonathan couldn't. He didn't trust in sudden changes of heart or professions of love. He didn't trust much of anything.

"I'll be mad if she gets hurt," he said finally. "But that's my default. I assume it's going to end badly because I've only ever seen these things end badly. I worked my ass off to keep the two of us off the streets. To make sure we had a roof over our heads, as much food in our stomachs as I could manage. I protected her." He shook his head. "And there's no protecting somebody if you aren't always looking out for what might go wrong. For what might hurt them."

"I guess I can't blame you for not trusting the good in people. You haven't seen it very many times."

He snorted. "Understatement of the century." He straightened, undoing the girth and taking the saddle off the bay in a fluid movement, then draping it over the fence. "But my cynicism has served me just fine. Look at where I am now. I started out in a single-wide trailer, and I spent years working just to keep that much. I didn't advance to this place by letting down my guard, by stopping for even one minute." He shook his head again. "I probably owe my father a thank-you note. My mother, too, come to that. They taught me that I couldn't trust anyone but myself. And so far that lesson's served me pretty well."

Hayley was looking at him like she was sad for him, and he wanted to tell her to stop it. Contempt, disgust and distrust were what he was used to getting from people. And he had come to revel in that reaction, to draw strength from it.

Pity had been in short supply. And if it was ever tossed in his general direction, it was mostly directed at Rebecca. He wasn't comfortable receiving it himself.

"Don't look at me like I'm a sad puppy," he said.

"I'm not," she returned.

He untied the horse and began to walk back into the barn. "You are. I didn't ask for your pity." He unhooked the lead rope and urged the gelding into his stall. "Don't go feeling things for me, Hayley. I don't deserve it. In fact, what you should have done this morning was walked out and slapped me in the face, not given me a cup of coffee."

"Why?"

"Because I took advantage of you last night. And you should be upset about that."

She frowned. "I should be?" She blinked. "I'm not. I thought about it. And I'm not."

"I don't know what you're imagining this is. I don't know what you think might happen next…"

She jumped down from the fence and set her coffee cup on the ground. Then she took one quick step forward. She hooked an arm around his neck and pushed herself onto her tiptoes, pressing her lips to his.

He was too stunned to react. But only for a moment. He wrapped an arm around her waist, pressing his forefinger beneath her chin and urging the kiss deeper.

She didn't have a lot of skill. That had been apparent the first and second times they'd kissed. And when they had come together last night. But he didn't need skill, he just needed her.

Even though it was wrong, he consumed her, sated his hunger on her mouth.

She whimpered, a sweet little sound that only fueled the driving hunger roaring in his gut. He grabbed her hair, tilting her head back farther, abandoning her mouth to scrape his teeth over her chin and down her neck, where he kissed her again, deep and hard.

He couldn't remember ever feeling like this before. Couldn't remember ever wanting a woman so much it was beyond the need for air. Sure, he liked sex. He was a man, after all. But the need had never been this specific. Had never been for one woman in particular.

But what he was feeling wasn't about sex, or about lust or desire. It was about her. About Hayley. The sweet little sounds she made when he kissed the tender skin on her neck, when he licked his way back up to her lips. The way she trembled with her need for him. The way she had felt last night, soft and slick and made only for him.

This was beyond anything he had ever experienced before. And he was a man who had experienced a hell of a lot.

That's what it was, he thought dimly as he scraped his teeth along her lower lip. And that said awful things about him, but then so did a lot of choices in his life.

He had conducted business with hard, ruthless precision, and he had kept his personal life free of any kind of connection beyond Rebecca—who he was loyal to above anyone else.

So maybe that was the problem. Now that he'd arrived at this place in life, he was collecting those things he had always denied himself. The comfortable home, the expansive mountains and a sweet woman.

Maybe this was some kind of latent urge. He had the homestead, now he wanted to put a woman in it.

He shook off that thought and all the rest. He didn't want to think right now. He just wanted to feel. Wanted to embrace the heat firing through his veins, the need stoking the flame low in his gut, which burned even more with each pass of her tongue against his.

She pulled away from him, breathing hard, her pupils dilated, her lips swollen and rounded into a perfect O. "That," she said, breathlessly, "was what I was thinking might happen next. And that we might… Take me back to bed, please."

"I can't think of a single reason to refuse," he said—a lie, as a litany of reasons cycled through his mind.

But he wasn't going to listen to them. He was going to take her, for as long as she was on offer. And when it ended, he could only hope he hadn't damaged her too much. Could only hope he hadn't broken her beyond repair.

Because there were a couple things he knew for sure. It would end; everything always did. And he would be the one who destroyed it.

He just hoped he didn't destroy her, too.

Nine

It was late in the afternoon when Hayley and Jonathan finally got back out of bed. Hayley felt… Well, she didn't know quite what she felt. Good. Satisfied. Jonathan was… Well, if she'd ever had insecurities about whether or not she might be desirable to a man, he had done away with those completely. He had also taught her things about herself—about pleasure, about her own body—that she'd never in her wildest dreams conceived of.

She didn't know what would happen next, though. She had fallen asleep after their last time together, and when she'd awoken he was gone again. This morning, she had looked for him. She wasn't sure if she should do that twice.

Still, before she could even allow herself to ponder making the decision, she got out of bed, grabbed his T-shirt from the floor and pulled it over her head.

Then she padded down the hallway, hoping he didn't have any surprise visitors. That would be a nightmare. Getting caught wearing only a T-shirt in her boss's hallway. There would be a lot of questions about what they had just spent the last few hours doing, that was for sure.

She wondered if Jonathan might be outside again, but she decided to check his office first. And was rewarded when she saw him sitting at the computer, his head lowered over the keyboard, some of his dark hair falling over his face after coming loose from the braid he normally kept it in.

Her heart clenched painfully, and it disturbed her that her heart was the first part of her body to tighten. The rest of her followed shortly thereafter, but she really wished her reaction was more about her body than her feelings. She couldn't afford to have feelings for him. She wasn't staying in Copper Ridge. And even if she were, he wouldn't want her long-term, anyway.

She took a deep breath, trying to dispel the strange, constricted feeling that had overtaken her lungs. "I thought I might find you here," she said.

He looked up, his expression betraying absolutely no surprise. He sneaked up on her all the time, but of course, as always, Jonathan was unflappable. "I just had a few schematics to check over." He pushed the chair away from the desk and stood, reaching over his head to stretch.

She was held captive by the sight of him. Even fully dressed, he was a beautiful thing.

His shoulders and chest were broad and muscular, his waist trim. His face like sculpted rock, or hardened bronze, uncompromising. But she knew the secret way to make those lips soften. Only for her.

No, not only for you. He does this all the time. They are just softening for you right now.

It was good for her to remember that.

"I'm finished now," he said, treating her to a smile that made her feel like melting ice cream on a hot day.

"Good," she said, not quite sure why she said it, because it wasn't like they had made plans. She wondered when he would ask her to leave. Or maybe he wanted her to leave, but didn't want to tell her. "It's late," she said. "I could go."

"Do you need to go?"

"No," she said, a little too quickly.

"Then don't."

Relief washed over her, and she did her best not to show him just how pleased she was by that statement. "Okay," she said, "then I won't go."

"I was thinking. About your list."

She blinked. "My list?"

"Yeah, your list. You had dancing on there. Pretty sure you had a kiss. And whether or not it was on the list…you did lose your virginity. Since I helped you with those items, I figured I might help you with some of the others."

A deep sense of pleasure and something that felt a lot like delight washed through her. "Really?"

"Yes," he said, "really. I figure we started all of this, so we might as well keep going."

"I don't have an official list."

"Well, that's ridiculous. If you're going to do this thing, you have to do it right." He grabbed a sheet of paper out of the printer and settled back down in the office chair. "Let's make a list."

He picked up a pen and started writing.

"What are you doing? I didn't tell you what I wanted yet."

"I'm writing down what we already did so you have the satisfaction of checking those off."

Her stomach turned over. "Don't write down all of it."

"Oh," he said, "I am. All of it. In detail."

"No!" She crossed the space between them and stood behind him, wrapping her arms around his broad shoulders as if she might restrain him. He kept on writing. She peered around his head, then slapped the pen out of his hand when she saw him writing a very dirty word. "Stop it. If anybody finds that list I could be… incriminated."

He laughed and swiveled the chair to the side. He wrapped his arm around her waist and pulled her onto his lap. "Oh no. We would hate for you to be incriminated. But on the other hand, the world would know you spent the afternoon with a very firm grip on my—"

"No!"

He looked at her and defiantly put a checkmark by what he had just written. She huffed, but settled into his hold. She liked this too much. Him smiling, him holding her when they had clothes on as if he just wanted to hold her.

It was nice to have him want her in bed. Very nice. But this was something else, and it was nice, too.

"Okay, so we have dancing, kissing, sex, and all of the many achievements beneath the sex," he said, ignoring her small noises of protest. "So what else?"

"I want to go to a place where I need a passport," she said.

"We could drive to Canada."

She laughed. "I was thinking more like Europe. But... Could we really drive to Canada?"

"Well," he said, "maybe not today, since I have to be back here by Monday."

"That's fine. I was thinking more Paris than Vancouver."

"Hey, they speak French in Canada."

"Just write it down," she said, poking his shoulder.

"Fine. What next?"

"I feel like I should try alcohol," she said slowly. "Just so I know."

"Fair enough." He wrote *get hammered*.

"That is not what I said."

"Sorry. I got so excited about the idea of getting you drunk. Lowering your inhibitions."

She rolled her eyes. "I'm already more uninhibited with you than I've ever been with anyone else." It was true, she realized, as soon as she said it. She was more herself with Jonathan than she had ever been with anyone, including her family, who had known her for her entire life.

Maybe it was the fact that, in a town full of people who were familiar with her, at least by reputation, he was someone she hadn't known at all until a couple weeks ago.

Maybe it was the fact that he had no expectations of her beyond what they'd shared. Whatever the case, around him she felt none of the pressure that she felt around other people in the community.

No need to censor herself, or hide; no need to be respectable or serene when she felt like being disreputable and wild.

"I want to kiss in the rain," she said.

"Given weather patterns," he said slowly, "we should be able to accomplish that, too."

She was ridiculously pleased he wanted to be a part of that, pleased that he hadn't said anything about her finding a guy to kiss in the rain in Paris. She shouldn't be happy he was assuming he would be the person to help her fulfill these things. She should be annoyed. She should feel like he was inserting himself into her independence, but she didn't. Mostly because he made her independence seem…well, like *more*.

"You're very useful, aren't you?"

He looked at her, putting his hand on her cheek, his dark gaze serious as it met hers. "I'm glad I can be useful to you."

She felt him getting hard beneath her backside, and that pleased her, too. "Parts of you are very useful," she said, reaching behind her and slowly stroking his length.

The light in his eyes changed, turning much more intense. "Hayley Thompson," he said, "I would say that's shocking behavior."

"I would say you're responsible, Jonathan Bear."

He shook his head. "No, princess, you're responsible for this. For all of this. This is you. It's what you want, right? The things on your list that you don't even want to write down. It's part of you. You don't get to blame it all on me."

She felt strangely empowered by his words. By the idea that this was her, and not just him leading her somewhere.

"That's very… Well, that's very… I like it." She furthered her exploration of him, increasing the pressure of her touch. "At least, I like it with you."

"I'm not complaining."

"That's good," she said softly, continuing to stroke him through the fabric of his pants.

She looked down, watched herself touching him. It was...well, now that she had started, she didn't want to stop.

"I would be careful if I were you," he said, his tone laced with warning, "because you're about to start something, and it's very likely you need to take a break from all that."

"Do I? Why would I need a break?"

"Because you're going to get sore," he said, maddeningly pragmatic.

And, just as maddeningly, it made her blush to hear him say it. "I don't really mind," she said finally.

"You don't?" His tone was calm, but heat flared in the depths of his dark eyes.

"No," she replied, still trailing her fingertips over his hardening body. "I like feeling the difference. In me. I like being so...aware of everything we've done." For her, that was a pretty brazen proclamation, though she had a feeling it paled in comparison to the kinds of things other women had said to him in the past.

But she wasn't one of those other women. And right now he was responding to her, so she wasn't going to waste a single thought on anyone who had come before her. She held his interest now. That was enough.

"There's something else on my list," she said, fighting to keep her voice steady, fighting against the nerves firing through her.

"Is that so?"

She sucked in a sharp breath. "Yes. I want to… That is… What you did for me… A couple of times now… I want to… I want to…" She gave up trying to get the words out. She wasn't sure she had the right words for what she wanted to do, anyway, and she didn't want to humiliate herself by saying something wrong.

So, with unsteady hands, she undid the closure on his jeans and lowered the zipper. She looked up at him. If she expected to get any guidance, she was out of luck. He just stared at her, his dark eyes unfathomable, his jaw tight, a muscle in his cheek ticking.

She shifted on his lap, sliding gracefully to the floor in front of the chair. Then she went to her knees and turned to face him, flicking her hair out of her face.

He still said nothing, watching her closely, unnervingly so. But she wasn't going to turn back now. She lifted the waistband of his underwear, pulling it out in order to clear his impressive erection, then she pulled the fabric partway down his hips, as far as she could go with him sitting.

He was beautiful.

That feeling of intimidation she'd felt the first time she'd seen him had faded completely. Now she knew what he could do, and she appreciated it greatly. He had shown her so many things; he'd made her pleasure the number one priority. And she wanted to give to him in return.

Well, she also knew this would be for her, too.

She slid her hands up his thighs, then curled her fingers around his hardened length, squeezing him firmly. She was learning that he wasn't breakable there. That he liked a little bit of pressure.

"Hayley," he said, his voice rough, "I don't think you know what you're doing."

"No," she said, "I probably don't. But I know what I want. And it's been so much fun having what I want." She rose up slightly, then leaned in, pressing her lips to the head of his shaft. He jerked beneath her touch, and she took that as approval.

A couple hours ago she would have been afraid that she'd hurt him. But male pleasure, she was discovering, sometimes looked a little like pain. Heck, female pleasure was a little like pain. Sex was somewhere between. The aching need to have it all and the intense rush of satisfaction that followed.

She shivered just thinking about it.

And then she flicked her tongue out, slowly testing this new territory. She hummed, a low sound in the back of her throat, as she explored the taste of him, the texture. Jonathan Bear was her favorite indulgence, she was coming to realize. There was nothing about him she didn't like. Nothing he had done to her she didn't love. She liked the way he felt, and apparently she liked the way he tasted, too.

She parted her lips slowly, worked them over the head, then swallowed down as much of him as she could. The accompanying sound he made hollowed out her stomach, made her feel weak and powerful at the same time.

His body was such an amazing thing. So strong, like it had been carved straight from the mountain. Yet it wasn't in any way cold or unmovable; it was hot. His body had changed hers. Yes, he'd taken her virginity, but he had also taught her to feel pleasure she hadn't realized she had the capacity to feel.

Such power in his body, and yet, right now, it trembled beneath her touch. The whisper-soft touch of her lips possessed the power to rock him, to make him shake. To make him shatter.

Right now, desire was enough. She didn't need skill. She didn't need experience. And she felt completely confident in that.

She slipped her tongue over his length as she took him in deep, and he bucked his hips lightly, touching the back of her throat. Her throat contracted and he jerked back.

"Sorry," he said, his voice strained.

"No," she said, gripping him with one hand and bringing her lips back against him. "Don't apologize. I like it."

"You're inexperienced."

She nodded slowly, then traced him with the tip of her tongue. "Yes," she agreed, "I am. I've never done this for any other man. I've never even thought about it before." His hips jerked again, and she realized he liked this. That he—however much he tried to pretend he didn't—liked that her desire was all for him.

"I think you might be corrupting me," she said, keeping her eyes wide as she took him back into her mouth.

He grunted, fisting his hands in her hair, but he didn't pull her away again.

The muscles in his thighs twitched beneath her fingertips, and he seemed to grow larger, harder in her mouth. She increased the suction, increased the friction, used her hands as well as her mouth to drive him as crazy as she possibly could.

There was no plan. There was no skill. There was

just the need to make him even half as mindless as he'd made her over the past couple days.

He had changed her. He had taken her from innocence...to this. She would be marked by him forever. He would always be her first. But society didn't have a term for a person's experience after virginity. So she didn't have a label for the impact she wanted to make on him.

Jonathan hadn't been a virgin for a very long time, she suspected. And she probably wasn't particularly special as a sexual partner.

So she had to try to make herself special.

She had no tricks to make this the best experience he'd ever had. She had only herself. And so she gave it to him. All of her. Everything.

"Hayley," he said, his voice rough, ragged. "You better stop."

She didn't. She ignored him. She had a feeling he was close; she recognized the signs now. She had watched him reach the point of pleasure enough times that she had a fair idea of what it looked like. Of what it felt like. His whole body tensing, his movements becoming less controlled.

She squeezed the base of him tightly, pulling him in deeper, and then he shattered. And she swallowed down every last shudder of need that racked his big body.

In the aftermath, she was dazed, her heart pounding hard, her entire body buzzing. She looked up at him from her position on the floor, and he looked down at her, his dark eyes blazing with...anger, maybe? Passion? A kind of sharp, raw need she hadn't ever seen before.

"You're going to pay for that," he said.

"Oh," she returned, "I hope so."

He swept her up, crushed her against his chest. "You have to put it on my list first," she said.

Then he brought his mouth down to hers, and whatever she'd intended to write down was forgotten until morning.

Ten

Sometime on Sunday afternoon Hayley had gone home. Because, she had insisted, she wasn't able to work in either his T-shirt or the dress she had worn to the bar on Friday.

He hadn't agreed, but he had been relieved to have the reprieve. He didn't feel comfortable sharing the bed with her while he slept. Which had meant sleeping on the couch in the office after she drifted off.

He just… He didn't sleep with women. He didn't see the point in inviting that kind of intimacy. Having her spend the night in his bed was bad enough. But he hadn't wanted to send her home, either. He didn't want to think about why. Maybe it was because she expected to stay, because of her general inexperience.

Which made him think of the moment she had taken him into her mouth, letting him know he was the first man she had ever considered doing that for. Just the thought of it made his eyes roll back in his head.

Now, it was late Monday afternoon and she had been slowly driving him crazy with the prim little outfit she had come back to work in, as though he didn't know what she looked like underneath it.

Who knew he'd like a good girl who gave head like a dream.

She had also insisted that they stay professional during work hours, and it was making it hard for him to concentrate. Of course, it was always hard for him to concentrate on office work. In general, he hated it.

Though bringing Hayley into the office certainly made it easier to bear.

Except for the part where it was torture.

He stood up from his chair and stretched slowly, trying to work the tension out of his body. But he had a feeling that until he was buried inside Hayley's body again, tension was just going to be the state of things.

"Oh," Hayley said, "Joshua Grayson just emailed and said he needs you to go by the county office and sign a form. And no, it can't be faxed."

For the first time in his life, Johathan was relieved to encounter bureaucracy. He needed to get out of this space. He needed to get his head on straight.

"Great," he said.

"Maybe I should go with you," she said. "I've never been down to the building and planning office, and you might need me to run errands in the future."

He gritted his teeth. "Yeah, probably."

"I'll drive my own car." She stood, grabbing her purse off the desk. "Because by the time we're done it will be time for me to get off."

He ground his teeth together even harder, because he couldn't ignore her double entendre even though he knew it had been accidental. And because, in addition to the double meaning, it was clear she intended to stay in town tonight and not at his place.

He should probably be grateful she wasn't being clingy. He didn't like to encourage women to get too attached to him, not at all.

"Great idea," he said.

But he didn't think it was a great idea, and he grumbled the entire way to town in the solitude of his pickup truck, not missing the irony that he had been wanting alone time, and was now getting it, and was upset about it.

The errand really did take only a few minutes, and afterward it still wasn't quite time for Hayley to clock out.

"Do you want to grab something to eat?" he asked, though he had no earthly idea why. He should get something for himself and go home, deal with that tension he had been pondering earlier.

She looked back and forth, clearly edgy. "In town?"

"Yes," he returned, "in town."

"Oh. I don't... I guess so."

"Calm down," he said. "I'm not asking you to Beaches. Let's just stop by the Crab Shanty."

She looked visibly relieved, and again he couldn't quantify why that annoyed him.

He knew they shouldn't be seen together in town. He had a feeling she also liked the casual nature of the restaurant. It was much more likely to look like a boss and employee grabbing something to eat than it was to look like a date.

They walked from where they had parked a few streets over, and paused at the crosswalk. They waited for one car to crawl by, clearly not interested in heeding the law that said pedestrians had the right-of-way. Then Jonathan charged ahead of her across the street and up to the faded yellow building. A small line was already forming outside the order window, and he noticed that Hayley took pains to stand slightly behind him.

When it was their turn to order, he decided he wasn't having any of her missish circumspection. They shouldn't be seen together as anything more than a boss and an assistant.

But right now, hell if he cared. "Two orders of fish and chips, the halibut. Two beers and a Diet Coke."

He pulled his wallet out and paid before Hayley could protest, then he grabbed the plastic number from the window, and the two of them walked over to a picnic table positioned outside the ramshackle building. There was no indoor seating, which could be a little bracing on windy days, and there weren't very many days that didn't have wind on the Oregon coast.

Jonathan set the number on the wooden table, then sat down heavily, looking up at the blue-and-white-striped umbrella wiggling in the breeze.

"Two beers?"

"One of them is for you," he said, his words verging on a growl.

"I'm not going to drink a beer." She looked sideways. "At least not here."

"Yeah, right out here on Main Street in front of God and everybody? You're a lot braver in my bedroom."

He was goading her, but he didn't much care. He was... Well dammit, it pissed him off. To see how ashamed she was to be with him. How desperate she was to hide it. Even if he understood it, it was like a branding iron straight to the gut.

"You can't say that so loud," she hissed, leaning forward, grabbing the plastic number and pulling it to her chest. "What if people heard you?"

"I thought you were reinventing yourself, Hayley Thompson."

"Not for the benefit of…the town. It's about me."

"It's going to be about you not getting dinner if you keep hiding our number." He snatched the plastic triangle from her hands.

She let out a heavy sigh and leaned back, crossing her arms. "Well, the extra beer is for you. Put it in your pocket."

"You can put it in your own pocket. Drink it back at your place."

"No, thanks."

"Don't you want to tick that box on your list? We ticked off some pretty interesting ones last night."

Her face turned scarlet. "You're being obnoxious, Jonathan."

"I've been obnoxious from day one. You just found it easy to ignore when I had my hand in your pants."

Her mouth dropped open, then she snapped it shut again. Their conversation was cut off when their food was placed in front of them.

She dragged the white cardboard box toward her and opened it, removing the container of coleslaw and setting it to the side before grabbing a french fry and biting into it fiercely. Her annoyance was clearly telegraphed by the ferocity with which she ate each bite of food. And the determination that went into her looking at anything and everything around them except for him.

"Enjoying the view?" he asked after a moment.

"The ocean is very pretty," she snapped.

"And you don't see it every day?"

"I never tire of the majesty of nature."

His lips twitched, in spite of his irritation. "Of course not."

The wind whipped up, blowing a strand of dark hair into Hayley's face. Reflexively, he reached across the table and pushed it out of her eyes. She jerked back, her lips going slack, her expression shocked.

"You're my boss," she said, her voice low. "As far as everyone is concerned."

"Well," he said, "I'm your lover. As far as I'm concerned."

"Stop."

"I thought you wanted new experiences? I thought you were tired of hiding? And here you are, hiding."

"I don't want to...perform," she said. "My new experiences are for me. Not for everyone else's consumption. That's why I'm leaving. So I can...do things without an audience."

"You want your dirty secrets, is that it? You want me to be your dirty secret."

"It's five o'clock," she said, her tone stiff. "I'm going to go home now."

She collected her food, and left the beer, standing up in a huff and taking off down the street in the opposite direction from where they had parked.

"Where are you going?"

"Home," she said sharply.

He gathered up the rest of the food and stomped after her. "You parked the other way."

"I'll get it in the morning."

"Then you better leave your house early. Unless this is you tendering your resignation."

"I'm not quitting," she said, the color heightening in her face. "I'm just… I'm irritated with you."

She turned away from him, continuing to walk quickly down the street. He took two strides and caught up with her. "I see that." He kept pace with her, but she seemed bound and determined not to look at him. "Would you care to share why?"

"Not even a little bit."

"So you're insisting that you're my employee, and that you want to be treated like my employee in public. But that clearly excludes when you decide to run off having a temper tantrum."

She whirled around then, stopping in her tracks. "Why are you acting like this? You've been…much more careful than this up till now." She sniffed. "Out of deference to my innocence?"

"What innocence, baby? Because I took that." He smiled, knowing he was getting to her. That he was making her feel as bad as he did. "Pretty damn thoroughly."

"I can't do this with you. Not here." She paused at the street corner and looked both ways before hurrying across the two-lane road. He followed suit. She walked down the sidewalk, passed the coffeehouse, which was closing up for the day, then rounded the side of the brick building and headed toward the back.

"Is this where you live?" he asked.

"Maybe," she returned, sounding almost comically stubborn. Except he didn't feel like much was funny about this situation.

"Here in the alley?" he asked, waving his hand around the mostly vacant space.

"Yes. In the Dumpster with the mice. It's not so bad. I shredded up a bunch of newspaper and made a little bed."

"I suspect this is the real reason you've been spending the night at my place, then."

She scowled. "If you want to fight with me, come upstairs."

He didn't want to fight with her. He wanted to grab her, pull her into his arms and kiss her. He wanted to stop talking. Wanted to act logical instead of being wounded by something he knew he should want to avoid.

It didn't benefit him to have anyone in town know what he was doing with Hayley. He should want to hide it as badly as she did.

But the idea that she was enjoying his body, enjoying slumming it with him in the sheets, and was damned ashamed of him in the streets burned like hell.

But he followed her through the back door to a little hallway that contained two other doors. She unlocked one of them and held it open for him. Then she gestured to the narrow staircase. "Come on."

"Who's the boss around here?"

"I'm off the clock," she said.

He shrugged, then walked up the stairs and into an open-plan living room with exposed beams and brick. It was a much bigger space than he had expected it to be, though it was also mostly empty. As if she had only half committed to living there.

But then, he supposed, her plan *was* to travel the world.

"Nice place," he said.

"Yeah," she said. "Cassie gave me a deal."

"Nice of her."

"Some people are nice, Jonathan."

"Meaning I'm not?" he asked.

She nodded in response, her mouth firmly sealed, her chin jutting out stubbornly.

"Right. Because I bought you fish and french fries and beer. And I give you really great orgasms. I'm a monster."

"I don't know what game you're playing," she said, suddenly looking much less stubborn and a little more wobbly. And that made him feel something close to guilty. "What's the point in blurring the lines while we walk through town? We both know this isn't a relationship. It's…it's boxes being ticked on a list."

"Sure. But why does it matter if people in town know you're doing that?"

"You know why it matters. Don't play like you don't understand. You do. I know you do. You know who I am, and you know that I feel like I'm under a microscope. I shared all of that with you. Don't act surprised by it now."

"Well," he said, opting for honesty even though he knew it was a damned bad idea. "Maybe I don't like being your dirty secret."

"It's not about you. Any guy that I was… Anyone that I was…doing this with. It would be a secret. It has to be."

"Why?"

"Because!" she exploded. "Because everyone will be…disappointed."

"Honey," he said, "I don't think people spend half as much time thinking about you as you think they do."

"No," she said. "They do. You know Ace. He's the pastor's son. He ran away from home, he got married, he got divorced. Then he came back and opened a bar. My parents...they're great. They really are. But they had a lot of backlash over that. People saying that the Bible itself says if you train up a child the way he should go, he's not going to depart from it. Well, he departed from it, at least as far as a lot of the congregants were concerned. People actually left the church." She sucked in a sharp breath, then let it out slowly. "I wanted to do better than that for them. It was important. For me to be...the good one."

Caring about what people thought was a strange concept. Appearances had never mattered to Jonathan. For him, it had always been about actions. What the hell did Rebecca care if he had been good? All she cared about was being taken care of. He couldn't imagine being bound by rules like that.

For the first time, he wondered if there wasn't some kind of freedom in no one having a single good expectation of you.

"But you don't like being the good one. At least, not by these standards."

Her eyes glittered with tears now. She shook her head. "I don't know. I just... I don't know. I'm afraid. Afraid of what people will think. Afraid of what my parents will think. Afraid of them being disappointed. And hurt. They've always put a lot of stock in me being what Ace wasn't. They love Ace, don't get me wrong. It's just..."

"He made things hard for them."

Hayley nodded, looking miserable. "Yes. He did. And I don't want to do that. Only…only, I was the good one and he still ended up with the kind of life I want."

"Is that all?" Jonathan asked. "Or are you afraid of who you might be if you don't have all those rules to follow?"

A flash of fear showed in her eyes, and he felt a little guilty about putting it there. Not guilty enough to take it back. Not guilty enough to stay away from her. Not guilty enough to keep his hands to himself. He reached out, cupping her cheek, then wrapped his arm around her waist and drew her toward him. "Does it scare you? Who you might be if no one told you what to do? I don't care about the rules, Hayley. You can be whoever you want with me. Say whatever you want. Drink whatever you want. Do whatever you want."

"I don't know," she said, wiggling against him, trying to pull away. "I don't know what I want."

"I think you do. I just think you wish you wanted something else." He brushed his thumb over her cheekbone. "I think you like having rules because it keeps you from going after what scares you."

He ignored the strange reverberation those words set off inside him. The chain reaction that seemed to burst all the way down his spine.

Recognition.

Truth.

Yeah, he ignored all that, and he dipped his head, claiming her mouth with his own.

Suddenly, it seemed imperative that he have her here. In her apartment. That he wreck this place with his desire for her. That he have her on every surface, against every wall, so that whenever she walked in, whenever she looked around, he was what she thought of. So that she couldn't escape this. So that she couldn't escape him.

"You think you know me now?" she asked, her eyes squinting with challenge. Clearly, she wasn't going to back down without a fight. And that was one of the things he liked about her. For all that she was an innocent church secretary, she had spirit. She had the kind of steel backbone that he admired, that he respected. The kind of strength that could get you through anything. But there was a softness to her as well, and that was something more foreign to him. Something he had never been exposed to, had never really been allowed to have.

"Yeah," he said, tightening his hold and drawing her against his body. "I know you. I know what you look like naked. I know every inch of your skin. How it feels, how it tastes. I know you better than anybody does, baby. You can tell yourself that's not true. You can say that this, what we have, is the crazy thing. That it's a break from your real life. That it's some detour you don't want anyone in town to know you're taking. But I know the truth. And I think somewhere deep down you know it, too. This isn't the break. All that other stuff... prim, proper church girl. That's what isn't real." He cupped her face, smoothing his thumbs over her cheeks. "You're fire, honey, and together we are an explosion."

He kissed her then, proving his point. She tasted like anger, like need, and he was of a mind to consume both. Whatever was on offer. Whatever she would give him.

He was beyond himself. He had never wanted a woman like this before. He had never wanted anything quite like this before. Not money, not security, not his damned house on the hill.

All that want, all that need, paled in comparison to what he felt for Hayley Thompson. The innocent little miss who should have bored him to tears by now, had him aching, panting and begging for more.

He was so hard he was in physical pain.

And when she finally capitulated, when she gave herself over to the kiss, soft fingertips skimming his shoulders, down his back, all the way to his ass, he groaned in appreciation.

There was something extra dirty about Hayley exploring his body. About her wanting him the way she did, because she had never wanted another man like she wanted him. By her own admission. And she had never had a man the way she'd had him, which was an admission she didn't have to make.

He gripped her hips, then slipped his hands down her thighs, grabbing them and pulling her up, urging her legs around his waist. Then he propelled them both across the living room, down onto the couch. He covered her, pressing his hardness against the soft, sweet apex of her thighs. She gasped as he rolled his hips forward.

"Not so ashamed of this now, are you?" He growled, pressing a kiss to her neck, then to her collarbone, then to the edge of her T-shirt.

"I'm not ashamed," she said, gasping for air.

"You could've fooled me, princess."

"It's not about you." She sifted her fingers through his hair. "I'm not ashamed of you."

"Not ashamed of your dirty, wrong-side-of-the-tracks boyfriend?"

Her eyes flashed with hurt and then fascination. "I've never thought of you that way. I never... *Boyfriend?*"

Something burned hot in his chest. "Lover. Whatever."

"I'm not ashamed of you," she reiterated. "Nothing about you. You're so beautiful. If anything, you ought to be ashamed of me. I'm not pretty. Not like you. And I don't even know what I'm doing. I just know what I want. I want you. And I'm afraid for anybody to know the truth. I'm so scared. The only time I'm not scared is when you're holding me."

He didn't want to talk anymore. He consumed her mouth, tasting her deeply, ramping up the arousal between them with each sweet stroke of his tongue across hers. With each deep taste of the sweet flavor that could only ever be Hayley.

He gripped the hem of her top, yanking it over her head, making quick work of her bra. Exposing small, perfect breasts to his inspection. She was pale. All over. Ivory skin, coral-pink nipples. He loved the look of her. Loved the feel of her. Loved so many things about her that it was tempting to just go ahead and say he loved *her*.

That thought swam thick and dizzy in his head. He could barely grab hold of it, didn't want to. So he shoved it to the side. He wasn't going to claim that. Hell no.

He didn't love people. He loved *things*.

He could love her tits, and he could love her skin, could love the way it felt to slide inside her, slick and tight. But he sure as hell couldn't love *her*.

He bent his head, taking one hardened nipple into his mouth, sucking hard, relishing the horse sound of pleasure on her lips as he did so. Then he kissed his way down her stomach, to the edge of her pants, pulling them down her thighs, leaving her bare and open.

He pressed his hand between her legs, slicked his thumb over her, teased her entrance with one finger. She began to whimper, rolling her hips under him, arching them to meet him, and he watched. Watched as she took one finger inside, then another.

He damn well watched himself corrupt her, and he let himself enjoy it. Because he was sick, because he was broken, but at least it wasn't a surprise.

Everyone in his life was familiar with it.

His father had tried to beat it out of him. His mother had run from it.

Only Rebecca had ever stayed, and it was partly because she didn't know any better.

Hayley didn't know any better, either, come to that. Not really. Not when it came to men. Not when it came to sex. She was blinded by what he could make her body feel, so she had an easy enough time ignoring the rest. But that wouldn't last forever.

Fair enough, since they wouldn't last forever, anyway. They both knew it. So there was no point in worrying about it. Not really.

Instead, he would embrace this, embrace the rush. Embrace the hollowed out feeling in his gut that bordered on sickness. The tension in his body that verged on pain. The need that rendered him hard as iron and hot as fire.

"Come for me," he commanded, his voice hoarse. All other words, all other thoughts were lost to him. All he could do was watch her writhing beneath his touch, so hot, so wet for him, arching her hips and taking his fingers in deeper.

"Not yet," she gasped, emitting little broken sounds.

"Yes," he said. "You will. You're going to come for

me now, Hayley, because I told you to. Your body is mine. You're mine." He slid his thumb over the delicate bundle of nerves there.

And then he felt her shatter beneath his touch. Felt her internal muscles pulse around his knuckles.

He reached into his back pocket, took out his wallet and found a condom quickly. He tore it open, then wrenched free his belt buckle and took down the zipper. He pushed his jeans partway down his hips, rolled the condom on his hard length and thrust inside her, all the way to the hilt. She was wet and ready for him, and he had to grit his teeth to keep from embarrassing himself, to keep it from being over before it had begun.

She gasped as he filled her, and then grabbed his ass when he retreated. Her fingernails dug into his skin, and he relished the pain this petite little thing could inflict on him. Of course, it was nothing compared to the pain he felt from his arousal. From the great, burning need inside him.

No, nothing compared to that. Nothing at all.

He adjusted their positions, dragging her sideways on the couch, bringing her hips to the edge of the cushion, going down on his knees to the hardwood floor.

He knelt there, gripping her hips and pulling her tightly against him, urging her to wrap her legs around him. The floor bit into his knees, but he didn't care. All he cared about was having her, taking her, claiming her. He gripped her tightly, his blunt fingertips digging into her flesh.

He wondered if he would leave a mark. He hoped he might.

Hoped that she would see for days to come where he had held her. Even if she wouldn't hold his hand in public, she would remember when he'd held her hips in private, when he'd driven himself deep inside her, clinging to her like she might be the source of all life.

Yeah, she would remember that. She would remember this.

He watched as a deep red flush spread over her skin, covering her breasts, creeping up her neck. She was on the verge of another orgasm. He loved that. Another thing he was allowed to love.

Loved watching her lose control. Loved watching her so close to giving it up for him again, completely. Utterly. He was going to ruin her for any other man. That was his vow, there and then, on the floor of her apartment, with a ragged splinter digging into his knee through the fabric of his jeans. She was never going to fuck anyone else without thinking of him. Without wanting him. Without wishing it were him.

She would go to Paris, and some guy would do her with a view of the Eiffel tower in the background. And she would wish she were here, counting the familiar beams on her ceiling.

And when she came home for a visit and she passed him on the street, she would shiver with a longing that she would never quite get rid of.

So many people in his life had left him. As far as he'd known, they had done it without a backward glance. But Hayley would never forget him. He would make sure of it. Damn sure.

His own arousal ratcheted up to impossible proportions. He was made entirely of his need for her. Of his need for release. And he forgot what he was trying to do. Forgot that this was about her. That this was about making her tremble, making her shake. Because he was trembling. He was shaking.

He was afraid he might be the one who was indelibly marked by all this.

He was the one who wouldn't be able to forget. The one who would never be with anyone else without thinking of her. No matter how skilled the woman was who might come after her, it would never be the same as the sweet, genuine urging of Hayley's hips against his. It would never be quite like the tight, wet clasp of her body.

He had been entirely reshaped, remade, to fit inside her, and no one else would do.

That thought ignited in his stomach, overtook him completely, lit him on fire.

When he came, it was with her name on his lips, with a strange satisfaction washing through him that left him only hungrier in the end, emptier. Because this was ending, and he knew it.

She wasn't going to work for him forever. She wasn't going to stay in Copper Ridge. She might hold on to him in secret, but in public, she would never touch him.

And as time passed, she would let go of him by inches, walking off to the life of freedom she was so desperate for.

Walking off like everyone else.

Right now, she was looking up at him, a mixture of wonder and deep emotion visible in her blue eyes. She reached up, stroking his face. Some of his hair had been tugged from the leather strap, and she brushed the strands out of his eyes.

It was weird how that hit him. How it touched him. After all the overtly sexual ways she'd put her hands on him, why that sweet gesture impacted him low and deep.

"Stay with me," she said, her voice soft. "The night. In my bed."

That hit even harder.

He had never slept with her. He didn't sleep with women. But that was all about to change. He was going to sleep with her because he wanted to. Because he didn't want to release his hold on her for one moment, not while he still had her.

"Okay," he said.

Then, still buried deep inside her, he picked her up from the couch, brought them both to a standing position and started walking toward the door at the back of the room. "Bedroom is this way?"

"How did you know?"

"Important things, I know. Where the bedroom is." He kissed her lips. "How to make you scream my name. That I know."

"Care to make me scream it a few more times?"

"The neighbors might hear."

It was a joke, but he could still see her hesitation. "That's okay," she said slowly.

And even though he was reasonably confident that was a lie, he carried her into her bedroom and lay down on the bed with her.

It didn't matter if it was a lie. Because they had all night to live in it. And that was good enough for him.

Eleven

When he woke up the next morning he was disoriented. He was lying in a bed that was too small for his large frame, and he had a woman wrapped around him. Of course, he knew immediately which woman it was. It couldn't be anyone else. Even in the fog of sleep, he wasn't confused about Hayley's identity.

She smelled like sunshine and wildflowers. Or maybe she just smelled like soap and skin and only reminded him of sunshine and wildflowers, because they were innocent things. New things. The kinds of things that could never be corrupted by the world around them.

The kinds of things not even he could wreck.

She was that kind of beautiful.

But the other reason he was certain it was Hayley was that there was no other woman he would have fallen asleep with. It was far too intimate a thing, sharing a bed with someone when you weren't angling for an orgasm. He had never seen the point of it. It was basically the same as sharing a toothbrush, and he wasn't interested in that, either.

He looked at Hayley, curled up at his side, her brown hair falling across her face, her soft lips parted, her breathing easy and deep. The feeling carved out in his chest was a strange one.

Hell, lying there in the early morning, sharing a toothbrush with Hayley didn't even seem so insane.

He sat up, shaking off the last cobwebs of sleep and extricating himself from Hayley's hold. He groaned when her fingertips brushed the lower part of his stomach, grazing his insistent morning erection. He had half a mind to wake her up the best way he knew how.

But the longer the realization of what had happened last night sat with him, the more eager he was to put some distance between them.

He could get some coffee, get his head on straight and come back fully clothed. Then maybe the two of them could prepare for the workday.

He needed to compartmentalize. He had forgotten that yesterday. He had let himself get annoyed about something that never should have bothered him. Had allowed old hurts to sink in when he shouldn't give a damn whether or not Hayley wanted to hold his hand when they walked down the street. She wasn't his girlfriend. And all the words that had passed between them in the apartment, all the anger that had been rattling around inside him, seemed strange now. Like it had all happened to somebody else. The morning had brought clarity, and it was much needed.

He hunted around the room, collecting his clothes

and tugging them on quickly, then he walked over to the window, drew back the curtains and tried to get a sense of what time it was. She didn't have a clock in her room. He wondered if she just looked at her phone.

The sky was pink, so it had to be nearing six. He really needed to get home and take care of the horses. He didn't want to mess up their routine. But he would come back. Or maybe Hayley would just come to his place on time.

Then he cursed, realizing he had left his car at the other end of Main Street. He walked back to the living room, pulled on his boots and headed out the door, down the stairs. His vision was blurry, and he was in desperate need of caffeine. There were two doors in the hallway, and he reached for the one closest to him.

And nearly ran right into Cassie Caldwell as he walked into The Grind.

The morning sounds of the coffee shop filled his ears, the intense smell of the roast assaulting him in the best way.

But Cassie was staring at him, wide-eyed, as were the ten people sitting inside the dining room. One of whom happened to be Pastor John Thompson.

Jonathan froze, mumbled something about coming in through the back door, and then walked up to the counter. He was going to act like there was nothing remarkable about where he had just come from. Was going to do his very best to look like there was nothing at all strange about him coming through what he now realized was a private entrance used only by the tenant upstairs. It didn't escape his notice that the pastor was eyeballing him closely. And so was Cassie. Really, so was everybody. Damn small town.

Now, he could see why Hayley had been so vigilant yesterday.

If only he could go back and be vigilant in his door choice.

"Black coffee," he said, "two shots of espresso."

Cassie's gaze turned hard. "I know."

"I came through the wrong door," he said.

She walked over to the espresso machine, wrapped a damp cloth around the wand that steamed the milk and twisted it, a puff of steam coming out as she jerked the cloth up and down roughly, her eyes never leaving his. "Uh-huh."

"I did."

"And it's just a coincidence that my tenant happens to live upstairs. My tenant who works for you." She said that part softly, and he was sure nobody else in the room heard it.

"That's right," he said. "Just a coincidence."

Suddenly, the door to the coffee shop opened again, and Hayley appeared, wearing a T-shirt and jeans, her hair wild, like she had just rolled out of bed.

Her eyes widened when she saw her father. Then she looked over at the counter and her eyes widened even further when she saw Jonathan.

"Good morning," he said, his voice hard. "Fancy meeting you here before work."

"Yes," she said. "I'm just gonna go get ready."

She turned around and walked back out of the coffee shop, as quickly as she had come in. So much for being casual. If he hadn't already given it away, he was pretty sure Hayley's scampering had.

"You were saying?" Cassie said, her tone brittle.

"I'm sorry," he said, leaning in. "Is she your sister?"

"No."

"Best friend?"

"No."

"Is she your daughter? Because I have a feeling I'm about to catch hell from the reverend here in a few minutes, but I'm not really sure why I'm catching it from you."

"Because I know her. I know all about you. I am friends with your sister, and I know enough through her."

"Undoubtedly all about my great personal sacrifice and sparkling personality," he said.

Cassie's expression softened. "Rebecca loves you. But she's also realistic about the fact that you aren't a love-and-commitment kind of guy. Also, I do believe Ms. Hayley Thompson is younger than your sister."

"And last I checked, I wasn't committing any crimes. I will just take the coffee. You can keep the lecture."

He was not going to get chased out of the coffee shop, no matter how many people looked at him. No matter how much Cassie lectured him.

He was not the poor kid he'd once been. He was more than just a boy who had been abandoned by both parents. He was a damned boon to the town. His business brought in good money. *He* brought in good money. He wasn't going to be treated like dirt beneath anybody's shoe.

Maybe Hayley was too good for him, but she was sleeping with him. She wanted him. So it wasn't really up to anybody to say that she shouldn't.

When he turned around after Cassie gave him his coffee, the pastor stood up at his table and began to make his way over to Jonathan.

"Hello. Jonathan, right?" the older man said, his voice shot through with the same kind of steel that Jonathan often heard in Hayley's voice. Clearly, she got her strength from her father. It was also clear to Jonathan that he was not being spoken to by a pastor at the moment. But by a fairly angry dad.

"Pastor John," Jonathan said by way of greeting.

"Why don't you join me for a cup of coffee?"

Not exactly the words Jonathan had expected, all things considered. He could sense the tension in the room, sense the tension coming off Hayley's father.

People were doing their very best to watch, without appearing to do so. Any hope Jonathan had retained that they were oblivious to what it meant that he had come down from the upstairs apartment was dashed by just how fascinated they all were. And by the steady intent on Pastor John's face.

If the old man wanted to sit him down and humiliate him in front of the town, wanted to talk about how Jonathan wasn't fit to lick the dust off Hayley's boots, Jonathan wouldn't be surprised. Hell, he welcomed it. It was true, after all.

"I think I will," Jonathan said, following the other man back to his table.

He took a seat, his hand curled tightly around his coffee cup.

"I don't think we've ever formally met," John said, leaning back in his chair.

"No," Jonathan said, "we wouldn't have. I don't recall darkening the door of the church in my lifetime. Unless it was to repair something."

Let him know just what kind of man Jonathan was. That's where this was headed, anyway. Jonathan had never met a woman's parents before. He had never been in a relationship that was serious enough to do so. And this wasn't serious, either. But because of this damn small town and Hayley's role in it, he was being forced into a position he had never wanted to be in.

"I see," the pastor said. "Hayley has been working for you for the past couple of weeks, I believe."

He was cutting right to the chase now. To Jonathan's connection to Hayley, which was undeniable. "Yes."

"I've been very protective of Hayley. Possibly over-protective. But when my son, Ace, went out on his own, he didn't find much but heartbreak. I transferred some of my fear of that happening again onto Hayley, to an unfair degree. So I kept her close. I encouraged her to keep working at the church. To live at home for as long as possible. You have a sister, don't you?"

Damn this man and his ironclad memory for detail. "I didn't think it was Christian to gossip. But I can see that you've certainly heard your share about me."

"I do know a little something about you, yes. My son is married to one of Nathan West's children, as I'm sure you know. And your sister has a connection to that family, as well."

Jonathan gritted his teeth. "Yes. My sister is with Gage. Though only God knows why. Maybe you could ask Him."

"Matters of the heart are rarely straightforward. Whether it's in the case of romantic love, or the love you feel for your children, or your sister. It's a big emotion. And it is scary at times. Not always the most rational. What you feel about Rebecca being with Gage I suppose is similar to the concerns I have about Hayley."

"That she's with a bastard who doesn't deserve her?"

The pastor didn't even flinch. "That she's involved deeply enough that she could be hurt. And if we're going to speak plainly, I suppose the question I could ask you is whether or not you would think any man was good enough for Rebecca, or if you would be concerned—no matter who it was—that he wouldn't handle her with the care you would want."

Jonathan didn't have much to say about that. Only because he was trying to be angry. Trying to take offense at the fact that the older man was questioning him. Trying to connect this conversation to what he knew to be true—everybody looked at him and saw someone who wasn't worthy. He certainly didn't deserve kindness from this man, not at all. Didn't deserve for him to sit here and try to forge some kind of connection.

Jonathan had taken advantage of Hayley. Regardless of her level of experience, she was his employee. Even if she had been with a hundred men, what he had done would be problematic. But, as far as he was concerned, the problem was compounded by the fact that Hayley had been innocent.

So he waited. He waited for that hammer to fall. For the accusations to fly.

But they didn't come. So he figured he might try to create a few.

"I'm sure there's a certain type of man you would prefer your daughter be with. But it's definitely not the guy with the bad reputation you'd want stumbling out of her apartment early in the morning."

John nodded slowly, and Jonathan thought—with a certain amount of triumph—that he saw anger flicker briefly in the older man's eyes.

"I told you already that I feel very protective of her,"

Pastor John said. "But I wonder if, by protecting her as much as I did, I shielded her too effectively from the reality of life. I don't want her to get hurt." He let out a long, slow breath. "But that is not within my control."

"Is this the part where you ask me about my intentions toward your daughter? Because I highly doubt we're ever going to sit around a dinner table and try to make small talk. This isn't that sort of thing." With those words, Jonathan effectively told Hayley's father that all he was doing was fooling around with her. And that wasn't strictly true. Also, he hated himself a little bit for pretending it was.

For saying that sort of thing to her father when he knew it would embarrass her.

But in a way, it would be a mercy. She cared what people in town thought about her. She cared about her father's opinion. And this conversation would make it so much easier for her to let Jonathan go when the time came.

She was always going to let you go. She has traveling to do, places to see. You were her dirty detour along the way. You're the one who needs distance. You're the one who needs to find a way to make it easier.

He ignored that voice, ignored the tightening in his chest.

"Why isn't it that sort of thing?" The question, issued from Hayley's father, his tone firm but steady, reached something deep inside Jonathan, twisted it, cracked it.

It couldn't be anything more than temporary. Because of him. Because of what he was. Who he was. That should be obvious. It would have been even more obvious if Pastor John had simply sat down and started hurling recriminations. About how Jonathan was beneath the man's pure, innocent daughter. About why a formerly impoverished man from the wrong side of the tracks could never be good enough for a woman like her.

It didn't matter that he had money now. He was the same person he had been born to be. The same boy who had been beaten by his father, abandoned by his mother. All that was still in him. And no custom home, no amount of money in his bank account, was ever going to fix it.

If John Thompson wouldn't look at him and see that, if he wouldn't shout it from across a crowded coffee shop so the whole town would hear, then Jonathan was going to have to make it clear.

"Because it's not something I do," he returned, his voice hard. "I'm in for temporary. That's all I've got."

"Well," John said, "that's a pretty neat lie you've been telling yourself, son. But the fact of the matter is, it's only the most you're willing to give, not the most you have the ability to give."

"And you're saying you want me to dig down deep and find it inside myself to be with your daughter forever? Something tells me that probably wouldn't be an ideal situation as far as you're concerned."

"That's between you and Hayley. I have my own personal feelings about it, to be sure. No father wants to believe that his daughter is being used. But if I believe that, then it means I don't see anything good in you, and that isn't true. Everybody knows how you took care of your sister. Whatever you think the people in this town believe about you, they do know that. I can't say you haven't been mistreated by the people here, and it grieves me to think about it."

He shook his head, and Jonathan was forced to be-

lieve the older man was being genuine. He didn't quite
know what to do with that fact, but he saw the same
honesty shining from John that he often saw in Hayley's eyes. An emotional honesty Jonathan had limited
experience with.

The older man continued. "You think you don't have
the capacity for love? When you've already mentioned
your concern for Rebecca a couple of times in this conversation? When the past decade and a half of your
life was devoted to caring for her? It's no secret how
hard you've worked. I may never have formally met
you until this moment, but I know about you, Jonathan
Bear, and what I know isn't the reputation you seem to
think you have."

"Well, regardless of my reputation, you should be
concerned about Hayley's. When I came through that
door this morning, it was unintentional. But it's important to Hayley that nobody realizes what's happening between us. So the longer I sit here talking to you,
the more risk there is of exposing her to unnecessary
chatter. And that's not what I want. So," he said, "out
of respect for keeping it a secret, like Hayley wants—"

"That's not what I want."

Twelve

Hayley was shaking. She had been shaking from the moment she had walked into The Grind and seen Jonathan there, with her father in the background.

Somehow, she had known—just known—that everyone in the room was putting two and two together and coming up with sex.

And she also knew she had definitely made it worse by running away. If she had sauntered in and acted surprised to see Jonathan there, she might have made people think it really was coincidental that the two of them were both in the coffeehouse early in the morning, coming through the same private door. For reasons that had nothing to do with him spending the night upstairs with her.

But she had spent the past five minutes pacing around upstairs, waiting for her breath to normalize, waiting for her heart to stop beating so hard. Neither thing had happened.

Then she had cautiously crept back downstairs and come in to see her father sitting at the table with Jonathan. Fortunately, Jonathan hadn't looked like he'd been punched in the face. But the conversation had definitely seemed tense.

And standing there, looking at what had been her worst nightmare not so long ago, she realized that it just...wasn't. She'd never been ashamed of Jonathan. He was...the most determined, hardworking, wonderful man she had ever known. He had spent his life raising his sister. He had experienced a childhood where he had known nothing but abandonment and abuse, and he had turned around and given love to his sister, unconditionally and tirelessly.

And, yeah, maybe it wasn't ideal to announce her physical affair with him at the coffee shop, all things considered, but...whatever she had expected to feel... She didn't.

So, it had been the easiest thing in the world to walk over to their table and say that she really didn't need to keep their relationship a secret. Of course, now both Jonathan and her father were looking at her like she had grown a second head.

When she didn't get a response from either of them, she repeated, "That's not what I want."

"Hayley," Jonathan said, his tone firm. "You don't know what you're saying."

"Oh, please," she returned. "Jonathan, that tone wouldn't work on me in private, and it's not going to work on me here, either."

She took a deep breath, shifting her weight from

foot to foot, gazing at her father, waiting for him to say something. He looked... Well, it was very difficult to say if John Thompson could ever really be surprised. In his line of work, he had seen it all, heard it all. While Protestants weren't much for confession, people often used him as a confessional, she knew.

Still, he looked a little surprised to be in this situation.

She searched his face for signs of disappointment. That was her deepest fear. That he would be disappointed in her. Because she had tried, she really had, to be the child Ace wasn't.

Except, as she stood there, she realized that was a steaming pile of bull-pucky. Her behavior wasn't about being what Ace hadn't been. It was all about desperately wanting to please people while at the same time wishing there was a way to please herself. And the fact of the matter was, she couldn't have both those things. Not always.

That contradiction was why she had been hell-bent on running away, less because she wanted to experience the wonders of the world and more because she wanted to go off and do what she wanted without disappointing anyone.

"Jonathan isn't just my boss," she said to her dad. "He's my... Well, I don't really know. But...you know." Her throat tightened, tears burning behind her eyes.

Yes, she wanted to admit to the relationship, and she wanted to live out in the open, but that didn't make the transition from good girl to her own woman any easier.

She wanted to beg her dad for his approval. He wasn't a judgmental man, her father, but he had certainly raised her in a specific fashion, and this was not it. So while he might not condemn her, she knew she wasn't going to get his wholesale approval.

And she would have to live with that.

Living without his approval was hard. Much harder than she had thought it might be. Especially given the fact that she thought she'd accepted it just a few moments ago. But being willing to experience disapproval and truly accepting it were apparently two different things.

"Why don't you have a seat, Hayley," her father said slowly.

"No, thank you," she replied. "I'm going to stand, because if I sit down... Well, I don't know. I have too much energy to sit down. But I—I care about him." She turned to Jonathan. "I care about you. I really do. I'm so sorry I made you feel like you were a dirty secret. Like I was ashamed of you. Because any woman would be proud to be involved with you." She took a deep breath and looked around the coffee shop. "I'm dating him," she said, pointing at Jonathan. "Just so you all know."

"Hayley," her father said, standing up, "come to dinner this week."

"With him?"

"If you want to. But please know that we want to know about your life. Even if it isn't what we would choose for you, we want to know." He didn't mean Jonathan specifically. He meant being in a physical relationship without the benefit of any kind of commitment, much less marriage.

But the way he looked at her, with nothing but love, made her ache all over. Made her throat feel so tight she could scarcely breathe.

She felt miserable. And she felt strong. She wasn't

sure which emotion was more prominent. She had seen her father look at Ace like this countless times, had seen him talk about her brother with a similar expression on his face. Her father was loving, and he was as supportive as he could be, but he also had hard lines.

"I guess we'll see," she said.

"I suppose. I also imagine you need to have a talk with him," he said, tilting his head toward Jonathan, who was looking uncertain. She'd never seen Jonathan look uncertain before.

"Oh," she said, "I imagine I do."

"Come home if you need anything."

For some reason, she suddenly became aware of the tension in her father's expression. He was the pastor of Copper Ridge. And the entire town was watching him. So whether he wanted to or not, he couldn't haul off and punch Jonathan. He couldn't yell at her—though he never had yelled in all her life. And he was leaving her to sort out her own circumstances, when she could feel that he very much wanted to stay and sort them out for her.

Maybe Jonathan was right. Maybe she had never put a foot out of line because the rules were easier. There were no rules to what she was doing now, and no one was going to step in and tell her what to do. No one was going to pull her back if she went too far. Not even her father. Maybe that had been her real issue with taking this relationship public. Not so much the disappointment as the loss of a safety net.

Right now, Hayley felt like she was standing on the edge of an abyss. She had no idea how far she might fall, how bad it might hurt when she landed. If she would even survive it.

She was out here, living her potential mistakes, standing on the edge of a lot of potential pain.

Because with the barrier of following the rules removed, with no need to leave to experience things... Well, it was just her. Her heart and what she felt for Jonathan.

There was nothing in the way. No excuses. No false idea that this could never be anything, because she was leaving in the end.

As her father walked out of the coffeehouse, taking with him an entire truckload of her excuses, she realized exactly what she had been protecting herself from.

Falling in love. With Jonathan. With a man who might never love her back. Wanting more, wanting everything, with the man least likely to give it to her.

She had been hiding behind the secretary desk at the church, listening to everybody else's problems, without ever incurring any of her own. She had witnessed a whole lot of heartbreak, a whole lot of struggle, but she had always been removed from it.

She didn't want to protect herself from this. She didn't want to hide.

"Why did you do that?" Jonathan asked.

"Because you were mad at me yesterday. I hurt your feelings."

He laughed, a dark, humorless sound. "Hayley," he said, "I don't exactly have feelings to hurt."

"That's not true," she said. "I know you do."

"Honey, that stuff was beaten out of me by my father before I was five years old. And whatever was left... It pretty much dissolved when my mother walked away and left me with a wounded sister to care for. That stuff just kind of leaves you numb. All you can do is survive.

Work on through life as hard as you can, worry about putting food on the table. Worry about trying to do right by a kid who's had every unfair thing come down on her. You think you being embarrassed to hold my hand in public is going to hurt my feelings after that?"

She hated when he did this. When he drew lines between their levels of experience and made her feel silly.

She closed the distance between them and put her fingertips on his shoulder. Then she leaned in and kissed him, in full view of everybody in the coffeehouse. He put his hand on her hip, and even though he didn't enthusiastically kiss her back, he made no move to end it, either.

"Why do I get the feeling you are a little embarrassed to be with *me*?" she asked, when she pulled away from him.

He arched his brow. "I'm not embarrassed to be with you."

Maybe he wasn't. But there was something bothering him. "You're upset because everyone knows. And now there will be consequences if you do something to hurt me."

"When," he said, his tone uncompromising. "*When* I do something. That's what everyone is thinking. Trust me, Hayley, they don't think for one second that this might end in some fairy-tale wedding bullshit."

Hayley jerked back, trying to fight the feeling that she had just been slapped in the face. For whatever reason, he was trying to elicit exactly that response, and she really didn't want to give it to him. "Fine. Maybe that is what they think. But why does it matter? That's the question, isn't it? Why does what other people think matter more than what you or I might want?

"You were right about me. My choices were less about what other people might think, and more about what might happen to me if I found out I had never actually been reined in." She shook her head. "If I discovered that all along I could have done exactly what I wanted to, with no limit on it. Before now, I never took the chance to find out who I was. I was happy to be told. And I think I've been a little afraid of who I might be beneath all of these expectations."

"Why? Because you might harbor secret fantasies of shoplifting doilies out of the Trading Post?"

"No," Hayley said, "because I might go and get myself hurt. If I had continued working at the church, if I'd kept on gazing at the kind of men I met there from across the room, never making a move because waiting for them to do it was right, pushing down all of my desires because it was lust I shouldn't feel… I would have been safe. I wouldn't be sitting here in this coffee shop with you, shaking because I'm scared, because I'm a little bit turned on thinking about what we did last night."

"I understand the turned on part," he said, his voice rough like gravel. He lifted his hand, dragging his thumb over her lower lip. "Why are you afraid?"

"I'm afraid because just like you said… There's a very low chance of this ending in some fairy-tale wedding…nonsense. And I want all of that." Her chest seized tight, her throat closing up to a painful degree. "With you. If you were wondering. And that is… That's so scary. Because I knew you would look at me like that if I told you."

His face was flat, his dark eyes blazing. He was… well, he was angry, rather than indifferent. Somehow, she had known he would be.

"You shouldn't be afraid of not getting your fairy tale with me. If anything, you should be relieved. Nobody wants to stay with me for the rest of their life, Hayley, trust me. You're supposed to go to Paris. And you're going to Paris."

"I don't want to go," she said, because she wanted to stay here, with him. Or take him with her. But she didn't want to be without him.

"Dammit," he said, his voice like ground-up glass. "Hayley, you're not going to change your plans because of me. That would last how long? Maybe a year? Maybe two if you're really dedicated. But I know exactly how that ends—with you deciding you would rather be anywhere but stuck in my house, stuck in this town."

"But I don't feel stuck. I never did. It was all…me being afraid. But the thing is, Jonathan, I never wanted anything more than I wanted my safety. Thinking I needed to escape was just a response to this missing piece inside of me that I couldn't put a name to. But I know what it is now."

"Don't," he bit out.

"It was you," she said. "All of this time it was you. Don't you see? I never wanted anyone or anything badly enough to take the chance. To take the risk. To expose myself, to step out of line. But you… I do want you that badly."

"Because you were forced to take the risk. You had to own it. Yesterday, you didn't have to, and so you didn't. You pulled away from me when we walked down the street, didn't want anyone to see."

"That wasn't about you. It was about me. It was about the fact that…basically, everybody in town knows I've never dated anybody. So in my case it's a little bit like announcing that I lost my virginity, and it's embarrassing."

Except now she was having this conversation with him in a coffeehouse, where people she knew were sitting only a few feet away, undoubtedly straining to hear her over the sound of the espresso machine. But whatever. She didn't care. For the first time in her life, she really, really didn't care. She cared about him. She cared about this relationship. About doing whatever she needed to do to make him see that everything she was saying was true.

"I'm over it," she added. "I just had to decide that I was. Well, now I have. Because it doesn't get any more horrifying than having to admit that you were having your first affair to your father."

"You see," he said. "I wouldn't know. Nobody was all that invested in me when I lost my virginity, or why. I was fifteen, if you were curious. So forgive me if your concerns seem foreign to me. It's just that I know how this all plays out. People say they love you, then they punch you in the face. You take care of somebody all of their damn life, and then they take off with the one person you spent all that time protecting them from. Yeah, they say they love you, and then they leave. That's life."

Hayley's chest tightened, her heart squeezing painfully. "I didn't say I loved you."

He looked stricken by that. "Well, good. At least you didn't lie to me."

She did love him, though. But he had introduced the word. Love and its effects were clearly the things that scared him most about what was happening between them.

Love loomed large between them. Love was clearly on the table here. Even if he didn't want it to be, there it was. Even if he was going to deny it, there it was.

Already in his mind, in his heart, whether she said it or not.

She opened her mouth to say it, but it stuck in her throat.

Because he had already decided it would be a lie if she spoke the words. He was so dedicated to that idea. To his story about who Jonathan Bear was, and who he had to be, and how people treated him. His behavior was so very close to what she had been doing for so long.

"Jonathan—"

He cut her off. "I don't love people," he said. "You know what I love? I love things. I love my house. I love my money. I love that company that I've spent so many hours investing in. I love the fact that I own a mountain, and can ride a horse from one end of my land to the other, and get a sense of everything that can never be taken from me. But I'll never love another person, not again." He stood up, gripping her chin with his thumb and forefinger. "Not even you. Because I will never love anything I can't buy right back, do you understand?"

She nodded, swallowing hard. "Yes," she said.

His pain was hemorrhaging from him, bleeding out of every pore, and there was nothing she could do to stop it. He was made of fury, of rage, and he was made of hurt, whether he would admit it or not.

"I think we're done then, Hayley."

He moved away from her, crossing the coffeehouse and walking out the door. Every eye in the room was on her, everybody watching to see what she would do next. So she did the only thing she could.

She stood up and she ran after Jonathan Bear for the entire town to see.

Jonathan strode down the street. The heavy gray sky was starting to crack, raindrops falling onto his head. His shoulders. Good. That was just about perfect.

It took him a few more strides to realize he was headed away from his car, but he couldn't think clearly enough to really grasp where he was going. His head was pounding like horse hooves over the grass, and he couldn't grab hold of a thought to save his life.

"Jonathan!"

He turned, looking down the mostly empty street, to see Hayley running after him, her dark hair flying behind her, rain flying into her face. She was making a spectacle of herself, right here on Main, and she didn't seem to care at all. Something about that made him feel like he'd been turned to stone, rooted to the spot, his heart thundering heavily in his chest.

"Don't run from me," she said, coming to a stop in front of him, breathing hard. "Don't run from us."

"You're the one who's running, honey," he said, keeping his voice deliberately flat.

"We're not done," she said. "We're not going to be done just because you say so. You might be the boss at your house, but you're not the boss here." Her words were jumbled up, fierce and ferocious. "What about what I want?"

He gritted his teeth. "Well, the problem is you made the mistake of assuming I might care what you want."

She sprang forward, pounding a closed fist on his

shoulder. The gesture was so aggressive, so very unlike Hayley that it immobilized him. "You do care. You're not a mountain, you're just a man, and you do care. But you're awfully desperate to prove that you don't. You're awfully desperate to prove you have no worth. And I have to wonder why that is."

"I don't have to prove it. Everyone who's ever wandered through my life has proved it, Hayley. You're a little bit late to this party. You're hardly going to take thirty-five years of neglect and make me feel differently about it. Make me come to different conclusions than I've spent the past three decades drawing."

"Why not?" she asked. "That's kind of the point of knowing someone. Of being with them. They change you. You've certainly changed me. You made me...well, more me than I've ever been."

"I never said I needed to change."

"That's ridiculous. Of course you need to change. You live in that big house all by yourself, you're angry at your sister because she figured out how to let something go when you can't. And you're about ready to blow this up—to blow us up—to keep yourself safe." She shivered, the rain making dark spots on her top, drops rolling down her face.

"There's no reason any of this has to end, Hayley." He gritted his teeth, fighting against the slow, expanding feeling growing in his chest, fighting against the pain starting to push against the back of his eyes. "But you have to accept what I'm willing to give. And it may not be what you want, what you're looking for. If it's not, if that makes you leave, then you're no different from anyone else who's ever come through my life, and you won't be any surprise to me."

Hayley looked stricken by that, pale. And he could see her carefully considering her words. "Wow. That's a very smart way to build yourself an impenetrable fort there, Jonathan. How can anyone demand something of you, if you're determined to equate high expectations with the people who abandoned you? If you're determined to believe that someone asking anything of you is the same as not loving you at all?"

"You haven't said you loved me." His voice was deliberately hard. He didn't know why he was bringing that up again. Didn't know why he was suspended between the desire for her to tell him she didn't, and the need—the intense, soul-shattering need—to hear her say it, even if he could never accept it. Even if he could never return it.

"My mistake," she said, her voice thin. "What will you do if I tell you, Jonathan? Will you say it doesn't matter, that it isn't real? Because you know everything, don't you? Even my heart."

"I know more about the world than you do, little girl," he said, his throat feeling tight for some reason. "Whatever your intentions, I have a better idea of what the actual outcome might be."

She shocked him by taking two steps forward, eliminating the air between them, pressing her hand against his chest. His heart raged beneath her touch, and he had a feeling she could tell.

"I love you." She stared at him for a moment, then she stretched up on her toes and pressed a kiss to his lips. Her lips were slick and cold from the rain, and he wanted to consume her. Wanted to pretend that words didn't matter. That there was nothing but this kiss.

For a moment, a heartbeat, he pretended that was true.

"I love you," she said again, when they parted. "But that doesn't mean I won't expect something from you. In fact, that would be pretty sorry love if I expected to come into your life and change nothing, mean nothing. I want you to love me back, Jonathan. I want you to open yourself up. I want you to let me in. I want you to be brave."

He grabbed hold of her arms, held her against his chest. He didn't give a damn who might see them. "You're telling me to be brave? What have you ever faced down that scared you? Tell me, Hayley."

"You," she said breathlessly.

He released his hold on her and took a step back, swearing violently. "All the more reason you should walk away, I expect."

"Do you know why you scare me, Jonathan? You make me want something I can't control. You make me want something I can't predict. There are no rules for this. There is no safety. Loving you... I have no guarantees. There is no neat map for how this might work out. It's not a math equation, where I can add doing the right things with saying the right things and make you change. You have to decide. You have to choose this. You have to choose us. The rewards for being afraid, or being good, aren't worth as much as the reward for being brave. So I'm going to be brave.

"I love you. And I want you to love me back. I want you to take a chance—on me."

She was gazing at him, her eyes blazing with light and intensity. How long would it take for that light to dim? How long would it take for him to kill it? How long would it take for her to decide—like everyone else in his life—that he wasn't worth the effort?

It was inevitable. That was how it always ended.

"No," he said, the word scraping his throat raw as it escaped.

"No?" The devastation in her voice cut him like a knife.

"No. But hey, one more for your list," he said, hating himself with every syllable.

"What?"

"You got your kiss in the rain. I did a lot for you, checked off a lot of your boxes. Go find some other man to fill in the rest."

Then he turned and left her standing in the street.

And in front of God and everybody, Jonathan Bear walked away from Hayley Thompson, and left whatever remained of his heart behind with her.

Thirteen

This was hell. Perhaps even literally. Hayley had wondered about hell a few times, growing up the daughter of a pastor. Now, she thought that if hell were simply living with a broken heart, with the rejection of the person you loved more than anything else echoing in your ears, it would be pretty effective eternal damnation.

She was lying on her couch, tears streaming down her face. She was miserable, and she didn't even want to do anything about it. She just wanted to sit in it.

Oh, she had been so cavalier about the pain that would come when Jonathan ended things. Back in the beginning, when she had been justifying losing her virginity to him, she had been free and easy about the possibility of heartbreak.

But she hadn't loved him then. So she really hadn't known.

Hadn't known that it would be like shards of glass digging into her chest every time she took a breath. Hadn't known that it was actual, physical pain. That her head would throb and her eyes would feel like sandpaper from all the crying.

That her body, and her soul, would feel like they had been twisted, wrung out and draped over a wire to dry in the brutal, unfeeling coastal air.

This was the experience he had talked about. The one that wasn't worth having.

She rolled onto her back, thinking over the past weeks with Jonathan. Going to his house, getting her first job away from the church. How nervous she had been. How fluttery she had felt around him.

Strangely, she felt her lips curve into a smile.

It was hard to reconcile the woman she was now with the girl who had first knocked on his door for that job interview.

She hadn't even realized what all that fluttering meant. What the tightening in her nipples, the pressure between her thighs had meant. She knew now. Desire. Need. Things she would associate with Jonathan for the rest of her life, no matter where she went, no matter who else she might be with.

He'd told her to find someone else.

Right now, the idea of being with another man made her cringe.

She wasn't ready to think about that. She was too raw. And she still wanted him. Only him.

Jonathan was more than an experience.

He had wrenched her open. Pulled her out of the safe space she'd spent so many years hiding in. He had shown her a love that was bigger than fear.

Unfortunately, because that love was so big, the desolation of it was crippling.

She sat up, scrubbing her arm over her eyes. She needed to figure out what she was going to do next.

Something had crystallized for her earlier today, during the encounter with Jonathan and her father. She didn't need to run away. She didn't need to leave town, or gain anonymity, in order to have what she wanted. To be who she wanted.

She didn't need to be the church secretary, didn't need to be perfect or hide what she was doing. She could still go to her father's church on Sunday, and go to dinner at her parents' house on Sunday evening.

She didn't have to abandon her home, her family, her faith. Sure, it might be uncomfortable to unite her family and her need to find herself, but if there was one thing loving Jonathan had taught her, it was that sometimes uncomfortable was worth it.

She wasn't going to let heartbreak stop her.

She thought back to how he had looked at her earlier today, those black eyes impassive as he told her he wouldn't love her back.

Part of her wanted to believe she was right about him. That he was afraid. That he was protecting himself.

Another part of her felt that was a little too hopeful. Maybe that gorgeous, experienced man simply couldn't love his recently-a-virgin assistant.

Except…she had been so certain, during a few small moments, that she had given something to him, too. Just like he had given so much to her.

For some reason, he was dedicated to the idea that nobody stayed. That people looked at him and saw the worst. She couldn't understand why he would find that comforting, and yet a part of him must.

It made her ache. Her heart wasn't broken only for her, but for him, too. For all the love he wouldn't allow himself to accept.

She shook her head. Later. Later she would feel sorry for him. Right now, she was going to wallow in her own pain.

Because at the end of the day, Jonathan had made the choice to turn away from her, to turn away from love.

Right now, she would feel sorry for herself. Then maybe she would plan a trip to Paris.

"Do you want to invite me in?"

Jonathan looked at his sister, standing on the porch, looking deceptively calm.

"Do I have a choice?"

Rebecca shook her head, her long dark hair swinging behind her like a curtain. "Not really. I didn't drive all the way out here to have this conversation with moths buzzing around me."

It was dark out, and just as Rebecca had said, there were bugs fluttering around the porch light near her face.

"Come in, then," he said, moving aside.

She blinked when she stepped over the threshold, a soft smile touching her lips. The scar tissue on the left side of her mouth pulled slightly. Scar tissue that had been given to her by the man she was going to marry. Oh, it had been an accident, and Jonathan knew it. But with all the pain and suffering the accident had caused Rebecca, intent had never much mattered to him.

"This is beautiful, Jonathan," she said, her dark eyes

flickering to him. "I haven't been here since it was finished."

He shrugged. "Well, that was your choice."

"You don't like my fiancé. And you haven't made much of an effort to change that. I don't know what you expect from me."

"Appreciation, maybe, for all the years I spent taking care of you?" He wanted to cut his own balls off for saying that. Basically, right about now he wanted to escape his own skin. He was a bastard. Even he thought so.

He was sitting in his misery now, existing fully in the knowledge of the pain he had caused Hayley.

He should never have had that much power over her. He never should have touched her. This misery was the only possible way it could have turned out. His only real defense was that he hadn't imagined a woman like Hayley would ever fall in love with a man like him.

"Right. Because we've never had that discussion."

His sister's tone was dry, and he could tell she was pretty unimpressed with him. Well, fair enough. He was unimpressed with himself.

"I still don't understand why you love him, Rebecca. I really don't."

"What is love to you, Jonathan?"

An image of Hayley's face swam before his mind's eye. "What the hell kind of question is that?"

"A relevant one," she said. "I think. Particularly when we get down to why exactly I'm here. Congratulations. After spending most of your life avoiding being part of the rumor mill, you're officially hot small-town gossip."

"Am I?" He wasn't very surprised to hear that.

"Something about kissing the pastor's daughter on Main Street in the rain. And having a fight with her."

"That's accurate."

"What's going on?"

"What it looks like. I was sleeping with her. We had a fight. Now we're not sleeping together."

Rebecca tilted her head to the side. "I feel like I'm missing some information."

"Hayley was working for me—I assume you knew that."

"Vaguely," she said, her eyes glittering with curiosity.

"And I'm an asshole. So when I found out my assistant was a virgin, I figured I would help her with that." It was a lie, but one he was comfortable with. He was comfortable painting himself as the villain. Everybody would, anyway. So why not add his own embellishment to the tale.

"Right," Rebecca said, sarcasm dripping from her voice. "Because you're a known seducer of innocent women."

Jonathan turned away, running his hand over his hair. "I'm not the nicest guy, Rebecca. We all know that."

"I know *you* think that," Rebecca said. "And I know we've had our differences. But when I needed you, you were there for me. Always. Even when Gage broke my heart, and you couldn't understand why it mattered, why I wanted to be with him, in the end, you supported me. Always. Every day of my life. I don't even remember my father. I remember you. You taught me how to ride a bike, how to ride a horse. You fought for me, tirelessly. Worked for me. You don't think I don't know how tired you were? How much you put into making our home…a home? Bad men don't do that. Bad men hit their wives, hit their children. Abandon their daughters. Our fathers were bad men, Jonathan. But you never were."

Something about those words struck him square in the chest. Their fathers *were* bad men.

He had always known that.

But he had always believed somewhere deep down that he must be bad, too. Not because he thought being an abusive bastard was hereditary. But because if his father had beaten him, and his mother had left him, there must be something about him that was bad.

Something visible. Something that the whole town could see.

He thought back to all the kindness on Pastor John Thompson's face, kindness Jonathan certainly hadn't deserved from the old man when he was doing his absolute damnedest to start a fight in the middle of The Grind.

He had been so determined to have John confirm that Jonathan was bad. That he was wrong.

Because there was something freeing about the anger that belief created deep inside his soul.

It had been fuel. All his life that belief had been his fuel. Gave him something to fight against. Something to be angry about.

An excuse to never get close to anyone.

Because underneath all the anger was nothing but despair. Despair because his parents had left him, because they couldn't love him enough. Because he wasn't worth…anything.

His need for love had never gone away, but he'd

shoved it down deep. Easier to do when you had convinced yourself you could never have it.

He looked at Rebecca and realized he had despaired over her, too. When she had chosen Gage. Jonathan had decided it was just one more person who loved him and didn't want to stay.

Yeah, it was much easier, much less painful to believe that he was bad. Because it let him keep his distance from the pain. Because it meant he didn't have to try.

"What do you think love is?" Rebecca asked again, more persistent this time.

He didn't have an answer. Not one with words. All he had were images, feelings. Watching Rebecca sleep after a particularly hard day. Praying child services wouldn't come by to check on her while he was at work, and find her alone and him negligent.

And Hayley. Her soft hands on his body, her sweet surrender. The trust it represented. The way she made him feel. Like he was on fire, burning up from the inside out. Like he could happily stay for the rest of his life in a one-room cabin, without any of the money or power he had acquired over the past few years, and be perfectly content.

The problem was, he couldn't make her stay with him.

This house, his company, those things were his. In a way that Hayley could never be. In a way that no one ever could be.

People were always able to leave.

He felt like a petulant child even having that thought. But he didn't know how the hell else he could feel secure. And he didn't think he could stand having another person walk away.

"I don't know," he said.

Rebecca shook her head, her expression sad. "That's a damn shame, Jonathan, because you show me love all the time. Whether you know what to call it or not, you've given it to me tirelessly over the years, and without you, without it, I don't know where I would be. You stayed with me when everybody else left."

"But who stayed with me?" he asked, feeling like an ass for even voicing that question. "You had to stay. I had to take care of you. But the minute you could go out on your own you did."

"Because that's what your love did for me, you idiot."

"Not very well. Because you were always worried I thought of you as a burden, weren't you? It almost ruined your relationship with Gage, if I recall correctly."

"Yes," she said, "but that wasn't about you. That was my baggage. And you did everything in your power to help me, even when you knew the result would be me going back to Gage. That's love, Jonathan." She shook her head. "I love you, too. I love you enough to want you to have your own life, one that doesn't revolve around taking care of me. That doesn't revolve around what happened to us in the past."

He looked around the room, at the house that meant so much to him. A symbol of security, of his ability to care for Rebecca, if her relationship went to hell. And he realized that creating this security for her somehow enabled him to deny his own weaknesses. His own fears.

This house had only ever been for him. A fortress to barricade himself in.

Wasn't that what Hayley had accused him of? Building himself a perfect fortress to hide in?

If everybody hated him, he didn't have to try. If there was something wrong with him, he never had to do what was right. If all he loved were things, he never had to risk loss.

They were lies. Lies he told himself because he was a coward.

And it had taken a virginal church secretary to uncover the truth.

She had stood in front of him and said she wanted love more than she wanted to be safe. And he had turned her down.

He was afraid. Had been all his life. But before this very moment, he would have rather cut out his own heart than admit it.

But now, standing with his sister looking at him like he was the saddest damn thing she'd ever seen, a hole opened in his chest. A hole Hayley had filled.

"But doesn't it scare you?" he asked, his voice rough. "What if he leaves?"

She reached out, putting her hand on his. "It would break my heart. But I would be okay. I would have you. And I would…still be more whole than I was before I loved him. That's the thing about love. It doesn't make you weak, Jonathan, it makes you stronger. Opening yourself up, letting people in…that makes your life bigger. It makes your life richer. Maybe it's a cliché, but from where I'm standing you need to hear the cliché. You need to start believing it."

"I don't understand why she would want to be with me," Jonathan said. "She's…sweet. And she's never been hurt. I'm…well, I'm a mess. That's not what she deserves. She deserves to have a man who's in mint condition, like she is."

"But that's not how love works. If love made sense, if it was perfectly fair, then Gage West would not have been the man for me. He was the last man on earth I should have wanted, Jonathan. Nobody knows that more than me, and him. It took a miracle for me to let go of all my anger and love him. At the same time… I couldn't help myself.

"Love is strange that way. You fall into it whether you want to or not. Then the real fight is figuring out how to live it. How to become the person you need to be so you can hold on to that love. But I'm willing to bet you are the man she needs. Not some mint condition, new-in-the-box guy. But a strong man who has proved, time and time again, that no matter how hard life is, no matter how intensely the storm rages, he'll be there for you. And more than that, he'll throw his body over yours to protect you if it comes to that. That's what I see when I look at you, Jonathan. What's it going to take for you to see that in yourself?"

"I don't think I'm ever going to," he said slowly, imagining Hayley again, picturing her as she stared up at him on the street. Fury, hurt, love shining from her eyes. "But…if she sees it…"

"That's a start," Rebecca said. "As long as you don't let her get away. As long as you don't push her away."

"It's too late for that. She's probably not going to want to see me again. She's probably not going to want me back."

"Well, you won't know unless you ask." Rebecca took a deep breath. "The best thing about love is it has the capacity to forgive on a pretty incredible level. But if there's one thing you and I both know, it's that it's hard to forgive someone leaving. Don't make that the story. Go back. Ask for forgiveness. Change what needs to be changed. Mostly…love her. The rest kind of takes care of itself."

Fourteen

Hayley had just settled back onto her couch for more quality sitting and weeping when she heard a knock at her door.

She stood up, brushing potato chip crumbs off her pajamas and grimacing. Maybe it was Cassie, bringing up baked goods. The other woman had done that earlier; maybe now she was bringing more. Hayley could only hope.

She had a gaping wound in her chest that could be only temporarily soothed by butter.

Without bothering to fix her hair—which was on top of her head in a messy knot—she jerked the door open.

And there he was. Dark eyes glittering, gorgeous mouth pressed into a thin line. His dark hair tied back low on his neck, the way she was accustomed to seeing him during the day.

Her heart lurched up into her throat, trying to make a break for it.

She hadn't been expecting him, but she imagined expecting him wouldn't have helped. Jonathan Bear wasn't someone you could anticipate.

"What are you doing here?"

He looked around. "I came here to talk to you. Were you...expecting someone else?"

"Yes. A French male prostitute." He lifted his brows. "Well, you told me to find another man to tick my boxes."

"I think you mean a gigolo."

"I don't know what they're called," she said, exasperated.

The corner of his mouth twitched. "Well, I promise to be quick. I won't interrupt your sex date."

She stepped to the side, ignoring the way her whole body hurt as she did. "I don't have a sex date." She cleared her throat. "Just so you know."

"Somehow, I didn't think you did."

"You don't know me," she grumbled, turning away from him, pressing her hand to her chest to see if her heart was beating as hard and fast as she felt like it was.

It was.

"I do, Hayley. I know you pretty damn well. Maybe better than I know myself. And... I think you might know me better than I know myself, too." He sounded different. Sad. Tired.

She turned around to face him, and with his expression more fully illuminated by the light, she saw weariness written there. Exhaustion.

"For all the good it did me," she said, crossing her arms tightly in a bid to protect herself. Really, though, it was too late. There wasn't anything left to protect. He had shattered her irrevocably.

"Yeah, well. It did me a hell of a lot of good. At least, I hope it's going to. I hope I'm not too late."

"Too late for what? To stick the knife in again or...?"

"To tell you I love you," he said.

Everything froze inside her. Absolutely everything. The air in her lungs, her heart, the blood in her veins.

"You...you just said... Don't tease me, Jonathan. Don't play with me. I know I'm younger than you. I know that I'm innocent. But if you came back here to lie to me, to say what you think I need to hear so you can...keep having me in your bed, or whatever—"

Suddenly, she found herself being hauled forward into his arms, against his chest. "I do want you in my bed," he said, "make no mistake about that. But sex is just sex, Hayley, even when it's good. And what we have is good.

"But here's something you don't know, because you don't have experience with it. Sex isn't love. And it doesn't feel like this. I feel...like everything in me is broken and stronger at the same time, and I don't know how in the hell that can be true. And when you told me you loved me... I knew I could either let go of everything in the past or hold on to it harder to protect myself." He shook his head. "I protected myself."

"Yeah, well. What about protecting me?"

"I thought maybe I was protecting you, too. But it's all tangled up in this big lie that I've been telling myself for years. I told you I didn't love people, that I love things. But I said that only because I've had way too much experience with people I love leaving. A house can't walk away, Hayley. A mountain can't up and abandon you. But you could.

"One day, you could wake up and regret that you tied your future to me. When you could have done better... When you could have had a man who wasn't so damn broken." He cupped her cheek, bent down and kissed her lips. "What did I do to earn the love of someone like you? Someone so beautiful...so soft. You're everything I'm not, Hayley Thompson, and all the reasons I love you make perfect sense to me. But why do you love me? That's what I can't quite figure out."

Hayley looked into his eyes, so full of pain, so deeply wounded. She would have never thought a man like him would need reassurance from anyone, least of all a woman like her.

"I know I don't have a lot of experience, Jonathan. Well, any experience apart from you. I know that I haven't seen the whole world. I haven't even seen the whole state. But I've seen your heart. The kind of man you are. The change that knowing you, loving you, created in me. And I know...perfect love casts out all fear.

"I can't say I haven't been afraid these past couple of days. Afraid I couldn't be with you. That things might not work out with us. But when I stood on Main Street... I knew fear couldn't be allowed to win. It was your love that brought me to that conclusion. Your love was bigger than the fear inside me. I don't need experience to understand that. I don't need to travel the world or date other men for the sake of experience. I need you. Because whether or not you're perfect, you're perfect for me."

"*You're* perfect," he said, his voice rough. "So damned perfect. I want...to take you to Canada."

She blinked. "Well. That's not exactly an offer to run off to Vegas."

"You want to use your passport. Why wait? Let's go now. Your boss will let you off. I'm sure of it."

Something giddy bubbled up in her chest. Something wonderful. "Right now? Really?"

"Right the hell now."

"Yes," she said. "Yes, let's go to Canada."

"It's not the Eiffel Tower," he said, "but I will take you there someday. I promise you that."

"The only thing I need is you," she said. "The rest is negotiable."

His lips crashed down on hers, his kiss desperate and intense, saying the deep, poetic things she doubted her stoic cowboy would ever say out loud. But that was okay. The kiss said plenty all on its own.

Epilogue

Jonathan hated wearing a suit. He'd never done it before, but he had come to a swift and decisive conclusion the moment he'd finished doing up his tie.

Hayley was standing in their bedroom, looking amused. The ring on her left hand glittered as bright as her eyes, and suddenly, it wasn't the tie that was strangling him. It was just her. The love on her beautiful face. The fact she loved him.

He still hadn't quite figured out why. Still wasn't sure he saw all the things in himself that Rebecca had spoken of that day, all the things Hayley talked about when she said she loved him.

But Hayley did love him. And that was a gift he cherished.

"You're not going to make me wear a suit when we do this, are you?" he asked.

"I might," she said. "You look really hot in a suit."

He wrapped his arm around her waist and pulled her to his chest. "You look hottest in nothing at all. Think we could compromise?"

"We've created enough scandal already without me showing up naked to my wedding. Anyway, I'm wearing white. I am a traditional girl, after all."

"Honey, you oughta wear red."

"Are you calling me a scarlet woman?"

He nodded. "Yes, and I think you proved your status earlier this morning."

She blushed. She still blushed, even after being with him for six months. Blushed in bed, when he whispered dirty things into her ear. He loved it.

He loved *her*.

He couldn't wait to be her husband, and that was something he hadn't imagined ever feeling. Looking forward to being a husband.

Of course, he was looking forward to the honeymoon even more. To staying in a little apartment in Paris with a view of the Eiffel Tower.

For him, trading in a view of the mountains for a view of the city didn't hold much appeal. But she wanted it. And the joy he got from giving Hayley what she wanted was the biggest thing in his world.

Waiting to surprise her with the trip was damn near killing him.

"You have to hurry," she said, pushing at his shoulder. "You're giving the bride away, after all."

Jonathan took a deep breath. Yeah, it was time. Time to give his sister to that Gage West, who would never deserve her, but who loved her, so Jonathan was willing to let it go. Willing to give them his blessing.

Actually, over the past few months he'd gotten kind of attached to the bastard who would be his brother-in-law. Something he'd thought would never be possible only a little while ago.

But love changed you. Rebecca had been right about that.

"All right," he said. "Let's go then."

Hayley kissed his cheek and took his hand, leading him out of the bedroom and down the stairs. The wedding guests were out on the back lawn, waiting for the event to start. When he and Hayley exited the house, they all turned to look.

He and Hayley still turned heads, and he had a feeling they always would.

Jonathan Bear had always been seen as a bad boy. In all the ways that phrase applied. The kind of boy no parent wanted their daughter to bring home to Sunday dinner. And yet the pastor's daughter had.

He'd definitely started out that way. But somehow, through some miracle, he'd earned the love of a good woman.

And because of her love, he was determined to be the best man he could possibly be.

* * * * *

MILLS & BOON®

PASSIONATE AND DRAMATIC LOVE STORIES

A sneak peek at next month's titles...

In stores from 9th March 2017:

- **The Ten-Day Baby Takeover** – Karen Booth *and*
  Pride and Pregnancy – Sarah M. Anderson

- **Expecting the Billionaire's Baby** – Andrea Laurence
  and **The Magnate's Mail-Order Bride** – Joanne Roc

- **A Beauty for the Billionaire** – Elizabeth Bevarly *and*
  His Ex's Well-Kept Secret – Joss Wood

Just can't wait?
Buy our books online before they hit the shops!
www.millsandboon.co.uk

Also available as eBooks.

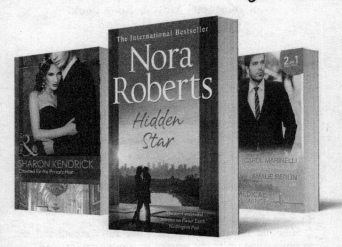

MILLS & BOON®

Congratulations
Carol Marinelli
on your 100th Mills & Boon book!

Read on for an exclusive extract

How did she walk away? Lydia wondered.

How did she go over and kiss that sulky mouth and say goodbye when really she wanted to climb back into bed?

But rather than reveal her thoughts she flicked that internal default switch which had been permanently set to 'polite'.

'Thank you so much for last night.'

'I haven't finished being your tour guide yet.'

He stretched out his arm and held out his hand but Lydia didn't go over. She did not want to let in hope, so she just stood there as Raul spoke.

'It would be remiss of me to let you go home without seeing Venice as it should be seen.'

'Venice?'

'I'm heading there today. Why don't you come with me? Fly home tomorrow instead.'

There was another night between now and then, and Lydia knew that even while he offered her an extension he made it clear there was a cut-off.

Time added on for good behaviour.

And Raul's version of 'good behaviour' was that there would

be no tears or drama as she walked away. Lydia knew that. If she were to accept his offer then she had to remember that.

'I'd like that.' The calm of her voice belied the trembling she felt inside. 'It sounds wonderful.'

'Only if you're sure?' Raul added.

'Of course.'

But how could she be sure of anything now she had set foot in Raul's world?

He made her dizzy.

Disorientated.

Not just her head, but every cell in her body seemed to be spinning as he hauled himself from the bed and unlike Lydia, with her sheet-covered dash to the bathroom, his body was hers to view.

And that blasted default switch was stuck, because Lydia did the right thing and averted her eyes.

Yet he didn't walk past. Instead Raul walked right over to her and stood in front of her.

She could feel the heat—not just from his naked body but her own—and it felt as if her dress might disintegrate.

He put his fingers on her chin, tilted her head so that she met his eyes, and it killed that he did not kiss her, nor drag her back to his bed. Instead he checked again. 'Are you sure?'

'Of course,' Lydia said, and tried to make light of it. 'I never say no to a free trip.'

It was a joke but it put her in an unflattering light. She was about to correct herself, to say that it hadn't come out as she had meant, but then she saw his slight smile and it spelt approval.

A gold-digger he could handle, Lydia realised.

Her emerging feelings for him—perhaps not.

At every turn her world changed, and she fought for a semblance of control. Fought to convince not just Raul but herself that she could handle this.

Don't miss
THE INNOCENT'S SECRET BABY
by Carol Marinelli
OUT NOW

BUY YOUR COPY TODAY
www.millsandboon.co.uk